YOU'RE STILL THE ONE

ERIKA KELLY

CW01496976

YOU'RE STILL THE ONE

Erika Kelly

ISBN-13: 978-1-955462-03-7

Copyright 2021 EK Publishing, LLC

Cover design and Formatting by Serendipity Formatting
Editing by Kristy DeBoer
Editing by Olivia Kalb Editing
Proofreading by Jamie McHugh

this is a not-to-be-missed book!" —Sharon Slick Reads, Guilty Pleasures Book Reviews

"Erika Kelly damn near pulled my heart from my chest with Delilah and Will's story. It's so well-written that you feel everything. My heart got tugged so hard! I honestly cried at a few moments in the book. I fell all the way in love with "Wooby." It's hard not to, really." —Ree Cee's Books

THE VERY THOUGHT OF YOU

"Wow, THE VERY THOUGHT OF YOU was simply OUTSTANDING! This second chance, friends to lovers romance is enchanting and entertaining." —Spellbound Stories

"I just finished this story, and I want to start all over again. Or maybe at the start of series. To once again feel the events, the emotions, that brought these amazing characters together. To hear the banter and the arguments, the sorrow, the loss and the happiness that brought a family together and closer." —Nerdy, Dirty, and Flirty

JUST THE WAY YOU ARE

"An alpha cowboy and a smart, sassy princess collide in JUST THE WAY YOU ARE in Erika Kelly's latest, and it was fabulous! I was cheering for Brodie and Rosalina with every page. If you love stories with heart, steam, and plenty of swoon, don't miss this one!" —USA Today Bestselling Author J.H. Croix

"With the Calamity Falls series, Kelly doesn't shy away from charming. She captivates with delectable characters that wrap themselves around a heart. From the first hello to the final goodbye, Rosalina and Brodie are a match made out of the unpredictable, but the sweetest kind of heaven. JUST THE WAY YOU ARE is the perfect example of why I am hooked on this series. SWOONWORTHY READ!" —Hopeless Romantic Book Reviews

IT WAS ALWAYS YOU

"This book was full of every emotion you could ever feel. Gigi and Cassian proved you can conquer anything with true love." —Cat's Guilty Pleasure

"I could not put this book down! Erika Kelly always delivers a great love story and never disappoints! I recommend this book for romance lovers looking to get lost in a great love story." —Reading in Pajamas

CAN'T HELP FALLING IN LOVE

"I love everything about this emotional and sexy, second chance story. Erika Kelly writes a story that makes me feel like I'm right there with the two main characters, Beckett and Coco. It is a slow burn, passionate story with lots of underlying tension. I not only enjoyed this story, but I found it impossible to put down." —Cocktails and Books

"I loved everything about this book. I loved all the characters, from Beckett, 'I don't believe in love,' to single mom, small business-owning, closed-off Coco, to a fairy-believing five-year-old who will steal your heart! I cannot gush enough about how spectacular I thought this book was." – Bookcase and Coffee

WHOLE LOTTA LOVE

"BRILLIANT! This book was incredible, I could not put this book down, that is how good Lu and Xander's story was. I fell in love with these two characters instantly." – Harlequin Junkie

"Whole Lotta Love was absolutely perfect! You will instantly love this couple and their journey to find happiness!" – Just Love Books

YOU'RE STILL THE ONE

"Griffin and Stella really are soulmates. They bring out the best of each other, and when they're together, everything is better. Their world is better with the love they feel for each other. And I think they made my world better a bit, too." – Jersey Girl's Bookshelf

"WOW! WOW! WOW! Welcome to all the feels! I ADORED Stella and Griffin's story. I was completely lost in this book and didn't want to put it down. I FELT everything, and I can't tell you how much I loved it." – Books According to Abby

Titles by Erika Kelly

The Calamity Falls series
KEEP ON LOVING YOU
WE BELONG TOGETHER
THE VERY THOUGHT OF YOU
JUST THE WAY YOU ARE
IT WAS ALWAYS YOU
CAN'T HELP FALLING IN LOVE
COME AWAY WITH ME
WHOLE LOTTA LOVE
YOU'RE STILL THE ONE
THE DEEPER I FALL
LOVE ME LIKE YOU DO

Rock Star Romance series
YOU REALLY GOT ME
I WANT YOU TO WANT ME
TAKE ME HOME TONIGHT
MORE THAN A FEELING

Wild Love series
MINE FOR NOW
MINE FOR THE WEEK

Sign up for my newsletter to read the EXCLUSIVE novella for my readers only! You'll get two chapters a month of this super sexy, fun romance! #rockstarromance #teenidolturnedboyfriend Also, get PLANES, TRAINS, AND HEAD OVER HEELS for FREE! I hope you'll come hang out with me on Facebook, Twitter, Instagram, Goodreads, and Pinterest or in my private reader group.

This book is dedicated to Olivia because she's patient and wise…and she gave me my epilogue!

Acknowledgments

- Thank you to Superman for knowing so much about so many things, for dropping your work when I interrupt you with, "Can I just ask you one thing?" and for loving me so wholly and unconditionally.
- Thank you to Sharon for being the best friend in the world.
- Thank you to Erica for your patience and for never letting me down.
- Thank you to Melissa for your willingness to always jump in and for always going the distance.
- Thank you, as always, to Kristy, for making my books richer, deeper, and better.
- Thank you to Olivia for enduring all my plotting talk—and always coming up with just the right solution!
- Thank you to Jamie McHugh for taking on FIVE books!

Prologue

GRIFFIN JAMES HAD SCREWED UP.

Badly.

The roar of the motorcycle couldn't drown out his regrets, and the Texas sun beating down on him couldn't burn through the fear that he might've lost her for good.

No. Not possible.

They were too good together, too strong.

She's my heart.

And I'm here now. We'll work it out.

The anxiety crashing through him made him jittery.

Not good when you're tearing down the highway.

His GPS signaled his exit, and he began easing over across lanes. He was close now. Soon, he'd get her back. And when he did, his world would finally be right again.

Getting off the freeway, he turned at the light. He'd tell her he loved her, that he was sorry, and that he'd never meant to say those two stupid, fatal words.

We're done.

What kind of asshole said that to the woman he loved?

Sure, she'd kissed her sister's fiancé at the rehearsal

dinner, but he knew Stella. Knew her intentions. She couldn't stand to see her sister marry the wrong man. The dirtbag wanted to be part of the Cavanaugh family—the Hall of Fame quarterback dad, the former supermodel mom, the pop star older sister. It had nothing to do with his fiancée.

So, Stella had tested the guy, and he'd failed. In front of everyone they'd ever known.

That whole night, she'd been threatening to expose him, but Griffin kept telling her to knock it off, that she'd done what she could by warning her sister. But Stella wouldn't listen. She loved fiercely, and she wouldn't stand around and watch her sister get screwed over by some asshole.

Yeah, it was bad, but I didn't have to break up with her. Fuck.

Of course, he hadn't known she'd take off like that. No one had. And now…six months later…Jesus, when he thought of how alone she'd been all this time. How… scared. How hurt and rejected she must feel.

He couldn't fucking stand it.

But he'd make things right.

Braking at a light, Griffin glanced down at the GPS. He was two minutes from his destination. Two minutes from putting himself out of his misery, from relieving Stella of the guilt and sadness she'd undoubtedly carried with her all these months.

Hammering down, he raced through the quiet streets until he hit the parking lot.

The corporate headquarters of the Wildcats was in a suburb of Dallas. The massive, modern building spread over acres with its training center, stadium, and practice fields.

Pulling into a spot, he cut the engine and swung a leg off his bike. *Ah, damn.* He ached. He'd ridden twelve hours yesterday and ten today, only taking short breaks. Last night, he'd slept in a campground in Burlington, Colorado.

But he didn't care. None of that mattered.

The only thing he could think about was seeing her.

And apologizing.

Entering the building, he took in the tinted windows and display cases filled with jerseys, awards, and photos of players. The walls, carpet, couches, and chairs all reflected the team colors—teal and metallic silver.

He headed to an enormous reception desk. "Hey, I'm here to see Stella Cavanaugh."

"Um, okay?" Looking flustered, the young woman flipped open a notebook and ran a finger along a list of names and phone numbers. Her forehead creased in confusion. "Um. Just give me a sec."

It struck him that Stella worked in PR. Maybe that was in a different building. "She's an intern with the publicity department."

"Oh, okay." She skipped ahead several pages and scanned a smaller list of names. "I don't see her. Let me make a quick call." Picking up the phone, she punched a few numbers. Then, she glanced up at him with an apologetic expression. "I'm new here. First day."

"No problem." He felt better, lighter than he had in months. At first, her parents had refused to give him any information. They'd said they had to honor her request— she didn't want anyone from her old life to know where she was—but last week—*finally*—they'd changed their minds. They were worried and wanted someone to check in.

They didn't know where she lived, only where she worked.

Fuck, but he missed her.

Seems crazy to fall in love when you're a kid, to know down to your bones that you've found the one person for you. But he'd known, all right. He'd never had a doubt.

We're done.

He fucking hated himself.

For most of his life, he couldn't have her, and it wasn't because of the nearly two-year age difference. It was because of her sister's crush. Not that he'd known about it at the time. Lulu had barely ever spoken to him.

But Stella knew, and she'd kept him at arm's length because she loved her sister.

Which was why, the minute Griffin had heard about Lulu falling in love, he'd dropped out of college and come home, taken a full-time job at the bike shop where he'd worked in high school, just so he could finally be with Stella. His heart.

My whole fucking heart.

What if she was pissed? Refused to see him?

Panic squeezed his lungs.

No, no. She loves me. I know she does.

He'd come to fix it, and he wouldn't leave until he'd won her back.

"Hi, this is Ashley at reception. There's someone here to see Stella Cavanaugh. He says she's in PR."

It killed him to remember how she'd begged him to forgive her, pleaded with him to stay with her. He'd been too angry at the time to think clearly, so he'd told her they were done.

Fuck, he'd do anything to go back and torch those words, turn them to ash.

"Is there something you needed?" the woman asked, one hand covering the mouthpiece.

Shit. He'd been so driven to get here he hadn't considered how it might look if she got a personal visit during work hours. Then again, it was nearly five in the afternoon. It couldn't be that bad to show up at the end of the day. "I'm a friend from home."

"He's her friend," she said into the receiver.

If only Stella had given him time. He could never have anticipated her leaving town only two weeks after the rehearsal dinner. She'd cut him—everyone—off from social media. She'd even blocked him on her phone.

Fortunately, her parents had tracked her through an emergency credit card, so they'd convinced her to take the job with the Wildcats.

"I'm afraid she's not here," the receptionist said.

"Not here, as in, she's already left for the day?" *Please don't tell me she quit her job and moved somewhere else.* How would he find her?

"Like I said, I'm new..." She gave a helpless shrug.

Leaning forward, he pressed his clammy hands on the desk. "I just drove twenty-two hours from Wyoming to get here. Please, if there's any way I can get in touch with her, I'd appreciate it. I..." *I miss her. I need her.* "It's a surprise."

She thinks everyone she loved turned against her.
Including me.
I hurt the person I love most in the world.

If only she'd given him a chance to work through his anger. Of course, he would've gotten back with her.

"I don't know if I should say this…" She glanced over her shoulder, but no one was around. "But she's not Stella Cavanaugh anymore. She goes by Rocky Miller now."

"Thank you." He slapped the counter. "Thank you so much."

The woman looked anxious.

And that's my fault. "I'm sorry for dragging you into this, and I won't tell anyone what you told me. Thanks again." Armed with enough information to get her back, he headed out into the blinding sunlight,

When he got to his bike, he checked the saddlebag for the little velvet box. He did it every time he stopped, worried it would fall out or someone would nab it. It wasn't much—he couldn't afford shit on his salary—but it was the message it delivered that mattered.

I'm going to marry her.

He couldn't wait to see her expression when he dropped to a knee and popped the question. Pulling out his phone, he tapped the Splashagram app. As soon as he found her, he'd message her. He smiled when he imagined her eyes lighting up at the sight of his name in her notifications, the relief she would feel.

It had to be killing her to be cut off from her family, to not be with him. He knew because he hadn't been able to function since they'd broken up.

He could barely eat or sleep. Every time his boss walked past him, he smacked him on the back of his head. *Get your head out of the clouds.*

The idea of her all alone in this big city, feeling rejected…it consumed him.

He typed Rocky Miller into the search bar.

Found her.

Fuck, yes. My girl.

My fucking heart.

But his stomach plummeted when he saw the images.

She sure as hell wasn't in the office. She wasn't even in Dallas.

She was on the beach.

With a guy.

On her fucking honeymoon.

Stella had gotten married.

Chapter One

SNOWFLAKES DUSTING HER CHEEKS, STELLA Cavanaugh gazed up at the heavy, gray sky.

She'd never felt so far from home.

Maybe because Thanksgiving was just weeks away, or maybe because she'd hurt her sister so badly, but tonight, she felt the distance more than ever.

Stepping off the curb to hail a cab, she had to smile. How was she supposed to stay in a funk when she was surrounded by all *this?* New York City during the holidays was magical. Christmas lights lit up the buildings on Fifth Avenue, garlands were strung across crosswalks, and department store windows competed for the most fantastical displays.

It was beautiful and festive and totally made her think of her mom, who always made such a big deal out of the holidays.

Cars whizzed by, but not a single cab had its available sign lit. And that was the frustrating part. *You can never get a cab here when it rains or snows.* Clutching her leopard print faux fur jacket to keep out the cold air, she took a sip of her quickly cooling mocha latte.

Her phone vibrated, and Taji's name flashed on the screen. *Great.* She loved her job. In fact, she was pretty sure she'd been born to plan weddings, but her boss was unreasonable and demanding, calling at all hours of the day and night.

As the top event planner in the city, though, Taji Nash could get away with anything. And since Stella had scored the coveted job with zero experience in the business, she put up with all the woman's crazy demands—even knowing she'd only gotten it because of her model mom and football Hall of Fame dad. Stella didn't care.

She'd take it and make it her own.

Taji: Can you come back to the office? I can't find the Davenport file.

Stella: You took it into the conference room. Did you leave it there?

Taji: Of course not.

With heavy snow predicted, Stella wanted to get back to her apartment. It had been a long, hellish week—who knew so many socialites wanted winter weddings?—and now she wanted to kick off her heels, heat up some soup, and not think about work...

Or the damage she'd done to her sister.

Again.

Because no matter how hard she pushed forward and tried to build a life independent of her family, guilt pulsed in rhythm with her heartbeat. There was no escaping it.

She'd blown up her sister's latest relationship.

Strike two. I'm out.

Lulu would never forgive her this time.

Of course, it had all been a huge misunderstanding. This time, Stella hadn't even touched her sister's boyfriend.

How could I have known the new quarterback was dating Lulu?

She couldn't.

But the images were splashed all over the tabloids, making it look like she and Xander had been engaged in some torrid affair. They'd failed to mention, of course, that Stella was his publicist, that she'd literally just met the guy, and her job had been to check him into his hotel and deliver him to the team dinner.

Whatever. The damage had been done, and Lulu had broken up with him.

And I can't do a damn thing to fix it.

A cab slowed, edging closer to the curb. Did she take it or go back to the office?

Stella: Do you still need me?

Taji: No, I found it.

Yeah? Was it in the conference room? But there was no point in antagonizing her boss.

Sliding into the backseat, Stella said, "Jane Street and Greenwich, please."

For seven long years, she'd stayed away from home in the hopes enough time would pass for Lulu to eventually forgive her.

Instead, Stella had reset the clock.

As she settled in for the long ride to her studio apartment in the West Village, she checked her emails. Even though she'd worked with an NFL team for years, she'd still had to start at the bottom with this new job. *It's fine.* She didn't mind. This was a new industry, and she needed to learn it. But she'd rise quickly—nobody worked harder or smarter, and nobody came up with better ideas than she did.

She might not have a particular talent like her sisters—she was no singer or chef or chocolatier—but she had big ideas.

Her phone vibrated. *Nooo.*

Can't find your keys, Taji?

You tossed them across the room when the Hilton bride canceled her wedding, so check the planter by the window.

But it wasn't her boss. It was a Calamity area code. She hadn't seen that one in a while. "Hello?"

"Stella?"

She didn't recognize the voice, so she grew anxious. "Yes." Were her parents okay?

"This is Diane Petersen. You might remember me from some of the projects your mother and I have worked on together over the years."

"Of course I remember. How are you?"

"I'm doing well, but let me tell you why I think you're the one who can make things even better."

She smiled. "Okay."

"About a year ago, Brodie Bowie built a lovely chapel in the mountains and asked me to launch a destination wedding business for the Owl Hoot Resort and Spa."

"That sounds fun."

"Oh, it is, and the response has been overwhelming. But I only agreed to get it started on one condition, that I'd train someone to take over for me. Well, let me tell you, I've interviewed countless professionals and hired quite a few people, but no one's worked out."

"It's a tough business."

"Yes, and when I was talking to your mother the other

day, she told me you'd recently moved to New York to work with Taji Nash Events, and I thought, Bingo."

How did Mom find out about that? Had Taji called her for a reference? "Let me stop you right there. I've only been here a few months."

And I ruined my sister's love life for the second time, so there's no way in hell I'm going back to Calamity.

And yet…this strange yearning reared up.

To go home.

To be with her family.

And worse…

To be in Griffin's arms again.

Plain and simple, Griffin James was her person. And she had a Griffin-shaped hole in her heart that would never heal.

"Here's the thing. Everyone I've hired has had experience. Know what they don't have? The ability to manage people. That's the key in a business filled with pushy moms, bridezillas, wedding party backstabbers, and in-law temper tantrums. I think you know exactly what I mean."

"I do."

"And do you know what I remember about you?"

"No, but I'd love to hear it." She glanced out the window, at the mad dash of cars cutting each other off and the pedestrians striding down crowded streets, shoulders hunched against the light snow.

"How gracious you were to everyone. You were the perfect hostess at your family's events, popular in school and in town, and you always knew just what to say. You know how to handle difficult personalities. You're a go-getter, you have sensational ideas, you've worked in PR… Stella, I want you to take over the wedding planning business here at the resort. I'll teach you everything you need to know to be successful."

Her heart pounded, making her acutely aware of how badly she wanted this job. But after what she'd done, how would that work? Maybe if she hadn't just ruined Lulu's latest relationship, she could do it. But she had. And no one would welcome her.

Griffin certainly wouldn't. He hated her.

Could she stand living in a town where he might be married?

Might have *children?*

The image of Griffin holding hands with a little girl, another baby strapped to his chest in a sling, slashed across her heart.

Those babies should be mine. Ours.

Her heart ached for all she'd lost—all she still longed for with every fiber of her being.

No way. She couldn't go home. Seeing that would kill her.

"I'm sorry, Diane. I love working with Taji"—*lies.* The woman was a narcissist—"and I'm learning so much here, but it's just not the right time. Maybe we can revisit this a year from now."

But what if Griffin hadn't moved on? What if he missed her just as badly?

What if she could heal the rift in her family and win back the love of her life?

That was too much to ask, though…wasn't it?

After what she'd done?

"I understand." Diane sounded disappointed. "It's a shame, though. I can't think of anyone better to plan Gigi and Cassian's wedding."

Whoa. "My sister's getting married?"

"Yep."

"And you're planning it?"

"Well, I'd like to hand it over to you, but yes, they've hired us. So, what do you say? Feel like creating your sister's dream wedding?"

Clamping the sheet metal over the hammerform, Griffin James tried to focus, but with the air compressor busted, his best welder in the hospital—the dumbass got cocky and spun out his Roadster on a snowy road—and more orders than ever, he had a lot on his mind.

Over the rat-a-tat of the power hammer and the whine of a drill, he heard a deep voice call, "Yo, Boss Man. Company."

When Griffin glanced over, he found Miss Carol ambling across the busy bike shop. His spirits crashed. Any hope he'd had of knocking out this front panel today died with her grim expression. He set down the metal and hurried over, so she didn't have to walk any farther. She'd recently had hip surgery, and it looked like she needed to get the other one done sooner than she'd expected—

Oh, hell.

Is that what she'd come to tell him? That she'd scheduled the next one?

All right, well, he'd just have to find another babysitter. She shouldn't have to live with so much pain. "Hey, Miss Carol. How you doing?"

Hand on her hip, she winced. "We had a little trouble today."

Worry struck like a match. "Okay." He went into fix-it mode. "What happened?"

"He got suspended."

"Dammit." The boy had begged not to live with his grandparents, and yet he'd just sent up a flare. "What'd he do?"

"Vandalism."

What? No way. That wasn't like Austin at all. "I'll talk to him." He tipped his chin. "How's your hip?"

Her features pulled in concern. "Well, that's the other thing. We've scheduled the surgery. I'm really sorry, but—"

"No, no, listen. Your health comes first."

She knew the score, though. During winter in this small mountain town, everyone dropped their bikes off for tune-ups and repairs. It was also his chance to work on spec and custom motorcycles. But he'd put everything on hold. Of course, he would.

He'd do anything for that boy.

"I'd ask my sister to cover for me, but I could be out a couple of months." Her cheeks were red from the cold, and her gray hair looked disheveled, as though she'd just yanked off her knit cap. "I don't know anyone who can watch him that long. Especially with the holidays coming."

"I understand. Don't worry about it. Just take care of yourself."

She took in his busy shop. "I hate leaving you in a bind."

They both knew the real concern wasn't Griffin's work. It was Austin. Being alone after school left him vulnerable to his grandparent's inevitable and frequent surprise visits. "I've got a big family. Between my sister, brothers, and parents, we've got it." That wasn't entirely true—everyone had busy, full lives— but she didn't object. Which meant she really was hurting. "How 'bout I drive you home?"

"I can finish out today." She tried to smile, but her features seized when the pain got hold of her. "I sent him up to the apartment. I can sit with him till you're done."

"I don't want you climbing those stairs. Go home and take care of yourself."

"Well, if you're sure, I wouldn't say no to a painkiller."

"You go. And let me know how surgery goes." He walked her to the door. Once outside, he gripped her elbow as they headed across the recently plowed asphalt to her truck. He waited until she left the parking lot to face his reality.

No help after school meant three hours less a day to work. And since the priority was getting the bikes to his customers in the spring, that meant he'd have to quit working on the specs.

But that was the least of his problems. The retired judge and former mayor had eyes and ears everywhere in Calamity. Without a doubt, they already knew about the suspension and would be stopping by for a visit any time now.

And nothing made them crazier than knowing their grandson lived with the tattooed owner of a motorcycle shop instead of them.

Okay, time to manage the situation.

He climbed the icy metal stairs. At the landing, he saw the blue screen of his TV through the curtained window. Letting himself in, he found Austin sitting on the couch, game controller in his hand, playing like he didn't have a care in the world. The coffee table was littered with a bag of chips, a box of chocolate doughnuts, and a liter of Coke.

He chuckled. *The little shit must've run across the street to the convenience store the minute Miss Carol came inside to talk to me.*

The gust of cold air sweeping in got the kid's attention, and his spine went ramrod straight. With the sleeve of his hoodie, he wiped orange powder residue off his mouth.

Griffin closed the door, headed for the TV, and flipped it off. He sat on the coffee table. "We've got bigger fish to fry than you sneaking out to buy junk food."

"I didn't sneak."

"You know I don't want you eating that crap."

"There's no food here. I'm hungry."

That's because I moved to the Inn, so your grandparents couldn't use my apartment over the shop as an excuse to take you from me. But he wouldn't let the boy distract him from the matter at hand. "So, what's going on? Miss Carol says you got suspended."

Guilt had the kid looking away. And that always made Griffin uneasy. For fourteen years, this boy had moved from one military base to another. That meant new schools, new friends, and new caregivers. On his dad's first deployment two years ago, he'd stayed with his grandparents. This time, he'd pleaded to stay with Griffin.

"You want to tell me what happened?" He hoped his tone sounded as free of judgment as he felt.

Looking uneasy, Austin pulled a piece of paper out of the back pocket of his jeans. "You need to sign it."

"Yeah, okay. Let's see what we've got here." He skimmed the details. "I don't know, man. I've known you since you were a little kid, and I'm not buying that you intentionally broke something."

Since he wasn't the boy's legal guardian, Griffin was in a tough position. He wanted to knock some sense into the kid, since getting suspended was just the kind of excuse the Pilsons were looking for. *You can't fuck up like this, not if you want to stay with me.*

But that's not what Austin needed. Right now, he needed Griffin to listen. "Can you tell me what happened?"

"I broke the wall."

"Right, but out of anger? Did you go all Hulk and smash it?"

"No."

Griffin was a man of few words, too, so he could hardly call Austin out for it. But he also needed to make sure the boy felt wanted and loved and just, well, *safe* enough to open up to him. "Hey, you're not alone. You know that, right? I'm here, and even when your dad's in another country, you're still his boy, and he loves you. That means you don't have to shoulder your troubles on your own. You can give them to me." He flexed his muscles. "See? I bench two-fifty. I can share the load."

"It's not a big deal. I sat on top of a bench. It fell over and took out a chunk of the wall behind it."

"Did you get hurt?" He got up to check the back of Austin's head, but the boy just waved him off. Fingers moving gently across the boy's scalp, Griffin found the swelling. "That's a big bump."

"It's fine."

Griffin sat back down. "Did you explain what happened?"

"No." He gave the first sign of emotion with his heated response. "No one asked."

So, they just assumed the new kid was a troublemaker? *That's bullshit.* But he'd deal with *that* later. Right now, he needed to get Austin on the right track. "All right, knob head." That got a small grin. "Listen up. Two things. One, you've got to talk to the principal tomorrow and explain what happened. Because even if they don't ask, you still have to stand up for yourself. You're the new kid in school, and they don't get to make assumptions about you."

Austin gave him a blank look—it was the one he used when he shut down. And Griffin got it. The boy had no control over anything in his life. He just got dragged from one base, one school, one situation to another. He'd adopted the *why bother?* attitude a few years ago.

"And number two…your grandparents are probably on their way right now."

It was like a shadow moved across him, and Griffin couldn't stand the haunted look in the boy's eyes. The Pilsons were powerful people in this town. All it took was a conversation with one of the judge's cronies, and a court order would be drawn up requiring Austin to live under their roof.

"So, we've got to get going." Griffin headed for the door. "While you're cleaning this mess, I'll try to get a hold of your dad, give him a heads-up. Meet me in the shop."

Griffin didn't want Austin to hear the conversation, so he took the form and headed downstairs. *Damn, it's cold.* His breath formed a cloud in front of his face.

Once inside his office, he texted his friend.

Griffin: Can you talk?

It didn't take long to hear back.

Peyton: Yeah, sure. Give me sixty seconds to get my SAT and step out of my bunk.

It would take that long to place the call, so Griffin pulled the international calling card out of his desk and punched in the number.

"Hey, man." Peyton sounded tired. "Everything all right?"

"It's nothing to worry about—"

"Fast forward, buddy. Is Austin all right?"

"He got suspended."

"What the fuck?" Peyton sounded as pissed as he was surprised.

"I know. That was my reaction. But Austin didn't do anything wrong. It says vandalism—"

"Bullshit. My boy's a lot of things, but he's not a vandal."

"No, I know. He sat on a bench, and it tipped over and hit the wall. But no one bothered to ask him what happened."

"Of course not." Peyton blew out an obscenity. "They just see this big, quiet kid in baggy jeans and a sweatshirt. I keep telling him to knock that broody shit off, stop scaring people."

"I told him to talk to the principal tomorrow, but I think we both know he won't, so I'll stop by the school in the morning. I'm sure everything's going to be all right, but we agreed the only way this'll work is if I keep you up to date on everything, so…here you go."

"No, I'm glad you did. I wouldn't be able to sleep at night if I thought you were deciding what I should and shouldn't know. Even if you have to wake me up at three in the morning, I still want to hear about it. But listen…" He lowered his voice. "Remember I told you, if there's any activity in the area, comm might go down?"

He'd explained the situation to both Griffin and Austin repeatedly. They knew the drill.

"So, yeah. I never know how long it'll last, but it could be as much as six weeks." Peyton was on a Combat Operating Base, and when things heated up, the Army shut down communication.

Which sucked. He might need Peyton's help. "Understood. You just do what you've got to do. I've got this. Nothing to worry about."

"I've got nothing to worry about because he's with *you*."

Griffin got hit with a wallop of fear. "You know that's working against us. You know what they think of me." He'd tried to tell Peyton. When he'd first asked him to watch his son, Griffin had reminded him about his connection to the judge.

"That was ten years ago. Nobody holds that night against you. Besides, anyone can see the man you've become."

Griffin hadn't realized how much he'd needed to hear that. "There's something else."

"Tell me this list is short."

"Yep. Miss Carol's scheduled her second hip surgery, so she's not going to be watching Austin after school."

"Ah, hell. You know the Pilsons heard about the suspension a half hour before you did, so they're probably pulling up to your house right now. And once they find out there's no sitter…"

Griffin knew what was coming, but he let his friend get it out.

"They're going to want to take Austin home with them. They're going to tell you he's better off with them, that they're retired and can give him all the attention he needs." His friend was getting all wound up.

"Soon as you get me that letter giving me temporary guardianship, we can take this threat off the table."

"My CO said a JAG lawyer's making the rounds, and he'll get here when he gets here. We're pretty remote."

Leaving Austin in Griffin's care had been a last-minute decision since the boy had pitched a fit about living with his grandparents. The normally chill kid had threatened to run away. "Okay, well, in the meantime, let me get him home so I can deal with them."

"If they give you any trouble, call me, and I'll talk to them. While I still can." Peyton exhaled heavily. "I wanted to put in my twenty years, but now I'm thinking about not re-upping. I've done enough damage to my boy."

"Nah, come on. You're a great dad." But Griffin knew the real issue was that nothing could compensate for having a mother who didn't want anything to do with her son. "But if you're serious, you know you've always got a job at the shop."

"Yeah, and I appreciate that. I've just got to get through the next eight months. I told Austin he could say no to his grandparents, that he doesn't have to visit if he doesn't want, but he just goes along with everything they say."

"He hasn't found his voice with them yet, but he'll get there." Leonard Pilson was an intimidating man. Griffin knew that first-hand.

"They make him miserable." No matter what Peyton told them about how he wanted his son raised, the Pilsons insisted on doing things their way. Since they had so little time with Austin, they tended to shove a lifetime of lessons into an overnight stay. Every time the boy came home from a visit, he had a suitcase full of khakis, golf shirts, and loafers. He always came back dejected.

Worst of all, they'd destroyed the thing that mattered most to him: his guitar.

Griffin knew his friend needed sleep. "All right, I'll let you go. We'll talk later."

"Well, wait, what're we going to do without a sitter?"

"He'll hang out with me. I'll be there when he gets off the bus. And if I can't, I'll send him to Quinn's." Griffin's cousin worked at the Owl Hoot Resort and Spa, and she never minded if Austin hung out there. "He likes it there anyway." A living museum, the town had costumed actors and staged shoot-outs. Plus, the hotel had a gym and an indoor pool, and he got access to room service—free of charge.

"Okay." Peyton sounded relieved. "I couldn't do this without you. Just…whatever you do, stay under the radar, so they don't get their hands on my son."

"You have my word."

Chapter Two

STELLA'S WORLD HAD FLIPPED UPSIDE DOWN. IN THE space of twelve hours, she'd gone from concrete and skyscrapers to pine needle-strewn trails and mountain lodges.

And she loved it.

She hadn't seen her family yet. *Nope. Not ready for that.* As soon as she'd landed, she'd come straight to the Owl Hoot resort to check into the room Diane had reserved for her—part of the employment package Stella had requested.

Since she wasn't about to move back home with her parents—*God, no, I'm too old for that*—and she wasn't sure how her family would react to her after the most recent Lulu debacle, she figured she'd give herself a few days to adjust to her new job and ease herself into seeing them. So, she'd dumped her suitcases in her room and come straight to the office to get started.

Only…it wasn't exactly the bustling environment she'd anticipated.

In fact, it was empty.

"Hello?" With no one seated behind the receptionist's desk, Stella wandered further in. Everything looked fancy and brand new, and it smelled like leather and just-installed carpet. *Nice.* "Is anyone here?" A rustling sound came from the conference room, and inside she found a tall teenager wearing a black hoodie and jeans. "Oh, hey. I'm Stella Cavanaugh. Is Diane around?"

The boy stood at one end of the long table, surrounded by cardstock, envelopes, and stamps. "No." He barely spared her a glance.

"Mailed invitations. How retro." She'd meant it as a joke, considering some brides wanted to save paper and send digitally, but the boy ignored her. "So, any idea when she'll be back?" She glanced around the elegant office. "Where is everyone?"

"Ugh," a voice called. "We are screwed halfway to Sunday." The voice moved closer. "You want a doughnut? I got your hot chocolate, but—*oh*." A young woman stood there holding a carry-out tray of drinks and a wax paper bag. "Are you Stella?"

"Yes. Here, let me grab those." She stepped forward to relieve her of the tray. "You're not Diane, are you?" Wasn't her boss her mom's age?

"Uh, no." The woman seemed flustered. "Would you like a hot chocolate? I got four. I don't know why, though." She gestured helplessly at the empty desks. "I'm Quinn, the part-time receptionist, and that's Austin."

"It's wonderful to meet you. I know Diane said you guys are swamped, so I came straight from the airport, ready to jump right in. Is everyone out on job sites?"

"So, here's the thing." Quinn set the bag on the table.

"Diane's mom had a stroke, and she's gone to New Jersey to take care of her."

Stella's smile faltered. "Oh, no. Is she all right?"

"It literally just happened, so we don't have any news yet. I mean, her mom's alive. So, that's a good thing. But honestly, we haven't heard from Diane since she landed in Newark."

"Okay. Well, who's second in charge?"

"That's the other thing. We had two full-time employees, and when they found out they weren't being promoted, that Diane hired an outsider to step into her shoes…they quit."

Oh, my God. "I packed up and moved across the country, and there's no job? Why didn't anyone tell me before I left the city?"

"I can't say why Elise didn't do it. I mean, I was there when Diane asked her to fill you in."

"No one told me anything."

"I'm so sorry about that. We're right in the middle of some high-profile weddings, and Elise didn't give notice, so I guess I shouldn't be surprised. I know this looks awful. A week ago, we were swamped, phones ringing off the hook, brides fighting over the available dates, and now…"

"And now what? You're shutting down the business?"

"Oh, no, no, no. We can't do that. Oh, my gosh, no. Princess Rosalina's wedding is in five weeks."

"A princess?" In *Calamity*? What world had she dropped into?

"Yes, she's having two, actually. A royal wedding in St. Christophe, and another, smaller one, here."

"This is unbelievable. So, are you hiring someone to step in during Diane's absence?"

Quinn cringed like she'd just gotten a paper cut. "We

already did. It's you." Her shoulder-length, choppy hair kept flopping into her eyes, and she shoved it back. "But don't worry about a thing. Diane promises she'll walk you through everything."

"Walk me through? I'm in no way equipped to plan a wedding for a princess." And what about Gigi? There wasn't a chance in hell she'd risk ruining her sister's wedding.

Not when she'd hoped it could be her chance to mend fences with her family.

"Everything's already taken care of. You just have to see it through. Come on. I'll show you." Quinn was on the move, leading Stella to a large, airy, well-appointed office. "Diane's the most organized person you'll ever meet. There's not a single detail that isn't written down in multiple places." She tapped the wall. "This is the calendar for the year. One glance, and you'll know exactly what's going on every day." She headed to the other wall. "This whiteboard has the most pressing matters on the to-do list. Diane updates it at the end of every day so she can hit the ground running when she gets here in the morning."

"This is all great, but I can't just pick up where she left off."

"Well, Diane seemed to think you could, and her instincts have never been wrong." She motioned to the wall facing the desk. "These are the mood boards." She headed over. "Come take a look at next May's outdoor wedding."

She'd worked for Taji Nash, so Stella had seen the most lavish, wildly imaginative events ever planned, but these images were stunning. A wooden bridge, dripping in tiny white lights, a black matte-finish food truck, the menu written in white chalk, a candle set in a jelly jar, covered in coarse string and decorated with a single pink heather blossom…a soaring canopy of trees, the bride and groom facing each other like dolls against the grandeur of the forest. "Wow."

"And it's all yours to bring to life."

"Oh, you're good." Stella's gaze drifted across the other boards—a reception in a barn, a ceremony on top of a glacier. Energy rushed in so fast, her fingertips tingled.

I was born to do this.

Quinn stood right beside her. "You'll stay, right? Diane can't do it without your help."

The rational part of her brain said, *Hell, no.* But her heart…well, it had been engaged from the moment she'd looked out the airplane window and taken in the Rocky Mountains.

With every mile marker she'd passed on the highway from the Idaho Falls airport, hope had unfolded its tightly packed wings, and by the time she'd seen the *Welcome to Calamity* sign, it had flooded her body.

I'm home.

And if Gigi let her, Stella would plan the perfect wedding.

At some point, she assumed, she'd run into Griffin… who might still be single.

Who knows, maybe he still has feelings for me?

Anything else seemed impossible—they'd loved each other so passionately.

She didn't know, but she had to find out. "I don't know if I can, but I'm sure as hell going to try."

"Good. Because your first appointment's in fifteen minutes." And with that, Quinn walked out of the room.

Toss me into the deep end, why don't you? "Well, hang

on," Stella called after her. "Where do I begin?" But Quinn was already answering the phone.

Stella sat behind the massive desk. It was clear from the disarray that Diane had dropped everything and abandoned ship. A pen discarded on top of a notepad, a business card perched in front of the landline, and a candle recently burned, its lavender scent still lingering in the air.

She read the words on the notepad.

Emory St. Joseph's
First three to four months critical
Physical therapy.

Diane had underlined the last two words multiple times. Stella's heart squeezed for the woman. She'd go nuts if her mom had a stroke. She'd drop everything.

Determination seized her. She'd missed seven years in her family's life.

And all because she'd done something stupid. No one questioned her motives—they knew she'd had no interest in Trace, knew she'd been madly in love with Griffin.

Still am.

But she'd been drunk, and Lulu had stubbornly refused to listen to the truth about her fiancé, and so Stella had flirted with the dickhead, got him all worked up until he'd kissed her.

Right there at the rehearsal dinner.

In front of all their friends and family. Pretty much the whole town.

Stella lowered her head. She'd give anything to go back to that moment in time. Griffin had warned her to stay out of it. Why hadn't she listened? Because she'd been desperate to save her sister from heartbreak.

Okay, enough wallowing in the past. She had eleven minutes until her first client arrived.

Where do I even begin?

Just then, the teenager came in and dropped a stack of envelopes on a desk by the window. "What should I do next?"

"Well, aren't we a pair? I was just thinking the same thing. I guess I need the file for the bride who'll be here in ten minutes."

Pulling a folder out of a leather organizer, Austin checked the name against the wall calendar before handing it over.

Smart kid. I like him. "Thank you." The phone rang— a landline. "Chapel in the Woods. This is Stella speaking." She put the call on speakerphone so she could skim through the folder.

"*Stella?* No, I want Diane." The woman sounded frantic. "Can you put Diane on the phone?"

"I'm afraid I can't do that. An emergency called her away, but I'm here in her place. What can I help you with?"

"We have to change the time of the rehearsal dinner. My daughter's future mother-in-law booked the wrong flight, and now she's thrown the whole day out of whack."

"Okay, I'm sure we can fix this. Give me a little more information."

"I can't believe this is happening. She had all the information." And then she muttered, "That fucking bitch."

Stella shot a look to Austin, but he seemed unfazed by the language.

"She did it intentionally. She just has to be the center of attention."

"When's the rehearsal—" Stella began.

"But she's not going to ruin my daughter's wedding."

"No, of course not. We won't let her."

Austin pointed to the calendar, tapping Friday night.

She nodded to him gratefully. "Here's what I'll do. I'll get in touch with the restaur—"

The boy shook his head and whispered, "It's at Wally's, here in the hotel. They rented it out for the night, so she can start whenever she wants."

She grinned. "Since you've booked Wally's, you can just let me know what time you'd like to start, and I'll tell —" She looked at the boy, who mouthed, *Delilah*. "Delilah."

"We need to push the rehearsal to four, so let's start dinner at seven."

"Consider it done."

"Just like that?" the frantic woman asked.

"Just like that."

"Well, thank you very much. I'll be in touch." The woman hung up.

"Whew." Stella smiled at the boy. "How about *you* take Diane's place?"

With a broody expression, he plopped into a chair.

"But seriously, thank you. I appreciate your help."

He barely acknowledged her. "Yeah."

"Say you're welcome, Austin," Quinn shouted from her desk.

He just rolled his eyes.

Stella smiled at him. "So, tell me what you do here?"

He shrugged. "I'm supposed to be doing homework."

"True story," Quinn shouted. "But since he's so smart, he gets it all done in an hour, and then I put him to work. He's a huge help."

Stella didn't have time to dig deeper. "Okay, well, maybe you can tell me about this meeting that starts in five minutes. Are they already booked? Is this their first appointment?"

"First time here." Quinn entered the office. "Some of these couples come in and know every detail of what they want, and others don't have a clue. Either way…" Coming around the desk, she clicked around on the keyboard. "This is the list of questions Diane asks." She reached for a thick, leather-bound notebook. "She records everything in this, and then I type it all up and send it to the clients, keeping a copy for the bride's file. That way there's no chance anyone can pull the *Hey, that's not I said* crap. She's so serious about it, the queen of England could walk into the room, and Diane would keep her waiting while she finished taking notes."

"Got it. I'll make that my top priority." Stella smiled. "It's actually something I learned in my last job. I did publicity for the Wildcats, and I always made sure to send the guys a copy of the marketing plan and get them to sign off on it. Not that it mattered. They're like bison. Impossible to get them to do anything."

"Hello?" a woman called from the foyer.

"Ready or not…" Quinn gave her a sympathetic look. "Here you go."

"I got this." Stella gave her a confident smile.
Because that's part of the game.
You fake it until you make it.
And she would make it.
She'd make this job her bitch.

．．．

33

She'd only worked two hours, but Stella's head was spinning. She was overwhelmed and unquestionably in over her head…but she was happy.

I love this job. After she finished writing her to-do list on the white board, she grabbed her purse and headed out.

A college student here at University of Western Wyoming, Quinn worked irregular hours. She'd left a while ago, so Stella was surprised to find Austin sitting in the receptionist's chair, spinning around and playing on his phone. "You need a ride?"

"No, my uncle's going to get me."

"Okay." Well, she couldn't leave him here alone. "Where does he live?"

"At the Inn."

"Which Inn? The Homesteader?"

He nodded.

Anxiety zinged through her. Griffin's parents owned that place. How many times had they met in a guest cottage and spent hours hanging out? Laughing, eating, talking…and making love.

Because they hadn't been able to keep their hands off each other.

She shook it off. He owned the Boneyard now. He wouldn't just happen to be at the Inn on a random Thursday evening. "I can save him a trip and give you a ride if you want." She needed to go into town and pick up some food anyway. No way could she afford room service, and the prices at the resort restaurants were way beyond her means. "Why don't you text him and tell him I'll take you?"

He stilled, watching her warily.

"You're not going to get in trouble for accepting a ride

from a stranger, are you? You can tell him I'm working for Diane now."

She gave him a moment to answer, but when he didn't, she made an executive decision. "This morning at four AM, I was in New York City. Other than a latte and a protein bar, I haven't had anything to eat since landing in Idaho Falls. I'm dead on my feet and starving, so I'm heading out now, and there's no way I'm leaving you here alone."

"Fine." Reluctantly, he shot off a text message. As he grabbed his heavy backpack off the floor, his phone vibrated, and he read the screen. As usual, his expression gave nothing away. Not even a flicker of emotion.

God, when she'd been his age, she'd been a hormonal mess. Crazy in love with Griffin and unable to be with him because of Lulu's crush, jealous of all the time her sisters got with her mom, frustrated beyond reason that she didn't have a passion the way Lulu and Gigi did.

So, for this boy to be so flat…made her wonder what had happened to him. She couldn't help the clutch of protectiveness. "Let's go." Heading out of the office, she locked the door behind her and stood in the long hallway. "I forget which way I came in."

"Where did you park?"

"Employee lot."

He pointed left. "This way."

With everyone gone for the night, the only sound was their footsteps on the plush carpet.

"How old are you?" she asked.

"Fourteen." He mumbled it. "I'll be fifteen in six weeks."

"Really?" He looked older. Or maybe he just had an old soul. The moment she pushed on the release bar, the cold evening air seized her. "Oh, my God. I forgot how cold it gets in the mountains." She thumbed the remote keypad for her car, and the taillights blinked. As part of her package, Diane had rented it for two weeks, but after that, Stella was on her own. She'd need to buy something.

So many expenses.

She couldn't afford to buy a house, but where would she find a rental during ski season in Calamity? And without a secure job, she didn't want to commit to a long lease. What if she screwed up majorly and got fired? She'd only worked with Taji for three months.

Well, she just had to hope Diane would be back soon. She'd do great with guidance, but she didn't have the experience to run the show on her own.

The minute she got inside the car, she cranked up the heat.

"You have to wait for the engine to warm up." Austin didn't sound impatient or annoyed, just like he was stating a simple fact. "Otherwise, you're just blowing out cold air."

"And the proof of your theory is that my nose is turning into an icicle right this minute." Closing the vent, she pulled out of the lot. "Okay, so tell me what a fourteen-year-old boy's doing in a wedding planner's office."

"I don't know. I just help sometimes."

Not much of an answer. "But you're staying at the Inn, so are you and your uncle visiting for the holidays?"

"No, I'm staying with him while my dad's deployed."

"Ah, okay. So, you're not from Calamity."

"I mean, I was born here, but I only lived here as a baby."

"And how long are you here this time?"

"Nine months." His tone suggested a prison sentence. "Eight to go."

She grinned at him. "Can't wait to get out of here?"

Slumping in the seat, he didn't answer.

"You really dislike it here that much?"

"I don't care about it."

"Oh, okay." She smacked the steering wheel. "You just threw down on my hometown. Challenge accepted. Next time you come to the office we're going for a drive. Give me an hour, and I'll turn you into a Calamity fanatic." When he didn't even crack a smile, she said, "You are coming back, aren't you?"

"No idea. I think something's wrong with my babysitter."

The whole situation was very odd. *First, he's fourteen and has a babysitter?* But then, staying in a hotel with his uncle? And how does he know his way around the office? *None of this adds up.* "So, you can tell me to mind my own business, but if you're just visiting, how do you know so much about Diane's business?"

"When my babysitter's got an appointment or something, I get off the bus there. Usually, I know before school, but today my uncle dropped me off and told me to hang out with Quinn until he came back to get me."

His uncle sounds shady as fuck. "Owl Hoot's pretty cool, huh? Bet you've never seen anything like it."

It hadn't existed seven years ago. As the original settlement of Calamity, the Bowie family had purchased the ghost town to keep it preserved. But they'd turned it into a living museum and high-end resort. It was the coolest place Stella had ever seen, and she loved that she got to work in a town where people dressed like gunslingers from the late eighteen-hundreds.

Her headlights lit up the two-lane road that led from Owl Hoot to Highway 191. Once there, she turned to get to the Inn. "Well, I'd have been lost without you today, so I'd be happy to pay you if you'd like to earn some extra cash."

He flicked a glance at her. "How much?"

"Minimum wage. Under the table, of course."

His eyes narrowed, and his interest sharpened, but he didn't say anything.

"You want to do it?" she asked.

"Yes."

"What're you going to spend that money on?"

"Guitar lessons."

Gigi. How badly did she want to tell him her sister was a musician and could teach him everything he needed to know? But nope. She'd keep her mouth shut. Since she hadn't talked to her sister in years, it seemed a little premature to offer her services. So, she changed the topic. "You're in ninth grade, right? Does Ms. Marshall still teach Geometry? I swear that woman *wanted* to fail me."

His phone chimed, and he checked it, his forehead creasing in concern.

"Everything all right?"

"My uncle says to wait."

"Wait where?" *It's like zero degrees outside.* Finally, they turned onto the Inn's long driveway. "Tell me where I'm going."

"Just drop me off here."

"No way." His dull tone worried her. "It's too cold." *This whole situation's just weird.* "I've got a bunch of messages to catch up on anyway, so I'll wait in the car with you. You can tell him that." *So, whatever drug deal his uncle's doing, he'll at least know someone's looking out for his nephew.*

With a few hand gestures, he led her toward the most remote cottages on the property—exactly where she and Griffin used to hook up. They'd had a hard time finding places where they could be alone, so they'd come here, and…God, it all came rushing back.

That jittery feeling of anticipation. The buildup, all day, of texting him, looking forward to the final bell after sixth period, when she could race over here and finally be with him.

That explosive connection when their bodies would slam together, their mouths fusing.

It hurt so much to remember his hunger, the way he'd devour her.

Sometimes, she just ached for him.

Nearing the last row of cabins, Austin grabbed his backpack off the floorboard. "This is good." He didn't even give her a chance to brake, before throwing the door open.

"Would you wait a second?" Nothing felt right about this. Parking, she left her rental car on the side of the two-lane road. Their boots crunched on the fresh show, and when the top of her head brushed a low hanging branch, ice rained down on her. It went under the collar of her coat, sending pinpricks of cold through her. "Oh, my God, it's like the Arctic here."

"You have to be quiet." He whispered it harshly. Not like he was scared—more like it was vitally important. And then, just before they broke through a clearing between the trees, his steps faltered, and he jerked to a stop.

A second later, he darted behind a tree.

Every protective cell in her body sounded the alarm, and she followed him. "What's going on?"

"Shh."

An older couple—covered head to toe in expensive winter wear—stood talking to a tall, broad-shouldered man on the front porch of a cottage. Wait…

That long, dark hair, that sexy facial scruff, and loose-limbed stance…her body reacted before her mind could catch up.

Griffin.

Chapter Three

SHOCK ROCKETED THROUGH HER, AS JARRING AS IF Stella had touched a light socket.

My Griffin.

She'd kissed every inch of that hard, inked body.

She'd loved him with every ounce of her soul.

And then she'd kissed another man and lost him for good.

"*Griffin's* your uncle?" she asked in a low voice.

"I'm serious. You have to be quiet. They can't know I'm here."

"Who are they?" And why would Griffin be involved with bad people?

"They're my grandparents."

Okay, wow. What is going on?

First of all, Griffin couldn't possibly be this teenager's uncle. He was the oldest of the seven James siblings. *And this boy is fourteen…*

I've only been gone seven years.

Secondly, Griffin was one of the best men she'd ever known. He wouldn't be involved in anything shady.

Even when he'd wanted her beyond reason, he'd never touched her until her sister had gone off to college and fallen for someone else.

After that…it had been *on*. It was like they'd made up for lost time—constantly touching, kissing, making love.

"They're leaving," he said.

The three of them headed down the walkway toward a Mercedes SUV. Now, they stood close enough for Stella to hear the conversation.

"Well, I'm not going to argue with you," the older woman said. "The situation speaks for itself. If he'd been staying with us, this never would've happened."

"As I said, he didn't actually do anything wrong, and I'll clear it up with the principal tomorrow." Griffin kept his voice calm, but she knew him. She knew the set of his shoulders, the tension in his jaw.

"I think we all know he should be staying with us. We have the time to give him."

Stella didn't like what this woman was suggesting. Sure, he'd been a hell-raiser when he was a kid, but Griffin had always taken his responsibilities seriously. His siblings all came to him when they needed something. He was a rock.

"As always, you're welcome to see him whenever you like," Griffin said.

The grandmother gave him a scolding look. "He should be *living* with us. We're retired. We can give him the discipline and structure he so obviously needs."

"The problem with kids today is that parents don't hold them accountable." The grandfather wagged a finger. "And you speaking to the principal is the perfect example. *Austin* needs to do that. He needs to go in there and apologize and accept the consequence of his behavior. Look, it's clear the boy's already showing signs of running off the rails under your care. He needs discipline. He needs *family*."

"And living in a hotel?" The woman gestured around them. "You must see this is no place to raise a boy."

"I'm not raising him." Though still calm, Griffin's tone tightened. "He's staying with me until his dad gets back."

"That's not for eight months." The woman's voice rose along with her agitation. "We're coming up on the holidays, and he'll be spending them with us anyway. We'll just take him home with us tonight and bring him back after New Year's."

"The fact that Peyton entrusted a man like you with a teenage boy is troublesome enough," the grandfather said. "But perhaps when he hears his son's already been suspended— not one month into his deployment—it will drive home our point about your character."

"What a dick." *But if* I'm *getting this upset, imagine Austin's reaction.* He didn't need to hear this. "Come on. It's freezing. Let's wait in the car."

But the boy was riveted. He wasn't going anywhere.

"Austin's doing just fine here," Griffin said.

"He's not doing *fine*." The woman lifted both arms and let them drop to her sides. "That's the whole point. He got *suspended*."

The grandfather pointed toward the cottage. "The boy's not home, and it's six o'clock? He should be doing his homework and sitting down to dinner. He should be doing chores. The fact that he's galivanting around town proves our point."

It struck her that Griffin didn't suggest they take the issue up with Austin's dad. And wasn't that just like him? To carry such a huge weight on his own?

43

ERIKA KELLY

"The problem is that you're not invested in him the way his family is," the grandfather said.

"I'm invested," Griffin said. "I love that boy. I spend as much time with him as I can, and we sit down to dinner together every night. Again, the door is always open for you to visit."

Stella had so many questions, but when she glanced at Austin, she knew she couldn't ask. He was practically vibrating with tension. She wanted to help, but she didn't know how.

"Leonard, let's go." The woman tugged on her husband's arm.

But the man didn't budge. "We're going to get dinner in the restaurant. By the time we're done, I expect Austin to be home. We'll have a conversation with him then."

"This is why you were hanging out in the office, isn't it?" Stella whispered. "Griffin didn't want you to hear this conversation."

But the boy paid her no attention.

"I've already talked to him," Griffin said. "He told me exactly what happened at school today. His grades are good. Everything's under control."

"Nothing is under control," the woman said. "Our grandson's living in a hotel room with a single man."

The grandfather folded his arms across his burly chest. "A man whose business is attached to a biker bar."

Stella's hackles went up. What was all this about Griffin's character?

It had been a long time since he and his friends had used Town Hall for parkour or turned the high school into a skatepark.

And it's a two-bedroom cottage. Not a room.

"Our businesses aren't attached. In any event, Austin will look forward to seeing you after dinner."

"Look, you're taking this the wrong way." The woman softened her tone. "You're a single man, a business owner, and we're retired. We can give him the cultural advantages he's not getting. With us, he'll join a sports team, get involved with our church. We have the resources and the time to take care of him."

"Cultural—" Griffin's jaw snapped shut, and his gaze dropped to his boots. Drawing a breath, he looked back at them. "I have the resources to give him whatever he needs. I own the shop, so I make my own hours. He knows he's welcome to join teams or do anything he likes—we've discussed his options. Right now, he's just happy to hang out."

"Kids need to be busy," the grandfather said. "They get in trouble when they have too much time on their hands."

"Do you have any idea what that boy's life has been like? How many times he's moved? This is his dad's second deployment."

Stella could've sworn Austin stopped breathing.

"High school is brutal," Griffin continued. "Try to imagine being the new kid in a small town where all the friend groups have been set for years. I'm not going to force him to sign up for anything right now, because in my book, there's nothing more important than greeting him with a snack when he gets off the bus and just being there for him in case he feels like talking. The last thing I want to do is shuttle him off to some class he doesn't care about. Right now, stability far outweighs 'cultural advantages.'"

He'd rendered them silent, and Stella's heart ached for the man she'd lost.

Griffin was a protector. Once, he'd cared about her with the same passion he showed Austin.

She would never forgive herself for losing him.

"And you think he's going to find stability in a hotel?" the grandfather asked. "This is the last place he'll find that. There's nothing but transients coming and going."

"Yeah, a lot of transients stay in five-star hotels." She said it quietly, hoping to break the tension. "This isn't exactly a truck stop."

It broke nothing.

The grandmother's spine remained rigid, but her cheeks had spots of red that had nothing to do with the cold.

Griffin held up his hands in a conciliatory gesture. "Look, I know you want the best for him."

"That's all we want."

"But while his dad's a thousand miles away, the worst thing we can do is fight over him. I'm asking you to accept that while he's in my care, he's my number one priority. I'm choosing to meet his very real need for stability and security before I consider bonus things like cultural opportunities."

Her heart beat for this man. He was fierce, loyal...he was everything.

She could barely stand to live in her own skin, knowing she'd lost him.

"I think it's in Austin's best interests if we think of ourselves as a team, taking care of him together," Griffin said.

"He will never be your priority because you're not his family. We are." The grandmother leveled a hard gaze at Griffin. "And, frankly, we have to wonder why a grown man *wants* to spend so much time with a teenage boy."

Rage enflamed her. Both because the woman had just accused an amazing man like Griffin of something so heinous *and* that Austin had to hear the sickening implication. Emerging from behind the tree, she marched toward the walkway. Not a chance would she let them get away with calling him a predator.

As the soles of her boots crunched on the hard-packed snow, multiple thoughts hit her at once. One, Austin was listening, so she couldn't go off on them and make things worse. Two, this was a difficult situation, and she probably shouldn't be inserting herself.

And three, it was too late since they'd all turned to her.

So, she did the only thing she could think of.

She flashed a big smile and slid her arm through Griffin's. "Hey, baby." She got up on her toes and kissed his cheek. "Sorry I'm late. I had three brides call with last-minute crises." She turned to the grandparents. "Hello. I'm Stella Cavanaugh, Griffin's fiancée. You must be Austin's grandparents. I'm so glad to finally meet you."

Griffin went hard as a rock.

Oh, God.

What had she done?

Fiancée?

Of all the things she could've thrown out there…

The woman looked from her to Griffin, her gaze lingering, as if verifying the truth.

But she had to go with it, had to keep the smile in place.

"When did this happen?" the woman asked.

"Oh, we've been together off and on since we were kids. For the past few years, I've been working in Dallas and most recently in New York, but now that he's got Austin with him, I knew it was time to come home. To be a family." Smiling, Stella gazed up at him with adoration. "I hadn't been home a day before he proposed…and of course, I said yes."

"You never mentioned a girlfriend," the grandmother said to Griffin.

Stella only gave him a single beat to respond, and when he didn't, she jumped right in. "Oh, you know Griffin. He's a man of few words." She gave him a warm smile. "And I love that about him. Besides, we've just always known we're it for each other. But we're ready for the next stage now."

"You said Cavanaugh?" The grandfather's gaze rested on Stella's hand on Griffin's arm.

She nodded.

"Tyler Cavanaugh's a good man." He seemed impressed, so that was a good thing.

"Oh, yeah. My parents are the best."

"Your family does good work." The grandfather gave Griffin an approving look. "All right, then. We'll get some dinner and be back to visit with Austin."

They watched the grandparents get into their SUV.

The anger radiating off Griffin made her pull her arm out of his. "Oh, my God, did it work? Did they back off?" She really couldn't tell.

But the look in his eyes told her she'd only made things worse.

After giving Austin instructions to set the table and warm the rolls, Griffin led Stella into the master bedroom bathroom and shut the door. "What the hell have you done?" Anger lit him up like a bottle rocket, and he needed to hold onto it, stoke it, fucking *accelerate* it.

Because standing right here in front of him was the woman who made his heart thunder, his body heat up, and his dick go hard.

And it was damn confusing to have a reaction like that to the woman who'd just thrown his world into chaos.

"They accused you of being a *monster*, so I stepped in. I *had* to. And it worked. They backed off."

Always so fiery, Stella never backed down. Never just fucking apologized. She drove him crazy.

But she was so beautiful. She used to be a brunette, but this blonde hair was sexy as fuck. And that lush mouth he'd kissed countless times? Jesus, he could feel it, the sensuous slide of their tongues, the indescribable softness. *Dammit.* Why did his body have to respond to her?

The only way to shut it down was to remind himself she hadn't changed at all. She was still impulsive and wreaking havoc.

Only this time, the stakes were so much higher. "They didn't back off. They'll never back off." *Not as long as I'm the one taking care of their grandson.* "You know nothing about the situation."

Her mouth opened as if she were about to argue, but then she deflated. "No, I don't. You're right. I shouldn't have jumped into a situation I knew nothing about."

"Then why did you? It's none of your damn business."

"It became my business when Austin overheard the conversation. I was with him, Griffin. He was standing right next to me when they accused you of being a *pedophile*."

Griffin closed his eyes. With all the moves and deployments, this kid had been through more than enough. He couldn't think of the last time he'd seen Austin laugh, relax, have a good time. And now, she'd made his situation worse. "Stella."

Why did he bother trying to get through to her? She'd always been this way.

A gorgeous, sexy, avenging angel.

Who obviously hadn't learned anything from her past mistakes. Because here she was standing in front him seven years later, battle-ready, as if a fake engagement was a fine solution to his problem. Dark eyes sparkling, cheeks pink, sexy lips pressed together so tightly his tongue was dying to lick them open.

He let out a breath. "Do you know who they are?"

"I know they're assholes for making you look bad, and I know Austin's afraid of them."

His skin went tight. "Afraid?"

"He was hiding in the woods, telling me to be quiet, so we didn't draw attention to ourselves."

"He wasn't hiding because he's afraid of them. They're not bad people. They're just strict. I told him to get off the bus at Owl Hoot because I knew they'd be coming over to discipline him about the suspension, and I don't want—I will *not* let them make him feel bad or punish him for something he didn't do."

Her features melted, like she was going all soft and sweet on him. And he didn't want that. Couldn't deal with it. "That's Judge Pilson."

She sucked in a sharp breath. "Oh."

Yeah. That's right. The Hanging Judge of Calamity.

The same judge Griffin and his friends had stood before in his courtroom.

The man had eviscerated them.

"I have to get back out there, but dammit, Stella. I

don't have legal rights to Austin, so I'm one court order away from him living with those people." And why the *fuck* did she have to smell so good? "It's been hard enough fending them off. I don't need you showing up and blowing it all to hell."

"I'm pretty sure Austin did that by getting suspended. I was just trying to fix an ugly situation. But you're right, and I'm sorry. What can I do to fix this?"

"Once I break their trust, there's no coming back."

"So, we won't lie." That simple shift closer to him caused a stir in the air, and her familiar scent floated around him, drifting into his sensibilities and making him *remember*.

Their naked bodies under the sheets, her soft, smooth skin.

In his truck, racing to get somewhere with a bed and some privacy so he could strip her naked and feast on her sexy body.

Fuck.

Fuck.

Fuck.

She touched his arm. "It doesn't have to be a big deal. We can just consider ourselves officially engaged. Everyone in Jackson County knows our story, and they'll totally believe we got back together."

"I'm not lying to everyone I know. That's a shitty thing to do."

"Sure, it is, but you know what's worse? The Pilsons dropping the suggestion that you're a creeper. You think a court order's bad? Wait until it gets out that you're perving on the teenager who's living with you. Trust me. Once they put that thought in someone's head, there's no coming back from it."

She was right about that.

"Look, let's just play it out for now. They're coming back after they eat, so I'll stay and have dinner with you guys. If being engaged makes them back off, then we go with the lie. If it's the same old song and dance, then I'll be the one to come clean. I'll say I jumped the gun and got carried away. Unless..." Her eyes went wide, and she sucked in a quick breath. "Tell me you're not married."

"Not married."

"Girlfriend?"

"Nope."

"Oh, thank God." She sounded genuinely relieved. "So, what do you think? Wait and see their reaction or do you want me to kill the whole thing right now?"

"It's not that simple." And that's the core of the problem right there. Her bold ideas fit her big, beautiful personality, but she never thought through the consequences. "How long are you here? Are you just visiting through Thanksgiving?"

"I'm not visiting. I moved here."

"You moved back home?" *Oh, Jesus.* This town wasn't big enough to keep him safe from this woman but posing as her fiancé?

Fuck my life.

"Yes, Diane hired me. She's training me to take over the wedding planning business at the resort."

Unbelievable. Okay, well, like it or not, she was back, and there wasn't a damn thing he could do about it.

"So, I really think we can pull this off. I'll be working crazy, long hours, but one text, and I'll come right over and be your fake fiancée."

She tossed out the idea carelessly. As if it wouldn't cost her a damn thing. *This is why we don't work. She's reckless.*

And that's how people get hurt.

"And what about you, Stella? Have you considered how this will affect you?"

"What do you mean? I just told you I'm willing to play the part." That jut of her chin, the challenging look in her eyes should've pissed him off.

Instead, it made his blood burn.

Because she didn't back down. She was strong, intense. He'd once loved that about her.

Shake it off. "Cool. So, you've made peace with your family?" The last time he'd talked to her older sister, she'd just ended her relationship because the tabloids had made it look like Stella and Lulu's boyfriend were having a torrid affair. It wound up being a total fabrication, but the damage had been done. After what had happened seven years earlier, it'd been a blow to Lulu to see the photos.

"No."

He watched while it sank in. "I don't know how you're going to do that when you're lying to them."

Indecision flickered across her features. "They'll understand when they find out why."

"Maybe." He hunched a shoulder. "Or maybe not."

"What do you want me to do here, Griffin? Let them spread disgusting rumors about you? This is a small town, and I'm not going to stand by and let them plant that seed in people's heads. So, if I have to pretend we're engaged for a few months, I'll do it. I'll do it for you."

"And what about Austin?"

"That's the whole point. If this works, they'll back off, and he'll get to stay with you."

"Right, but my point is that we'll be making him lie, too."

"Okay, okay. God." With a defeated sigh, she lowered

her face into her hands. "What've I done? I haven't even told my parents I'm back in town yet. The last thing I want to do is lie to their faces. And, no, of course, I don't want to put Austin in that position." She tipped her chin and straightened her shoulders. "I'm sorry. I jumped in without thinking."

It was impossible to stay angry at this woman. "I appreciate what you were trying to do, and I get where it came from, but I'll tell you right now, you can hurt your sister, and you can hurt me, but you cannot hurt Austin. That boy's had it tough enough, but on my watch? He gets the good stuff."

"You didn't see his reaction. I had to do *something*." Her voice came out like she barely had any breath left in her. "But okay, I'll fix it. When they get here, I'll tell them I jumped the gun. That we're not officially engaged." She gazed up at him, her soft lips parted, her skin so creamy and smooth. "And I never meant to hurt you. You have to know that."

Clearly, she was thinking of the rehearsal dinner. She didn't know he'd come to Dallas.

And she never would.

"Sure." It wasn't her fault she hadn't loved him the same way he'd loved her. "I have to get back out there."

As soon as they opened the door, they heard voices. Mrs. Pilson talked to Austin like he was a toddler, and the judge spoke with his deep, authoritative tone.

Before turning into the living area, Stella stalled. In the dark hallway, she gazed up at him. "I'm really sorry." Nervous, she licked her lips. "But I'll take care of it, okay?"

And this was the power she had over him. Because he knew her heart. And it was good and kind and pure. For whatever reason, Stella had latched onto Austin, become his Mama Bear, and she'd lied both to protect Griffin and the boy.

He'd only had her for eighteen months, but he'd been damn lucky to be one of the people she loved so fiercely.

With a curt nod, he pushed past her, because he couldn't get caught up in her again. Stella threw herself into life wholly and recklessly. She was a passionate woman who fell in love fast and hard, while he…well, he'd only ever loved her.

"Hey." He swept past the Pilsons and turned off the slow cooker. As he listened to them chat, he felt Stella behind him. It was that slow churn of air that stirred up her scent, causing electrical impulses to fire at the back of his neck and cascade down his back.

And even after seven years apart—probably in the kitchen of the same cottage where they'd once spent so much time together—they fell into sync. She pulled down plates, while he gathered silverware. She got napkins, and he found the ladle.

Lifting the slow cooker lid, Stella breathed in the scent of herbs and roasted meat. "Don't tell me you made this?"

"Ha. Good one. No, some mornings, my dad drops dinner off before work."

"He's such a sweetheart."

"It helps that work is about a hundred yards away."

"I'll bet it does. Tell him to bring over his lemon tart." She glanced at the stove. "Should we make some vegetables? Shouldn't Austin have something green?"

"I don't…uh…" He stood in front of the refrigerator as if a bunch of spinach or broccoli might magically appear. "We don't really like…"

Standing beside him and peering inside, she playfully

smacked his arm. "He's a growing boy. He has to eat good food. I literally just got into town today, and I went straight to the office, so I haven't gone shopping yet, but when I do, I'm going to buy you guys some fruit and vegetables."

His pulse ticked in his throat. Noise roared in his ear, and he couldn't have stepped away from her if someone had shouted, *Fire!*

This is what she does. She makes people feel like they've known her forever.

He couldn't fall for it again.

The judge cleared his throat, and they both whipped around to find the grandparents staring at them. Mrs. Pilson grinned. "We're going to head out now."

"We'll pick Austin up at our usual time on Saturday." The judge gave them a nod that felt very much like acceptance. And then he turned and headed for the door.

Mrs. Pilson lingered a moment longer, watching them with a big smile, making him acutely aware of how close Stella stood to him in front of the refrigerator. "I can tell you've known each other a long time. You've got that familiarity with each other. Have a wonderful rest of the week." And then she followed her husband out the door.

Stella looked up at him. "Did that just happen? Are they backing off?"

"Seems like it."

Her eyes went wide, and she looked at him like they'd just pulled off a heist. "It worked."

He stepped back, closing the door. "It worked."

"So, does that mean we're doing this?" she asked.

How the hell was he supposed to look his parents in the eyes and tell them he was engaged? Lie to his friends, his employees? But until he got that document from the

JAG attorney, he didn't see another choice. "As long as you understand, it means you can't tell anyone. Not your sisters, not your parents...no one."

She reached out a hand. "For Austin, okay?"

A handshake shouldn't carry so much weight. But this hand—this one had sifted through his hair, smoothed the worry lines off his brow, and gripped his ass while they'd fucked, pulling him in deeper. It had fisted his cock while she'd licked him like an ice cream cone.

"Yeah, for Austin's sake." He reached for her, but the minute he felt her delicate hand—the warmth, the firm grip, the sizzle of their connection—he knew he was in big trouble.

Chapter Four

STELLA STOOD IN FRONT OF AN ENORMOUS SCREEN IN the conference room, beyond impressed with the stunning images splashed across it. Taji's office didn't have this kind of technology, so it was a learning curve, but Stella loved the way each wedding was displayed like a digital wish book.

"I'm in awe of your work." Stella smiled at her boss, whose face appeared in a box at the top of the screen.

"Oh, thank you. That's lovely to hear. I feel terrible that I'm not there to help you but extremely grateful you didn't jump ship like the others."

"Well, I'm definitely in over my head—I'll be honest with you about that—but between Quinn and Austin, I think we're doing all right."

"Austin?" Diane sounded amused.

"I'm not even joking. He was here my first day, and he saved me. For a fourteen-year-old, he's surprisingly knowledgeable and insightful."

Someone caught Diane's attention, and she held up a finger. "Excuse me a moment."

Right then, Quinn walked in. "A glacier wedding? I'm born and raised in Calamity, and I can't even imagine jumping out of a helicopter and standing on the side of a mountain to exchange vows."

Stella laughed. "Actually, the view's spectacular at the summit. And the ride down's a blast."

"What's your dream venue?"

"For a wedding?" As if she hadn't visualized it a thousand times. "I definitely want it here in Calamity. Probably something small." She couldn't imagine marrying without her sisters standing beside her and her dad walking her down the aisle.

Her heart squeezed so hard. She still hadn't told her parents she was back, and she just didn't know how to. How did she explain not talking to them for seven years? How did she make that first move?

"Have you seen Mountain Chapel yet?" Quinn asked. "It's small and intimate. It's just so romantic."

She'd seen the images on the website. And, honest to God, she could picture herself in a wedding gown facing her groom. He had dark, tousled hair, the perfect amount of scruff, tattoos everywhere, and a look in his eyes that said *The minute I get you alone, I'm stripping you bare.*

And that man was Griffin. The only man she could ever imagine spending her life with.

"It really is." Built of river stone and reclaimed wood, its stained-glass windows and rustic timber trusses and beams gave it an old-world feel. "It's perfect."

Diane's voice cut into her reverie. "Sorry. That was the nurse. The doctor will be here in a few minutes, so let's move ahead to the princess since that's the most important one." Clicking forward, she landed on the royal wedding.

ERIKA KELLY

So far, everything her boss had shown her was impressive, but this one? She blew out a slow breath.

"Right? Diane's a goddess." Quinn threw an arm around Stella's shoulders. "But this one's a goddess-in-training. You picked a good one. She's doing an amazing job."

"Oh, I know." Diane gave her an approving grin. "Believe me, I knew what I was doing when I made that call. Now, let's finish this up because we, ladies, are going to crush this."

Stella smiled because she hadn't expected that phrase to come out of this elegant woman's mouth.

"Okay, so this wedding is not quite what the bride wanted," Diane said. "But she's very happy with the outcome."

Lavish bouquets of white flowers, massive crystal chandeliers, the finest bone china, and silverware…it all looked perfectly royal to Stella. The bride would walk down a grand staircase with gleaming banisters. "What did she want?"

"Since she's having a formal ceremony at the palace, she'd hoped for something simpler here. Something that better reflected her and Brodie's personalities. Unfortunately, once her mother got involved, it slowly transformed into a mirror image of the royal wedding."

"Mostly, it's because of the guest list," Quinn said. "They didn't expect so many royals to fly out here for a second ceremony. But since they're coming, they can't exactly throw a hoe-down."

"Why not?" *That's the best part about wedding planning—coming up with wild ideas, thinking outside the box.*

Until she remembered her *wild* idea to be "engaged" to Griffin.

And then she deflated like a popped balloon.

Because, boy, had she blown it. *Big-time.*

If she'd had any hope of getting back with him, she'd ruined it with a stunt like that. Instead of helping him, she'd put him in a position to lie. To make *Austin* lie.

She didn't think there was any way to come back from this one.

Fortunately, Diane kept talking, forcing her back into the moment. "At this point, Rosie's fine with it. But for obvious reasons, we need to stay on top of this one. We can't afford to have anything go wrong, which is why, I suppose, my two assistants quit, to impress upon me that I can't function without them."

"I'm so sorry." Quinn looked apologetic. "I wish I could give you more time—"

"Nope," Diane said. "That's not what you signed on for. I'm grateful for the time you give me."

"Well, thank you," Quinn said. "But I do wish I could help more. In any event, we've got three experienced event planners interviewing on Monday. We've got this."

"Thank you, sweetheart." Diane smiled warmly. "Well, I must go, but you'll find all the details in Rosie's file. It includes contact information for all the venues and service providers and a log of past conversations. I'll try not to micromanage you, but you'll forgive me if we do a lot of video-conference calls, so I can see what you're doing in real-time."

Stella smiled at her. "I'll want you with me every step of the way."

"As I'm sure Quinn already told you, I encourage you to record the details of all your conversations. Emotions run high during wedding planning, and I've been grateful more times than I can count to forward my notes to those who swear I've gotten it all wrong."

"I hear you, and I get it. I actually love how you do things here. It's far less chaotic than the other offices I've worked in."

"As for new clients, please remember to do all the work in the shared file so I can follow along. That way, I can catch anything early in the process that might not work with our location or vendors."

"Perfect. Oh, I just wanted to ask…Austin's babysitter's having surgery, so how do you feel about him coming here after school when Griffin's got a meeting or a project he can't miss?"

"I don't mind at all. He's always welcome."

Stella didn't miss the look Quinn and Diane gave each other. "What?"

And then Quinn broke out in a big grin. "It's just really nice that you make him feel so important and valued. He doesn't get enough of that."

"Okay, well, I wish I had better news about my mother's health, but I do hope to get her home and with a caregiver in the next couple of weeks. I can't apologize enough for not being physically present, but I'm available any time of day or night to jump in and help. And Stella? As daunting as it all seems, I can't think of anyone better to handle the situation than you. Good luck you two. Bye, now."

Once the screen went blank, silence weighed heavily in the room.

And then Quinn got busy, gathering up files. "I know why Diane hired you, you know."

"Because of my mom?"

"Nope. The two who used to work here would be all

stressed out and snapping orders, but you're really chill, and from what little I've seen, you've got great ideas."

"Thank you for saying that. It makes me feel better about taking this on."

"All right, back to work for both of us." Quinn gave her a big grin, before heading out of the conference room.

Back at her desk, Stella dove right in. Checking her to-do list, she saw she had to return six calls and dozens of emails, check in with three vendors, and figure out orders for some future events. *Oh, brother.*

Well, as her dad liked to say, *You reach the summit by taking one step at a time*. So, that's what she'd do, check off one item after another. And as soon as they hired a few people, her load would ease.

Truthfully, she didn't mind having so much on her plate. Not only did it give her a crash course in wedding planning at the Owl Hoot Resort and Spa, but it kept her mind occupied, so it didn't stray where she didn't want it to go.

Toward Griffin.

How she'd done a spectacular job of reminding him why he'd broken up with her.

On the plane from New York, she'd fantasized about getting back together with him. Picnicking on the ledge, holding hands, and gazing up at the bright blue sky through a canopy of pine trees. She'd wanted to explore each of his new tattoos and find out what they meant. Because everything Griffin did had a purpose.

She wanted to catch up on everything he'd done the last seven years.

What happened to his friends? Did any of them still live in town? That night had changed Griffin. Before, he'd been wild and reckless. After, he'd become this super-responsible, think-everything-through-first kind of man. And she got it. Of course, she did.

But also…had he fallen in love?

A lot happened over seven years.

But now was not the time to wallow in what she'd lost.

Now, she needed to return the florist's call. But just as she reached for the phone, Quinn walked in with a huge smile. "You've got a visitor."

Automatically, Stella checked the wall calendar. She didn't see any appointments.

"It's your sister." Quinn made it sound like the greatest gift in the world. "You want me to send her in or…?"

And yet, for Stella, it was like hearing the cops say she was under arrest. That terrible fight-or-flight instinct kicked in.

Of course, she'd known she was planning Gigi's wedding—that was the main reason she'd taken the job— but she hadn't talked to her or set up an appointment yet, so she wasn't prepared to see her.

Quinn's smile wavered. "She just wanted to drop something off for Diane, so I told her I'd see if you could chat with her for a sec. Figured you didn't want me sending your sister away." She watched Stella carefully.

"Of course. Absolutely, send her in." Fear numbed her legs, keeping her rooted to the chair.

"Great, one sec."

She didn't even have a moment to check her lipstick or smooth her hair, as Gigi breezed right into her office, coming to an abrupt stop when she saw Stella.

"*Stella?*"

"Hey, yes. Surprise." Her brain sent multiple commands at once.

Stand up.

Say hello.

Drop to the floor and curl up in the fetal position until she leaves.

And then her sister came barreling around the desk, arms open wide. Forced to get up, Stella had barely cleared her chair when Gigi wrapped her in her arms, holding onto her as if the office were slowly sinking into the earth.

She only realized she'd braced for Gigi's wrath when it didn't come. So, when she got nothing but love and warmth, Stella's body went weak with relief. She sank into the embrace, breathed in the essential essence that was Gigi—a summer outdoor concert with fresh-cut grass, clear blue skies, and bright yellow sunshine.

Truthfully, as the baby of the family, Stella hadn't been super close to her oldest sister. Gigi had always been larger than life, like a celebrity visiting your house that barely interacted with you. While Stella had admired her, she hadn't really known her.

But she'd always loved her.

"I am *so* happy to see you." Gigi lifted a strand of hair. "You went blonde."

"I did."

"You look like a movie star." Her sister lifted both hands in a helpless gesture. "I can't believe this. What in the world is going on? I fully expected to see Diane."

"I know. Crazy, right?" She smoothed shaky hands down her skinny black pants. Her legs felt weak. "Well, surprise. You've got me instead. I was going to call you, but I just got in yesterday, and I've been thrown right into the job." Her mind was revving so fast, it was hard to think. "Diane's training me to take over the business, but her mom's sick, and she had to leave unexpectedly, so…it's just me. I mean, Diane's still around. We'll talk every day."

"Hey, slow down. It's me."

Stella let out a shaky breath. "Yeah, but you're a big deal to me. You're my sister, and I…" *Now is not the time to get emotional.* "And I'm just really nervous."

Gigi's expression clouded. "So, I don't understand. You've moved back to Calamity? You live here now?"

"That's right."

"And no one told me? Do Mom and Dad know?"

This is way more awful than I ever imagined. "No."

"I don't get it." Gigi stepped back. "How long have you known that you were moving here?"

"I got the call two weeks ago, but I had to give my notice, pack up my apartment…I got into town yesterday."

"You've known for *two weeks*? Okay, I'm super confused right now. If Mom and Diane are friends, why doesn't Mom know about this?"

"Because I asked Diane not to say anything. She knows I haven't been home in a while, and—"

"In a while?" Gigi took another step back. "A while is a semester abroad. A while is a summer internship. You haven't been home in *seven* years. We haven't even heard from you. We only found out three months ago that Dad and Mom knew where you were this whole time."

"I know. I'm sorry."

"You're *sorry*? Sorry doesn't cut it. What did we do to deserve a punishment like *that?* I mean, *you're* the one who kissed Lulu's fiancé. Why punish us?"

"Okay, whoa. Just…" As shame and embarrassment came crashing in, she had to make a concerted effort to hold it at bay. "*This* is why I haven't told anyone I'm here."

"Well, if you'd warned us you were coming home

instead of springing it on me in my wedding planner's office, it might have gone better."

"I know that. I know." God, she was shaking. "I really am sorry. I thought I had a little more time—"

"You needed more than seven years to figure out what to say?"

"Can you stop attacking me, please? I get that you're angry. I get that I haven't handled things well, but I'm here. I'm home, and I'll do everything I can to make things right with you, with Lulu, with everyone." She placed a cool palm on her forehead. "You have to understand...I did it *again*. And after blowing up another one of her relationships, did you think I could just pop in and say, Hey, guys, I'm back! She'll *never* forgive me now. None of you will."

"Lulu?" Gigi waved a hand. "She's fine. She and Xander got married."

"They did?" *Oh, thank God.* The relief nearly dropped her to her knees. Maybe it wouldn't be so hard to see Lulu after all. "I'm so happy to hear that. You have no idea." Finally calming down, she let out a breath. "In any event, I really just need you to back off and give me a chance, okay?"

"Yes, of course. I'm sorry. It's just...you're the last person I expected to see when I walked in here. I mean, if it had been Oprah Winfrey, I'd have been less surprised."

"I know. Believe me, I know I have a lot of explaining to do, and I have a lot to make up for, but I've been thrown into the deep end of a job I'm not experienced enough to handle." She took a calming breath. "I can't get into family issues at work. So, if you want to talk about your wedding, please sit down and let's do it. But for God's sake, you're going to have to wait until tonight and a bottle of tequila before we get into the hardcore conversations that I owe you. Fair?"

It took a long moment filled with tension before Gigi's features softened. "Who are you, and what have you done with my baby sister?"

"I've been living on my own for a long time now, so I've grown up." Feeling more in command, she said, "Now, are you okay with me working on your wedding, or would you rather wait for Diane to come back?"

"Are we really going to talk about weddings right now?"

"Either that or you're going to have to leave so I can get back to work. I'm barely keeping my nose above the water line here, and the only way to survive is to get through it one task at a time." Stella gave her sister a look that said, *What's it going to be?*

Her sister sat in the chair. "This is weird." She pulled a magazine out of her tote bag. "But yes, I want you to plan it. To be honest, I can't imagine anyone I'd want more than you to do it."

"I really appreciate that, but I don't have a lot of experience with this stuff."

"That makes two of us."

"Okay, so Quinn said you wanted to drop something off?"

"Just this." She tapped the magazine. "When Diane asked me what I wanted, I told her I didn't have a single clue."

"You were never the girl who dreamed of weddings."

"I was the girl who dreamed of being married to Cassian Ellis."

Warmth rushed through her. Her sister had loved that boy so hard. He'd loved her too, but their dad had made him promise to keep his hands off Gigi. "I'm so glad you two finally got together." Her phone buzzed, and she silenced it. "We'll talk about that later, too. So, you didn't have a single clue…"

"Right, and she told me to start looking around. She said to check out bridal galleries, magazines, that kind of thing. And let me just tell you, I saw mountains of tulle and fairy lights and…ugh. I *still* didn't have a clue. But then I was at the airport, and I saw this…" She set the magazine on the desk and flipped through the pages. "I love this."

Stella pulled it closer to look at the photographs. It was kitschy—a doughnut truck, a candy table, a wall of paper flowers in teal blue, orange, yellow, cream, pink, and sea green. "Are you going to wear go-go boots? A white patent leather miniskirt?"

Gigi looked horrified. "No, why? Does this give a whole seventies vibe?"

"I don't know what a seventies vibe looks like, but this is very fun. I can totally make this happen."

Her sister looked uneasy.

"You don't have to wear go-go boots. I was kidding. You can do whatever you want."

"That's the thing. I don't know what I want."

"But this caught your attention because it wasn't traditional?"

"Right. Exactly."

"Okay, great." Stella took out a sheet of paper and wrote down *Traditional* and drew a line through it. "There. We've just eliminated something."

Gigi smiled. "It worked, that little technique of yours. I feel better already. One less thing on my list of possibilities."

"Exactly. So, let me ask a few questions, okay?"

"Sure. Hit me."

"How many people are you thinking of inviting? Are we talking about everyone you, Cassian, and our parents have ever known? Or something small and intimate, with just close friends and family? Or somewhere in between?"

"It's football season, so we haven't talked about the details, but I'm pretty sure we want to keep it small."

"And when you imagine yourself in a wedding gown, what does it look like? Because anything goes. You can be a princess with miles of tulle or a go-go girl with a mini skirt."

"You know, I've spent half my life wearing costumes. For auditions and concerts and appearances. I think if I'm going to exchange vows with the love of my life, I want to be as real as I can." She grinned. "Wait, scratch that. That sounds like I'm wearing leggings and no make-up. There will be no bed-head on my wedding day."

"I get it. You want to look beautiful, but you don't want to feel like your wedding is a performance. Let me show you something." She turned to her computer screen and opened up a file. "I call this look Understated." Nudging it toward Gigi, she said, "Does this feel right to you?"

"Ew, no."

Stella wrote down Understated and then crossed it out.

Her sister smiled. "Okay, this is good. There's nothing understated about me."

"It's possible you've spent half your life wearing costumes because you love dressing up. And you can have an intimate wedding and still wear a magnificent ball gown. Literally, anything goes." An image dropped into Stella's mind. A sleeveless, off-white gown, plunging necklines in front and back, sparkling with crystals. A fitted top and gobs of flowing skirt. "Something like…" She tapped the keyboard, opening up the Flair file, and clicked through until she found the exact dress she had in mind.

"Oh…" Gigi looked in awe. "That's…dramatic. And gorgeous. Because when you said ball gown, I was thinking Cinderella, and I guess that's what I associate traditional with."

"And you don't want it."

"Right. I like that one because it's unique and sexy and a show-stopper."

"Perfect. Now, do you have a date in mind?"

"Nothing in particular. It just can't be between August and February."

"So, we know it'll be in spring—either next May or the year after. Check with Cassian and let me know." She opened up her spring wedding file. "We'll go with fresh and lighthearted elements. We can give you a free-flowing bouquet, cocktails with an edible flower garnish…is any of this working for you?"

"Yes. Oh, my God, yes." Gigi sat back in her chair. "I'm really just blown away right now. I've been all over the place. Happy to be getting married but really lost in all the details, and it's like the more magazines I look at the more confused I get. But right now, I feel like I'm in really good hands. And I have to say, knowing that it's my *sister's hands?* It's just…I'm really happy right now."

"Me, too." *This is going to be okay.* Stella was going to get back to her family, and it was all going to work out.

For the first time, she was so glad she'd taken this job. Happiness reared up, and she had to fight back tears.

She wanted to hug Gigi. She'd missed her family so much, and she hadn't seen a path back to them. "I'm sorry

I didn't stay in touch with you. I'm sorry I created so much drama."

"Why, though? That's the thing I don't get. I mean, I know it was a horrible time. Lulu took off to Paris, and Griffin broke up with you, but the rest of us, we were there for you."

"No, Gigi, you weren't. You were a Lollipop. And I'm not blaming you, but you were on a world tour during the whole time Lulu was dating that jerk. And Coco was in college. I'm not blaming anyone, I swear. But I was the only one at home, and honestly? I'd never felt all that close to you and—"

"Can I go in?" the most familiar voice in the world said from the outer office.

The shock to her system shorted out Stella's brain.

"Sure," Quinn said. "Your sister's already in there."

Lulu Cavanaugh strode right into the room. "Sorry, I'm late. It's snowing like mad—" Lulu froze solid as an ice sculpture. "Stella?" Her gaze snapped to Gigi as though her sister had set her up.

"I know. I was shocked, too." Gigi got up cautiously. "Surprise, Stella's home. She's going to plan my wedding. Isn't that great?"

The clash of emotions playing out across Lulu's features sent a knife through Stella's heart. Confusion, torment, anger…it was like her sister didn't know where to land.

And then, Lulu turned on her heel and walked right back out the door.

Her presence hung in the room, a rebuke, a reminder of her failures. If scents triggered emotions, Lulu's perfume was devastation.

It took her back to the rehearsal dinner.

To the awful taste of too much champagne in her mouth.

The growing desperation that her sister wasn't listening to her, that she'd actually go through with marrying this guy who was using her.

The sickening twist in her stomach as Trace's eyes had glazed over when his hand had clamped onto her ass.

When his disgusting mouth had closed over hers, and he'd kissed her.

God.

And then Gigi came around the desk and rubbed her back. "She'll come around. She was just surprised."

"*This* is why I stayed away." Because there was nothing she could say or do to make up for kissing Lulu's fiancé at the rehearsal dinner.

There just wasn't.

Chapter Five

Stella was shaking.

And it was two hours after her sister had run away from her.

In the chapel, the staging team moved around her hauling lights, candles, and ribbons, while Stella stood off to the side comparing their work with Diane's schematics.

What have I done?

Lulu had been her best friend, her person, and no one else in the world would ever come close to filling that role.

That night, when she'd kissed Trace, it had been to save her sister from a lonely, terrible life with a man who'd only wanted to marry into a celebrity family.

He hadn't loved Lulu. He hadn't appreciated her sister for the beautiful, intense, caring, kind soul that she is.

Yes, of course, she knew now how wrong she'd been.

But through all these years, she'd believed that one day she could make peace with her sister, *redeem* herself. She'd imagined coming back into town for some big event like their parent's thirtieth wedding anniversary. Lulu would enter the room, see her, and tears would spring to her eyes, as she raced across the room to hug her. "I missed you so much," Lulu would say.

But then pictures of her and Xander had hit the tabloids, and Stella had figured she'd set the clock back. This time, maybe she'd be exiled forever.

Why hadn't she told her family she was coming home? She'd had two weeks to do it. Her sisters should never have found out by bumping into her.

She'd convinced herself that Taji had extracted every second of her time and energy during those final weeks in the city. *I'll tell them once I'm settled.*

And then she'd told herself she was in over her head. *I'll tell them once I get the hang of things here.*

But those were excuses.

The truth is that I don't know what to say. I don't know how to explain being away for seven years.

And I don't know how to begin making things right.

Obviously, step one was calling her mom. And of course, she'd thought about it every minute since she'd gotten Diane's job offer. Whether she'd been riding the subway or racing across town for supplies, she'd worked on that conversation.

Hey, Mom. Guess what?! I'm moving back to Calamity.

But how do you call your mom out of the blue when you haven't talked to her in seven years?

And she couldn't be flippant. *Hey, Mom. Long time no speak.*

She couldn't pretend as if nothing had happened. It had to be real, genuine.

Mom, I know I haven't talked to you in a long time.

And that right there was why she hadn't done it. Because being real required her to plow through the bravado and bear her soul. The conversation was just too deep and wide to handle on a phone call. She needed to do it in person when they could look each other in the eyes and really see each other.

"That's not where it goes." Austin's voice startled her out of her thoughts.

She landed back in the warm, cozy chapel, surrounded by the smells of furniture polish and melting wax. "Sorry, where what goes?" She followed his gaze to the ceiling. Between the wooden beams, swaths of tulle draped like soggy diapers. "What's it supposed to look like?"

He took the iPad from her, clicked around till he found what he wanted, and handed it back. She checked the image against the actual work. "Oh, I see. That's much better." She smiled at him. "What, do you have like an eidetic memory?"

He ignored her and slid back into the pew where he'd been working on his homework.

She held out the iPad. "Here, show them how it should be done."

He looked at it with big, round eyes.

She shook the device. "Come on."

"I'm not telling them they screwed up."

"Of course not. That would put them on the defensive. You look at the screen, glance up at the ceiling, and go, 'Huh, does something look off to you?' And then they'll figure out the mistake on their own."

"Why don't you do it?"

"Because I'm not the one who caught it."

He hesitated, and she remembered the way he'd cowered behind the tree, hanging onto every word but unable to charge forward and tell his grandparents he wanted to stay with Griffin.

It struck her how little agency this young man had in his life.

She'd grown up here, so she couldn't imagine what it had been like to pick up and move again and again. She could picture him as a little boy saying goodbye to his friends, maybe even having a going away party. Trying again in the new school. But after a third and fourth move? Would he even bother trying anymore?

And what must it feel like to have your dad stationed overseas on a military base? Did Austin ever get a decent night's sleep? Or did he jolt awake with worry that his dad had gotten hurt?

This boy must feel like he didn't have power over anything. She tipped her chin. "Go on. The sooner we get this done, the sooner we can get out of here."

He watched the crew for a moment, particularly Carl, the man who ran the staging company, and then he slid out of the pew, snatched the iPad out of her hand, and stomped off.

Slowly, he made his way to the altar, crossed in front of the wide section of seats, and headed up the middle aisle. Then, he waited for Carl to notice him. *Come on, Austin.* She was about to march over there—even though she knew she shouldn't—when the man turned abruptly and knocked right into him. He looked annoyed, and she hoped the boy wouldn't slink away.

Crap. He did. Austin stepped aside, letting the stager rush by. But then the boy looked at her, chin lowered, long hair in his eyes, and she gave him a warm and encouraging smile.

He held her gaze for one…two…three seconds…and then, with a long-suffering look, he set off after the stager.

Tapping him on the shoulder, Austin showed the man the iPad and pointed to the ceiling.

Once again, Stella held her breath. Because the guy might be mean. She hadn't considered that. She'd been so intent on giving him agency that it hadn't occurred to her the stager could be a total asshole. Being called out by a kid? If he did…

Stella geared up to march over there, but then Carl smiled. A moment later, he burst out laughing. Setting his hand on the boy's head, he playfully pushed him back, and Stella knew everything would be all right.

Austin came back, thrust the iPad at her, and said, "Okay?"

"Yep. Great." She dumped the device into her bag. "Is your uncle picking you up?"

"He told me to text him when I'm ready."

"Well, great news. I got Diane to trade my room at the resort for a cottage at the Inn"—*just in case your grandparents stop by and expect to see us together*—"so, we're neighbors now—yay."

He was unimpressed with her jazz hands.

"Which means I can drive you home." She led the way up the aisle, weighed down by knowing she'd forced him to lie. She'd have to address it in the car.

When she opened the door, the cold air smacked her in the face. Her first step had the sole of her leather boot sliding on the stone walkway. "Whoa."

Austin caught her elbow, steadying her.

"Thanks. That was gonna hurt."

He released her. "Why do you dress like that?"

"Like what?" Growing up in Calamity, she'd never worn the uniform of her classmates: jeans, Uggs, and hoodies. Where her mom had taken her oldest sisters to auditions and cooking classes, she'd taken Stella on shopping trips. Stella had always loved clothes, purses, jewelry, shoes, and she'd had an appreciation for quality from the time she was little. Since living on her own, she hadn't been able to afford designer things, but she'd become an expert on finding the best values.

"Get some winter clothes."

Glancing down, she could see dampness darkening the edges of her stiletto boots, ruining them. "You're right, but I'm a wedding planner. I have to impress brides and their families with my style and panache."

"You impress them with your ideas. And you show them you're smart by wearing winter boots."

She grinned. "Anyone ever tell you you're wise for your age?"

He didn't answer, but she was getting used to him by now. Wishing she had a parka, she dug her keys out of her purse. In Texas, she hadn't had to wear bulky clothes. She despised layering, but okay, fine. She'd go into Wolf Village and shop at their fancy skiwear boutiques.

It's cold as balls.

By the time they reached her rental car, her boots were crusted in snow and completely wet. She got inside and cranked the engine. "Hey, so, I want to apologize for lying to your grandparents. Obviously, Griffin and I aren't engaged."

Ignoring her, he stuffed his backpack between his feet and buckled in.

"I have this terrible thing I do, where my mouth gets ahead of my brain, and I blurt things out—"

"It was a good idea."

Oh. She wasn't sure how she felt about that. "It puts you and Griffin in a crappy situation. It's just that there's nothing more important than a person's reputation. It's our currency in life, you know? If your grandparents put that idea in anyone's head…it would change the way people see Griffin permanently. Do you know what I mean?"

She could feel his eyes on her, but she kept her focus on the road. "Griffin doesn't deserve that. He's a good man. And when I heard them question his character… well, I couldn't just stand there and let them do that. So, even if the lie turns out to have a great outcome, I never should've done that to either of you."

He kept looking at her, and she wanted to ask him what he was thinking, but her gut told her that would just shut him down. So, she kept talking. "You shouldn't have to lie to your family."

"But I do. All the time."

On edge, she waited for more.

"I'm not allowed to chew with my mouth open or put my feet on the table. I can't bring food into my room, use my phone after nine o'clock, or play video games for more than an hour a day. I can't play guitar." His voice went hard with that last one.

"They don't know about the guitar Griffin bought you?" She'd heard him strumming behind a closed door the other night when she'd dropped off some groceries.

He shook his head.

She wanted to tell him he could ask them to back off a little, to give him some room to be himself, but she'd seen them in action. They were intimidating people. "I hate that they're so strict, but I know you're turning fifteen in a few weeks, so the older you get, the less control they'll have over you." Though, she did see a pattern here of him not being able to speak up for himself. And since he was talking… "Hey, so good news. Griffin said he talked to the principal, and you're not suspended anymore."

He didn't respond.

"Which is great." She headed out of the lot. "But he also said you never told Mr. De Luca what happened. How come?" She had to slow for a delivery truck, and when she glanced over at him, she could tell he had no intention of answering.

By the time she reached 191, she knew she'd already become invested in this boy, so she tried again. "Why do I get the feeling you'd rather be suspended than go to school?"

Slouched, he looked out the window, pressing his forehead to the glass.

"Where were you living before this?"

"San Diego."

"Oh, nice. I've never been, but I have this idea in my head that Southern Californians are all laid-back surfers."

"I live on a military base."

"You and your friends don't surf?"

Beneath that shuttered look, she felt his isolation, his deep hurt. She got the feeling he didn't have friends in San Diego. Well, he was in town for eight more months. He could make some here. *What can I do about that?*

"Have you ever taken karate?" That was a good one because it would give him goals to reach, and he'd make friends outside of school.

"Yes, I hate it. Can you stop?"

Right. She should've expected that.

"I just want to get through this." He sounded glum.

She turned down the driveway toward the Inn. "Okay, I'll drop it, but I really do want to show you how cool this town is. Maybe I'll take you to Wild Billy's so you can ride the mechanical bull."

"I'm not riding a bull."

"Said no one ever." *This town's so awesome.* Had he ever been on a ranch? Ridden a horse? "Hey, did you know Calamity was actually founded by outlaws? In the eighteen-hundreds, when people were settling in the west, they figured out pretty quickly that they couldn't make a go of it here. How do you plant food in metamorphic rock, right? Not to mention the harsh weather."

He turned to look at her. *Yes.* Finally, something interested him.

"This land was so inhospitable that it became a haven for outlaws. There was only one way in—the Owl Hoot Pass—and they'd bring stolen horses and cattle in from the east, give them new brands, and then lead them out west and sell them. I love that about our history. So, I just think the people here are naturally quirkier and more independent, which means they're really accepting of everyone else's quirky ways. Like, it doesn't matter who you are, you can't help but fit in."

"I don't care about fitting in."

"Right, I'm saying you don't even have to try. You just have to be yourself. I know you like playing guitar, but maybe while you're in town, you might want to try some other things."

"This isn't my first time here. Before my grandpa Mack died, I came here a lot."

Right. Of course. How else would he know Griffin so well? She gestured to the mountain. "So, you've done it all? Snowboarding, skiing, hiking, rappelling…?"

"No, my grandpa was too old, and Griffin doesn't do stuff like that."

Anymore. Griffin used to do it all the time. But she'd definitely snagged Austin's interest. "You know people come here for the extreme sports, right? Will Bowie's an Olympic gold medalist, and I don't even know how many snowboarding medals his brothers have won." She could totally imagine Austin looking all badass in ski pants and a helmet, his board on his shoulder. *Yessss.* She was dying to ask him about it, but she had to talk to Griffin first.

She parked, and in her shiny-soled boots, she followed him across a snowy embankment, high-stepping to keep from slipping. "We could go ice skating this weekend, if you want."

"No." With his back to her, his voice came out muffled.

She followed him to the door of Griffin's cottage. He stomped his boots on the welcome mat and reached for the handle.

"Hang on, Austin."

He stopped and turned to her, wary, cautious.

"I know it sucks to be dumped into a new school, and I know it's scary to have your dad so far away, but you can either hide out in your bedroom and 'get through this' or you can take advantage of this wild, crazy town. Will you just do me a favor? Give me one day. We'll ride the gondola up the mountain and jump in the hot springs. I'll take you to the Antigravity Center, and we'll bounce on the trampolines. Let's have some fun." She flashed him a smile, hoping she'd convinced him to emerge from his cave of misery.

"I'm good." And with that, he walked into the house, leaving the door open.

She supposed that was an invitation of sorts, so she

stepped into the living area of this two-bedroom cottage tucked deep into the woods.

Oh, man. Every time she was in here, she got knocked back in time.

She remembered reaching to open the door, only to have it thrown open, Griffin's hand on her wrist yanking her inside, kicking the door shut, his hungry mouth on hers, his hands gripping her ass.

He loved my ass.

She'd laughed so hard with him she'd cried. They'd cooked together, watched movies, and made love on every flat surface. One time, they'd had such a big shouting match a groundskeeper had knocked on the door to make sure everything was all right.

She'd had other lovers since then, but she'd never had that kind of passion with anyone other than Griffin.

Then why have I given up?

Yeah, I messed up again—so what?

She had to try to win him back.

Determination flooded in.

They were doing this whole fake engagement thing—that meant they *had* to be together.

When had she ever accepted defeat? It wasn't in her DNA.

She'd use this time together to get to know him again, flirt her ass off…and she'd win Griffin James back.

Because he was her one and only. She'd known it then, and she knew it now.

She just had to earn his forgiveness. *That's the only thing that'll clear the way for us to get back together.*

She found Austin in the kitchen, the refrigerator door open. "Tomorrow after school, get off the bus at my office. Bring your sneakers, sweats, and a T-shirt."

"I'm not doing soccer, and I hate karate, so you can just forget it." He poured himself a glass of milk and snagged a sleeve of cookies from the top shelf of the cabinet. Shoving an Oreo into his mouth, he headed for the couch and reached for his controller.

"You've got a choice. You can hide out in this cabin and play video games and eat junk food, or you can come with me to the Antigravity Training Center and get a fitness trainer who'll get you ready to try some of the outdoor activities this town offers."

He put his headphones on.

"Ah, Austin, Austin, Austin." She grinned at him. "You've finally met your match."

At the training center, Griffin held the door open, and Stella sailed right past him.

She'd been in their lives for what, a week? And she acted like she was part of the family.

And he fucking loved it.

Because I'm an asshole.

A glutton for punishment.

She hadn't changed a bit in seven years. The evidence? The ring she wore on her left hand.

He'd meant to pick up a cheap one, but nothing in the jewelry store had looked like something Stella would wear. And a modest or boring ring would be a dead giveaway the engagement wasn't real. So, he'd wound up spending way the hell too much money on a ruse.

Because that's what he did. He got caught up in her.

She consumed him. Mind, spirit...

And body, as was obvious by the way his gaze was riveted on her perfect peach-shaped ass.

That he wanted to bite.

Which he'd done countless times. Yeah, he'd sunk his teeth into those fleshy cheeks.

Fuck. Not this again.

But he knew how to shut it down. All he had to do was call up the images he'd seen on Splashagram so many years ago.

Two sets of feet in the sand, one with cherry red-painted toenails, the other big and hairy, and the ocean blurred in the background.

A selfie of Stella laughing, eyes sparkling, her head tucked into the shoulder of her new husband.

Pain radiated through him, as vivid as an uppercut to the jaw.

Yep.

That did the trick.

At the desk, Stella waited while the receptionist finished a phone call.

Standing so close to her, his senses went on high alert —aware of the smooth skin of her cheek, the curve of her generous mouth, the scent of an elegant, sexy woman. And it pissed him off. Because what he'd viewed as love had been nothing more than chemistry. "You didn't need to come with me."

"I want to see if he likes it." She touched his hand. "Hey, you never answered my question earlier. Was it hard to convince him this morning?"

"I didn't have to say anything. Last night before bed, he asked if I had a gym bag he could use. Then, this morning, right before he got on the bus, he said he was getting off at the center."

She grinned, and it was like looking up at a sunburst through pine branches. "That makes me happy."

"How can I help you?" The receptionist got up from his desk and moved toward the counter, his attention fixed on Stella. Because she had that effect on everyone.

"Hi, we're here to pick up Austin Greene. He had a session with a personal trainer."

"Okay, sure. Can you tell me which one?"

"It was Jonathan."

The man—clearly a trainer himself, with his workout clothes and strong physique—picked up a cell phone and dialed. "Hey, man, I've got Austin's parents here."

A bolt shot through him.

Parents.

It was like going home to an empty house, only to open the door and have all the lights thrown on and your best friends jumping out of their hiding places shouting, *Surprise!*

He couldn't believe the way his body responded to the idea of being bonded to Stella for life, raising kids together. Well, he *could* believe it. But that was nothing more than a knee-jerk response. Once, he couldn't have imagined having a family with anyone other than her.

"Great, I'll tell them. Thanks." Disconnecting, the man smiled. "He's in the tramp gym. I can take you there if you like."

You can fuck right off, buddy. But before he could tell the guy they'd find it on their own, and he could pull his eyes off Stella's tits right the fuck now, she said, "I remember where it is but thank you."

Stella led the way out of the main building and across a snow-packed path. "I don't know what to expect. Half of me is afraid to find him sitting alone on a bench, while the other kids are having the time of their lives." She hunched her shoulders against the cold.

He fought the impulse to wrap an arm around her. She was a big girl. She could buy herself the right kind of coat. Besides, it would send the wrong message. And he wasn't about to blur the lines between the ruse and real life.

Because he'd learned his lesson with this woman. She flared up hot in the moment…and forgot all about you when you were gone.

He tried to ignore her trembling lower lip. *Ah, hell.* He shrugged off his leather coat and set it over her ridiculously light-weight jacket. "And the other?"

Tilting her face toward the collar, her eyelids fluttered closed. A flash of happiness softened her features—*and holy shit*, was she sniffing it? Was she as affected by his scent as he was hers?

But then she said, "The other half fully expects to see him totally into it."

"The only thing I've seen him care about is his video game. Why do you think he'll like a fitness trainer?"

"I don't know. I was wondering how to make his time in Calamity fun, and I thought, well, what are we known for? Winter sports." She looked at him like, *Right?* "But he's not in the kind of shape to do sports even if he wanted to. So, I guess if we have a hope in hell of getting him off the couch, maybe it starts with getting him in shape."

Griffin slowed.

"What?"

"I get so pissed at you, but then you say something like that, and I remember why you pull these stunts."

"I don't know what you're talking about."

"I think you process things a lot quicker than the rest of us. Like with the fake engagement. I couldn't believe you'd jump into a situation you knew nothing about, but you'd already put the pieces together. And you were right. The Pilsons would absolutely have planted that seed into the next dinner party conversation. 'Why *would* a grown man want to take care of a teenage boy?' And you figured out how to shut it down. You figured *them* out."

"Thank you for saying that. I mean, I know you're still angry about it, but I'm glad you understand where it came from."

"You've known Austin a few days, and you already care about him."

"I do. And I'm worried that sitting on a couch and playing games and eating cookies is going to lead to depression, so…this just made sense." She gestured to the building in front of them, a massive gym with floor-to-ceiling windows.

Before opening the door, he touched her shoulder.

She startled and looked up at him.

Jesus Christ, she was stunning.

"It means a lot that you care about him. Thank you."

"You're welcome." She broke out into a devastatingly beautiful grin that popped a bubble of warmth in his chest. And then, she pulled the door open, and he followed her inside.

"Hey, how'd you know where the tramp gym was?" he asked.

"I stopped by this afternoon and asked for a tour. I wanted to see what they offered." Following a sign that said *Viewing Room*, she led the way up a staircase.

"You went out of your way to come here?"

"I did." Her leather soles clicked on the galvanized steel stairs.

"Why?" Didn't she have enough on her plate with her own work?

"I was already out, and since I was driving by…"

At the top, they stood side by side in front of the wall of windows that overlooked the gym. "You didn't have to do that."

"I wanted to," she said softly.

This crazy energy tore through him. He'd call it gratitude. *That's all it is.* He stuttered out a laugh. "It's…you have no idea what Austin's been through. He's lucky to have you in his corner."

"Well, we don't know that yet. He might be sitting on the sidelines playing a game on his phone." She touched his arm. "But I'm happy to hear you say that. Sometimes it feels like you can't stand me. That you wish I were anywhere but here, in your life."

"That's because it's true."

Chapter Six

HURT CREASED THE SKIN AROUND HER EYES AND tightened that lush mouth.

"Come on. You know I don't mean it like that. You've always been my weakness." He stared at his own reflection in the window. "And even after all this time…after everything that's happened between us…let's just say my mind and my body aren't on the same page."

"What does that mean?"

He shrugged. "We've always had chemistry."

"Okay, you can be angry with me, and you can be done with me, but you're not going to reduce what we had to 'chemistry.' If you're going to stand here and tell me you don't feel this connection between us, then you're lying. Even when we're doing nothing more than talking about who's going to pick up Austin, we have this insane energy. We *like* each other."

He shoved a hand deep into his pocket. "No, you're right." It came out more a mumble.

"Excuse me?" She cupped an ear. "I don't think I heard you."

He chuckled. "I'm agreeing with you. It's more than chemistry."

Hope lit her from within until she glowed. "It's been seven years, Griff. We've both grown up. I'm not the same girl that kissed Trace."

He lifted her ring finger and gave her a challenging look.

She shook her head, disappointed. "Fine. I'm not asking you to date me, but you could at least let us be friends again."

Anger spread like a flash fire across his skin, and he leaned in close. "I've kissed you so deep we lost the line between your body and mine. I've seen you come so hard you nearly passed out."

Her hand trembled, and heat radiated off her body.

"I know you read Lulu's diary the summer she went to Idaho Falls for a cooking class, and I know you didn't pay for the ice cream cone you got at Bliss when they were crowded and forgot to charge you. I hold all your secrets in my heart. But sure, Stella, let's be pals." He dropped her hand and focused on the sea of trampolines. He needed a minute to pull himself together.

Friends? Why was he so worked up over this?

He'd had seven years to wrap his head around the fact that she'd married another man. She'd moved on a hell of a long time ago.

But to hear her say she's good just being buddies? Fuck, that ground his heart into a fine powder.

He could feel her gaze on him, but he wasn't ready to look at her.

Finally, she turned her attention to the gym. Touching a hand to the glass, she said, "Oh, wow. Look at this place."

Blue foam pads dotted the long, rectangular gym. Coaches in red golf shirts and navy blue training shorts worked in small groups.

He had to get over it. It was nothing but old history. *I'm here to see Austin.* He scanned the gym until he found him, then tipped his chin toward the far left. "There he is."

Stella's eyes went wide with recognition. "That's Austin?"

"Yep." As angry as he got with her, he'd never deny her the praise she deserved. "You did that."

She let out a rush of breath that sounded like, "Oh." Her cheeks pinkened. "I can't believe it."

Generally, Austin wore baggy jeans and hoodies, so his shorts and T-shirt revealed a lean, long body. He bounced easily, comfortably, each time going higher and higher, and then Will Bowie, a former Olympic athlete, called something out to him. Austin listened with a solemn expression. Then, he nodded before executing a series of flips.

"Oh, my God. Look at him. How is this possible?" She tugged on his sleeve. "He's so good."

Yeah, he saw, but he was so worked up with a heady mix of gratitude and relief that he couldn't put words together.

She noticed. Of course, she did. She turned towards him, tugging his T-shirt. "Hey, are you all right?"

He nodded. "I've never seen him do anything like that." He cleared his throat. "Let's get out of here. I don't want him to see us watching him." *I don't want him to shut down again.*

"No, he *should* see us. No more hiding for this kid. He's got more confidence than we knew. Come on. Let's tell him how awesome he is." She sat down on a bench to take off her high heeled boots. Shoving them into her tote, she got up and headed down the stairs.

Damn, she was something. He'd known Austin for years, had watched him turn from a quiet, watchful little boy into a broody teenager who kept his mouth shut.

I've never seen him like this.

He held the door open for her, and she strode right into the gym. The place was loud, with every trampoline in use. As they walked the perimeter, heads turned to watch the gorgeous woman stride by. Half the athletes were too intimidated to return her friendly wave. She walked with ease and grace, smiling at everyone as if they'd grown up together.

Stella was magic. All she had to do was walk by, and people bloomed.

As they neared, they watched Austin execute a few more flips. Griffin stopped beside Will. "Hey, man."

"Griffin." Will shook his hand. "Good to see. How's it going?"

"Good."

Will turned back to the boy. "Straighten your legs."

"He's never shown an interest in sports before. I expected to find him sitting on the floor playing a game on his phone." Griffin shook his head in awe. "How'd you get him to do this?"

Will never took his eyes off Austin. "See, that's the thing. A lot of kids show up expecting to be experts from the get-go. Or they're here because their parents are trying to turn them into champions. But this one? He's got fire in his belly."

Right then, Austin landed awkwardly, wobbled, arms waving like pinwheels before he landed in a sprawl. Griffin froze, worried the boy would be embarrassed and quit.

Not all the kids at the training center went to Calamity High, but some did. Fourteen was a rough age.

But Austin surprised him. Pushing to his feet, he stepped off the trampoline and said, "Can I try it again?"

Will checked his watch. "I think we're done for today, but if you want to continue working with me, talk to Griffin and let me know what you guys decide."

"Decide about what?" Griffin couldn't miss the look that passed between Will and Stella. "What's going on?"

Austin stood there, anxious, worried, almost like he was asking for permission. *Can I do this? Please say yes.* Hard to tell with him, but the vulnerability, the need, made Griffin's heart go all tender and soft. "I thought you were going to work with a trainer to get in shape, but…are you talking about learning how to *ski*?"

"Snowboarding. There's a class, and I want to take it." And then Austin's voice lowered. "Will said I should see if I liked it first. And I do."

Griffin's heart swelled so big he thought it might pop. To see this kid so invested in something? He gestured to the trampoline. "You did great, man." Damn, he had so much affection for this kid. And then it built so big he couldn't take it anymore. He pulled Austin into his arms. The boy was sweaty, hot, and breathing hard, but he let Griffin hug him. "I'm really proud of you." He might've squeezed a little too hard.

Stella turned to Will. "So, what do you think? Do we have a future gold medalist on our hands?"

"Kid's a natural." Will said it firmly, seriously. "He's got good balance, great athleticism. He just needs to develop his muscles."

Keeping an arm slung around Austin's shoulders, Griffin joined them. Once again, with this woman, he was caught between wanting to kiss her for making this happen and throttle her for not talking to him first. How had they gone from cardio and weights to snowboarding in the very first session?

Will must've picked up on the tension. "Why don't you grab your stuff?" he asked the boy.

Austin headed off to a row of benches overflowing with backpacks and gym bags.

"So, is this cool?" Will asked.

"I feel like I'm a few steps behind." Griffin looked to Stella.

She seemed to hover between apologetic and wanting to explode with excitement. "I ran into Will when I was on the tour. He said he'd hang out with Austin after his session, talk to him about the kinds of classes they offer here."

"He seems excited about boarding," Will said. "I'd be happy to spend some time with him if that's okay with you."

How could he argue with that? "I appreciate it. He'd be damn lucky to train with you but let me run it by his grandparents. Make sure they're good with it."

"They're not in charge of me." Austin never stood up for himself, so his wavery tone didn't match the words. "You are."

"I know, buddy. I just don't want to stir anything up. Let me talk to your dad."

"I haven't heard from him in three days."

Fuck. Normally, Peyton checked in every day. The fact that he hadn't meant communication had been shut down on the COP. Griffin had tried bringing it up, but Austin had shrugged it off like it was no big deal.

Of course, it's a big deal. He'd have to do a better job of checking in with the boy. "We'll talk about it. Hey, thanks a lot, Will."

"You got it." Will shook their hands and headed off.

Griffin clapped a hand on Austin's shoulder to get him going, but he stood firm. "The winter session already started, but Will said I could join, and he'll give me private lessons until I catch up. And he's not even the teacher. He's a freestyle skier. He's doing it for me."

"I don't want to say no to the opportunity to train with a gold medalist, but you know how it goes. I have to manage your grandparents, so they don't stir things up. Let me pass it by your dad first."

"No, you said yourself we might not hear from him for a while. And it's not like I'm jumping out of helicopters and boarding down glaciers. It's a beginner class."

"You're right." Fucking Pilsons. They had him working too hard to stay under the radar.

"I want to do this." As tough as he wanted to sound, Austin's tone held a plea.

And Griffin knew there was no way he'd crush this first show of independence. "Okay, I can see how much it means to you. It's still contingent on your dad's approval, but until we hear otherwise, let's do this."

Austin's chest expanded, but he didn't say a word. Just grabbed sweatpants out of his backpack and pulled them on over his shorts.

Stella leaned into Griffin. "I swear I was going to talk to you about it first, but when I was talking to Will, he threw out the suggestion, and it seemed like such a great opportunity. I didn't think it would hurt to at least let Austin meet with the guy, you know?"

Griffin opened the door, and Austin walked out. Stella lingered, one hand on his chest. "I had no idea he'd offer private lessons or that Austin would like it so much. I mean, I'm sorry—wait, what am I saying? I'm not sorry at all. Did you *see* him on that trampoline?"

The heat of her hand warmed his heart, and he wanted to kiss the smugness right out of her, until she turned all soft and pliant in his arms, until her body and heart opened to him.

The way his heart always did for her.

Austin stopped on the pathway. "Are we going?"

With twilight settling over the valley, the air had turned frigid. As they stomped across snow drifts to get to the parking lot, Griffin reached for Stella's arm to stop her. "Half of me wants to make you walk home for shaking up our lives like this." She really had no idea the threat the Pilsons posed.

Their mouths were a breath away. Her eyes went sultry, smokey, and she licked her lips. "What does the other half want to do to me? Because that's the only half I'm interested in."

Jesus, this woman.

After getting home, Griffin changed into pajama bottoms and a long-sleeve Boneyard T-shirt. He came into the kitchen to wash his hands. "What do you want for dinner?"

"Stella's making chicken enchiladas."

He smacked the faucet off and snatched a towel from the counter to dry his hands. "She's coming back here?"

Austin didn't even look up from his homework. "No, she's going to make them at an undisclosed location, and our mission is to find them."

"Wait, did you just make a joke?"

The corner of Austin's mouth lifted.

Well, look at that. Happiness soared through him. *This is a first.* "Tell her we're fine. I'm ordering a pizza." Griffin reached for the phone.

"I don't want pizza. I want enchiladas."

Oh, now he finds his voice? "Well, it's late, and I'm hungry." *And I don't want Stella here.*

"She said it's easy and quick."

"Text her and say we'll do it another night." He pulled the flyer out of a drawer and punched in the number.

"Hole in the Wall Pizza Joint," the guy said. "How can I help you?"

"Hey, yeah, can I get an extra-large—"

"Knock, knock, open up." Stella's voice came from outside.

Getting up so fast he practically knocked his chair back, Austin raced to the door and let her in. Cold air blew into the small cottage, but Griffin barely noticed. He was lost in that brilliant smile and those sparkling eyes.

"These enchiladas are so good." She breezed right into the kitchen. "You're going to love them."

"Sir?" the guy asked.

"Yeah, sorry," Griffin said. "Never mind. Got our signals crossed. Sorry about that."

"No problem." The man disconnected.

Tossing his phone on the counter, Griffin stepped aside as Stella and Austin started unpacking her canvas tote bags.

"Can you turn the oven on to three-fifty?" she called over her shoulder.

How did her presence change everything? This place so beige and flat, flashed into Technicolor. Every atom was charged and vibrating.

And it had to stop. "I was going to order a pizza."

"Well, lucky you. You get a homemade meal instead." She tipped her chin to the oven. "Preheat."

He tried to hold onto his irritation, but he actually really wanted enchiladas. So, he did as she asked and then grabbed himself a beer. Twisting the cap, he leaned back against the counter, watching the two of them in motion. Austin opened a can of sauce, while Stella heated a skillet and stacked the tortillas on a plate next to the stove.

"You like olives in it?" she asked.

"I don't care." As morose as Austin sounded, he took his job of spreading the sauce around the baking pan seriously.

"That's not much of an answer," she said. "I can add olives or leave them out. All I need is to know if you like them or not."

"I've never had one."

"Well, then." She thrust a can of olives at Griffin. "Can you please open this?"

Reluctantly, he set his beer down and pulled the can opener out of a drawer. Once he'd pried the top off, he dipped his fingers in and popped an olive into his mouth before handing it back to her. Their fingertips brushed, and her gaze flicked up to him.

For all her breezy flair, he caught a hint of *Is this all right?* in her expression.

He wanted to say *hell, no*, but it was hard to stay annoyed when anyone could see how Austin came to life around her.

Also, it was good for the boy to have a homecooked meal.

And, you know, for him to learn how to cook.

Ah, fuck it. He had to face that he liked her in his kitchen. Liked playing happy fucking family.

I'm a sucker for this woman, okay?

"Woo." She fanned her face. "It's hot in here."

"Thermostat's set at sixty-eight."

"Yeah, well, these cabins are small, and with more than one or two people, they get overheated fast."

"I'll lower it." He took the excuse to get away from her and hightailed it into the main room.

"No, it's all right. I'll take off twelve of my sixteen layers." She rinsed her fingers in the sink and then shrugged off the cropped cardigan sweater, tossing it onto the back of a chair.

He'd hoped she'd leave it at that. The blouse underneath was loose-fitting enough to only hint at the curves he knew so well.

The memory hit strong and hard, the feel of her plump breasts in his hands.

Fuck me.

Desire burned hot, rousing a deep, aching hunger, and when she reached for the top button of her silky shirt, he wanted to shout, *Stop. I'll turn off the heat. Just keep your damn clothes on.*

Too late, she'd pulled it off. As it went winging past him to land on the table, he got a whiff of her scent.

It filled his senses, driving him right back into the heart of them.

Alone in this cottage, so easy with each other, so… joyful. Always wanting her.

He'd never gotten his fill, no matter how times he'd kissed her, stroked her, licked her, tasted her…fucked her.

This isn't going to work.

He needed her gone. Striding back to the counter

where he'd left his beer, he clapped his hands together. "What can I do?" He'd hurry her along, get her out of here.

"Can you make a salad? I brought all kinds of veggies for it."

"Sure." They needed boundaries. They could pretend to be engaged in front of other people but not here in the privacy of his own home.

"Okay, so now let's pull the chicken off the bone and use a fork to shred it." She pulled the lid off the rotisserie chicken, the scent filling the small kitchen.

Austin took the fork from her and peeled back the skin.

"Have you ever cooked before?" she asked.

"No. I mean, I can make cereal or a sandwich or whatever. But not something like this."

As the two of them talked quietly, Stella's laughter entered his bloodstream, making him go weak. Opening a bag of mixed greens, he dumped matchstick carrots into the salad bowl and called it done. He had to get out of there. "I'm going to the store. Need anything?"

"Well, hang on. Let me get this in the oven, and I'll come with you. I need food for breakfast. I've got to start making a point of eating, otherwise, the day just gets away from me."

Griffin froze with one arm in his jacket. "You're not eating?"

"Not really. I haven't caught my groove here. In Dallas, the team had a cafeteria and a gym. It was pretty cushy. Of course, in New York, I didn't have anything like that, but I walked a ton, and there're food vendors on every street, so I could always grab something."

"You have to *eat*. That's ridiculous."

"I'll get some protein bars, stick them in my purse."

"Get a mini fridge. You can stock it with sandwiches and cheese, fruit salad…stuff like that."

"That's a great idea. I'll talk to Diane about that."

He headed for the door. "Just tell me what you want. I'll pick it up for you."

"Wait. Give me five minutes to get this in the oven. I want to go with you."

Yeah? Well, I don't want you in my truck.

I need fucking space.

But he'd never tell her that. Cursing his luck, he lowered his head and blew out a breath. Of all the ways for her to come home, of all the jobs she could've taken… somehow their paths had crossed in a way that tangled them up.

And he had to admit he wanted it as much as he hated it.

"Now, let's pour the rest of the sauce all over the enchiladas. I saved this bag of cheese for when it's done. We'll dump the whole thing over it ten minutes before we take it of the oven." She washed her hands. "Okay, you work on your homework, and when I get back, we'll tackle that algebra."

Moments later, they were locking the door and trudging through the snow to his truck. When her feet nearly flew out from under her, she let out a cry, but she caught herself on the hood.

"Why don't you get some winter boots?"

"Do you have any idea how crazy this job is? I'm slammed at work."

"And yet you had time to drive all the way out to the training center and hook Austin up with Will Bowie?"

"Priorities." She said in a sing-songy voice.

Chuckling, he slammed his door and cranked the engine.

She got in beside him. "Why are you not excited about this class? How many kids get Will Bowie for a coach?" She buckled up. "You saw how happy it made him."

"It's not about me. It's about his grandparents, not giving them a reason to take him from me."

She went quiet for a moment, thoughtful. "The judge still sees you as that eighteen-year-old boy."

"He sure as hell does." *And that's why I've got to prove myself to him.*

"I heard him. He thinks you haven't changed."

"Exactly. He's convinced I'll be reckless with Austin."

"This is a beginner class, though. He's not going to be riding black diamond trails."

"That's not the point."

"Of course not, but you can't keep Austin locked up for eight months because you're worried about Judge Pilson's opinion of you."

"I'll do whatever it takes to keep Austin with me. If he breaks a leg snowboarding, that's when the Pilsons will show up and start flexing. And you saw how far they're willing to go."

"I did. That was horrifying." She cut him a look. "I guess I was thinking since it's a beginner class, how could anyone object?" She shook her head. "No, I wasn't thinking that at all. Will made an offer, and I was so excited I just grabbed it."

"I know. I get that. And as long as you keep his grand-parents in the back of your mind, I think it's great that you care about him. The way he stood up for himself in the gym? That's a first. And getting him to help with dinner? He's never done that before, either. Most nights, I have to pry the controller out of his hands. So, you've been great. Don't misunderstand what I'm saying."

"If he broke his leg hotwiring a car and crashing into a tree, I could see them taking him away from you. But would they really do it if it happens while he's taking a snowboarding class?"

"It's not so much about the broken leg. It's the incident that proves I'm neglectful. But all these worries disappear when I know I can call Peyton, and he'll handle them. When he's out of touch? I'm screwed."

"That's not really fair. He should've taken care of this situation before he left."

"It was a last-minute decision, but he's working on it. He's waiting to meet with an attorney. Until then—"

"I know. One court order, and Austin's living with them."

"Right. My choices for their grandson don't hold up against their legal rights as blood relatives."

She reached over and folded her hand over his. "I'm sorry. I'm making everything more complicated for you."

"You are, but you're also making things better for Austin. And that's my highest priority."

The impulse to turn his hand over and thread his fingers with hers was the most natural thing in the world. But then he got hit with an image from her old Splasha-gram page.

Hands, one large and hairy, the other feminine, both sporting wedding rings.

And he just couldn't go there.

"Are you worried about Peyton?" she asked.

"Sure. He warned me this would happen, so I've half-expected it. But now that it's here, I just…"

"You're walking a tightrope."

"Yep."

"What are they like?"

"You mean you didn't get enough from hearing them the other day?"

She gave him a bittersweet grin. "Oh, I got more than enough. But what're they like with Austin?"

"They're strict and demanding. They think if they can control what he does, what he's exposed to, then he'll turn out to be a respectable man. Best example I can give you is his guitar. He's always loved music, so right before Peyton went on his first deployment, he gave Austin his guitar. Man, he loved that thing. Played it all the time...until the judge took it from him." He fingers tightened on the wheel. "Austin found it in a closet and started playing it when they weren't home, but I guess they came back early." It was the first and only time Griffin had ever seen the boy cry.

Shit. Fuck.

"What? I can tell from your expression something awful happened."

"The judge drove over it."

She sat forward. "He what? Why would he do that?"

"To make his point."

"You know, yesterday on the way home from work, I apologized for putting him in a position to lie, and he told me he does it all the time. Now, I know what he means." She tugged the fringe on her scarf. "Can I ask about the elephant in the room? Their daughter?"

As he pulled into the parking lot of the grocery store, she put her hand on his thigh. "I don't actually need anything."

"Neither do I." He shifted into Park and settled back in his seat, the leather creaking. "I just needed…"

"Just say it. Stop being so careful with me." She smiled softly. "That's what made us so strong. We didn't hold back. We said what we felt in the moment, and we dealt with it."

She was right about that. Though it was more her than him. Stella held nothing back.

"Everyone's so careful," she said. "We don't want to hurt people's feelings, but it's the honesty that breaks down walls. It's what makes people get closer to each other. I loved that about us." And then she said quietly, "I loved the way you loved me."

I'm sure you did.

He could feel her watching him, could feel her need for more. He might not be looking to bring them closer, but she deserved the truth. "I liked how you loved me, too." At the time, anyway. "You give everything you've got…and that's a hell of a lot."

And he was sure her ex-husband felt the same way.

"In any event, you wanted to know about Austin's mom…" They might as well go back home. Checking the mirrors, he headed out of the lot. "Peyton's four years older than me, so I didn't know him in school. He's Mack's son—you remember the guy who owned the bike shop?"

She nodded. Of course, she remembered. How many times had Mack cuffed Griffin on the back of his head because he was talking to his girlfriend instead of working?

"He didn't work in the shop because he was pretty much a pothead, but then he got his high school girlfriend pregnant."

"Wrong girl to knock up."

"Right? But they didn't find out until Mindy was pretty far along. In fact, it was her mom who figured it out—she recognized the symptoms. She wasn't ready to be a parent, so she'd planned on putting Austin up for adoption. At first, Peyton was okay with that. If you ask him now, he'd tell you he was high most of the time, so it never really sank in. But then they got in a car accident—nothing serious—and it changed him. He said it only became real when he thought they might've lost the baby. And that made him realize he was already a dad—whether he was ready or not. So, she signed away her parental rights, and he got his shit together. He didn't have any real hope of a career, so he joined the Army. Figured it would give him skills and direction."

"Well, I have to admire him for that. Where's Mindy now? Does she ever see him?"

"No, her parents gave her a rash of shit for signing away her rights."

"I'm sure. They both ran on family values platforms. That's their whole thing. If you lead clean, family-focused lives, society's problems will go away."

"Exactly. So, they cut her off, thinking it would scare her into falling in line, but instead she left and never came back. She lives in Wisconsin now, and she doesn't keep in touch with anyone."

"You mean, she doesn't even ask about Austin?" Stella sounded horrified.

He shook his head because if he opened his mouth, he'd go on a tear. He didn't know anything about Mindy, but he couldn't stand the idea that Austin lived with the fact that his own mother didn't want anything to do with him. The sense of rejection he must feel, the blow to his sense of worth…it killed Griffin.

"That must be so hard for him."

"I don't know. He doesn't talk about it, and I don't ask. I see my role as Austin's soft place to fall. I want to make the next eight months as good for him as I can."

She caressed his arm. "That's really sweet, Griffin. I just worry you take on too much."

"What does that mean?"

"You've always been the protector. Well, I guess that's why Peyton chose you to watch his son. You've always had this huge sense of responsibility for everyone."

"Well, I'm the oldest of seven."

"No, I think it's because of what happened that night."

Ten years later, and everyone still referred to it the same way. *That night.*

The night that five stupid kids—all on the cusp of greatness—had blown up their lives. Griffin had been with them, but he hadn't been an elite hockey player on track to play in the NHL. He hadn't gotten hurt.

Had that night changed him? *You bet your ass.* He'd stopped being reckless and wild. But none of that had anything to do with his current situation. "Austin's a complicated kid. I don't want to fail him."

"You could never fail anyone. You care too much. It's one of your best qualities, but you can't keep him locked up in your hotel room while his dad's gone. You have an opportunity here to help him grow. I think you should take it."

"You know I probably will."

"I do know." She smiled. "You just have to weigh things first. Look at it from all angles." The smile died. "The opposite from me."

"I don't know that we're opposites." He cut her a look. "I think we're two sides of the same coin. We both get invested in the people we care about. We just have different ways of handling it. Where I think things through, and you're intuitive. You pay attention to what people don't say, and then you give them the things they didn't even know they needed."

"I want to think that's a compliment, but because you look at me like I'm the neighbor who lets her dog poop on your lawn—I'm looking for the insult."

"No insult." He gave it some thought. "Is there a part of you that wants to be liked? Needed? Yeah. But it's not a bad thing. There's not a bad bone in your body."

"Well, thank you." Then, in the softest, most vulnerable voice, she said, "If that's true, why do you look at me like you want me gone? Why do you talk to me like you can barely tolerate my presence?"

Ah, Christ. If they weren't pretending to be engaged, he might've avoided this conversation for the rest of his life.

But they were.

And he couldn't, so...

"I guess we're doing this."

Chapter Seven

"Doing what?" she asked.

As much as he didn't want to have this conversation, his body sparked with the anticipation of it. This volatile thing he'd held inside for so many years—he hadn't even known how badly he'd wanted to confront her. He glanced at the dashboard clock. They had twenty minutes before the enchiladas came out of the oven.

But first, he had to get his head on right. He couldn't attack her. She hadn't done anything wrong.

It wasn't her fault she hadn't loved him the way he'd loved her. It didn't make her a bad person. It just made her bad for him.

So, where he would have braked for the turn to the Homesteader Inn, he pressed the accelerator and kept on going straight.

"Hey." She swung around in her seat. "You missed the turn-off."

"We need to get some things clear."

"Oh, that's rich. Do you actually think your attitude towards me isn't *clear*? Do you think I'm confused about the radioactive anger rolling off you when you so much as look at me? Believe me. You made yourself *crystal* clear when you dumped me. I get it. I can't be trusted because I'm impulsive. I don't think anything through. And, you know, if that's my worst flaw, then I think I'm doing all right."

"That's not what I was going to say."

"And since we're doing this, *I* think you were a dick for letting me go. Now, I strongly suggest you turn back around because I don't need a recap of all the reasons you don't want to be with me."

He shot her an incredulous look. "You're the one who asked me the question."

"Yeah, well, that's when you were open and nice. I don't want to hear about my flaws when you're all intense and dark and dangerous."

"I'm dangerous now?"

"Uh, considering you're breaking all posted speed limits, yeah. Besides, I don't need an answer. Your actions speak loud enough. But if you insist on speaking your mind, you'd better slow down because I really don't want to jump out of a speeding truck. These pants cost me two hundred and forty dollars at Barney's annual sale."

This energy—this is what it felt like to be with her. The excitement, the attraction, the connection—even when they were fighting. It was dazzling, so he sped up.

"Oh, for God's sake. Who's the impulsive one now?" She reached for the dashboard—*drama queen*. "Slow down. You're going to get a ticket."

"How about you stop talking for five seconds so I can answer the question *you* asked?"

"No, thanks. I don't need to hear all the reasons you hate me."

"I don't hate you. I could never hate you." *That's the whole fucking problem.* He gripped the steering wheel, pressing down on the accelerator.

"What's that about?" She made a circling motion toward his face. "See, there you go getting all dark and dangerous like we're going to drive off a cliff together."

"Can you stop talking?"

"No, I don't want to hear what you're going to say. Because the only way I can be here in Calamity, in this truck with you right now, is if I have one tiny kernel of hope that you'll forgive me."

Jesus, she thinks I'm still hung up on her kissing Trace.

"It's not about…"

She married *someone else.*

Six months after we ended.

While I was unable to eat or sleep, she was having the time of her life dating, falling in love, and eloping.

He would never get it out of his mind, those images of her on her honeymoon.

A selfie of them in bed, rumpled sheets, tousled hair, that just-got-laid smile on her gorgeous face.

Fuck this shit. He needed to be on his bike right now. He needed the highway cleared of snow, the chilled air scented with sage and pine trees. He needed speed and wind and wide, open roads. He needed to be anywhere but sitting next to the woman he couldn't stop wanting, who would never love him the way he'd once loved her.

"See?" she grumbled. "I knew you couldn't forgive me."

Because it wasn't her fault. *It just is what it is.* He slowed and pulled a U-turn in the deserted road.

"What're you doing? We haven't talked yet."

"You've talked enough for both of us. Besides, we have to get back to Austin."

"All right, fine. I'll shut my mouth." She shifted towards him, hitching up a knee, so it rested on the console. "I'm a strong, independent woman. I can take anything you have to say to me. So, go ahead. I'm giving you one free pass to let it rip. It's just me and you, and our big, huge, tangled ball of feelings, so go for it. I'm a big girl, and you can bet I'll punch back. You've got the ten minutes it'll take to get us back to the Inn."

Her permission shifted the tectonics of his heart, unleashing a toxic cloud of emotion. Wheeling the truck around, he got back onto the highway.

Not taking his eyes off the road, he said, "I fucking loved you, Stella."

Her jaw snapped shut. She obviously hadn't expected that.

Neither had he. "I've never loved anyone the way I loved you, and I never will. But you…" No, he couldn't talk about it in terms of what she'd done. That wouldn't be fair. He had to keep it about himself. His feelings. "You're —" Fuck, he'd done it again.

"Don't manage the conversation. See? That's what you do. You manage your brothers and sister's lives, you take care of Austin, and you don't need to do that with me."

He jerked the wheel, pulling back onto the shoulder and nosing the truck into snow-covered sage brush. "You're right. I was a dick for letting you go. I figured that out about two minutes after you ran. I spent a month burning off my anger and five trying to find you. I got to Dallas right about the time you'd taken your first vacation." He paused, barely able to say the words. "You were on your *honeymoon*."

It was like lightning hit the interior of his truck. The discharge of energy was so violent, Stella actually flinched. And then she went stone-still.

Idling in Park, he shifted towards her. "You got *married*, Stella."

Tears glittered, and she swiped under her eye. But she didn't say a word.

"Oh, now you have nothing to say?"

"You came to Dallas?" The whispered words sounded tortured.

He gave one curt nod.

"To get me back?" Tears spilled down her cheeks. "I didn't know."

"It wouldn't have changed anything. You were *married*."

"I can't even imagine…"

"You can't imagine what?"

"I would've died if you'd gotten married." The words came out like she'd scraped them off the asphalt.

That about sums it up.

"That's one of the main reasons I didn't come home. When I got the call from Diane, all I could think about was walking down the street and finding you with another woman, each of you holding the hand of a little girl. I couldn't do it. I just couldn't."

"Look, it's not your fault. I'm not blaming you for falling in love with someone else. But if you want to know why I'm not thrilled to see you, that's why."

"I didn't love him."

"Stella…" He let out a huff of breath. "I thought we were going to be honest with each other?"

"I didn't. I was so scared. My sister hated me, my boyfriend dumped me, and I was alone for the first time in my life. And then Logan came along and swept me away."

The blade sank into an old wound, the pain so sharp and lethal he sucked in a breath.

Her hand pressed to his arm. "No, no, I don't mean it like that. It was never about love. I meant that he swept me into his life. He's a charmer, and he makes everyone feel like they're his best friends. And I needed that. We barely knew each other, and there I was on video calls with his parents and his childhood friends. I had no one, and he stepped in and filled the void."

"I saw the pictures." His tone said *Cut the crap*.

"What pictures? What do you mean?"

"On Splashagram. Of your honeymoon."

"Oh, God." She tipped her head back, features twisted in pain. "Griffin, I'm so sorry. I had no idea anyone saw them. I deleted that account. I felt like such a fool." Her voice went thick with emotion. "I never loved him. I was still in love with you, and he knew that."

"You told him?"

"Of course I did. It was all I could think about. I'd lost the love of my life. But it's not like I had to say anything. God, I was a mess. It hit me at the most random times. I'd be driving to work or taking a shower, and bam. I'd have that memory of you saying *we're done*, and I'd start crying again. So hard, he'd come into the bathroom, wrap me in a towel, and spoon with me until I got ahold of myself."

He wanted to believe her, but those photographs had built a house he'd lived in for a very long time, and it would take more than words to burn it down. "That doesn't make any sense."

"What doesn't? Are you saying I'm *lying*?"

"No, I'm saying it doesn't make sense to marry someone who's still crying over her ex."

She let out a bitter laugh. "No, it doesn't. I don't know how to explain our relationship."

"Try."

Holding his gaze, she had to have seen how much it mattered to him because she gave a gentle nod. "I can only speak for myself, but I was scared and alone, and he gave me the big family I'd run away from. I can only assume he married *me* because I gave him a home base. I mean, he's in the NFL. His whole life is football and travel and press. I was someone to check in with at the end of the day, someone to come home to."

"You married him, Stella. You don't exchange vows unless you have strong feelings for each other." *And that's my issue.*

Because the idea of marrying anyone other than Stella…it just didn't compute. *Still.*

"Yes, I had big feelings. And they were fear, not love, so you can sit there and impose your judgment of what I felt when I was eighteen, or you can hear me when I tell you how scared I was. I grew up in a big family in a town where everyone knew me, where I was special. And it didn't take long to find out that, outside of the county limits, I was nobody."

But it was starting to make sense. Stella had only ever been celebrated and welcomed. The rehearsal dinner was the first time in her life she'd experienced rejection.

He could see that she'd run right into the arms of guy, a team, a family, who saw her with fresh eyes, who thought she was amazing.

"Of all places, how did you wind up in Dallas?"

"My parents caught me right away. I was using the

emergency credit card they'd given me, so I didn't make it too hard for them. But I didn't start there. I went to Los Angeles, thinking I'd be a model or an actress or something. Little did I know they were tracking every diet Coke I bought and every motel I stayed in."

"Credit card or not, that must've been hard to be on your own like that."

"It wasn't as awful as it sounds. Do you remember Lucy Banoff? She moved to LA in fifth grade, but we kept in touch, and she let me crash on her couch. So, it wasn't like I had nowhere to stay. The hard part was that I'd lost Lulu, and you'd just broken up with me."

"You fucking kissed Trace, Stella. Let's not forget that little part of the story. I'm not the bad guy here. I think it was fair for me to be a little pissed off."

"Of course, it was. I'm just trying to tell you what I was going through, what led me to marry Logan." Her voice lowered on the last bit of that sentence, and he could tell she was mortified.

And that eased the anger, the tension, because if she was embarrassed by her marriage…maybe those photographs *didn't* tell the whole story.

"I'm sorry. Go on. You stayed with Lucy?"

"Yes." She blinked back tears. "But that didn't go well because all I did was cry. I couldn't even get out of bed. And Lucy…she was beside herself. She'd expected her sunny, fun friend from Calamity. She wasn't equipped to handle a woman having a total breakdown."

"It didn't have to be like that. Your family would've been there for you."

"But *you* wouldn't. You made that clear. And I just couldn't live with myself knowing I'd lost you." She wiped the tears and shifted in her seat. "Anyhow, when my parents found me, I was a total mess. My dad said he had a friend who'd hire me. He let me keep the emergency credit card until I moved to Dallas and got my first paycheck as an intern for the team. And then I was on my own. And let me tell you, I threw myself into that job. It was about survival. I was living in a boarding house until I could afford my own apartment. I was totally on my own, and I had to make it work."

"Sounds scary."

"It was, but everyone was good to me."

He chuckled. "That's one of the things I loved about you. 'It was scary, but...' You always find the good in everything. 'I was devastated, but...' Most people aren't like that. I'm not like that."

"Well, I mean, everyone was so nice to me. The guys invited me out to parties and clubs, and I went along, but I had a broken heart and no interest in dating anyone."

"Except Logan."

She squeezed her eyes shut. "He's one of those fun guys who sweeps everyone into his orbit." She said it quietly, focused on the hands in her lap. "And I jumped right in, organizing dinners, renting out clubs. I was the party planner for the ultimate party boy."

He could see that. The walls of his house went from cement to paper.

And that made him uncomfortable. "But you *did* have feelings for him? You married him, so you obviously felt something. That's all I'm asking. That's all I want to know."

She went quiet for a moment, the only sound the occasional whoosh of a car sailing past on the highway. "I felt...relief. I felt...less alone. I don't know what you want me to say—well, actually, I do. You want me to say that it was some whirlwind romance, but it wasn't like that. It was a scary time. I was a mess, and then this guy comes along and takes my hand and says, Come on, follow me. I'll take care of you. And so, I did. I followed."

"What went wrong?"

"He cheated. The entire time he was on the road, he acted like he was still single. I'd never been cheated on, so I didn't even consider the possibility. But it wasn't like he tried to hide it. He's got this big personality. Everyone flocks to him. And he's just one of those go-with-the-flow kinds of people, so if someone wanted to get naked, he was down for it."

"Didn't he try to be discreet? For your sake?"

"Not at all. In fact, he was shocked I was upset. He was like, *This is what we do. We fuck around on the road, but we always come home to our families.*"

"He sounds like an asshole."

"Oh, I don't know. Pretty sure *I'm* the asshole for not paying attention, for only seeing what I wanted to see. Besides, I was more embarrassed than devastated. He didn't have my heart, so it's not like he could break it. Anyhow, I filed for divorce, and that's when I had to do the hard work. I was alone for the first time. It was just me, alone in my apartment, scared shitless. It took me a solid year after leaving him to get on my own two feet and make friends."

"I'm sorry you went through all that." But he knew he didn't sound it. Because he still had so much anger.

No. He should probably stop calling it anger.

Because that's not what it was. He was hurt. A hurt so deep it had sunk into his bones, making them ache.

She looked miserable. "I can't imagine what you're

thinking, me marrying somebody six months after we broke up. It sounds so awful."

He didn't answer. He couldn't. He just stared out the windshield, wanting to disappear into the sheer darkness of nighttime in the mountains.

Beside him, she shifted, her nervous energy filling the truck. "You can say it, you know. You can say you can't believe I did that. Hell, *I* can't believe I did it. Truth is, I loved you with everything I was back then, and I couldn't believe you threw me away over a kiss you *knew* meant nothing to me."

Only when she put her hand over his did he realize how hard he was gripping his knee. His other hand held the wheel so tightly his knuckles had gone white. "Talk to me, please. We're letting it all out, remember? Say it."

He felt strange. The emptiness—the hollowness—didn't mesh with the tension in his body. With the tightness of his lungs.

"Please?" she whispered urgently.

It was her softness, the openness, that broke through. It wasn't enough to tell her he knew she'd gotten married. She needed to see all the way down to the still-open wound. "I didn't do hockey with the other guys." After he and his friends had damaged private property building dirt bike courses, their parents had sat them down. But instead of a punishment, they'd all gotten hockey sticks. Instead of grounding the ten-year-olds, their parents had given them a focus for their wild energy.

And it had worked. They'd thrown all their energy into it. But the better they became the more training involved. And when his friends joined the Mountain West elite team, Griffin had bowed out. "Because it would've taken me away from you."

Her hand grew too hot, so he pulled his out. He didn't want to upset her. He never wanted to hurt this woman, but she asked, and so he'd answer. "Even if I couldn't have you, I wanted to be around you any chance I could." He didn't look at her when he said, "I dropped out of college to be with you."

"Griffin…"

She sounded remorseful, and he didn't want that. "That was my choice, and I don't regret it. I like owning the shop, and making custom and spec bikes? That's the little kid in me who tinkered with dirt bikes in the garage living his dream. I'm telling you I knew when we were kids, and I knew when I finally got to be with you at nineteen, that you were the only girl for me." He couldn't help himself from reaching for a lock of her silky blonde hair. "I will always want you. You're my barn owl."

"Your *what*?" She let out a shaky laugh. "They better be animals who mate for life."

He nodded. "And I'll never want anyone the way I wanted you, but you married someone else, and you can tell me you didn't love him, you can tell me you did it out of fear, but the truth is that I saw those photographs of you on your honeymoon. And, Stella, you were happy." He lowered his hand and looked away. "And I believe that you'll be happy again…with someone else." He shifted in his seat, ready to crank the engine. "So, there you go. We got it all out, and now we both need to move on. If we're going to be together because of Austin, there can't be any drama between us. My priority is him." *Conversation over.*

But Stella had fire in her eyes. "You saw some photographs on social media, and somehow you know what was in my heart? Well, let me tell you something, you smug ass, you want to know how I feel about something, you can ask me. But don't you ever get on your high horse again and tell me what or who I am."

"Okay." He hit the button to start his truck.

"No, it's not okay." She lunged over the console and punched it off. "I did a terrible, stupid thing, and I hurt you. And, yes, I'm embarrassed that I married Logan, but I can't take it back. I can't erase it. The only thing I can do is tell you I never loved him, and I'll never love anyone the way I loved you. Do you hear me? So, you can just drop this notion that somehow your love was loftier or purer than mine. You're just wrong."

"How am I wrong? I saw the pictures. You were laughing, having the time of your life. And it sure as hell looked like the sex was really fucking great. I don't know why you can't just admit it. You're an impulsive person, passionate person…that's just who you are."

"Oh, I see. I'm fickle. My emotions turn on a dime. I get it." Even though she tried to sound defiant, the fire in her had dimmed. "I don't know why I bother." She shook her head. "You know what? Fuck you. I'm a passionate woman, and I'm not going to apologize for who I am."

"I don't want you to apologize." A fireball of lust sped through his bloodstream, waking him the fuck up and making his senses sing. "I fucking love your passion. That's what makes this so damn hard." He wrapped his hand around her wrist and yanked her toward him, gripping the back of her neck, and pressing his mouth over hers. *Don't do it. Don't fucking do it.*

But she made this sexy little sound in the back of her throat, half moan, half cry, all aroused woman, and he broke. He licked inside her mouth, and the indescribable softness, the slick heat, made his heart burst. He coaxed her tongue into play, kissing her with all the frus-

123

tration and anger and regret he'd hoarded for seven long years.

She tasted so good, like strawberries and iced tea, and her scent filled his senses until he was nothing but a pulsing, throbbing ball of desire.

Fingers tightening on her neck, he pressed his forehead against hers. "You make me feel alive. Swear to God, Stella, I've been idling since you left."

"You don't have to idle. You know that, don't you? I'm right here."

Yes, and that was the problem. She hadn't simply shown up in town. He didn't get to glance at her as he drove down the street. He wasn't just passing her on the highway on his way to work.

She'd fucking dropped into his life in the role of fiancée.

When he didn't respond, when he forced himself to let go of her, she crumpled. "I ruined everything." She settled back in her seat, staring out the windshield. "You're never going to trust me again."

Chapter Eight

As they neared his cottage, Griffin knew they couldn't leave the conversation unfinished. "You're right. I shouldn't make assumptions about your feelings. I'm sorry I said that."

"It's not like I blame you. If I saw pictures of you on your honeymoon…" For one moment, she had a look of absolute desolation. "But you know something?" She sounded resigned. "I think we were doomed no matter how much we loved each other."

"What's that supposed to mean?"

"You're the oldest in your family, and I'm the youngest in mine. And like you said, we're two sides of the same coin. You look out for the people you love by trying to control everything. And my way is to go balls to the wall. You're keeping them safe and warm, while I'm throwing them a blow-out party."

"Stella, you *are* the party. You're the focal point in any group. You're the brightest light and the warmest heart, and I will always love you…"

"You just can't trust me." Her eyes glistened, and her bottom lip trembled.

He barely shook his head because this conversation made it all too real. Whatever hope might still simmer inside him had just died. "No, I can't."

"Okay…" She blinked back the tears and tilted her chin. "Good talk."

"I'm sorry—"

"No, it's good. Really. We got it all out there, and now we know where we both stand."

"Now we know." But he was sure it rang as hollow to her as it did to him.

As he rounded the bend, he saw the familiar black SUV parked in his spot. "Shit."

"Why are they back?" Stella leaned forward. "Don't tell me they've already heard about the training center? They can't be that well-connected. So help me, God, if they try to keep him out of this class…"

Affection surged right through the dread of seeing the Pilsons. Because Stella would never be intimidated by the Hanging Judge of Calamity or the former mayor. She'd go to the mat for a boy she'd just met.

"We're about to find out." He parked and cut the engine.

"Okay." She reached for her fancy leather purse on the back seat. "How do you want to play this?"

With her leaning halfway across the console, he could see into those warm hazel eyes and down the gaping neckline of her blouse to the plump mounds of cleavage. Sensation roared inside him.

This fucking chemistry between them…he just didn't know what the hell to do about it. "We're not playing anything. We'll hear what they have to say and go from there."

"I meant this is your last chance to get out of being engaged to me. We haven't actually lied to anyone but them yet, so…"

"It seems to be working. Let's just play it by ear." He reached for the handle, but she grabbed his arm and pulled.

"Kiss me."

"What?"

"You want to pull this off, kiss me."

"I'm not going in there with a fucking hard-on, Stella."

"I know." She grinned, all sultry and hot. "It took the whole ride home to get the last one to go down."

He laughed. "Stop looking at my dick, and maybe it won't last so long."

She grinned, looking at his lap. "It's literally like a third person in this truck. Now, come on, let's get into character."

Alarms went off in his head, but the draw of this woman was too strong, and he leaned in, slowly, taking in the sassy arch of her brows and the adorable dimples in her cheek, and then…he moved in close enough for their lips to brush.

What should've been nothing more than a staged kiss of affection set his pulse pounding. The world disappeared, as he fell into the slow dance of their tongues, the clasp of her hand at the back of his neck, and the sexy little moan that preceded the surrender of her body against his chest.

He kissed an apology into her mouth, sorry for being gruff and cold to her, sorry for making her feel she was anything but beautiful, sexy, smart, and the most caring, loving person he'd ever known.

He kissed the woman who owned his heart. Kissed her with a mind full of memories and a heart full of want.

Setting a hand on his chest, she pushed him away. "It's special for us, right? It's not just my imagination?"

"Nope." He caught her wrist, moving in for another kiss. "There's nothing better."

But she yanked her hand away. "Stop trusting a photograph over me, and you might just get another one." Throwing him a saucy look, she threw open the door and left him sitting alone in the truck.

As he sat there, the engine ticking, his blood pumping, he wondered if, when Peyton got back, and he was no longer responsible for Austin, he and Stella might have a chance for happiness together.

What would a little drama matter then? And if things went sideways again, well, he'd gotten over her once, he could get over her again.

Had he gotten over her, though?

I'm still single, I still ache for her…

Yeah, that'd be a hard no.

Right now, though, he had to deal with the judge. As soon as he got out, he joined the Pilsons and Stella on the walkway of his cottage.

"Hello." Mrs. Pilson looked between them with concern. "Where's Austin?" She gestured to the truck.

"We're making enchiladas tonight, and we didn't have avocado, so we ran out to the store," Stella said.

"Really? Austin helped you cook?" Mrs. Pilson sounded surprised but pleased.

"He sure did," Stella said.

"How nice," the older woman said. "Okay, well, we

just wanted to talk to him about Thanksgiving. I assume you'll spend it with your families, and of course, Austin will be with us."

"We haven't discussed our holiday plans yet," Stella said. "But we'll talk about it tonight after dinner and get back to you, okay?"

"We'd prefer to discuss it with him ourselves." Judge Pilson started up the walkway. "We've got plans that need to be finalized now."

His wife tugged on his coat. "They're about to sit down to dinner. We can come back." She smiled at them. "The holidays are for families, and with his father away, I'm sure you understand why it's important he needs us more than ever."

"Like Stella said, we haven't worked it out yet. We've got a lot to celebrate this year." Griffin nodded, a sign the conversation was done.

"All the more reason for him to be with us," Mrs. Pilson said. "You two can toast to your good news, and Austin will get to be with the extended family he so rarely gets to see. You understand."

"I do. And we'll discuss it." He started for the cabin.

The judge fell into place behind him. "We'd like to check on him before we go."

"Check on him?" *What the fuck's he insinuating now?*

"That's right. You've left him alone in a hotel."

Griffin stopped. "My parents own this place. He's perfectly safe here."

"Regardless of who owns it, it's a hotel with strangers coming and going." The judge tipped his chin to the cottage. "This is no place for a fourteen-year-old to live."

"Oh, this is temporary," Stella said. "The house we were buying fell through, and so now we're homeless. But we've got some other places we're interested in."

She did not just say that. I'm not buying a damn house. As soon as Peyton came home, Griffin would move back into his apartment over the shop. He worked so many hours, it only made sense.

But there was no denying how happy the idea made them. "That's wonderful." Relief relaxed Mrs. Pilson's features, making him wonder if he'd gotten her motivations all wrong. Maybe she really did want what's best for Austin. "What part of town are you looking at?"

Fuck my life. He couldn't stand the lies. They always backfired, and the truth always came out.

"We've narrowed it down to a few favorites, but we're not sure." Stella linked her arm through his. "We might just rent until we find our dream house."

The hell we will.

And why was she giving specifics?

"None of them are on 191, are they?" Mrs. Pilson asked. "That's a dangerous road."

He'd never house-hunted a day in his life. He didn't have a clue about neighborhoods.

But, of course, Stella stepped right in. "Would you like to see the listings?"

"Oh, I'd love that. Thank you so much, Stella." Mrs. Pilson looked tickled.

While Griffin wanted to shout at her. *What listings? What the hell are you talking about?*

"Let me go grab them. In the meantime, you go on inside." With a big grin, Stella shuddered. "It's freezing. Honey, get the enchiladas out of the oven, okay? Make them a hot cup of tea or coffee. I'll be right back."

Did she just call me honey?

"Oh, no, don't bother with us. We'll only stay a minute while you're getting the listings, but then we'll let you sit down to dinner." The woman couldn't have been more delighted.

Grumpy as hell, Griffin led them to the cottage. Where was she going to get fake listings? If she drove into town and talked to a realtor, it could take an hour or more. He wasn't entertaining these people that long.

Before he opened the door, he turned to them and said, "I don't want to discuss Thanksgiving right now. As I said, we need to discuss it with Austin first." He wouldn't let them ambush the boy.

The judge gave him a barely perceivable nod.

Griffin entered the warm cottage. "Austin, your grandparents are here." While the boy was nowhere to be found, the enchiladas were sitting on a trivet on the counter. *Responsible kid.* "He's probably in his room doing homework."

The judge started down the hallway.

"Hang on. I'll get him." Griffin strode ahead of him and knocked on Austin's door. "Hey, your grandparents are here. Come out and say hello."

A long, tense moment passed before the door opened, and a sulky teenager ambled out. His expression said, *Do I have to?*

Yep.

"Austin." The judge greeted him with a warm, kind smile. "How are you?"

It was painful to watch the stern and commanding man try to have a relationship with the boy when he couldn't get out of his own way. He couldn't seem to set down his gavel or do anything other than direct, teach, control. He didn't seem to know how to just love.

Wait a minute.

Holy shit.

Am I like that?

At that moment, Stella's comment about him protecting the people he loved hit him in the solar plexus. It rang true. Was he so busy making sure nothing went wrong that he hadn't made Austin feel loved? Wanted?

That would suck. And he had a horrible feeling it might be true.

Because it was Stella who'd taken him to the training center and arranged lessons with Will. It was Stella who'd gotten him to open up about his grandparents.

He'd have to do something about that.

Following Austin into the living area, he made a quick scan of the small but very nice space. He wasn't worried about a mess, but he did look at it through their eyes and couldn't see a damn thing wrong. "Can I make you some coffee?"

"We won't stay long," Judge Pilson said.

"We'll just take a quick peek at the houses and then let you eat." Mrs. Pilson followed her grandson into the kitchen. "I heard you helped make dinner tonight."

Austin reached into the refrigerator and pulled out a carton of milk.

"Austin." The judge's tone was scolding. "Answer your grandmother when she speaks to you."

"I didn't know you liked cooking. You can help me make Thanksgiving dinner." Mrs. Pilson smiled warmly at him as if Griffin hadn't specifically asked them not to bring it up.

Anyone could see the boy stiffen, and yet Mrs. Pilson kept on talking like nothing was wrong. "Do you remember our neighbors, the Gregorys? Their grandchildren are in town, and they've got a boy your age, so that will be fun for the two of you to play together. They'd like to ride the gondola to the top of the mountain and use the hot springs, so I want to make sure you bring your swimsuit."

Austin's clear discomfort got Griffin moving to his side. "As I told you, we're not sure about our plans yet."

The judge sent him a hard look.

Jesus, I'm a grown man, and he makes me feel like I've been caught driving a stolen car. But he held firm for Austin's sake. "We'll talk about it and let you know by this weekend."

"Oh, you know holidays are special family time," Mrs. Pilson said. "And with his father so far away, he needs to be with us."

"Traditions are important," the judge said. "They connect you to your history, build strong bonds, and reinforce that you belong. And Austin belongs with us."

Maybe if the judge had smiled or if his tone held even a hint of warmth, Austin might've relaxed. If he'd said, *Hey, it won't be the same without you.* Or *We're making your favorite spicy hot chocolate.*

Instead, Austin looked like bugs were crawling up his legs.

"Okay, well, have a seat. Austin and I are going to finish up the salad." He'd started it, but he'd done a half-ass job. He'd have Austin cut up a tomato or something. "Stella won't be long." Not that he knew what she was doing. Would she come back in and say she couldn't find them and then go into great detail about some imaginary listings?

That was the thing about her. With her dazzling personality, she could convince you of anything.

You *wanted* to believe her. You wanted to be her friend.

And then she'd do something stupid and leave you reeling.

"How did you and Stella meet?" Mrs. Pilson came into the kitchen, taking in the open bag of shredded cheese, the can of olives, the dark liquid spilled onto the counter.

Griffin set Austin up with a knife and the tomato. "I'm the same age as her sister, and Lulu used to cook in my dad's kitchen back in high school." At least he could answer this stuff honestly.

"And you've been together all this time?" Mrs. Pilson seemed surprised.

"No, like she said, it's been on and off."

"I see. How lovely. I assume you'll want kids of your own?"

Kids? He'd never given the idea much thought. But just the idea of having children with her sent a jolt of excitement rocketing through him.

Because it implied a future.

With Stella.

And there was no one else he wanted to spend his life with. "Absolutely."

"Well, that's nice. She's quite a catch."

"Stella's the best." He couldn't stop the flood of affection.

"She comes from an exemplary family," Mr. Pilson said. "They're quite active in philanthropy."

"Yes, they are."

The door flew open, and Stella burst in with her dazzling smile and a hand full of papers. "Who-ee, it's cold out there. I can't believe we're going to get more snow. It's not even December yet." She handed over the documents, before wrapping her arm around Griffin's waist and leaning against him. "Those are what we call our 'safeties.' They're in our budget. The last three are the rentals we're looking at."

Mrs. Pilson scanned the listings.

"Real estate's expensive in Calamity," Mr. Pilson said.

"It is, but we both have good, secure jobs." She reached up to play with the hair at the back of his neck.

For one brilliant moment, it wasn't a lie. Maybe it was because of that spectacular kiss in the truck a few minutes ago, or maybe she just fit back into his life so seamlessly, but it didn't feel like they were pretending.

Her body belonged up against his, and her hands should live in his hair, making him feel loved, wanted, and on fire. Nothing could stop his arm from wrapping around her, the heat of her skin an irresistible draw.

As they rambled on about the house that didn't exist, Griffin lowered his hand, slid it under her shirt, and skimmed her lower back. Sensory memories slammed him.

The slide of his palm on the back of her thigh, the dip of her waist and flare of her hip. He'd kissed a path from the curve of her neck all the way down to her toes, not missing a single patch of smooth skin. He knew the sensitive spots that made her writhe, and the erotic ones that made her neck arch.

And right then, it took every ounce of restraint not to slide his hand up her back and around to her chest, feel the bounce and weight of her breast, the hard nipple begging to be pinched.

Fuck, but he wanted to be alone with her.

"Ideally, I'd love to have an office in my home."

So he could spank her ass red for coming up with more lies.

"I'll keep working when we have kids, but I want to cut back my hours, and I'd love to actually do as much work from home as possible. That means a bigger house, but Griffin's handy, so we can get a fixer-upper and do most of the updating ourselves."

What a convincing liar she is.

Mrs. Pilson set the papers down. She glanced to her husband, and they shared a look of silent communication. "This is wonderful." She pressed a hand to her heart. "You have no idea how much peace of mind this gives us. When Peyton left our grandson in the care of a twenty-eight-year-old bachelor who runs a motorcycle shop…" She gave him a look that said, *I'm sure you understand.* "We had our concerns."

"The most significant impact on a child's behavior is the community around him," Mr. Pilson said. "Children might rebel against their parents, but with cousins, aunts, uncles, and church families around them, they're less inclined to stray off course."

Which course is that? he wanted to ask. *The one you set for him?*

"I think you know we only want the very best for our grandson." Mrs. Pilson set her hand on the boy's shoulder. "You know that, right? Everything we do comes from our love for you." She turned to the happy, fake couple. "But with Stella and her family involved, we can rest easier."

"Well, that's very nice to hear." Stella started toward the door.

Like sheep, they followed. They probably had no idea they'd just ceded control to her.

At the door, the judge turned to Austin. "We'll see you at Thanksgiving."

With Austin silent and stiff beside him, there wasn't a

chance Griffin could let the power play slide. "I'll get back to you with our plans."

Mrs. Pilson smiled at Stella. "I know the house on Blossom Lane. It's on a cul-de-sac and not far from town. It's a lovely neighborhood and the perfect home to raise a family. They're renting it out for now, but a little bird told me they might consider selling in the not-too-distant future. Act quickly, or it'll be gone."

Stella beamed her warm smile. "We plan on it."

"Take care, dear." She patted Stella's arm.

And with that, they left the cottage.

"I'm hungry." Austin went back to the kitchen, leaving them alone.

For a long moment, they both just stared at the door.

"Well." Stella raised her brows. "I don't think I gave you enough credit for the way you've handled them. They're…a lot to deal with."

"Yeah, but I really wish you hadn't lied about the house."

"Oh, my God, seriously? They backed off. Like, all the way off."

His annoyance only impressed on him how much he wanted to trust her. *But that's just the chemistry.* It was hard to keep his hands off her. "You're right."

"I thought they just wanted him, period. Like, to make up for the daughter they lost. But I think they really do want what's best for him."

They want him away from me. But whatever. They *had* backed off. "Looks like it."

"Honestly, if my grandson were living with my son's friend instead of me? In the same town? I'd be hurt."

He would be, too. "Yep."

"You're giving me these clipped answers. Are you seriously that mad at me about the house?"

He leaned in. "You're building a house of cards with all these lies, and it's going to come crashing down. You have to stop this."

"You don't have to actually *buy* one, but why not rent a place for a year? I mean, come on, you're going to be twenty-nine in May, and you're still living in an apartment over the shop like you did when you were nineteen. At least while Austin's living with you, give him a real home in a real neighborhood. Maybe part of the reason he's not making friends is because he's living out of a suitcase. Maybe it'll feel less like he's waiting for his dad to come home if he feels settled somewhere."

She made a good point. He started for the kitchen. "Maybe."

"So…do you want to go house hunting?"

"No, Stella. I absolutely don't want to go house hunting."

Chapter Nine

As soon as they got into the truck, Stella peered through the windshield at the house they'd just toured on Blossom Lane. "I love it. It's absolutely perfect."

They'd seen five so far—and since Griffin wouldn't even consider buying, they were all rentals. He was still insisting on moving back into his apartment over the shop once Peyton came back.

So stubborn.

What had she ever seen in him? Buckling in, she glanced over. He'd shoved the long sleeves of his blue Henley up to his elbows, exposing the inked, muscular forearms that flexed as he backed out of the driveway.

His dark, silky hair brushed his collar, and with his elbow propped on the windowsill, he ran a finger over the top of his sexy mouth. Always so thoughtful, always so intense.

Stella squirmed, looking away. She knew exactly what she'd seen in him. He was good, kind, honest, loyal. He was gorgeous and had a better body than most of the athletes she'd worked with.

But it was something about their connection. She'd met a lot of hot guys in her life—had worked with pro football players, for God's sake—but no one had ever lit her up the way Griffin did. "I think you should grab it."

"Maybe."

"Well, there are literally only five rentals in this entire town, and that was the best."

"It's ski season, and the only reason they're on the market is because of the price. They want way too much."

"You can't put a price on Austin's stability. I really think it'll change things for him."

"Yeah, I get that."

See? That willingness to concede? She loved that about him. He didn't have some big ego. He was reasonable, and she knew he truly wanted to do what was best for Austin.

As they headed back to the highway, she thought about the stupid way they'd ended their talk the other day.

We're not right for each other.

Okay, bye.

Yeah, she didn't think so. That just wasn't going to fly.

He thinks he can't trust me because my feelings are shallow. That I can love him one day, and Logan the next.

If she'd seen pictures of him on his honeymoon, she'd feel the same way.

Just the thought of it made her hurt.

But she wasn't going to give up that easily. Because she finally had a pathway forward. Now that she knew what held him back, she'd show him her feelings were constant, real. *Deep.*

Griffin was worth fighting for. "You seem lost in thought. Anything on your mind?"

"Just thinking it through." He tugged on his scruff. "It is pretty sketchy to live in a hotel. If Austin wanted to have friends over, their parents might not want their kid going to a single dude's hotel room."

"Ew. When you put it that way." She smiled.

"And it'll change the Pilsons perception of me, push them to see me as a responsible adult. So, yeah, okay. I'll take this one."

He was such a good guy, always thinking about other people, but…

Who took care of him?

I want to. I want to have his coffee waiting for him when he gets out of the shower. I want to leave the book he's dying to read on his nightstand.

I want to be the one who gets to offer him comfort and love. I want to be the source *of his comfort and love.*

And she couldn't do that when she posed as big of a threat to him as Austin's grandparents. With the lies that kept popping out of her mouth, she kept him on edge. If she wanted him—and she did. God, did she want him. Then, she'd have to think before speaking, talk to him about her ideas first. It didn't seem too much to ask.

"Do you want me to call and tell them?" she asked. "Before they give it to someone else?"

"I'll call after I drop you off. We're almost there."

Her stomach squeezed. As much as she wanted to see her parents, she dreaded it. They'd forgive her. She knew that. It was more that she'd missed out on *seven years* of their lives.

How selfish is that?

You don't do that to family.

They'd had health scares and crises, weddings and babies. They'd lived through big things, and she'd never checked in on them. "I'm a terrible person."

"What?" He whipped around to her. "No, you're not."

141

"I am. God, I feel sick."

"Hey." He reached for her hand. "No, don't do this. Your parents are excited to see you. They're happy you're home."

"Can I live in the house with you and Austin?"

"What? Where did that come from?"

"You know it's the first thing they're going to ask me. 'Where are you staying?' I've been here two weeks, and my free hotel room and car rental are up. They're going to tell me to move in with them, and I can't do that. I don't *want* to do that. We've just seen the rental situation. I can't afford anything during ski season on my salary. And you've got that cute carriage house. It's furnished…please?"

"Absolutely not." He accelerated, features going tense. "Why would you want to? Your parents have a guest house, too."

"I'm not living with my parents."

"Then live in Gigi's house. It's football season. They won't be back till January."

"Oh, come on. You know she comes and goes. She wants to wake up late, blast music, and jam in her studio. Eat cereal at the sink in her underwear."

"Do *you* eat cereal at the sink in your underwear?"

"Pretty sure you already know the answer to that."

For one hot second, they held a gaze, remembering how many times he'd come up behind her in the cabin, wrapped his arms around her, and nuzzled her neck. She'd set the bowl down and turned in his arms.

"You still like Golden Grahams?" he asked.

"I'm obsessed with it."

He cracked a grin before turning his attention back to the road. "I don't know why you'd want to live with us anyway."

"I want to live in the carriage house because it's furnished and affordable. *You* should want me to live with you because I'm fun."

"We don't need fun. We're just fine."

"Thank you for making my point. Your Friday night pizza delivery is the very definition of fine." She raised her arms. "Woo hoo, pizza…again."

He smirked. "I don't do pizza *every* Friday night."

She stared at him until the corner of his mouth turned up.

"There's nothing wrong with pizza. Austin likes it."

"You know what else is fine? Him playing video games while you read a book. Now, there's a wild night in the James hotel room. You know what's way more than fine?"

"Anything with you in it?"

Her smile burst from deep within, shooting glitter out to her entire body. "Taco night is fun. Sunday night ice cream sundaes? Now, that's ballin'. Karaoke while cooking? The bomb. And I can deliver all of that. Now, which do you want? Fine or fun?"

"Stella, you're not moving in with me."

"I didn't ask you that. I asked if I can crash in your carriage house until I save up enough to afford my own place. Besides, we're engaged. We're buying a house together…it makes sense. And then when you need me to play the happy fiancée, I can come right over. Unless…" Oh, God, it had never even occurred to her until just now.

"Unless what?"

"Well, if you don't want me to see what you're doing…" That would explain his reluctance.

"What I'm doing? Like taking out the garbage? Getting the mail?"

"No, you know, with women. I'm sure you get your

needs taken care of after Austin goes to sleep or when he visits his grandparents."

"My needs?" He shook his head before shock froze his features. "Wait, are *you* going to bring guys home?"

"Turn." She waved frantically.

Gripping the wheel, he made a hard left into her parent's driveway.

With a hand to her thundering heart, she said, "*Griffin.*"

"Sorry. You distracted me with the parade of men coming in and out of my guest house."

"I'm not…" She made a tsk sound with her tongue. "Do you know how many hours I work? I'm running a wedding planning business by myself. The rest of the time, I'm planning ice cream sundae parties for poor Austin who has to live with a boring roommate. Now, can I move in or not?"

"You always get your way, so I don't know why you even ask."

She hid her smile. She did, didn't she? "I don't always." But as they reached the gate, Stella's good mood got swallowed up by anxiety. "What's that? Why would they get a new gate?" The old wrought iron one had been original to the property when it was a working ranch eighty years ago. This new one was made of glossy wood. Her parents loved the history here, so she couldn't imagine why they'd remove one of the most fundamental pieces.

See, this is how much I missed.

"Do you think someone rammed the gate? You don't think someone tried to break in, do you?"

He braked and reached for the intercom button. "I don't know what you're talking about." Once it swung open, he drove through.

"My parents would never get rid of the original ranch gate unless there was a reason."

"And it has to be a bad one?"

"There's no good reason to get rid of a historic gate."

"Maybe it's in a museum."

"The museum of broken gates?" Although that wasn't as ridiculous as it sounded. Antiques, history…it was a big deal in Calamity.

"Do you remember Callie Belle?"

"Of course. She and Fin were my dream couple." She'd always wanted that kind of love. Instead, she'd hidden her feelings so she wouldn't hurt her sister.

"She created a museum. Well, she calls it an exhibition."

"Of broken gates?" She grinned.

"The Exhibition of Broken Hearts. Turned out to be a big hit. Her next one's Ghosts of the Past. She's invited everyone in the county to donate their historical artifacts."

"That sounds amazing."

He slowed in the horseshoe-shaped driveway and braked.

Seeing her childhood home for the first time in so many years…it was like taking a step in the dark and finding nothing but air. She was in freefall, completely disoriented.

"You okay?" He jerked the gearshift into Park.

Her stomach churned. "No." She looked beyond to the sage meadow surrounding her parent's property, the Teton Mountains jutting from the earth and presenting a striking backdrop. How could something feel so familiar and yet so foreign at the same time?

"Talk to me." He shifted toward her. "What're you thinking?"

"I stayed away too long, so now it's become this big thing. If I'd called, texted, emailed…if I'd sent a freaking postcard, this wouldn't be so bad."

"Why didn't you?" He said it kindly, and she appreciated that.

"I think the longer I was gone, the harder it was to reach out." *But that's not the real reason, is it?* "I missed everyone so much, and I was so sorry about what I'd done, but…" She shook her head, letting out a bitter laugh. "I got married. And it felt like I kept making a bigger and bigger mess of my life. I wasn't proud of anything, so why would I talk to them? 'Hey, guys, it's me. Living the life in Dallas as a lonely divorcée. Yep, killing it out here on my own.'"

"That's when you needed them the most."

Them. He'd excluded himself.

When all along, she'd needed him the most.

"Any time I found myself reaching for my phone to see what my sisters were doing or if I wanted to share good news with my parents, I remembered how long it had been since I'd talked to them, and it seemed selfish. So, I just kept coming up with excuses to put it off. And now…" She tipped her chin to the house. "I'm sitting here completely freaked out to go inside my childhood home."

"You want me to go in with you?"

Was it possible to love this man even more than she already did? She didn't think so. "You're amazing. But no, I have to do this alone. Thank you, though."

He sifted his fingers through her hair. And then his fist closed, and he shifted toward her. "You make it impossible not to kiss you—your honesty, your courage, the way you own your problems." He gently tugged, tipped her head back, and desire rocketed through her. "I'm starting to think you actually might've missed me the same way I missed you."

"That's what I've been trying to tell you." She gave him a teasing grin, but with the heat in his eyes, his gaze riveted on her mouth, and the tension in her scalp as pure evidence of what he wanted to do to her, the humor faded.

And then he kissed her. She opened to him right away, wanting him, all of him, and she sucked his tongue into her mouth. His hand went to the back of her neck as if to make sure she stayed right where she was.

She wasn't going anywhere. She wanted to live in his scent, in this lush kiss that hinted at the barely restrained desire rumbling under the surface. She wanted to kick down the barriers, let out the carnal man who took what he wanted.

And he'd always wanted her.

Her phone buzzed, startling them apart.

Mom: Are you coming in?
Stella: Yes. One second.

Dragging her purse from the footwell, Stella pulled out her make-up bag and reapplied her lipstick. But her hand was shaking, so she only swiped her lips and pressed them together. Recapping the tube, she tossed it back into the bag.

"Why do I feel sixteen again?" Smoothing her hair, she rested her hand on the spot that still vibrated from his touch. She wanted more. She would always want more from him. "Do you remember that day Mr. Ramirez called the police on us, and we all scattered—"

"And you and I wound up alone in that cabin? Yes, Stella. Of course, I remember. I finally had you all to myself, and yet I couldn't touch you."

"Yeah, but it was the best, wasn't it? Just the two of

us?" The energy between them had been wild and electric. They'd had so much fun.

The muscle in his jaw popped. "Yeah. It was."

"And then my dad called. And he might as well have burst into the room. I'll never forget that feeling. *Busted*." Her smile faltered, as she looked to the house made of wood, river stone, and glass, set on acres of sage meadow. "Well, this is it. Thanks for driving me."

"I can come in, tell them I need to use the bathroom?"

"You'd lie for me?" She held a hand over her heart, pretending to be touched.

"Considering I'm engaged and moving into a new house…yeah, I'd say so."

She smacked his arm. "Hey, I thought you were trying to make me feel better? But, no, I've got this. Thanks."

"You're returning the rental car tomorrow. Want to hit the dealership in Jackson?"

"I was thinking I'd buy one of your custom bikes."

A slow smile spread across his handsome features. "I can't think of anything sexier than you straddling a Harley in your high heels and leather pants. But since it's winter, we'll put a hold on fulfilling my fantasies."

"I didn't know there were more to be fulfilled?"

The grin widened. "I only had you for eighteen months. Not even close to running out of them."

She kept her smile in place, but she was confused. Had their conversation the other night enabled him to relax around her, now that getting back together was off the table?

Or was he softening toward her?

She couldn't begin to read his mind, and now wasn't the time anyway, so she reached for the handle. "Yeah, sure, let's buy me a car."

"Remember the Crosby brothers? They opened a dealership, and they'll give you a good deal on an SUV. Big enough to cart around all the wedding shit."

"Sounds good. I'll make some time tomorrow to get over there."

"If it's possible, shoot for after school. I like taking Austin with me for things like that, so he learns about negotiating, changing a flat, filling the truck with gas. That kind of thing."

"That's really nice. And while we're out, we can get him pants, gloves, a snowboard and all that stuff."

He shook his head. "You're an unstoppable force."

"Of good, right?"

And there it was—that connection—that arc of electricity between them. There was nothing like it in the world.

"Nearly all good." He gave a shrug of his eyebrows. "Ninety-nine percent good."

"Actually, if you track all the decisions I've made over a lifetime, there've only been three whammies—the kiss, the elopement, and the fake engagement—so, that makes it more like ninety-nine-point-nine-percent."

His grin widened. "Okay, I'll—"

Someone tapped on the window, and Stella startled. Her mom stood there with a big smile.

And the world stopped spinning.

Mom.

Every wall she'd built to be strong, to handle what life threw at her, to make all her own decisions and navigate the consequences by herself, crumbled, leaving nothing but deep, profound regret that she'd lost so much time with the people who mattered most.

Her mom read the anxiety flowing through Stella, and her smile wilted.

Nothing was her parent's fault, so she turned back to Griffin. "Bye."

He must've seen the anxiety in her eyes because he put his hand on hers. "Let me pick you up, okay? Text me, and I can be here in ten minutes."

Her mom pulled the door open, letting in cold air. "You coming in, Griffin?"

"No, I'm just dropping her off."

Her mom looked between them, as though trying to figure out the relationship. And then her gaze settled on the diamond sparkling on Stella's left ring finger. Her eyes went wide, and she straightened, backing right into Stella's dad. "You're engaged?"

Chapter Ten

Her mom glanced up at her husband with a confused expression. "They're engaged."

Stella got out of the car, dreading this moment. Griffin had warned her lying to her parents was the worst thing she could do when trying to repair the relationship.

He was right.

Her mom hugged her. "Oh my God. You and *Griffin*? I had no idea."

As her mom rocked her back and forth, her dad leaned into the car. "Come inside."

With an arm wrapped around her waist, her mom ushered her up the stone walkway, holding her tight as if she thought Stella might pull a runner.

She glanced over her shoulder to find Griffin getting out of the truck and following them.

Dammit. Just when they were starting to get along, now he had to lie to her parents. He was going to hate this.

Once inside, Stella shrugged off her parka and tossed it onto the back of a blue velvet love seat. How many times had she done the exact same thing, when she'd come racing in breathless, happy, hurrying through homework, dinner, chores, whatever she had to do, so she could get back out and join her friends or see Griffin?

Momentarily disoriented from flying back in time seven years, she reached out to steady herself, and a strong arm gripped her, grounding her. "You okay?" Griffin murmured.

She nodded, leaning into him like it was the most natural thing in the world.

"Stella?" Her mom stopped on the way to the kitchen. "Everything all right?"

Griffin answered for her. "She hasn't eaten since breakfast."

Stella looked up at him, wondering how he knew that. His love, it was like a blanket on a cold day. It was like hot cocoa in front of a fire. It enveloped her, comforted her, and strengthened her.

The past seven years had taught her a painful lesson. Several, actually. But number one was that Griffin James was the fabric of her soul, and she would never be complete without him.

It wasn't just the connection she felt when they kissed. And it wasn't some nostalgic sense of the history between them.

It was because Griffin James was the best man she knew, and the worst thing that had ever happened to her had been losing him.

She *had* to get him back.

"Let me grab some appetizers." Her mom hurried to the island. "You guys sit down. Hon, why don't you pour some drinks?"

Her dad, still as muscular and fit as his days as a pro

quarterback, shifted his gaze from Griffin to Stella. "I'm not thirsty."

Her dad was the most loving, generous man Stella had ever known. Even at her worst moments in her teen years, when he'd had to come up with some serious conse-quences for her actions, he'd never lost his temper.

He hardly ever got pissed like he was right then.

"Everyone sit down." That commanding tone, so rarely used, had all of them comply.

When Griffin headed to the couch, Stella grabbed the back of his Henley and pulled him onto the love seat. She needed him next to her.

"You're engaged?" Her dad's tone was flat.

They both stayed quiet a beat too long.

What do I do?

Was she actually going to lie to her parents? It was one thing when it was a concept, and her only concern was protecting Griffin and Austin.

It was entirely another thing to face her father and flat-out lie to him.

And to make Griffin party to this?

It's just wrong. And it's unfair to him.

But then what about the Pilsons?

It's working. They've backed off.

Dammit, she'd made such a mess of the situation.

Besides, I'm wearing a freaking engagement ring.

No, she had to do it. She had to lie.

"Stella." Her dad's tone made her palms go clammy.

I'm the worst liar. Everyone knew it. As a teenager, she'd dated a seasonal worker at Wolff Lodge. A few years older than her, he'd had a British accent, dressed like a punk rocker, and doused himself in a cologne so strong, they'd never gotten the scent out of her truck.

That scent was the giveaway every time she'd tell her parents she hadn't snuck out.

Whatever. You just have to do it. For Austin's sake.

But just as she opened her mouth, Griffin said, "No, sir."

Her dad's gaze dropped to the diamond ring. "Explain."

"You don't have to do this." She said it quietly but obviously her dad heard.

"Yes, Stella. He does."

"No, Dad, you don't know what—"

But Griffin cut her off. "I have a situation."

"Wait." Her mom came out carrying a platter of cheese, crackers, slices of sausage, and grapes. "So, you're *not* engaged?"

"No, but you have to listen," Stella said. "This is serious. You can't tell anyone."

Her dad made a rolling motion with his hand. *Explain.*

Griffin let out a breath. "I'm taking care of Judge Pilson's grandson."

Immediately, her parents understood the seriousness of the situation. Everyone knew the judge's reputation.

"If the Pilsons live here, why is their grandson living with you and not them?" her mom asked.

"I don't know if you remember Peyton Greene, Mack's son?" Griffin asked.

Her mom shook her head.

"He's four years older than me, so I didn't know him well. But by the time I started full-time at the shop, Peyton had a five-year-old. The mother wasn't in the picture—"

"That's the Pilsons daughter?" her dad asked.

"Right. And Peyton had enlisted to try to make a good life for his son, so I've spent a lot of time with Austin over the years when he's visited Mack. He's comfortable with me. And when his dad deployed last month, he said he'd rather stay with me. As you can imagine, the Pilsons don't understand that choice."

Her dad gave a curt nod.

"They're difficult and controlling, and Austin doesn't want to live with them." Griffin let out a breath. "He threatened to run away if his dad made him go there, and we believe he'd do it. He's got a will of iron, that kid."

"Look, this whole fake engagement thing is my fault," Stella said. "I was bringing Austin home, and we heard them talking to Griffin. They said something incredibly offensive, and I just couldn't let them get away with it."

"What did they say?" her dad asked.

She glanced at Griffin to make sure it was okay to tell them. He nodded. "They asked him why a 'grown man would want to spend time with a teenage boy.'" She looked at them with an expression that said *Can you believe it?* "Austin was standing right there. He heard it."

"That gives me chills," her mom said.

"Which is why she did it," Griffin said. "To save my reputation. She marched right over and charmed them…"

"And I told them I was his fiancée."

"Okay, but I'm confused," Her mom waved a finger between them. "Have you and Griffin been in touch all this time?"

"No, it was my first day back in town," Stella said. "I hadn't seen him until that moment."

Her mom looked disappointed in her. "So, you had no idea what you were walking into?"

She waited for Griffin to say, *Exactly*. But, instead, he

said, "You know their influence, and if they'd thrown that comment out to someone in town, it would've done serious damage to my reputation. Besides, it got them to back off. Turns out, all they want is for Austin to be raised in a wholesome environment, and knowing I'm marrying into the Cavanaugh family seems to make them happy."

"But you're not marrying into the family." Her dad sent her a pointed look. "This could backfire."

"It could." Griffin sat forward, resting his elbows on his knees. "It's a tough situation all around, but we chose this approach, and we're sticking with it. I don't like putting Austin in a position to lie, but it's better than forcing him to live with them."

"And running the risk of him running away." Thankfully, her mom got it.

"And now I've drawn you into our circle," Griffin said. "I apologize for that, but I know the last thing Stella wants is to ruin this reunion with lies."

"Understood," her dad said.

Her mom sat back. "Well, how far are you going to take this? Are you going to get married?"

"No." Griffin almost sounded offended by the suggestion. "I don't anticipate this lasting long."

Don't sound so happy about it.

"Peyton's talking to a JAG lawyer to make me Austin's legal guardian in his absence. Once I have that, the threat's gone."

"Well, at least you won't have a hard time pulling it off," her mom said.

"What does that mean?" Stella asked.

"Oh, come on. Look at you two. No one would doubt you're together." Her mom reached for a grape. "Well, I suppose it wouldn't be a Stella homecoming without some drama, now would it?" She pushed the charcuterie board over to Griffin. "Please, help yourselves."

Her dad remained silent, and Stella grew uncomfortable. "What're you thinking, Dad?"

"I'm thinking I'm damn glad to have you home. I missed you, sweetheart."

Stella leaped off the couch and threw herself into his arms. "I missed you, too. So much. I love you, Daddy."

He got up, holding her tightly, his body growing warm. "I love you, too."

And the tilted axis of her world righted. For the first time in years, she stood on solid ground.

"Can I get in on this?" Her mom's voice sounded thick with emotion.

Her dad got up, and the three clung to each other.

Warmth spilled into all the cold, empty crevices carved out by too many years spent alone and far from home. Comfort rose like a forgotten scent, driving her back to her childhood when she'd felt safe, loved, and whole.

Her mom smoothed Stella's hair. "Are you staying in Calamity? Please tell me you're staying."

Swiping the tears from under her eyes, Stella pulled away. "I'm scared."

"Oh, sweetheart. What're you scared of?" Her mom looked concerned.

"I don't know if I've ruined everything."

"What do you mean?"

"I've been gone so long. What if I can't fit back in? My sisters have gotten used to there only being three of them. They have adult relationships with each other now." Tears spilled hot down her cheeks. "Coco's had two babies, and I've missed everything. Lulu got married, and I wasn't there."

Strong arms wrapped around her waist and turned her around. The next thing she knew, she was enveloped in Griffin's embrace, his big hand at the back of her head. She slumped against him, giving him all her weight because she knew he could take it.

"I don't belong here anymore," she whispered.

"Then fix it," Griffin said.

The noise in her head shut down, and she gazed up at him.

"This is your family. They love you. So, just go on and fix what you broke."

"I don't know how." Not after what she'd done. Which was why she'd run in the first place.

"Stella," her dad said. "You don't have to do anything. You just have to show up. Everything will fall into place after that. You're here. That's the first step. One foot in front of the other."

"I can do that."

She could…with her parents, Gigi, and probably with Coco.

But what about Lulu?

It wouldn't be that easy with the sister of her heart. Lulu might never forgive her.

And then what would she do?

After dropping Austin off at the training center, they stopped in town for coffee.

Stella got out of the truck, stepped onto the sidewalk, and came to a hard stop. *Wait a minute.*

Where's Duke's?

In between Calamity Joe's and Coco's Chocolates sat

an historic building with plate glass windows. A sign said *Harley Lu Emporium.*

Griffin pocketed his keys and joined her. "What's up?"

"What happened to the toy store?"

"Duke moved to Arizona a couple of months ago. He sold the place to Lulu and Maureen's daughter Harley."

"Harley, the surfer?"

"She retired, but yeah."

"How could he do that? That store...that's my entire childhood." Shock turned to disbelief. "Every year on our birthdays, my dad would take us there. We got to buy three things. One for ourselves, one for all of our sisters, and one to donate to the Women and Children's Shelter." She didn't like change. Especially when it erased her childhood. "How could Duke just leave?"

"He wanted to be near his kids."

"But what about *all* the kids? Where do the children of Calamity get their toys?"

"They don't." He said it seriously. "The children of Calamity have no toys. They have no books. They sit on hardbacked chairs and do math problems. The Youth Center council grades them. If they fail, they get lashes on their bare backs."

"What?" She was totally confused.

"I'm kidding. You should see your face right now. It's okay. The children of Calamity are fine."

"But every town needs a toy store. That's as basic as a bakery."

"Where have you been living? You know the big box stores have killed a lot of Mom and Pop places." He gave a chin nod to Calamity Joe's. "Come on. Let's grab our drinks."

"Wait, why would Lulu buy a building?" Disbelief

shifted into something that squeezed her lungs and made it hard to pull in a full breath.

Does that mean she's here?

Now?

"I don't know. You'll have to ask her. But it's a cool place. Calamity's never had a gourmet store. It's got a bakery, a prepared foods section, and I hear they'll eventually have a café."

"But she lives in Dallas. How can she own a store here if she's not around to take care of it?" No one had mentioned Lulu owning a business here. "How often does she come to town?"

"They're in Dallas during the football season and here when it's not. But just like Gigi, she comes and goes. It's just a three-hour flight."

"So, that's why she showed up at the office. She was in town for her store."

"Probably. You want to go in and check it out? I can grab our coffees, while you look around."

"Are you kidding me? My sister took one look at me and ran out of the room. I'm not going to just wander around her store." *She doesn't want to see me.*

"Why are you being so weird about this?" He came in close enough for their shoulders to touch. "What's really going on?"

"I think I've just been in this bubble, you know? Since I landed, I've either been working or hanging out with you and Austin. And this…" She made a sweeping motion, taking in the coffee house, the sidewalk, and the town green across the street. "It's like the first slap of reality." She became keenly aware of the passersby. The population of Calamity might be under thirty thousand residents, but in the ski season, it swelled to a million. It wouldn't be uncommon to run into someone she knew.

She felt…exposed. Because if her own sister didn't want to see her, what about her old friends? All the people who'd once loved her and went out of their way to say hello and chat with her—did they all hate her, too?

"Hey." Hands on her shoulders, he turned her to face him. "What's going on in your head right now?"

His touch kept her from spiraling. "I should go."

"I thought you wanted a coffee. You said you wanted to warm up."

"I don't want to be here."

"Because of Lulu?"

"Because of everything."

He tipped her chin. "Sweetheart, talk to me."

Sweetheart. This man melted her into a hot puddle even on an icy cold day. Holding onto his gaze to keep her grounded, she let herself slow down enough to actually process her feelings. And once she did, the panic ebbed, and she could think clearly. "When I grew up here, everyone loved me. I couldn't even go to the grocery store without a dozen people stopping to say hello. And now…I mean, is everyone going to look at me and go, What the hell is she doing back in town?"

He tugged her wool hat so it covered her ears better. "You bet your ass everyone's going to look at you. Because you're gorgeous. Look at you. You're as glamorous as a movie star, and you give off this big, happy energy. You're the sun, and everyone who comes near you gets caught in your gravitational pull." His hand caressed her cheek till it cupped her jaw. "And if Lulu sees you and runs? That's on her. You're home, this is where you belong, and I know you won't stop until you fix the relationships that are broken."

She smiled at him. "I'm the sun?"

"Yeah, you are." His thumb stroked her chin. "And you know, maybe instead of worrying about other people, you should work on forgiving yourself. It's time to let it go. Everyone has moved on. So should you."

She grasped his wrists, awash in affection for this man. "Have you?" Their gazes locked, and her body vibrated with anticipation. "Moved on?"

She could tell from his expression he understood the importance of his answer. "No, Stella." He picked up her hand and pressed it over his heart. "I don't think I can do that."

It was a strange kind of happiness that flooded her. It was quiet, but it had lift and thrust, and if his hand hadn't been touching her, she thought she might just…float.

Until he looked away, and she landed on the snowy ground. "Let's go inside and get you warmed up. You're shivering."

"No, that's okay. I don't want coffee anymore. Besides, I need to get going." She glanced up at the gray sky. "I heard this storm's going to be worse than expected."

"You sure? I can run inside and grab one for you." He lifted her hands to his mouth, cradling them in his and blowing on them. "Let me warm you up."

Desire bloomed in her, warming her like sunshine. "That's okay. Thanks, though. Honestly, I'm not going to run scared in this town, and I'm not going to avoid Lulu. I mean, I live here now. I'm staying. But I have to turn on the generator and vent the water pipes of a cabin for one of my couples, and I don't want to get caught in a blizzard."

"Where is it?"

"It's the Montrose's place, about five miles from Moose."

"Moose is a twenty-minute drive from here, and then you have to get up the mountain."

"Yeah, I know. That's why I'm skipping the coffee."

He glanced up at the darkening sky. "Can you put it off till tomorrow?"

"No, the wedding's this weekend. They're going straight to the cabin Saturday night." *On a sled*. Which she still had to decorate. *Gah. So many things to do*. "It has to be ready for them."

"There must be someone who does that for Diane."

"It's too late now. Besides, it's my fault. I didn't make the connection between the storm and preparing the cabin. It's been a while since I've had to think about things like that."

"Look, if you put it off till tomorrow, I'll go there and do it myself."

"I appreciate that, but it's their honeymoon. I can't have anything go wrong."

"Fine." He turned back to his truck.

"What're you doing?"

"You're not going up the mountain alone with a snowstorm on the way."

"No, Griffin. You have to get back to the shop." Not only did he need to take advantage of the fact that Austin had after school activities now, but the Pilsons were picking Austin up for a sleepover. "You've got a big block of time to catch up on work."

"You're not going alone, so get in the truck. We'll stop at my parents' house and get the snowmobiles."

"Griffin—"

"We don't have time to argue. Get in."

"Okay, Mr. Bossy Pants." He might not be so insistent if he knew where they were going.

He didn't know it, but the Montroses had bought several cabins as part of a new rental business. And this one in particular…

It had been theirs.

Which meant she'd have to be alone with him in the cabin where they'd first made love.

Only this time, he wasn't hers to touch.

Chapter Eleven

GRIFFIN STOMPED HIS BOOTS ON THE SNOW-COVERED patio of the cabin. "You've got to be kidding me." Of all the cabins in the Tetons, she'd brought him to this one?

"Nope." Climbing off her snowmobile, Stella unbuckled her helmet and headed for the shed to turn on the generator. "Told you not to come with me." She'd grumbled it to herself.

But he'd heard.

Griffin hadn't been one of those people who'd always known what he wanted to do with his life. When his friends had headed down the hockey path, he'd gone with them. He was good at it, but he hadn't loved it the way they had. He could've worked at the Inn—there'd always be a job for him there. But he'd preferred working for Mack after school and tinkering with Harleys.

So, when it came time to apply to college, his only criteria was that it was close enough to Calamity that he could come and visit Stella whenever missing her became too big to bear.

And when he'd gotten her text in the first semester of

his sophomore year at USC, the decision to drop out had been simple.

Stella: Lulu's got a serious boyfriend!

He'd packed up his truck and headed home. His first stop had been the Cavanaughs. He'd lifted Stella off her feet and planted a kiss on her mouth that his body remembered to this day. It was like plugging in the lights. His body had just blazed.

His second stop had been the Boneyard. He'd told Mack he wanted to work there full-time.

Third stop: right here. They weren't going to risk interruptions at either of their homes or the Inn. And sex after a build up like that? It had been insane. They'd torn each other's clothes off. He'd taken her against the wall, on the kitchen table, and in the shower.

And then, for Valentine's Day—corny as it might've been—he'd arranged a whole weekend away with her here. He'd queued up movies, brought her favorite foods, and they'd hidden away, just the two of them.

It had been better than anything he'd ever experienced.

For a guy who didn't have a whole lot to say to people, he'd found himself talking to her. Stella made everything easy. His friends used to call him "a broody fuck," but he'd been downright playful around her. She'd brought out that side of him.

Thinking about it now, the way he'd always felt so desperate for her, so…*complete*…made it all come flooding back.

This is not good.

Well, fuck it. What could he do? He was here to help her get the place ready for use, so he'd get it done.

Unlocking the door, he let himself in. Sensation crept

across his skin, and he felt a pull, a drag back in time. But he wouldn't let himself go there.

He'd do what he did with everything else. He'd simply shut it down.

Stella came in, blowing into her clasped hands and stomping the snow off her boots onto the rubber mat. Their gazes locked, and tension billowed out so thick and fast it filled the space around them.

But then, as she always did, she broke out into a warm smile. "All right, let's do this." She swept past him and went into the kitchen. "With two of us, we'll be out of here in no-time." She pulled a dishtowel from a drawer and started dusting.

"I'll take care of the water."

"That'd be great. Thank you." Was she avoiding eye contact?

He wouldn't blame her. The memories took up so much space in this small cabin that it felt crowded. Right on that couch, they'd dozed like kittens, sprawled all over each other. She'd straddled him on that chair, her tits bouncing, her hair cascading down her back.

Shit, shit, shit.

Move. Get busy. He crossed the kitchen—completely upgraded since he'd last been here—and headed into the basement.

He turned on the valve, and the tank started rumbling. It belched out some trapped air, but then the flow of water started, so he climbed back up the wooden stairs.

Stella fluffed the pillows, her back to him, and he was pretty sure she was paying a little too much attention to the task.

"What else do you need me to do?" he asked.

167

ERIKA KELLY

"I'm going to put fresh sheets on the bed, so would you mind sweeping?"

"Sure."

"I'll come back on Friday and fill the propane tank, bring some fresh flowers. The toiletries look great, so…" She sounded tense, and it was killing him.

He touched her shoulder. "Hey." Lightly, he put his hand on her lower back, but she probably couldn't feel it through her down jacket.

She straightened, giving him a strained smile. "Of all the places, right?"

"Yeah. A lot of memories here."

"With their kids in college, the Montroses were looking for rental income, so they bought up a bunch of cabins. Diane suggested pitching them on the website as remote honeymoon hideaways. You can't believe how popular they are."

"I believe it." He brushed the hair off her cheek, and she gazed up at him.

The energy between them grew charged, the molecules heating, spinning out into a whirlwind of hunger and longing. His heart just felt so damn full, and he was overcome with this feeling of absolute rightness…*us, together. Here.* "You're so beautiful."

Color enflamed her cheeks, and she licked her lips. The intensity of her gaze stirred him into a frenzy of desire. No one had ever wanted him the way Stella did. His friends and brothers used to say their attraction had been fueled by the forbidden—because of their age difference and Lulu's crush—but they were wrong.

When they could finally be together, their love had grown bigger and brighter. It had deepened, the passion never subsiding.

But he also saw wariness in her eyes. He'd told her he'd never trust her heart again. Did he mean it? At that moment, he couldn't tell. He wanted her too much. "We really fucked things up."

She went soft as if he'd said the exact right thing. "We did."

"Why do you look relieved?"

"Because up until now, you've made me feel like it's all my fault. But Griffin, I might've made the mistake of kissing Trace, but you made the mistake of throwing me away. If you'd just been some guy I'd been dating, it would've been okay. But you weren't."

"No, I wasn't."

"You were...everything. The love of my life. I couldn't see a future that didn't have you in it. You have to understand how—"

He gripped her elbows. "I do. I do understand because I felt the same way. You don't know how hard I beat myself up after you left. For months, I couldn't sleep. I couldn't eat. All I could think about is why I'd done that. Why would I break up with the only woman I'll ever love? It killed me."

"Let's not do this." She brushed the hair off his forehead and turned away. "Not here." She got busy again, flipping the cushion of a leather club chair. Pulling sheets from the linen closet, she tossed them on the bench at the foot of the bed.

The whole time he watched her, he tried to find the words she needed to hear. He didn't know how to explain how he'd felt back then, but he knew he had to. "I..." *You what?* He sat on the arm of the chair, letting himself remember those days after she'd kissed her sister's fiancé.

And there was only one response that he could name. "I couldn't control you."

She'd tossed the pillows off the bed, hugging one to her stomach.

"And it scared me."

She waited for more.

"The closer we got to the wedding, the more worked up you got." He rubbed his jaw. "I could see you were headed for disaster, and I couldn't stop you. You wouldn't listen. And that night, you kept drinking. You got more and more determined to make Lulu see the truth. You were on this path of destruction, and I felt out of control. I wanted to stop you before things blew up, but I couldn't."

Setting the pillow down, she shrugged off her coat and tossed it on the bed. "I remember feeling so…panicked. Lulu wouldn't listen to me, and I just…if I didn't stop her, it would be the end of the world. I'd built it up to be this crazy, huge thing."

"Right, and then you got this look in your eye, and I knew…my gut told me you were going to do something terrible. I got so…I don't know how to explain it."

"Try."

He gave her a curt nod. She needed this. Maybe they both did. "I was sweating, my heart beating so fast I thought I'd have a heart attack. I lost sight of you, and that flipped me the fuck out because I knew you were doing something bad, something you couldn't come back from." *Like he'd done with Booker.* "And then Lulu's face. *Fuck.*" He lowered his head, remembering her sister's expression. "You didn't see it because you were across the room. But your sister was…to say she was devastated doesn't do it justice."

Her features crumpled in pain.

"I'm not saying it to make you feel bad."

"I know. Go on."

"And then I looked—we all looked—across the room. And there you were, against the wall, Trace's hands on your ass, and you were kissing him."

She closed her eyes. "I'm sorry."

"My instinct should've been to run over there, jump over tables, knock people down, and tear you from him. But I wasn't jealous. I knew you weren't cheating on me. I didn't feel betrayed. I felt like…"

"Like what?"

"Well, it wasn't even a year after the accident." He still had nightmares about that night, of watching Booker hit the ground, right there in front of him. "And I couldn't stand feeling out of control…that kind of…recklessness. That's the only way I can think to describe it. I just couldn't handle it."

"I want to say I understand, but I don't. I'm not like your friends. I didn't wear batsuits or go BASE jumping. I don't see myself as *dangerous*. But I guess it doesn't have to be physical. It can be emotional, too." She looked so damn defeated. "I can see that I'm still doing it, making you feel unsafe. I show up out of the blue and make myself your fake fiancée, and now you're renting a house you never wanted." She turned away from him, yanking back the blanket and sheet. "You should probably start sweeping."

"Yeah. Sure." He found a broom in the pantry and got to work, feeling unsettled and uneasy.

"Have you dated anyone?"

"What? How did we go from talking about that night to me dating?"

"I'm making conversation."

"Well, find another topic. I'm not talking about other women with you."

"It's not that big of a deal. It's been seven years."

"Fine. Sure, I've been on dates."

"Did you fall in love?" She stripped off the bottom sheet. "Have you had a girlfriend?"

"No, Stella. That's not going to happen for me."

"So, what, you're just going to be alone the rest of your life?"

Watching her in that soft cashmere sweater, the sunlight streaming in through the windows and accentuating those big, round breasts was making him crazy. "I don't know. I don't really think about it. I like my job. I have good friends, family…"

"Oh, come on. Everyone needs love. Even the bad boy biker who takes such good care of everyone around him."

Uncomfortable, he turned away and did an outstanding job of sweeping. He even shoved the chair aside to get the dust underneath it.

Because he already had love. Nothing had changed for him.

The room had gone quiet. No more shaking out sheets or lifting the mattress. He stopped what he was doing to find her watching him. "What?"

"You did fall in love." The sadness in her eyes gutted him. "Who was she?"

He went back to sweeping, but since there was no more dust, he nudged the chair back in place.

"You can tell me. I won't fall apart. It's…of course you've had relationships." Despite her words, her voice had gone thick with emotion.

"No girlfriends."

"You're lying to me right now." She sat on the edge of

the bed. "You really loved her. God, and you made me feel so bad about Logan."

Anger flared, igniting. "No, Stella, I don't work like that."

"Like what?" She shook her head. "Are we doing this again? Where you tell me how flighty I am? How easily I fall in and out of love? I told you I didn't love him."

"Okay."

She crossed over to him. "Not 'okay.' You've got something to say, say it."

"There's a storm coming. Let's get this done and get out of here."

"No, Griffin. You don't get to drop something like 'I don't work like that.' Because it makes me sound cheap and shallow compared to you. And I'm neither of those things."

"I know you're not. But if you think I could love someone else after what we had, then you don't know me at all."

She watched him for a moment like she was processing. "I do know you." She said it like a revelation. Her features cleared of worry, her shoulders went back, and she looked…happy. Pure joy lit her eyes. "Your love is constant. You…You still love me." She reeled away from him, a hand on her forehead. "Oh, my God. All this time, I could have had you. You still loved me. I could've been here with you instead of alone and scared and…I was so *sad*, Griffin, thinking I'd lost you forever."

"I don't know that we can be together, but I do know everything I felt for you is still here." He touched his chest. "There's no room for someone else."

"Griffin." Tears brimmed, and she looked almost desperate. "You have to believe me. I didn't love Logan. I don't know what you saw in those pictures, but I can tell you what I felt. I was frantic. There was a part of me that knew the marriage was all wrong, but I was so scared. You have to believe me. I have only ever loved you, but I thought I'd lost you. Forever."

He didn't answer because for some reason, her scent became more pronounced, the glossiness of her hair more distinct, and the amber in her eyes had turned molten. And if he stood this close to her much longer, he'd lose control.

That wasn't something he could afford to do. Austin was his highest priority, and he couldn't fall back into the high drama that would always be part of a relationship with Stella . His figures curled around the broom handle, and he swept so hard it smacked against the coffee table.

His body had gone hot and needy, and his every instinct was to toss aside all his concerns and just fucking be with his woman.

"No, sir." She grabbed his arm and jerked him back around. "This conversation isn't over. I want to know how you can love me the way you say you do and yet keep your distance? Because it's killing me. Do you understand what I'm saying? It kills me to be in the same room with you and not be yours. And you just told me it's the same for you. Am I wrong? Am I only hearing what I want to hear?"

"Jesus *fuck, Stella*. What do you want me to say?"

"I want you to say that you know me. You know my heart. I want you to say you can let it all go and just be with me."

And the friction of his heart constantly grinding against his fears finally erupted into flames, so when she opened her arms, when she made that first step toward him, he lost it.

He hauled her up against him and wrapped her in his arms. Their mouths met, tongues seeking, falling into a rhythm of desperate, urgent need.

All the work he'd done to keep his distance, every excuse he'd come up with to keep her out, went up in flames with the scorching release of suppressed desire. His hands slid down her back, resting on the rise of her ass. He had one second of clarity to stop this, to walk away, to get back on their snowmobiles and head home.

But need enveloped him, and he was gone. He cupped that fleshy ass and hauled her up against him. She let out a cry, as she shifted her hips restlessly over his hard cock.

When her hands pushed under his shirt, finally touching skin, gliding up his stomach, he went electric. Starved for this woman's touch, his body trembled. He couldn't resist her anymore. He didn't want to.

No one's touch lit him up the way hers did.

She hitched a leg up to press closer, and he caught it under her knee, grinding his aching cock right at the apex of her thighs. She slid a hand beneath the waistband of his jeans, and her fingers brushed the crown of his cock.

His body jerked, fireworks exploding in his chest. Lifting her, he carried her to the bed, holding her close as he lowered them both. Her legs spread for him, welcoming him, and he settled between them. Between her fingers gripping his hair, her tongue tangling with his, and her smooth, sweetly scented skin, he was lost, drowning in everything Stella.

She reached between them, fingers fumbling with his buttons, and the moment she popped them open, she grasped his hard cock. He nearly jumped out of his skin.

Surging into her hand, he murmured in her ear, "Let go, or this is going to be over before it starts."

Lifting her sweater, he helped ease it over her head. Then, his hands were on her breasts, pushing them together. He kissed the mounds spilling out of the lacey cups. She'd always loved her fancy lingerie.

"Everything about you is sexy." Peeling back the cups, he licked her nipples. "The way you walk, your laugh, the way you make everyone you meet feel special. You're magic, Stella. And when I'm with you, I feel…"

She reached underneath to unclasp her bra, and she quickly tugged down the straps and sent it sailing. When he sucked her nipple into his mouth, she arched her back, and her fingers scraped across his scalp.

"You feel what?" The words came out broken, breathy.

"Alive. When I'm with you, everything tastes better, smells better…feels better. You…" How did he explain it? "Amplify everything."

Pressing a trail of hot kisses all the way down her stomach, he sat back on his heels to peel off her jeans and panties, casting them aside. Pushing her thighs open, he licked inside her slick heat. She cried out, and then he gave her deep, lush kisses that made her back arch off the mattress.

He loved the way she responded to him. Stella abandoned herself to sex.

Had she done that with Logan?

The idea coldcocked him, sending a stinging jolt through his body. He shut down the train of thought. Couldn't go there. Not when he finally had her.

His tongue circled her clit, lavished it with attention, while he slid two fingers inside. He lost his sense of time and place, enclosed in the bubble of space meant only for him and his woman. Affection, desire, need slammed him all at once, making him wild.

"Oh, my God, Griffin." She planted her feet on the mattress, gripped the back of his head, and ground against him.

His tongue swirled faster, pressed harder, and he reached for her breast. He knew how sensitive her nipples were, so he caressed, then pinched them.

She cried out, her body writhing, and he stayed with her while she rode out her release. He'd never seen anything more beautiful than Stella losing herself to pleasure.

Collapsing onto the bed, she sighed and pushed the hair off her damp forehead. "Holy mother of God. You *wrecked* me. Either you've had a lot of practice, or it's just been a really long time since I got laid."

He barked out a laugh, giving her legs a playful shove, before settling beside her.

"Give me a minute to bask in the afterglow, and then I'll—" she began.

His phone buzzed. With his jeans on the floor next to her, he said, "Grab it. In case it's Austin."

She rolled to her side, and he could hear the rustle of clothes. "It is." She handed it over.

Accepting the call, he sat up. "Hey, man. Everything all right?"

"Can you come get me?" Austin sounded tense.

"Yeah, of course." Griffin glanced out the window. It was snowing hard but nothing he couldn't handle. "Everything all right?"

"I guess."

Tell me. He waited, but damn, the energy was rolling through him hard.

"They have all these plans for me in the morning, and I just want to come home."

"What kind of plans?"

"They're taking me shopping." He lowered his voice. "And to get a haircut."

"Okay, well, you turn fifteen in a few weeks. You can say no. Just tell them, No, thank you. I appreciate it, but I have enough clothes. Tell them your hair is fine the way it is. They can't just come at you with scissors."

"You don't know what it's like. When they want me to do something, it becomes this whole campaign. They make fun of me. They get their friends in on it, so everyone's telling me I look like a hippie or whatever."

"Yeah, well, they're idiots." Griffin was off the bed and rounding it to get to his clothes. He'd never spoken badly of the Pilsons before, but they were not going to bully him into cutting his hair. "I'm on my way. I'm up the mountain, so it'll take me about an hour to get there. Is that okay?"

"It's good. That way I can eat dinner with them. I just don't want to spend the night."

By the time he'd disconnected, Stella was already dressed. He really fucking loved that about her. She didn't know the situation, but she was down for the mission to extract Austin from the enemy camp.

Grabbing her boots, she sat on the couch. "What's going on?"

"They're taking him shopping and getting him a haircut in the morning, and he doesn't want to be there."

She tied her laces. "Will they mind you picking him up?"

"I'm sure they will."

"Just tell them one of the guys bailed on you, so we

need his help moving tomorrow." With a grin, she lifted her eyebrows.

Austin was spending the night so Griffin and his friends could get them settled into the new rental house. He stood, shaking his head. "Should I be worried that you come up with lies so easily?"

She got up and faced him. "I was in PR for seven years, and my job was to spin bad situations into harmless ones. So, you can tell them he's bailing because he doesn't want them cutting his hair and inflate their anger and control issues, or you can spin the truth so that Austin suffers the fewest consequences."

"What if I don't say anything?" He smiled, sifting his fingers through her tousled hair.

"Then they'll be resentful and try to spend more time with him."

She was right. "You're a bad influence on me."

"Oh, please." She headed to the dining room table to grab her jacket. "I'm the best thing that ever happened to you."

Chapter Twelve

WHITE CANDLES FLICKERED IN KNOX BOWIE'S couture wedding gown boutique. Gauzy curtains draped from plate glass windows overlooking the town of Owl Hoot, and a profusion of silk, tulle, chiffon, and lace exploded from the racks.

"Oh, my God." Stella stood in front of a stunning dress on a mannequin. She'd never seen anything like it. "I can't believe you get to make these for a living."

Knox smiled. "Me, neither. And it's as fun as it looks."

At the back of the store, Gigi scanned racks of gowns in every style. "I don't know how I'm supposed to choose one. I love them all. Ball gown, mermaid, sheath, A-line…"

"I like the separates." Reading glasses perched on her nose, her mom sat at a desk, scrolling Knox's online designs. "They're less fussy but still fun and different."

"I know it can be overwhelming." Knox headed toward Gigi. "So, what I always suggest is that you keep the process fun. This isn't a race to find the perfect dress in twenty-four hours or even two weeks. Take your time, look around, and keep your perspective."

"But we're getting married next spring. Can I get something tailored and delivered by then?"

"All the dresses you see on the website are produced in a factory. They're my designs, but you order them like you would a dress from a department store. So, yes, you can order it, and we'll take care of alterations during a fitting." Knox made a sweeping motion around the room. "Everything you see here is what I custom-make for my clients. And I don't take on more projects than I can comfortably handle."

"Assuming we want custom, when do you need us to place an order?" her mom asked.

"With the holidays coming up, I'd love for you to just be a happily engaged couple. And maybe over the next month, you can flip through bridal magazines, poke around some ateliers online. And then we'll get together the first week in January and get serious about this. Does that sound good?" She reached for Gigi. "I promise you this. You're going to look at dozens of gowns and think they're all lovely, but only one of them is going to grab you. The minute you look at it, you're going to say, *That one.*"

"That one," Stella murmured to the sparkling, mermaid-style dress.

Everyone stopped what they were doing to look.

"It's so you." Knox came back to her.

Stella eyed her curiously. "You think?"

"Only someone with a big personality can pull it off. It's a showstopper."

"I've never seen anything like it." She fingered the tulle flower petals covering the gown.

"Those are 3D appliqués. Each one is hand made. And look." Knox touched the feather shoulder accents. "These are detachable, so you can take them off when you're ready to dance. And this?" She turned the mannequin around to reveal a deeply cut back. "Pure drama."

"It's so you." Her mom gazed at it in awe. "It's going to hug your gorgeous figure—"

Gigi joined them. "The sweetheart neckline's perfect for your big boobs. You should try it on."

Stella laughed. "You guys, I'm not the one getting married." *Oh, crap. Oops.* "Yet." Flustered, she knew her cheeks had gone hot. *Don't look at them.*

If she did, Gigi would know something was up.

Stella felt sick to her stomach about lying.

Here I am planning my sister's wedding, getting closer to her, all while letting her think I'm engaged.

She forced her thoughts back to the moment. "Today's about you. Come on, let's look around." But as she stepped away, she got hit with a vision of her wearing that dress with a red flower tucked behind her ear, walking down the aisle toward her groom.

Griffin.

There could be no one else for her.

Instead of a tux, though, he wore a white shirt tucked into black jeans. And black biker boots in place of dress shoes.

And he was looking at her like she was his whole world.

Her heart thundered, and her spirits soared.

"What kind of wedding are you having?" Knox asked.

For one stupid moment, caught in her reverie, Stella thought the question was directed towards her. But, of course, they were here for Gigi's wedding. A real one.

And Stella's fantasy crashed and burned.

Her sister let out a frustrated sigh. "I don't really know."

When Knox shot a look to Stella, she felt the sting of failure clear down to the soles of her feet. "Well, we know a few things. She wants it simple, just close friends and family, and she doesn't want something traditional, so with that as our starting point, I thought we could look at dresses, figure out her sense of style from that."

"Oh, okay." Knox seemed on board. "That makes sense. So, you haven't chosen a venue yet?"

"No."

Stella felt every bit the inexperienced wedding planner that she was. She'd been stupid to start with a dress. What if they chose a Cinderella ball gown and then wound up having the ceremony in their backyard?

"All right, well, let me ask you a few questions." Knox went over to the desk and sat in the velvet armchair. Tapping on her keyboard, she said, "You spent a lot of time on stage with the Lollipops in elaborate costumes. Do you like the idea of making a grand entrance? Do you love dressing up?"

"That's what Stella asked me." Gigi collapsed on the loveseat. "And I realized I don't want to play dress-up for my wedding, but I want an amazing gown."

Knox smiled. "Excellent." She clicked away, then turned the screen to face them. "Okay, let's narrow it down. Do you like simple, structured…like this?"

Gigi scrunched her nose. "No, that's too…stark. Is that the right word?"

"Yes, it's a great word." While Knox was extremely chic and hip, she seemed so down-to-earth and caring.

"It feels like something a cool New York City woman

would wear. I like wearing pretty clothes, I just don't want to feel artificial with tons of hair and make-up."

"Got it. Okay, take a look at this one." Knox showed her a simple but lovely dress. "This is a fit and flare, which just means the top is fitted and the skirt flares out a bit—nothing as dramatic as a ball gown. We can do any kind of sleeve you want…hang on." She tapped again to show a page full of sleeves. "A cap sleeve, draping, long…anything you want."

A spark lit Gigi's eyes. "Okay, this is good. I definitely want sleeveless." She wheeled her arms. "So, I can move around."

"Perfect. Now, for a bodice, how sparkly are we going to go? Do you like pearls, beads, crystals? Here look at this one. See the beaded flowers up here?"

"Oh, pretty. I love it, just maybe instead of flowers we could do musical notes?" Gigi asked.

Knox gave her a beaming smile. "We can absolutely do that. What a great idea."

Bam. An image popped into Stella's head. "What if we had the reception in the Owl Hoot Amphitheater?"

Her sister grew excited. "Oh, that's a cool idea."

"We could get a bunch of food trucks—"

"Food trucks?" her mom sounded disappointed.

But Stella had a vision, and she kept going. "Imagine the trucks lined up at the back of the space in a semi-circle. We could have everything from salads and burgers to biryani and pad thai. We could have cake and ice cream sundaes and doughnuts. The guests would get to pick and choose what they wanted to eat. Just as if they were at a concert. And your friends could get up on stage and perform. Like, instead of speeches, they could sing to you and Cassian."

"Yes, yes, yes." Gigi jumped up and hugged her sister. "Oh, my God, I love that so much."

"Do you?" She pulled back to look into her eyes. "Really?"

Gigi pulled away. "I do. It's perfect."

Everyone was smiling hard, and Knox went back to her screen. "Maybe, since it's outdoors and you want room to move, you'd like something like this."

While the dress was feminine and flirty, the neck and hemlines sparkled with shiny silver grommets.

"That is so rock and roll." Gigi pumped her fists. "I love it."

"I could tell you were pretty lukewarm over the fit and flare," Knox said.

"It's pretty…I mean, they're all beautiful, but that one…that's so me."

"Are you sure, sweetheart?" Her mom asked. "Knox said you could take time over the holidays and look some more. You don't have to settle on the first dress you like."

"Positive. As soon as Stella talked about the amphitheater, it all came together for me. This dress is perfect."

"All right." Knox got up. "Why don't we take some measurements and get some details?"

"Well, hold on," her mom said. "I think we're being hasty. We started looking fifteen minutes ago."

"I know it might not make sense," Gigi said. "But the things that matter to me aren't who's catering or what flowers go in my bouquet. I just want my sister to plan it, and my mom to be with me every step of the way. I want Coco to make the cake and Lulu to do my hair. And this dress, it'll make me feel…like me." She reached for Stella and her mom's hands. "And now, with the major details taken care of, we can just look forward to the day I finally marry the boy I've loved for more than half my life."

In that moment of silence, while everyone let Gigi's words sink in, Stella was seized with an absolute sense of rightness.

In her job.

In her life.

In her family.

I'm exactly where I need to be.

The only thing that would make this moment more perfect—she looked down at her fake engagement ring—was if she and Griffin were together for real.

Hurt crashed over her.

Because even after that perfect afternoon in the cabin, nothing had changed. They'd picked up Austin, stopped at Bliss for ice cream, and then they'd gone back to the Inn.

Standing on the pathway, she'd hoped he'd invite her in. Expected him to. After what they'd shared only hours ago? How could he not want to be with her?

But he hadn't.

So, she'd gone back to her cottage alone.

Knox broke the silence by opening a drawer. "I love that. I seriously love everything you just said." She pulled out a notepad and pen. "Come with me to the dais. You two get comfy on the couch."

Her mom led them to a purple velvet love seat. "That was brilliant."

"What was?" While she loved her mom, she still didn't feel entirely comfortable with her. Not that they felt like strangers but more like there was a chasm between them. So much had happened in their years apart. It would take time to feel like they'd caught each other up.

"The way you read Gigi so well. I would've pushed her

to make some decisions, to get a handle on what direction we were going in. But you intuitively knew to back off and let her get a sense of what she wanted in her own time."

"Oh, thank you. The way Knox looked at me…I thought, Oh, my God, go back to Dallas and get your old job back. You have no idea what you're doing."

"You're not going anywhere." Her mom held her hand. "I finally got my baby girl back. But Diane sure knew what she was doing when she called you. You've always been so good at reading people. When you were little— I'm thinking three or four—your dad came home from his father's funeral. And the minute he walked in the door, your sisters jumped on him, so excited to have him back. But you…"

Her mom smiled. "He got down on his knees so the girls could hug him and throw a million questions at him, and when they got distracted opening the gifts he'd brought, you crawled onto his lap and wrapped your little arms around his neck. You patted his shoulder, and in the sweetest little voice, you said, 'It's all right, Daddy. It'll be all right.'" Her eyes glistened. "That was the first time your dad cried since getting the call about his father." She squeezed Stella's arm. "You've always been special like that. And now you've found a way to turn that into a business."

"I plan weddings. I'm not exactly a therapist."

"Well, thank God for that. Can you imagine how far you'd go with your patients? Signing them up for classes, taking them to the mall for make-overs?"

Stella started to disagree, but what could she say? "You're probably right about that."

Her mom wrapped an arm around her and tugged her in close, stroking her hair the way she used to do when Stella was little. "You'd be a terrible therapist because you'd get way too invested in each client. No, this is better. You get to make dreams come true. I can't think of a more perfect career for you." Her mom gave her a gentle shake. "Look at Gigi. She came in worried and anxious, and now she's glowing. You nailed it."

"Thanks, Mom. It means a lot to hear you say that."

"I'll be honest with you. It hasn't been easy, not knowing where you were or what you were doing." She picked up a lock of hair. "You've grown into a beautiful, elegant woman, and I missed out on all of it."

"I'm sorry. I'm sure I would've come home a lot sooner if I hadn't kept messing up."

"How did you mess up? You had a successful career in PR. You got a job with the top wedding planner in New York City. So what if you ran off and got married? That was a little blip."

"I was eighteen, and I…" Clarity struck with a jolt. She knew exactly why she'd gotten sucked into Logan's life. "I wanted to be someone else. I'd done such a terrible thing, and I could hardly stand myself. Every time I closed my eyes, I saw Lulu's expression when I tried to apologize. I couldn't get Griffin's voice out of my head when he told me he was done with me. And Logan…he literally swept me into a whole new world, where I could reinvent myself."

"That's why you changed your name? We thought it was so we couldn't find you."

"Oh, it was. If I'd been proud of my marriage, I doubt I would've changed my name. I made all new social media accounts, so that I could be this new person. I was just so ashamed, knowing I'd ruined my sister's life…"

"Okay, let's not be so dramatic. You didn't ruin her life. She's never been happier. That woman was born to be a chef, so moving to Paris was the right move. And of course, she wound up with Xander, and there really isn't a better man for her. No, what you did was betray her trust. You took away her agency. And there's a pathway back from that. You just have to find it."

"You're right. And I will. When things settle down…" She flicked a glance at her mom, and they both smiled.

"Or now. Now's always good."

Stella laughed. "Okay, Mom."

"Look, honey, you were eighteen. We all do stupid things at that age. I know I did. My point is that we would've been there for you. You didn't have to go through any of it alone." She shifted towards her. "You understand if you'd called to tell me about Logan cheating, I would've caught the next flight to Dallas, right? My first stop after landing would've been the grocery store to get you six pints of caramel dark chocolate ice cream." She stroked Stella's hair. "You're not alone. You have your family behind you."

"I think I get that now. But at the time, I had a lot of grieving to do. I'd lost it all, and I just had to figure out who I was outside of Calamity."

"I understand that, and I certainly did the same thing when I moved away from home when I was sixteen. That's why I feel so much for what you went through, because I went through it myself."

"Honestly, it made me stronger. That whole time, I never missed a day of work. It might not have been my best work, but I still showed up. And, you know, I started to feel better. And eventually I found my own groove. And then so much time had passed, I didn't know what to say."

"You could've said, Mom, want to come see my apartment in Dallas? And I would've come, no questions asked."

"I wanted to make something of myself. I wanted to come home as a sophisticated woman. I didn't want a trace of the stupid eighteen-year-old girl. And I thought I'd gotten there…until the Xander mess happened with the tabloids…and I couldn't believe it. I just…" She let out a huff of disbelief. "I ran to New York."

"Honey, look at me." Her mom cupped her cheeks and turned her so they looked each other in the eyes. "You're forgiven. Do you hear me? Would you like to know how everyone here remembers you? As the beautiful young woman who had a smile and a kind word for every single person she met. They remember you for the way you made them feel. Sweetheart…you are forgiven."

Love for her mom hit her so hard she slumped against her. There was nothing she'd missed more than her mom's strong, unshakable support. "I love you, Mom."

"I love you so much. With you gone, it was like walking around with half a heart." Her mom squeezed her. "Promise me, no matter where life takes you, you'll never leave us again."

"I promise." When she pulled away, she wiped the tears from under her eyes. "Do you think Lulu will ever forgive me?"

"I'm going to bet she feels the same way you did. So much time has passed, she doesn't know what to say or do. But honey, she's moved on, she's happy. And I think you're going to have to reach out to her, tell her you're here, you miss her, and you'd like to talk to her the next time she's in town."

"It's just that I'll never get back what I had with her. I

mean, she was my best friend. My person. And I ruined it forever."

"Well, relationships change. Don't you think life would've taken you in different directions anyways, once you left home and made your way in the world? All you can do is build something new, and maybe it'll even be healthier. Stronger."

Her mom was absolutely right about that. "I feel so much better. It's like I've been stuck in this sand trap, and I didn't see a way to climb out. But I do now. And it doesn't seem nearly so scary."

"She won't be here for Thanksgiving, you know."

"I didn't, but with the Wildcats playing that day, I figured she'd stay in Dallas to be with Xander."

Her mom leaned in. "How are you and Griffin going to handle the holidays? I know it won't be easy for him to lie to his family. Maybe he should come to our house."

"I'll bring it up, but I don't think he'd even consider that."

"This must be torture for you. To spend time with him, to pretend you're close, but to not really be with him."

Oh, but I did get to be with him. I had his body pressed to mine, his hands grabbing, stroking, claiming me. I had those deep, passionate kisses that reawakened every dormant feeling I've ever had for him.

And then…it was like it had never happened.

"It is. He's the only man in the world for me, Mom, and I don't think I get to be with him."

"Give him time." She touched Stella's arm. "So, what about Austin? What's he doing for Thanksgiving?"

"He's going to his grandparent's house."

"Oh. Is that what he wants?"

ERIKA KELLY

"Not at all, but he won't tell them that."

"What do you mean? Isn't it his choice?"

"No, they tell him what he's doing and when. They're super old school and believe kids should do as they're told. Like, they didn't want him playing guitar in their house and when he did it anyway, they took it from him."

"What?" Gigi strode over to them. "Playing an instrument is a good thing. It's good for your brain and your motor skills. Plus, it makes you super cool." She grinned.

"Right? Instant panache. But, yeah, I feel bad for him. His dad's been out of contact for a week now, his grandparents are tough on him…" And idea popped into her head. "He's turning fifteen in a few weeks. I wonder if he'd let me throw him a party. He doesn't really have friends at school yet, but maybe we can pull something together with just our two families."

"I think that's a lovely idea," her mom said.

"And Coco could make her amazingly decadent chocolate cake," Gigi said. "What if my birthday present to him is guitar lessons? We have enough time between now and then that Austin and I could do a little show for everyone."

"That's an amazing gift, and I think it might be just what he needs to come out of his shell. And it's just family so it's not like it could get out of hand."

See what I did there? I thought about consequences. How do you like that, Griffin?

Hm, maybe she could win him back after all.

Chapter Thirteen

HIS FIRST NIGHT IN THE NEW HOUSE HAD BEEN miserable. Since it came furnished, he and his friends had only needed to bring in boxes and a few pieces of furniture from his apartment over the shop. Everything had gone smoothly.

No, the issue had been knowing Stella slept a few feet away in the carriage house. She'd kept the lights on all night—and he only knew that because he'd kept checking. He had a perfect view from his bedroom window.

What had kept her up all night?

He'd finally crashed around four, and now he was late for work and hurrying to get ready. Coming out of the bathroom, he heard female laughter downstairs and banged his shin on the dresser. "Dammit."

So that's how it's going to be? She's going to come and go as she pleases?

Yes, please.

What? No. That would be unbearable. He'd had a hard enough time agreeing to let her live in the guest house—he'd lose his mind if she were under his roof all the damn time. Grabbing jeans off the back of a chair and a clean T-shirt from the middle drawer, he tossed them on the bed.

He'd have to set some damn boundaries.

Ha. As if Stella paid attention to boundaries.

Which, of course, is one of the things I love about her. If he had to be honest, he sometimes felt caged by this constant state of…vigilance. And Stella was unencumbered. She was free.

But the last thing he needed was her scent lingering in the house or her laughter filling up his head because the constant reminder of her presence would wreck him.

Jesus, that afternoon in the cabin? The way her back had arched, the feel of her hand on his cock…fuck, he was getting hard just thinking about it.

Which is why I'm not giving her a key to the house.

Forget it. He couldn't think about her right now. He had to get to the shop so he could be home when Austin got off the bus. If he had three fewer hours each day, he had to work harder and more efficiently with what he had.

Quickly pulling on his jeans, a long sleeve Boneyard T-shirt, and his black boots, he headed down the hallway. The whole place smelled like pancakes and syrup, coffee… and Stella. Music blasted, and he wanted to shout at her to turn it off. It was too damn early. But when he hit the dining room, he found Austin sitting at the table chewing and staring, mesmerized, into the kitchen.

He already knew what drew the boy's attention, and he didn't want to see it. Stella, shaking her ass as she sang along to the music, using the spatula as a microphone.

She'd danced for him plenty of times. Not to show-off. It was just what she did. She rocked out while she cooked, washed a truck, did laundry, or exercised.

She was fun, lively, and…

This isn't going to work. They needed boundaries.

If Austin hadn't called, interrupting them, Griffin would have made a huge mistake. She was his kryptonite, and being alone in a cabin with her?

Their cabin?

Just one taste of her, and he'd been a man possessed.

He breezed past Austin, catching a glance at his plate. "Morning." Of course, they weren't just plain pancakes. He saw the little specs of yellow—and by the scent, he knew she'd put lemon zest on them. "Are those lemon ricotta?" His mouth watered.

Austin shoved a forkful into his mouth and nodded, attention fixed on the kitchen.

And then Griffin did the one thing he shouldn't have.

He looked. Stella stood at the stove, flipping a pancake, her ass shaking as she rocked out to a Kings of Leon song. Her dance involved a dramatic flip of her thick, glossy blonde hair, and when she came back up, it fell around her shoulders like a shampoo commercial.

And it sent him right back in time.

He'd been what? Nineteen? Yeah, because he'd just started working full time at the shop, and all he could think about was meeting Stella in an empty cottage at the Inn. But Mack had kept jawing with a customer, and Griffin couldn't leave until he talked to him about the problem with a low boy someone had brought in.

By the time Griffin had gotten to their room, he'd been so worked up that when he'd opened the door and found her rocking out in nothing but pajama bottoms and one of his T-shirts, he'd lost it.

Jesus, even now, all these years later, the hunger slammed him.

He'd fucked her so hard they'd cracked the headboard.

And then, when they'd seen the damage, they'd laughed so hard they hadn't been able to catch their breath.

Fuck, but he'd loved her.

Grab your keys and get out of here. He came into the kitchen so swiftly, she startled, pressing a hand to her chest. She touched the screen on her phone and killed the music. "You scared me." She watched him pocket his keys. "Where are you going?"

"Work."

"Uh, I don't think so. Not today."

"Have to." If he didn't keep to a schedule, the jobs would pile up like a big car crash. He couldn't fall behind. Customers counted on him.

"I've got a stack of lemon ricotta pancakes with your name on them." She handed the plate to him with an arch of her brow. "Eat first."

He heard her unspoken message to sit and have breakfast with Austin. He accepted the plate. "Thank you." Of course, he'd sit with the boy. "Hey, man."

Austin gave him a chin nod.

"Smells good." He pulled out a chair, swiped a napkin out of the basket Stella must've put on the table, and sat down. "Beats cold cereal."

"Coffee?" Stella held up a mug.

"You've done enough. I can get it myself."

"Don't be silly. I'm standing right here." As she set down two drinks, the sleeve of her silk kimono brushed over his arm, and he got a whiff of her expensive perfume. "Coffee and juice."

Given the pulp, it looked fresh-squeezed. "This is good."

"I know, right? One of my brides is having a brunch, so I had to meet with the chef at Wally's."

"Delilah?" he asked.

"You know her?"

"Yeah, she's married to Will Bowie."

"First, I can't believe the Bowie brothers got married, but man, did they do well. Delilah's gorgeous and unbelievably talented. Anyhow, so we were talking about the menu, and she told me about the hydroponic farm and greenhouse orchards she runs so she can have fresh produce for her restaurant all year round. I was so impressed that she put together a box of her fruit and vegetables for me. We should go check it out. Want to take a tour with me?"

Acting as though he couldn't care less, Austin hunched a shoulder and dug into his pancakes, but the color flooding his cheeks showed how happy he was that she'd thought to include him in her plans. That she'd treated him like family.

It was then that Griffin noticed the boy wore pajama bottoms. "Hey, you're going to miss the bus."

"There's no school."

Griffin cut a look to Stella for confirmation.

"The teachers have meetings today." She brought her own plate of pancakes over and sat down. "And we've got big plans."

"Plans?"

"The winter market starts today, so we're heading over to Wolff Village. We're going ice skating and getting crepes and cocoa. Right, Austin?"

The boy kept his attention on his pancakes. "I'm not ice skating."

"Wolff Village is magical in winter. They have lights

and wreaths and the prettiest decorations you've ever seen. Carolers walk around the town square, and they have horse-drawn sleigh rides through the forest."

Austin dragged the last forkful of pancake through syrup. "I'll go to the village, but I'm not skating."

"That's fine." She looked to Griffin. "You sure you won't come with us? It's going to be fun."

"Can't. I've got too much work to do."

With a wool beanie on his head, gloves, and a parka, Griffin raced around the rink, laughing as Stella grabbed a handful of his coat to wing past him. That woman made everything fun.

He'd catch up on work later.

I'm a sucker for her.

With the rink this crowded, he had to slow down to avoid plowing into the families and kids all around him.

He skated to the wall and caught himself on the ledge. Nearby, people gathered to listen to the Christmas carolers, and the scent of warm crepes made his stomach grumble.

Stella came up beside him. "When he said he didn't want to skate, I thought it was because he didn't know how."

They watched as Austin whizzed past them. She slid an arm through his, like they were an actual couple, and he liked it. He liked this whole morning. Everything from breakfast with the three of them sitting around the table, having a conversation full of jokes and ribbing, to the trip to the village—something he'd never have thought to do, even though it was a fifteen-minute drive from his shop.

His heart was just so damn full.

"Look at him go." Stella stood back as Austin sped past them, as sure-footed as an Olympic speed skater. "He's so much like you, he could be your son."

"What does that mean?"

She gazed up at him, and just like that, the rink disappeared, his frozen nose turned warm, and a blanket of intimacy dropped over them, muffling the conversation and music. "You say no to everything. 'Do you want to go out to dinner?' 'No.'" She lowered her voice to imitate him. "'You want to go skating?' 'No.'"

He cracked a grin. "As if I don't wind up doing everything you want."

"You do. That's what makes it so funny. And now Austin's doing it too." She tracked the boy on the ice. "He's a natural athlete, isn't he?"

"Yeah, he is. I'm glad you got him into boarding."

Her lips softened, parted, and she looked at him like she wanted the same thing he did—a kiss, their bodies pressed together, hands roaming. Heat flashed through him.

Her skin looked so smooth he couldn't resist touching it. Biting the finger of his glove, he pulled it off and brushed her cheek. "You're cold."

"I don't feel cold right now."

He could kiss her. Right here and now, in front of everyone. They were *engaged*, after all. His heart thundered, his breathing went shallow, and he leaned in.

Austin skated right up to them, shaving off a layer of ice that spattered Griffin's jeans. "Can we go?"

"Sure." Griffin lowered his arm, shoving his hand back into the glove.

"Ready for lunch?" Stella started off the rink.

"I can eat later. I don't want to be late for my session."

Griffin glanced at the clock tower in the center of the village. "It's not for another hour and a half."

"There might be traffic."

"In Calamity?" he asked, but at the same time, Stella said, "Let's get some warm food in your belly first, okay? When I was a kid, my dad used to take me to the creperie. It was our special thing."

Griffin caught the affection in her tone. He knew that while her mom had been busy shuttling her sisters to auditions and cooking classes, Stella had often been left alone. She'd spent a lot of time with her dad. "Sounds good."

"I don't have time for a restaurant. Let's just get something from one of those carts."

"Sure." Griffin wasn't used to Austin taking a stand, so he wouldn't deny his request. They collapsed onto benches to remove their skates. "Did you bring your gym bag?"

"Yeah. It's in the truck."

Focused on his laces, Austin didn't look up, so he didn't catch the knowing grin Griffin and Stella shared. To see him this interested in something…damn. It was good. He couldn't wait to tell Peyton.

A shiver of fear ran through him. He needed to hear from his friend, needed the reassurance he was okay.

Of course, he is. I've known from the beginning there'd be pockets of time when we wouldn't hear from him.

He's fine.

After returning their skates to the rental counter, they headed for the crepe kiosk.

"Is there a reason you're in such a hurry?" Stella asked.

"Last week, when you dropped me off early because you had an appointment, Fin Bowie saw me in the gym and started talking to me." His voice was edged with wonder. "He gave me some suggestions that made everything make sense."

"Yeah?" Griffin pulled his wallet from his pocket. "That's really cool. Not everyone can teach. Would you rather get lessons from him?"

"No, I like Will. But I want to be around in case I can learn something else."

"I get it." He'd known this boy for most of his life, and he'd never seen him excited about anything. He reached for Stella's hand and gave it a squeeze. *Thank you.*

As they neared the food cart, the scent of maple syrup and warm butter grew stronger. He didn't care what he ordered, so he stepped aside, letting Austin get a better view of the chalkboard perched on a mound of hard-packed snow.

"You know what you want?" he asked Stella.

"Well, the menu's changed since I was a little girl. It's a lot fancier than when I used to get ham and cheese or strawberries and cream. Now, they have Nutella."

"I don't want dessert," Austin said. "Fin told me about the kinds of food I need to eat to be a good snowboarder."

"Look." Stella pointed to the flyer taped to the cart. "There's a special menu for athletes. The crepes are made with protein powder and egg whites."

"I'll get the one with spinach."

As Austin placed his order, Stella said, "You should talk to his grandparents, so they don't force him to eat pie or gravy or whatever. They have to respect his interest in nutrition."

"I'll talk to him about it, tell him it's okay to stand his ground."

Her eyes went wide. "You don't think they'll try to take away his snowboard, do you?"

"If they do, I'll buy him a new one."

She touched his arm. "He's so lucky to have you."

"Griffin." A big hand clapped on his shoulder.

He spun around to find his friend Declan surrounded by some of his former hockey players. "Hey. What the hell are you doing in town?"

But Declan's gaze had slid over to Stella, and his face lit up. "No way." He grabbed her and pulled her into a bear hug. "What the hell? You didn't tell me you were hanging out with the prettiest girl in all of Wyoming." Letting her go, he took her in. "How long are you in town?"

"It's great to see you." She pulled back. "I moved back home. I live here now."

Declan shifted his attention to Griffin. "Why didn't you say anything? This is big news."

Austin joined them, handing Griffin the change, and when Stella reached for a napkin, her diamond glinted in the sunlight.

Declan grabbed her hand.

Shit. Griffin hadn't told anyone at the shop, still hadn't told his family. He'd put it off just in case they changed their minds…or something happened.

He'd wanted to handle it in the best way possible.

Not here and now. He didn't want Austin to see him lying.

His friend's expression turned to shock, and he looked between them. "You're engaged?"

Griffin felt sick. How the hell was he supposed to look one of his oldest and closest friends in the eyes and lie? He felt queasy, and he wondered if he could tell Declan the truth. His friend could be trusted.

But the guys were standing there, listening. Word

would spread fast.

I have to do it. If Austin moved in with the Pilsons, he wouldn't be learning how to snowboard with the Bowies. He wouldn't have guitar lessons with Gigi Cavanaugh. He wouldn't be finding his voice.

And so, he smiled and said, "We are."

He saw the disbelief in Declan's eyes but appreciated the way his friend broke into a grin. "Best news ever." He hauled Griffin in for a hug, giving him hearty pats on the back. "You're full of shit, and we're having a conversation later." Releasing him, Declan moved onto Stella. "It's not too late, you know. You and me. It could happen." He held up her hand. "I could buy you a real ring. And you wouldn't even need a magnifying glass to see the stone."

"I'm good, thanks." She wrapped her arm around Griffin. "I'm keeping the ring and the guy."

As the two of them caught up, Griffin watched Austin dig into his crepe.

Am I doing the right thing?

Lies always come back to bite you in the ass.

When would his blow up in his face?

Pocketing his keys, Griffin climbed the mound of plowed snow bordering the parking lot and headed toward the bunny slope.

"You're angry with me." Somehow, Stella kept up with him in those stupid boots.

"I'm not."

At the top of the hill, the kids clustered around their instructor who demonstrated a stance.

"And yet you're not talking to me."

"It's not that I'm not talking to you." He stopped in a

stand of trees, so Austin wouldn't see them creeping on him. "I've just got a lot on my mind."

"Okay, but I was there when you lied to Declan. I saw what it cost you."

"And in a couple of days, I'll be lying to my family. That doesn't mean I'm angry with *you*. I chose to go along with this, but I don't have to like it."

"We can go inside, you know." Stella tipped her chin to the training center. Crowding the window of the second floor, parents stood watching the kids.

"You can go in if you're cold."

"No, I'm good." She huddled beside him.

"I'm sorry if I'm being quiet. Declan knows I'm lying, and he said he's going to talk to me about it later. I have to figure out if I'm going to tell him what's going on."

"For God's sake, Griff, you don't have to deal with everything by yourself. You can talk to me." And then, more softly, she said, "We're in this together."

She was right. As the oldest of seven, he tended to view himself as responsible for them—and not the other way around. "What do you think I should do?"

"Well, everything changes when you get that letter from Peyton's attorney, so maybe just hold off until then. Your friends and family will forgive you once they understand why."

"They will. And it's not like anyone would question us being together."

"True."

"And if Declan pushes, I'll at least be telling him the truth." He grew hot under his leather jacket.

"What truth is that exactly?"

His chest tightened, making his heart feel too big.

"That I've always loved you, that there's never been another woman for me."

She was silent beside him, and he didn't dare look at her.

"That I'm happy with her."

"I'm happy with us, too."

Warmth hit like whiskey, spreading through him, making his blood heat.

Stella. My Stella.

"Do you regret what we did in the cabin?" she asked quietly.

They still hadn't talked about it. And not just because they both worked so much, but because when they were together, Austin was around. "Fuck, no. You know I have feelings for you. I'm attracted to you." *I want you.* "But it's complicated. My focus has to be on Austin."

"I agree."

"You do?"

"Of course. He's the priority."

"So, what're you saying? You think it should be a one-time thing?"

"Oh, my God, Griffin, the two things don't connect. Because Austin's a priority, you can't have love in your life? You can't date? You can't have pleasure?" She nudged him. "Look. It's his turn."

In his snow pants, parka, and helmet, Austin stood at the top of the bunny slope, all of the other kids watching.

"You realize if he wipes out, Uncle Griffin can't charge over there and help him up, right?"

"I'd never do that." He pretended to be outraged at the suggestion.

"Well, if you try, I'll trip you, and when you land on

your face in the snow, I'm going to sit on your back and make sure you can't get up."

He fought a smile at the visual. "Okay, Stella. I'm just watching his first attempt to snowboard. I wouldn't embarrass him by running over there to 'save' him."

"Good. Because it's a bunny slope. He's not going to break his femur."

He cut her a sharp look, remembering what had happened to Booker.

But she was riveted on Austin, her excitement making her eyes sparkle. "He's going, he's going. Oh, my God, look."

The instructor stepped back, and Austin bobbed, gearing up for his run. Griffin felt a swell of pride. "I should film this for Peyton."

"You totally should."

He pulled out his phone, his frozen fingers fumbling with the camera app.

"Hurry." Stella tipped her chin to the slope. "There he goes."

For a kid who showed coordination and balance on the ice, he sure didn't have confidence on his board. He held both arms out like he was surfing, and his hips jerked back and forth and sideways.

Bend your knees.

Austin seemed stiff, intense, like everything was riding on getting it right. He wavered, arms pinwheeling.

Come on, Austin, find your center.

But his body twisted, and he landed face-first in the snow.

Griffin bolted, but he didn't even get three steps out before he felt a tug of resistance. Stella had a grip on his jacket. He looked at her like she was nuts until he realized what he'd been about to do.

Embarrass the hell out of Austin. And then, just as he shoved his phone back into his pocket, she jerked hard, sending him flying. With quick reflexes, he grabbed her arm and took her down with him.

Stella shrieked, scrambling onto her knees, straddling him, and pinning his wrists.

Her nose was red, her blonde hair hung down, the tips brushing his chin, and Stella laughing was the most beautiful sight he'd ever seen. She glanced up. "The teacher's got him."

A hand on her lower back, he jackknifed upright to find the instructor reaching out to Austin. The boy wavered, but the woman had a good grip on him.

"He's fine. He didn't get hurt."

His ass turned numb in the snow, but he'd sit there forever if it meant he got to be this close to Stella. "I just don't want him to quit because it's hard, or because he got embarrassed. I don't want him going back to Cheetos and video games."

Stella got to her feet, swiping snow off her knees. She reached out a hand, and he took it, standing up. They watched as Austin stared toward the bottom of the slope, doing that knee-bobbing thing again. And then, with a flick of his hips, he continued down.

"What makes you think he'll quit just because he fell?"

"That's what he does. He got hit in the head with a soccer ball and quit the team. A bunch of kids piled on him in a game of flag football, and he never went back to camp. And he bailed on karate before he got his yellow belt."

"That's because he didn't like soccer or flag football.

He told me he hated karate. This, he likes. He's not giving up."

They watched as Austin reached the base of the slope. He squatted and popped off the bindings. Picking up his board, he looked over at them.

"Oh, shit. He saw us."

He broke into a huge grin before turning around and heading back up the hill.

Griffin watched him with pride and relief. "It's going to be all right."

"It really is."

Chapter Fourteen

STELLA COULDN'T BELIEVE HE'D DONE THIS. PULLING a yogurt from her new mini refrigerator, she stood there for a moment taking in the contents. Salads, protein shakes, chicken stir fry...*don't tear up*.

You are not crying at work.

But come on, Griffin was an amazing, loving man. He didn't want her to miss meals, so he'd bought it for her. Didn't even tell her. She'd just walked in, got busy, and noticed a low hum in her office.

When she'd looked over to see it, her heart had nearly exploded.

Her phone buzzed, and she hurried over to her desk to open the text message.

Quinn: The princess is here!

Stella: Is she wearing a tiara?

Quinn: She's wearing RED cowboy boots. And they're badass!

Stella: Never keep a princess waiting. LOL. Send her in.

A moment later, Quinn swept in. "May I introduce

Princess Rosalina Anais Isabella Villeneuve." Then, with a flourish, she gestured to the doorway.

In walked a beautiful brunette wearing black leggings and a colorful blouse. "Oh, my God, look at your face right now." She laughed. "You were expecting crown jewels and a Chanel suit, weren't you?" When she reached the desk, she held out her hand. "Hi, I'm Rosie."

"Can I get you coffee?" Quinn asked. "Sparkling water? Prosecco?"

Stella laughed. "Yes, champagne for everyone! Here, we drink it instead of water…as one does."

Rosie laughed. "I'm fine, but thank you." The stunning woman could dress like a local all she wanted but nothing could hide her regal bearing.

"Hey, Rosie, I'm Stella, and I'm afraid to admit I'm a shabby stand-in for Diane. But fortunately, she's done all the work, and you're going to have a spectacular wedding."

The sparkled dimmed in the princess's eyes.

Now, what's that about? "Please, sit down, and let's talk." Stella hadn't even had a chance to clean up her desk. She'd been swamped for three weeks straight. *Nothing I can do about it now.*

Rosie dropped a stuffed diaper bag onto the chair next to her. She smoothed her hair behind her ears, revealing dangling silver and turquoise earrings.

Stella smiled.

"What's so funny?" Rosie glanced down at her blouse. "Don't tell me I've been walking around with spit-up on me. I left the house feeling like such a badass. I showered, put on make-up…I even brushed my teeth."

"No, that's not it at all. I just didn't expect a royal princess to be wearing red cowboy boots and turquoise earrings."

"Oh." Rosie smiled. "I've been here a couple of years now, and I still haven't had my fill of line dancing and bull riding. Have you been to the rodeo in Jackson?"

"More times than I can count. I'm actually from here, but I also lived in Dallas for several years and never missed an opportunity to hit the Stockyards." She got up. "Come on. Let's go into the conference room. We've got your wedding up on the screen."

The moment they entered, Rosie took in the photograph of the grand staircase with its plush burgundy carpet, and her features fell.

Okay, so I didn't imagine it. She's not happy.
But why?

"This is your chance to make last-minute tweaks." Though, she wasn't sure she could deliver on that promise. Everything was set. The wedding was in two weeks.

"No, no changes. It's perfect. Diane's done a lovely job."

It's me. She doesn't think I can pull it off. "Now, if you're concerned about me running it, keep in mind, Diane's taken care of every detail. All I have to do is hold my baton and conduct the production."

"Believe me. I'm not worried. With my mother running the show, I have no doubt everything will come off perfectly."

"Okay, great." *Then, why aren't you glowing?* "So, what can I do for you? Do you want to go over the details?"

"No. Actually, I'd like to add an event. A pre-wedding dinner for close friends. Well, and my sister and her husband, if they can get here in time. She's got a project due before the school break."

"Okay." Stella wasn't following. She didn't need a

wedding planner to put together a dinner. "What did you have in mind?"

"I was thinking…maybe the weekend before the wedding, we could rent out a space, like a community center or something like that."

"Not a restaurant?"

"No…I thought it might be fun to bring in a DJ and do line dancing. Could we rent a mechanical bull? Is that a thing?"

"Yes, we can absolutely do that. If you want, I could help your sister or your friends put together a bridal shower for you."

"Vivi's in business school in Boston. She's got enough on her plate, and I already told my friends not to do anything. But between the wedding and the holidays and all the guests visiting from St. Christophe…my mom's got one party after another planned."

Okay, so Mom's calling the shots here, Rosie can plan her own party, but she's asking me to do it…

A picture was forming. Stella sat on the edge of the table. "This could be fun. So, your parents won't be at this event, right?"

"Oh, God, no. They're uncomfortable with loud music and big crowds. Plus, with their security team, it always changes the tone. Everyone becomes hyper aware of the royals and tries to be on their best behavior. And I don't want that. I want everyone to have fun."

Yes, Stella was getting a clear picture. "So, if I plan it, you're not responsible for anything, and you can let go and have a good time and not worry what the queen will think."

Rosie stuttered out a laugh. "I feel so seen right now. Yes, that's exactly right."

"Why do I get the feeling that your wedding isn't exactly what you'd had in mind?"

"Way to read the room, lady." Rosie grinned. "My mom's great, and I love her, but once I started planning things here, she poked her royal nose in and started making suggestions. Then, she and Diane were having regular conversations, and by the next time I checked back in, they'd replicated the royal wedding in St. Christophe. Including the guest list. And I've been blaming my busy life—I just had my second baby, I've got a toddler and a business to run—but now, thanks to you, I have to accept that I let myself get cowed by my mother."

"What, you can't picture the queen on a mechanical bull?"

Rosie grinned. "Now I can. But, no, never in a million years would she go for that. She's too proper, and my dad's too…scholarly."

"But it's what you want, right?"

"Very much. I want beer and line dancing and a live band. My parents want Dom Perignon and orchestral pieces."

"Gotcha." Stella clicked to the page of a wedding she was planning next May. "So, for your pre-wedding party, you had something like this in mind?" On the screen, she had snapshots of a wild-ass country wedding. Under the bride's frothy Cinderella gown, she wore pink cowboy boots, and the groom wore a Stetson on the dance floor. All around them, the guests were two-stepping. Everyone was laughing and having a blast.

With a sudden intensity, Rosie sat forward. "Yes, just like that."

Creating a split screen, Stella put the formal wedding

on one side and the fun one on the other. "What if we could combine the two for your Calamity wedding?"

Hope flared in the princess's eyes but quickly died out. "We're getting married in two weeks. Besides, my mother's worked so hard on this."

"She has, but you specifically asked for something informal here, and she didn't listen. And…you only get one wedding." She smiled. "Well, in your case two. But your mom gets her ceremony in St. Christophe. So, here…what if we throw your dream wedding, but also make the king and queen and their guests comfortable?"

"That doesn't seem possible, but I'm listening." Rosie looked at her with so much interest—like she needed to hear the right words to convince her.

Stella rose to the challenge. "What if we keep the ceremony in the church, just as formal as your mom and Diane planned, but what if instead of the grand ballroom, we rent out Wild Billy's?"

Her eyes went wide. "You want the king and queen in a bar for my reception?"

"I do, but only after we transform it for the night. We can replace the bar stools and tables with linen-covered seating areas for the royals, make it formal with plush chairs and candles and dinner service—no buffet for them—and then we leave the dance floor as-is for the live band and line dancing. On the other side of the room, we hire a bunch of chefs with their jackets and toques to serve your friends buffet-style. What do you say? You get the wedding of your dreams, and your mom gets most of what she wants."

Rosie smiled at her. "I love it, but I can't do that to my mom."

"Well, the only thing we're changing is the reception

venue. Your mom still gets her formal ceremony in the church, the same food, and the chef she's already arranged. The only difference is that you get the party you and Brodie want." She grinned. "You get your mechanical bull."

Color rose in her cheeks, and Rosie grew animated. "I want that bull."

"I know you do. Look, things went off the rails. You just had a baby, so you let things get away from you, but it's not too late to course-correct." Stella's palms grew damp, and she felt a little nauseated. She was making promises she might not be able to keep. Why did she even think she could get Wild Billy's to shut down for a night during ski season? Worse, she might be causing trouble between Rosie and her mom.

Still, the princess had been railroaded, and anyone could see how very much she wanted a reception at Wild Billy's. "We don't have to actually do anything, but what if you test the waters, explain to your mom how things got so far away from what you'd wanted, and you've come up with a compromise to make both of you happy?" There, that would give Rosie the time she needed to decide if it was the right choice. If she came back and said she'd rather leave it be, then Stella wouldn't say another word.

"It can't hurt to bring it up." Rosie gave a cautious smile. "You really think you can pull this off?"

"I know I can." *What just came out of my mouth? I don't know anything.*

But if Rosie wanted this, Stella would move heaven and earth to make it happen.

Something happened to the princess. She went from anxious to thoughtful to…resolved. She smacked her hand on the desk. "Let's do it."

"You don't want to talk to your mom first?"

"I'm a grown woman, a mother of two, and this is my wedding. I told them very clearly, multiple times, what I wanted, and they both agreed to make it happen, and the next thing I knew…I was getting Royal Ceremony Redux. No, Stella. What you described is exactly what I want. It's on." Rosie got up and met her at the side of her desk. Hugging her she said, "Thank you so much." Her voice was filled with emotion. "It shouldn't matter this much to me."

"But it does."

"Yes, it does." When they pulled apart, Rosie swiped the dampness from under her eyes. "Sorry. New baby and all."

"We got this." *Maybe?*

Oh, my God, what have I done?

"I'll transform that bar. You'll see." *If they'll actually rent it out to me.*

Will they?

Already, her mind scrambled to think of who she knew with the kind of connections to make that happen.

"I just met you, but somehow I know you'll deliver."

The moment Rosie left, Stella collapsed into her chair. Anxiety spun through her system like a cyclone, wringing her out.

What if the queen calls Diane to ream her out, vowing to ruin the reputation her boss had so carefully built?

Energy started rolling in. *What if it's the best damn party this town has ever seen?*

What if I can make Rosie's dream come true and keep the queen happy?

She could dwell in fear, or she could get to work.

She needed to call Wild Billy's—wait, her mom might

know the owner. She would absolutely use her family's connections to make this happen. Just as she picked up her phone, Quinn came rushing in.

"Did that just happen? Did you just turn the royal wedding into a hoe-down?"

"Yes. Is that a bad thing?" She meant it as a joke, but Quinn didn't smile.

I just came back to town, I faked an engagement, and now I've thrown a Molotov cocktail into the most important and visible wedding Diane's ever done. "It won't be like that, I promise. It'll be amazing."

Quinn pressed a hand to her forehead. "Diane's been planning this wedding for a year. With the *queen*. She's going to have a fit."

"Well, then, I'd better get to work convincing her I did the right thing."

Griffin lowered the hydraulic platform, damn pleased with this bike. He was about finished, which meant he could move onto the vintage spec one he'd started a few weeks ago. And with Stella letting Austin hang out at the office on days he didn't have training, he could actually get other jobs done—

"Wow, that's cool." The clack of heels on the pavement had him looking over.

Stella. Every time he saw her, his body had the same reaction. His engines revved to full throttle.

Even when she'd just rolled out of bed and come over for breakfast. Or when he glanced out his window and saw her doing yoga—and no, he wasn't creeping on her. She did it with the curtains open and the lights on in the carriage house.

And sometimes, usually when Austin was in school, she wore this tiny peach-colored sports bra and bike shorts that made it look like she was naked.

Kill me now.

Strutting toward him, she looked like a runway model. Skin-tight black pants with tiny crystals on them, leather ankle boots, an oversize scarf, and an enormous coat that hung well below her knees, made her look like she belonged at a film festival in Cannes.

Winter in the mountains, you'd think she'd look ridiculous.

She didn't. Every single person in the shop stopped what they were doing to track her. It had always been that way, all the way back to elementary school. Stella was the girl everyone wanted to be, every guy wanted to date, and when she sat down at your table in the cafeteria, you couldn't believe she'd chosen you.

And yet, she had no idea. She didn't know there were kids you didn't hang out with. Stella lived in the moment, so if she were looking for a place to sit and saw someone from her chemistry class, she'd plop right down and start up a conversation about the cool project they were working on.

Then, she'd get to talking and include you in her plans that weekend.

"Does it need a test rider? Because I'm game."

"Ha. I've just spent three months on this. Soon as the roads are cleared, I'm taking her out."

"What is it?"

"It's got the heart of a '47 Harley. I added more

chrome and rubber elements to give it a more elegant feel."

Her fingertips traced the hand-formed metalwork. "You're an artist. I can't believe you did this. Is it Owl Hoot?"

"It's the original settlement of Calamity, yes."

"It's amazing." She glanced up at him. "Who ordered this? I'm guessing a Bowie."

He chuckled.

"What?"

"You've got a gift. Yes, Lachlan Bowie's, actually."

"Oh, man, I can totally see him riding through town on a bike like this with his white pompadour."

"Boss." Jinx strode by, heading to his station. He gave Stella a nod.

Stella watched him for a moment. "Whoa, who's that?"

"Settle down. That's Skylar's husband." He'd discovered the insanely talented artist when a group of bikers had stopped in for repairs one summer day. They'd all had custom paint jobs, and Griffin had asked about the work. Best he'd ever seen. They'd told him about Jinx Costello.

"Your sister's married?"

"Yep. Two kids."

Her features softened. "Why does that make my heart so happy?"

"Because she had a rough go of it, thanks to her asshole boyfriend."

"What does Jinx do?"

"Here." He walked her over to a freshly painted tank.

"Oh, wow. It doesn't even look airbrushed. That's art."

"Yeah, it is. He's talented."

"That's putting it mildly. Who're these faces?"

If you looked closely, a chalky design came through on the matte tank finish. A house, a lawn, a swing set. But on either side, faces were captured, as if stored inside the tank, peering out. "He does memorials, mostly."

"Oh." She cut him a surprised look. "All these people died?"

"Yeah, fire."

"Oh, my God."

"Jinx lost his brother and dad, so he's made a career out of keeping loved ones close, even after they're gone."

"That's strangely beautiful."

"He's got more work than he can handle. So, what brings you by?"

"Sorry, I'm interrupting you. I just…"

"You're good. Talk to me."

"Well, I was talking to Austin at work this afternoon, and he really opened up and…God, it's just so unsettling. I should've waited till you got home from work, but I needed to talk."

His body went tight. "No, it's fine. What did he say?"

"We were talking about Thanksgiving, what kind of traditions his grandparents had, and he didn't say much, but when I asked what he did for fun when he stayed there, he said, 'Nothing.' And I don't know why, but that got him to open up. He said he doesn't want to do anything when he's there because then he'll have to listen to them telling him how to do it. They correct the way he holds a fork, the way he chews, how he dresses and brushes his teeth. They won't let him slouch or give one-word answers. They make him leave his bedroom door open."

"What? Why?"

"He said it's a rule in their house because that's how

people get into trouble, behind closed doors. Griffin, they don't give him any privacy. They do these random checks of his laptop and phone."

"Jesus, what's wrong with these people? I'm going to talk to them. If they want to see him, they're going to have to respect his privacy."

"I said that. I said, Griffin will talk to them, and then he just clammed up. I hate that I shut him down, but I'm sure he doesn't want you interfering because he thinks it'll make things worse."

He nodded. "Yeah, I know. That's what makes this situation so hard. I want to help him, but there's not much I can do. Where is he now?"

"I couldn't concentrate at work, so I brought him home. And then I came here. I just needed to tell you."

"I'm glad you did." He put his tools away and cleaned up his station.

"What're you doing?"

"Going home. I won't tell him you talked to me, but I just want to be with him right now. I can't fix the problem, but I can hang out with him, let him know he's loved." It's about all he could do.

Everything about her went soft and sweet. That worry she'd walked in with melted away, and now she just looked all hot and sexy.

"Don't look at me like that."

She looked at him through her lashes. "Like what?"

"Like you want me to drape you over that bike and fuck you."

"I always did wear my heart on my sleeve."

Lust seized him, a fierce hunger sweeping through him. "Woman, get out of here. Go back to work."

She gave him a sassy pout. "Hmpf." And then she turned and strutted her sexy ass away from him.

Fuck, but he wanted her. "Where you going?"

"Home." Her hips sashayed. "To do yoga in my living room." She threw a sexy glance over her shoulder and winked.

And he knew exactly what that meant.

She'd be in that skimpy peach sports bra.

Chapter Fifteen

GRIFFIN STOOD AT HIS WINDOW, GAZING UP AT A SKY full of glittering stars. With Thanksgiving two days away, the Pilsons were picking up Austin the day after tomorrow, and he was worried.

If he could get ahold of Peyton, he could have his friend talk to them, tell them to ease up, or they'd be seeing much less of their grandson.

Movement in the carriage house caught his attention, and when Stella came to the window and looked up at him, his pulse quickened. She pressed her hand to the glass, and he could feel the ghost of that touch on his chest.

Wanted it there.

Wanted her.

All of her.

He grabbed his phone off the nightstand and hit her number.

When she stepped away to answer, the gauzy curtain swung shut "Hey. How'd it go tonight?"

"He doesn't open up to me the way he does with you."

He willed her to come back to the window, needed to see her.

She didn't make him wait long. "Did you tell him he doesn't have to go there for Thanksgiving?"

"I did, but he said he'd go. He's told me it makes things worse when he speaks up for himself or defies them."

"*Defies* them. Can you imagine? Not going along with everything they ask of him is viewed as defiance? I would love to give them a piece of my mind."

"Yeah, I don't mind if he spends time with them, but I don't want him spending the night anymore." He touched his forehead to the cold glass. "Nothing's going to change, though, until I talk to Peyton."

"You worried about him?"

"Yes." How could he be anything but?

"And it's only been three weeks."

"Right, and he said it could be as long as six weeks." Which also meant he could come back online before that. "I just want to talk to him before the holidays. The less time Austin spends with his grandparents, the better." He needed her here, with him. The distance physically hurt. "You eat dinner?"

"Well, I had a really nice salad I found in my mini fridge. I seem to have a secret chef who loads it up every now and then. Wonder who it could be?"

He couldn't deny how good it made him feel to know she had something to eat when she worked such long hours.

"I can see that, you know. That sexy little man-grin you try so hard not to show."

He broke into a full-on smile. "I'm not hiding anything. Hey, speaking of shows. Thank you for not doing yoga in your living room tonight. There's only so much a man can take."

"I prefer to save those kinds of activities for when there isn't a fourteen-year-old boy in the house."

"I could send him to boarding school."

She laughed. And when emotion took up too much space inside him, he went quiet.

She went quiet, too, and it made him wonder...why did he only notice his beating heart when she was around?

Because she is my heart.

She just is.

"Stella?"

"Yes?" Her voice was all breathy, a little eager, a little scared.

"You want me to make you some tea?"

"Yes. Very much."

The urgency pounded like a drum in his throat. "What kind?"

"Anything. I want anything you have to give."

Fuck. This woman. "Get over here."

He disconnected, let the curtain fall shut, and headed downstairs. Body strung tight, he felt brittle, like if he tripped and fell, he'd shatter. By the time he hit the kitchen, she was there. In her leggings, fluffy slippers, and an oversize sweatshirt, she was everything he'd ever wanted in a woman.

She gazed up at him, that look in her eyes that made his blood heat. And he kissed her. Oh, hell, did he kiss her. It all came roaring out of him, the desire, the need. It broke down the restraints he'd put in place to guard his heart from this reckless, wonderful woman.

But she wasn't reckless. He just couldn't control her, and that was his issue, not hers. Because Stella was fierce.

And he wanted that fierceness—wanted to taste it on his tongue and feel it in her touch. He wanted it in his bed, and he wanted it in his life.

Cupping her ass, he lifted her onto the counter. Stepping between her legs, he slid his hands under her sweatshirt to feel the warm, smooth skin of her back.

She scraped her fingernails across his scalp and tilted her head to deepen the kiss. His heart thundered, and a current of hot pleasure ran through him. When she reached between them and rubbed his hard cock, he growled.

She pulled her mouth away. "I don't want Austin to catch us."

"Good point." He scooped her off the counter and, never taking his mouth off hers, carried her to the door. Pressing her against the wall in the mudroom, he ground his cock against her hot center, and she rocked her hips, tugging fistfuls of his hair.

One hand under her ass, he reached for the doorknob.

"Wait." Her tone cut through his hunger.

"I don't want to be with you if you're going to pretend like nothing happened. Like last time. You can't mess with me, Griffin. I want…I want everything with you."

He tipped his forehead to hers. "I'm sorry. I'm trying to keep everything together for Austin, and I keep telling myself I can't have any complications. But I want you, sweetheart. I've never wanted anyone the way I want you—"

"I know you want me. That's not what I'm saying. You have to accept me the way I am. You have to know…this is me."

"The worst thing I've ever done is make you feel like you're not good enough. You're the best person I know, and I'm so fucking lucky you want to be with me. I want to try with you, okay? Can we do that? Can we try again?"

"I'm not the one who has to answer that question. If you can't get over what I did when I was eighteen, then I'm not sure—"

He kissed her hard and fast. "It hurt. Knowing you'd moved on so quickly destroyed me. And I held onto those pictures for seven years. But now that you're back, now that we've spent time together…I know you couldn't have loved anyone the way you love me. Because I know *us*. I know what we are, what we've been, and what we'll always be."

She wrapped her hands around his neck and kissed him until he was hot and frantic to feel more of her. Reaching behind her, he felt for the doorknob and stepped outside.

She wriggled her hips. "Put me down."

"Like hell, I will." Shutting the door behind him, he made his way carefully down the stairs, loving the feel of her arms around his neck, the jiggle of her tits against his chest. "Fuck, it's cold." In his T-shirt, sweatpants, and bare feet, he dashed across the freezing patio, shoveled clear of snow, across the patch of icy grass, to her front door.

He hurried in, kicking it shut behind him. "I can be nice and take you to bed, or I can strip you right here and bend you over the couch."

"If you take the time to carry me into the bedroom, I'll think you don't like me very much." Twisting free, she got down and went straight for the curtains, whisking them shut.

By the time she'd turned back around, his sweats had dropped to his ankles.

Her expression went hot, hungry. "Commando. That's

so hot." She stripped off her sweatshirt and yanked down her leggings, standing before him in nothing but sexy black lace panties. No bra.

"Jesus." He lost his mind for this woman.

When her hands went to the waistband, he advanced, batting them away. Gripping her hips, he spun her around, pressing on her lower back and bending her over the arm of the couch. He dropped to his knees, pulling one side of her panties aside to reveal a perfect ass cheek. It was so plump, he smacked it, just to watch it jiggle. She was delicious. Every inch of this woman turned him the fuck on.

She shifted restlessly, popping her ass out, clearly wanting more.

"Temptress." He took a bite of her peachy flesh.

"Come on, Griffin. *God*. I've waited so long."

"And you'll wait longer." He teased a finger along her slick, hot center, loving how aroused she was. Peeling off the panties, he let them fall to the carpet, as he spread her open and licked her clit.

She cried out, her body shuddering, and he eased two fingers inside her—fuck, she was wet—and licked her into a frenzy, until her legs shook, her cries turned frantic, and she buried her head in the cushion.

Every twist of her hips, every moan, wound him tighter, sent him closer to the edge, and he had to grip his cock to relieve the pressure. He loved the taste and smell of her, loved the way she let herself go so completely.

Loved *them*.

Together, they were fire.

And then she came on his tongue, her hips writhing, as she cried out. "Oh, my fucking God."

When she finished, her knees buckled.

As he stood, he swatted her ass. "You been tested?"

"Huh?"

"Condom or no?"

That perked her up. "Oh, I'm clean, and I'm on the pill." She swished her ass, as she peeked at him through the curtain of blonde hair that fell across her eyes. "Do it."

"I haven't been with anyone in a while, so this is going to be fast." A hand on her hip, he gripped his cock and lined himself up. "And hard." He eased into her, a gentle push and retreat, covering his cock with her slickness. With every press into her hot channel, electrical explosions lit him up. Back when he was nineteen, he'd always used a condom with her. Couldn't risk a pregnancy.

But now? He wanted everything with this woman. Whatever happened…he was done fighting.

Once he'd reached as deep as he could go, he took a moment to watch his cock slide in and out of her, and desire ignited him into a fervor. Pulling all the way out, he choked out, "Brace."

Her eyes flared, and a shudder went through her. With a punch of his hips, he thrust back in, letting his hand travel up that beautiful back, taking in her hourglass shape. He reached under and cupped her full breast, squeezed it, and thumbed the nipple.

"So good." That voice, coated in sex, fueled him. "Harder."

He gave it to her. Fingers digging into her hips, he yanked her back onto his cock, as he pounded into her. He'd never felt anything so good. With her, he'd never had to hold back. She took it all and gave right back.

Combustible, explosive…she made him lose control.

Nothing made Griffin lose control. Nothing.

Except this woman.

Every time he slammed into her, her ass bounced, her neck arched, and she moaned like she was lost in erotic bliss. The tension ramped up until he couldn't take it anymore. Couldn't think, couldn't breathe, couldn't feel anything but the frantic imperative to come.

And there it was, the tingling, the pressure at the base of his spine. He clamped onto her and slammed home, hips punching, each blast of his release a shock to his system.

His vision went white, and he soared right out of his body into a state of euphoria.

Griffin must've dozed because the bathroom light startled him. It flicked off, and Stella came back to the bed. He felt sated, content.

She pulled back the covers and slid in next to him, curling up when he wrapped an arm around her. But he could feel the tension in her body. She wasn't going to sleep anytime soon.

"You okay?" He trailed his fingertips down her inner forearm.

"I'm fine. Go back to sleep."

Which of course, woke him all the way up. "What's on your mind?"

"Well." She drew the word out like taffy. "Princess Rosalina came in today."

"Okay." He kissed her temple.

She drew in a breath. "You're the last person I should talk about this with but the only one I *want* to talk to."

"She's not canceling, is she?" She and Brodie were rock solid, so that wouldn't be the issue. Unless… "Do they not trust anyone but Diane to run the wedding? Because that's not on you. Diane put you in an impossible situation."

"Look at you, always rushing in to protect me. No, she's not cancelling. But her wedding's in two weeks, and I could tell she was dreading it."

Oh, shit, Stella. What have you done? He hiked up on an elbow. "You could tell?"

"Yes, and I was right, so don't look at me like that. That's why I shouldn't be telling you this."

"But I'm the only person you want to tell. So, go on."

"She came in to see if I'd throw a party for her close friends, and the more we talked, the clearer it became that she wasn't happy about her wedding. Her mom had taken over, and Rosie's vision got lost in the process."

"And I'm guessing you resurrected Rosie's vision for her?" *That's so Stella. She knows what you want, and she makes it happen for you.*

She ran her fingertips over his chest, and he broke out in goosebumps. "Yes, but only because Rosie had been very clear about what she wanted, and her mom and Diane ignored her. They wound up recreating the royal wedding, only this time in Calamity."

He didn't like to see her so full of anxiety. "So, you found a way to give her the wedding of her dreams?"

Her searching gaze told him she wasn't sure if he was mocking her, but he wasn't, and when she saw it, the tension in her shoulders eased. "I told her we could keep the ceremony in the church, but instead of the grand ballroom, we could have the reception at Wild Billy's."

"What's that now? You told the princess of St. Christophe to have her reception in a bar?"

"Well, when you say it like that…" She gave a nervous laugh. "No, but listen, I can transform the place. The reason I missed dinner with you guys tonight is because I talked to the owners. They're actually really excited about it. So, you know how it's got three sections? We're going to turn the bar area into a formal dining room for the royal family. We'll make it every bit as fancy as the Grand Ballroom."

"I can picture that."

"Right? And we're transforming the whole place. We'll borrow chandeliers from Carter's—you know that fancy lighting shop in Jackson? And we'll polish the floor, so it looks shiny and new, hire a band and do line-dancing, and we'll let the guests ride the mechanical bull." It all came out in a rush like she was ripping duct tape off a hairy arm.

It was hard for him to see her so worried and not want to make things better. "And she agreed to this?"

"She loved it. I'm telling you she was so relieved we'd found a compromise."

"You. You found the compromise. Which was Diane's job, so it sounds like a win. What's the problem?"

She gave him a genuine smile this time. "You don't know how much I needed to hear that. I'm pretty sure Diane won't agree, though. She might fire me."

"Is she happy with your work so far?"

"I think so."

"Are you happy being there?"

"I love it. I love it more than anything I've ever done." She kissed his chest. "Except having sex with you. That's the bomb."

He lowered back down, and she nestled in against him again. His hand caressed down her back, cupped her ass, and he drew her even closer. "There's nothing like it."

"I've just been so out of my depths with all of this, but

my dad used to say something that I try to keep in mind. Whenever I was overwhelmed, he'd tell me to be methodical about it. I know that sounds obvious, but it calms me down to know that there might be a hundred things on my calendar that need to get done, but I can only tackle one of them at a time." She looked away. "I just…I haven't told Diane yet, and I could punch myself in the face for just blurting out my idea before running it by her."

"Diane's not here. She hired you to run the place in her absence, and that's what you're doing. You can't effectively run the business if you're getting her approval for every move you make. She hired *you*. That means she trusts you to make decisions."

"Well, this one involves a king and a queen. It could make or break her business."

"Possibly, but if they're not happy with the reception, isn't that on Rosie, not you? She's a grown woman who makes her own choices. If she comes back tomorrow saying she's changed her mind, it's not worth upsetting her mom, are you going to back off, or are you going to push her into following your new plan?"

"No, I won't push. I don't think she'll be happy with her mom's plans—like, what's the point of doing the same thing all over again? But I won't argue with her final decision."

"Then, as far as I can see, you're good. Your job is to give brides the wedding of their dreams. This bride wasn't happy, so you changed things. You made her happy. Diane can't fault you for that. In fact, she'll have to credit you for it and kick herself in the ass for kowtowing to the bride's mom."

"God, Griffin." She flung her arm across his chest and

hugged him. "Thank you. I thought you'd tell me I'd gone and done it again, that I should stop being so impulsive."

"I don't want you to stop being anything, sweetheart. You're amazing. You're perfect."

"I want to believe you. I do. I'm just afraid…"

"Yeah, I know. But this time, I know what it's like to be without you. I won't make that mistake again."

"Promise?"

"I promise."

———

Stella lounged in Griffin's arms.

Repeat: I'm lounging on the couch with the love of my life, acting like we're an old married couple. And I've got an engagement ring on my finger.

It almost felt real, like those seven years had never happened. Like they'd stayed together as she'd always hoped they would.

But it wasn't real.

Because no matter how perfect this moment felt, she lived with a niggling fear that if she made one mistake— well, come on, she knew they were more than mistakes. Kissing Trace? Pretending they were engaged?

Pretty big whoppers. And for another man, maybe they wouldn't be reasons to break up with someone you loved. But for Griffin, who'd watched his friend plummet to the ground, who'd sat with him in pain so agonizing he'd passed out, it was a whole other story. Especially since the accident never should've happened. They'd made a reckless, stupid mistake that had nearly cost Booker his life.

It *had* cost him his dreams of playing in the NHL.

So, yeah, she understood why Griffin had become cautious. And that, combined with being the oldest of seven…well, the man had legitimate triggers.

But it wasn't like she could snap her fingers and stop being impetuous. She'd do *something* again.

She believed they were wired for each other. She believed he cared about her, wanted her, even needed her. In bed, they were explosive.

But she could no more change her impulsive nature than he could change his need to control situations. The very things they loved about each other were what could drive them apart.

Which meant she'd dive right in, immerse herself in all this gooey loveliness—and try not to run this joyride off the rails.

Griffin lowered his book, listening to Austin strum. "Best thing I ever did was buy him a new guitar."

"He's good, too." She sat up a little straighter. "I still can't believe they took his last one away. What a terrible thing to do. I mean, his *dad* gave it to him. What right did they have? They're such awful people."

"I agree, but the weird part is that they believe they're doing what's best for him. When they destroyed his guitar, they thought they were saving him from going down the wrong path. In their minds, they helped him."

"That's awful. You'd think you'd change your ways if your own child cut you off."

"True, but when Peyton got their daughter pregnant, he was a hard-partying bass player in a grunge band. So, I believe they're genuinely trying to keep Austin from going down that path."

"You have a nice way of looking at things."

"The difference between us is that when *you* care about

someone, you want to fix the world for them. I want to keep them locked in my basement."

She laughed. "You're not that bad." She pretended to look scared. "Are you?" She started to get up. "I mean, I've never really been *in* the basement. Should I be worried?"

He yanked her back down. "Oh, come on. You know I have to reveal my secrets to you slowly, over time." He patted her hair clunkily with his big paw, and she pushed him away.

"Creeper." She kissed him on the mouth. "But you're my creeper, so if you've got people in the basement, I'll make sure to double my next batch of enchiladas."

"See what a good team we make?"

"The best." She deepened the kiss, smoothing the hair off his face. But they heard a voice…and she pulled back. "Oh, my God, is he *singing*?"

Chapter Sixteen

THEY BOTH STILLED, LISTENING.

"He's good." She looked to Griffin, who nodded. "He's really coming into his own, you know? I wish he didn't have to spend Thanksgiving with them."

He set his book on the coffee table. "You can see how much he's dreading it."

"I hate the way he accepts these awful things. I want him to know life can be anything he wants it to be. That if he uses his voice, if he goes after what he wants, he can be happy."

"And I think life's a balance. It's not just about what makes you happy. It's about meeting your obligations. He thinks he has to spend time with his grandparents. And who knows? Maybe there's a small part of him that wants a connection to his mom."

She kissed his cheek, running her fingers through the scruff. "You're a smart man. I never thought of it that way, but I'll bet you're right. He has to be curious about this woman who gave birth to him and walked away."

Griffin lifted his arm and wrapped it around her. She

loved the way he always had his hands on her. He seemed to unconsciously need her tucked in close. The sense of belonging, of being wanted…she got it all with him.

There's nothing like it in the world.

Austin didn't have that. And she really, really needed him to find it. "I'll be right back." She got up.

"Where're you going?"

"I'm just going to talk to him." She didn't have anything specific to say. She just needed to see him, give him a smile, let him know he was loved.

"Okay."

Wait. He was just going to let her go? One hand on the banister, she stopped and turned to him. "Thank you."

"For what?"

"For trusting me to talk to him. For all you know, I could throw some wild-ass idea at him that'll make him run off and join the circus."

He grinned. "You're in his corner, and he needs that. He's damn lucky to have you care about him."

As she started up the stairs, she heard, "Like I could stop your wild-ass ideas anyway."

She stuck her tongue out at him and continued climbing. But she felt good. Really good. He accepted her, and that made her breathe a little easier.

When she reached Austin's room, she stood outside his door and listened.

Savannah, I wanna, I gotta,
I'm gonna be your man
Savannah, my only, my truly,
I'm your number one fan
Oh, oh, oh, life is fine when you're on my mind
Oh, oh, oh, wherever I look you're who I find

Okay, what in the world? Mr. Broody wrote a pop song? Well, not pop. It had an indie-rock edge, but it was pretty lively.

And who's Savannah? She thought he didn't have any friends at school. She knocked, and the strumming stopped. "Austin?"

"What?"

"Can I come in?"

She heard a rustling sound, and then he said, "Fine."

When she entered, she found him putting the guitar back in its case.

He glanced up at her. "What?"

She loved everything about this bedroom. The cheerful navy, white, and yellow comforter, the sturdy wooden frame of the bed, the interesting shade of blue on the walls. And the window facing the mountain had a spectacular view. "Hey, so, I was wondering if you wanted to get a gift for your dad for the holidays."

"What do you mean?"

"Maybe after school tomorrow, we could stop by the holiday market in Wolff Village and get him some things. I'm not sure what he's into, but we could just put together a care package."

He perked up. "I want to do that."

"Cool. What's your dad into?"

"What do they sell?"

"Like candles and jewelry and knit hats and scarves and…" His disinterest had her petering out. "Yeah, nothing a soldier would be into. Oh, you know what?" She'd barely talked to Coco since she'd come home. Her sister had texted to say, *I heard you're in town??? What's up with that?* And Stella had promised to visit her, but she hadn't done it yet. "My sister owns a chocolate

ERIKA KELLY

shop. We could buy a big box from her. Would he like that?"

"Yes."

"What if we got enough for everyone in his bunk or unit or whatever?" By his expression, she knew she'd hit on a winning idea.

The only reason she'd held off seeing Coco was because her sister had gotten married and had two babies, and Stella didn't know where to begin, having missed out on so much in her life.

But Coco was the least intimidating person in her family, so she was just making excuses.

That all changes now.

"So, you'll go with me?"

He nodded.

She was glad he wanted to go with her, but…a little worried about just showing up and surprising her sister. Should she call first?

See, that's the whole thing. When you don't talk to people for seven years, it's hard just to pick up the phone. Though, with Coco, it would probably be all right.

Funny how Stella could be bold in all other areas of her life, but when it came to confronting her family, she folded like a cheap T-shirt.

"Cool. We'll go tomorrow after school." *Oh, wait.* What time was she meeting the Taylors? "Just get off the bus at the office. I've got a meeting at two-thirty, but we can leave right after."

He hunched a shoulder. *Sure.*

Stella rolled her eyes. "You're just like your uncle. Man of few words. Hey, I couldn't help overhearing that song you were playing. It's really good. Who wrote it?"

"Me." He looked away.

"Sweetie, I'm not kidding when I tell you it was fantastic. I'd buy that song if I heard it playing somewhere."

Color spread across his cheeks.

"Griffin said your dad used to play guitar, and that he gave you his before he left for his first deployment."

"Yeah." Anger sparked in his eyes.

"It makes me so angry that your grandfather broke it."

"He *drove over* it."

"That's horrible. He had no right to do that. I mean, it's their house. They have their own rules, and if they don't want you playing guitar, that's just how it goes. But they didn't have to destroy it. Did you tell them how angry you were?"

"No, he was angry at *me*."

Ah, so there's no room for anyone else's emotions in that family. Got it.

"Well, here's the thing. We're here, so if anything like that goes down or is about to go down, text us, and we'll come right over."

He watched her for a moment, his expression guarded, almost like he didn't believe he could rely on them.

She moved closer, so he'd look at her, *hear* her. "I'm serious. They live fifteen minutes from us. One text, and we're on our way." She couldn't tell for sure, but he might've gotten a little bit of comfort from that. "And you don't have to go for the whole weekend, you know. I know that's what they expect, but we can pick you up earlier. It's truly up to you."

"No. It's fine."

"Well, I don't know about you, but fine has never cut it for me. I guess I'm one of those people who thinks every choice matters. And the thing is, what *you* want matters.

Every bit as much as what your grandparents want. I guess I just want you to know that you have a say in where you go and what you do."

He wouldn't budge—she could see that—but she did have an idea that might give him something to look forward to. "So, I was going to wait until your birthday to give you this present, but now that I've heard your song, I'll tell you now. My sister—you know Gigi Cavanaugh, right? She used to be a Lollipop?"

"That's your *sister*?"

"Yep. And she's offered to give you guitar lessons." *Oh, oh, oh.* "Wait, do they still do the Holiday Musicale? I graduated seven years ago, so I don't even know if it's still a thing."

"It is. There are signs up all over school."

"What do you think?"

"I'm not performing."

She had to smile at his curtness. Because she knew the richness that lay beneath the hard surface. And it had become her goal to crack it wide open. "Not even if Gigi did it with you?" Oh, man, had she just offered up her sister's services without asking? *Yes, yes, I did.* "She'll be here for Thanksgiving. She could give you your first lesson, and you could work on a song for the show."

"She'd do a song with me?"

"Yes."

"Why would she do that? I'm nobody."

"I don't even know how to answer that. You're somebody special to a lot of people, but in this situation, you're *my* somebody, and my sister just happens to want to give you guitar lessons. And since you're a seriously amazing singer and songwriter, I think you should go for it." Okay, she'd planted the seed. Time to go. As she headed for the door, she said, "Think about it. Rehearsing a duet for the Musicale with Gigi Cavanaugh is a legit excuse to cut short your visit with your grandparents and hang out with her for a day to work on the song, am I right?"

And then he surprised the hell out of her. "Okay. I'll do it."

The adorable chocolate shop faced the town green. Plate glass windows topped with half-moons were set into the glossy green façade, and a striped canvas awning hung over the doorway.

"Are we going in?" Austin pulled his wool cap down and stomped on the recently shoveled pavement.

"Yes. *But.*" She clapped her mittened hands together. "You should know that I haven't seen my sister in a long time."

"How long?"

She lifted her scarf, so it covered her mouth, and exhaled, her breath warming her nose. "Years."

"How many years?"

"Seven."

"Why so long?"

Because I'm an asshole. But he didn't need to hear that.

"I did something stupid, and instead of dealing with it, I moved away. And one month turned into a year and then time got away from me. It just became so much harder to come home and say, I'm sorry, I miss you, please, can I come home?"

"You don't think they'll forgive you?"

"I don't forgive myself." *Ah. And there it is. The real reason I haven't talked to anyone. If I'm still holding onto it, then I certainly can't imagine anyone else letting it go.* "God, it sounds stupid now that I'm saying it to you. I mean, if I were giving you advice, I'd say, She's your sister. She loves you. Just go in and tell her you're sorry."

"She's your sister. She loves you. Just go in and tell her you're sorry." And then…Austin smiled.

And warmth bloomed in her heart, making her forget all about the bitter cold. "Okay. I will." She started forward and found Coco standing in the doorway.

Her stomach plummeted to her toes.

"You going to stand there and turn into ice sculptures, or are you going to get over here and give me a hug?"

Stella dashed up the walkway and into her sister's arms. They clung to each other like Coco had just yanked her to safety from a raft in the ocean.

"This is Austin." Stella blinked back tears. "He's staying with Griffin while his dad's on deployment."

"Nice to meet you." Coco shook his hand, before turning back to her. "Is your GPS broken? It took you this long to find my store? It's literally in the center of town."

"No, I knew where it was. I'm sorry. I've been…embarrassed."

Coco ushered them inside, and they were immediately enveloped in the lovely scent of warm chocolate.

"This place is unbelievable." All three walls had floor-to-ceiling built-in bookcases arranged with colorful planters, chocolate gift bags, and fancy boxes. The glass display cases had row upon row of artfully designed chocolates, and the marble table in the center of the shop held antique cake stands with clusters of specialty treats.

"Chandra?" Coco called to the clerk behind the register, pointing to Austin. "Can you please put together a box of whatever he wants?" The moment Austin took off to wander, her sister turned to her. "Why the hell would you be embarrassed to see your sister? You're not going to kiss my husband, are you?"

Floored by the comment, Stella just stared at her. And then she said, "You already married him. Where's the fun in that?"

"You dummy. Come on, show me the engagement ring."

It hit again, that punch of shame. Her arm hung limply.

"I can't believe you're engaged." Coco flicked her fingers. *Show me.*

Oh, God, this is terrible. Horrible. How could she lie to her sister?

Do it. With a smile, she showed her sister the modest diamond.

"It's beautiful. You're beautiful. I'm so glad you're home. And marrying Griffin? That's the best news in the world. When did you guys get in touch with each other because Lulu saw him last summer, and he said you guys hadn't talked since you left town?"

She flicked a glance to Austin, who was peering into a display case. "It's a long story. We can talk more over Thanksgiving. I have to get him to his snowboarding class, but I wanted to see you and pick up some chocolates for his dad. He's deployed, and I thought it would be a pretty awesome care package."

"Sending my chocolates to one soldier is just plain cruel. How about we send enough for everyone in his unit?"

Stella broke out laughing since she'd pretty much said the same thing to Austin. "I love how the Cavanaugh women think."

"Go big or go home. Come on. Let's box up every

chocolate I've got in this shop. My thank you to the Armed Service members who defend our country and miss out on the holidays with their own families."

But before Coco could go, Stella reached out to her. "I'm sorry. I've been ashamed of myself for so long, and I didn't know how to come back. So, thank you for making it so easy. I've really missed you." She pulled her sister in for a hug.

"I missed you, too, and we have a lot of catching up to do."

So far, Gigi, her parents, and Coco had made it super easy.

That just left Lulu.

And she had a feeling that wouldn't be easy at all.

***

Joe: Found your template on top of the printer. Want me to bring it?

Griffin: Nah. Leave it. About to take my knucklehead on a spin.

Pocketing his phone, Griffin stared at the beauty in front of him. He'd worked on this bike for months and couldn't wait to get it out on the road. Boots on concrete made him smile. He figured Joe would want to hear the engine purr.

But when he turned around, it was Declan. His friend handed him the template. "I like what you've done to the place."

He'd transformed the original garage, modernized and expanded it, but he knew his friend was teasing. "What're you still doing in town? It's hockey season."

"Just got some shit to deal with." Declan patted the

bike. "This the forty-eight knucklehead you told me about?"

"Yeah."

"You need me to give it a ride?" Meeting Declan in a dark alley might give a guy a little scare. With his scruff and worn jeans, his ink, and ancient biker boots, he looked rough. But he was the nicest, most loyal friend Griffin had ever known.

"After I christen it, you're next."

"Cool. I'm in town a couple more days. You want to get a drink?"

"Absolutely. Does that mean you're in town for Thanksgiving?"

"Sure am. Text me when you want to meet up." Declan had been raised by his grandpa, his only family. After the old man died, he was pretty much alone in the world.

"Declan." The sharpness in his tone had his friend turning around. But there wasn't a chance in hell he'd be alone for the holidays.

"Flag football in the Sundance Room at one on Thursday."

Declan broke out in a slow grin. "You sure about that? I'd hate to embarrass you with your *fiancée* watching."

A prickle at the back of his neck alerted him to the fact that Declan knew about the lie. "Stella's going to be with her family. First time in seven years. It's a big deal."

"Shouldn't you go with her? You are *engaged*, after all."

"Not this year. She needs to work shit out. It's just family."

"Uh huh."

"Whatever you think's going on, keep your theories to yourself." He'd known Declan since preschool and trusted him with his life. He probably should tell him. *But where does it end?* He should tell his parents, too. His brothers, Skylar, Jinx…

Best to just play the game.

Shouldn't be for much longer.

"Oh, I got theories, all right. You want to hear one of them?"

"No."

Declan grinned. "You've been in love with that woman half your life. Doesn't matter how you got a ring on her finger…don't fuck it up."

"Okay." Griffin's tone was dismissive, meant to shut the conversation down, but heat flushed through him. A jumble of emotions hit him all at once.

"You want her, but she's way out of your comfort zone."

"I don't have a zone."

"Oh yeah? It ever occur to you that you fix bikes for a living?"

"Yes, daily. When I come to work and fix bikes."

"Don't be obtuse."

"I'm glad you only had a year and a half of college. I'd hate to hear your vocabulary if you'd had more."

Declan's grin burst right through all that scruff. "You design motorcycles, my man. To make sure the owners don't crash. You keep people safe."

"Yeah, it'd be bad for business if my customers crashed."

"Look, man, what happened that night sucked. But we'd done that kind of thing hundreds of times before, and no one had ever gotten hurt. It was a fluke." He hunched a shoulder. "We fucked up."

"I fucked up. Jamie fucked up. Cole fucked up. You and Booker had nothing to do with it."

"And I lost my shot anyway. See? That's my point. Shit happens. If you live your life trying not to fuck up, you're not really living." He exhaled. "Griff, your heart chose one woman. Now, you've got to get over your issues so you can keep her." Declan turned and walked off.

"What issues?" When his friend didn't even break stride, Griffin shouted, "What fucking issues?"

Chapter Seventeen

MOM: GREAT NEWS! LULU'S HERE!

As the gate opened, Stella stared at the text message.

Griffin reached for her hand, threading their fingers together. "What's going on?"

She lifted her phone. "I just found out Lulu's here."

"Isn't Xander playing today?"

"He is." She shrugged. "But she came home."

She'd talk to her sister for the first time in seven and a half years.

And it made her feel sick.

"Would it help if I came with you?" he asked.

Yes. "You're amazing. You really are." But he'd been avoiding his family because of her lie, so she wasn't about to keep him away from them today. "I'll be fine once I get inside. Thank you, though." Besides, he was so close to them. He was the best big brother his siblings could ask for. "You have to see Rocco and Nico."

He cracked a grin. "Yeah, I do."

See? He loved his nephews.

"We could divide the day. Your family eats a lot earlier than mine."

She shifted toward him. "You'd do that for me?"

The gate opened, and he drove through. "I think you know I'd do anything for you."

She launched herself across the console to hug him. And right in the middle of the driveway, he shifted into Park so he could hug her back. "You don't know how... happy I am." She tucked her face into his neck. "Happy isn't even the right word. Every minute of every day these past seven years, I've ached for you. No matter where I was, who I was with, what I was doing, I felt you in my heart, and it hurt. I knew I'd lost the love of my life, and I knew I'd done it to myself."

He thumbed away a tear. "I know. Believe me, I know. Life without you...it's going through the motions. It's eating without tasting and laughing without finding anything funny."

She kissed him, giving him her whole heart through her mouth, her tongue, and the hands cupping the back of his neck.

He pulled back and shifted into Drive. "Come on, let's get you home."

I'm already there.

Because home is with you.

He braked behind a line of trucks and SUVs. She glanced toward the house, imagining the easy laughter, the way her mom finished her dad's sentences, the conversations that overlapped and veered in new directions.

"I'm a guest." She glanced at him. "They've got a new normal now with just the five of them. Well, six with Cassian. Seven and eight with Xander and Beckett. And when I walk in, everyone will stop talking. It'll become stilted. No one's going to tease me about rushing in late because I met my friends for brunch at the diner. No one's going to give me shit for not helping out in the kitchen. Instead, it'll be like, So, how did you like working for the Wildcats? I heard you moved to New York. How did you like living there? You know what I mean? I gave up my place in this amazing family."

He broke into a soft smile. "Now, that's where you're wrong. The magic of you is that no one's a stranger. I don't think you realize how special you make someone feel just by sitting next to them at the airport gate. But next time, pay attention. Watch them sit up a little straighter and wipe the crumbs off their shirt. You'll see exactly what I mean." He reached for her hair, rubbed a lock between two fingers. "*Forget* you? Sweetheart, you're the heart and soul of this family, so get that fear out of your head." He cupped her chin, his gaze sinking into her. "You are loved, you are missed, and you are irreplaceable."

"Oh, my God, Griffin." And once again, she was leaning across the console, holding him like she never wanted to let him go.

And she wouldn't.

She wouldn't do anything to jeopardize their relationship this time around.

Always unrattled, he smoothed her hair and kissed her mouth. He cut the engine. "Come on. I'm going in with you. I'll stay until you feel comfortable."

"You make everything better." She unbuckled, pulled her purse from the backseat, and opened her door. "Let's do this." With each step up the walkway, her stomach tightened. "I wish I didn't have to lie to them."

"Yeah, I know, but I keep reminding myself that as soon as I get that letter, we'll be able to explain ourselves."

They climbed the steps and stood under the shelter of the porch. She reached to open the door, but he caught her wrist and pressed a kiss to her hand. "Just be yourself. They can't help but love you. No one can."

Do you love me?

I'd do anything to earn his love again. And that's when she realized, he couldn't come in. He couldn't miss time with his family to hold her hand through a problem she'd caused. "Griffin."

He waited, patient, kind, as always.

"Go to your family."

"I will. At least let me stay for your mom's famous hot crab pinwheels. Those things are awesome."

"I'll put some in my purse for you. Now, go play flag football with your brothers and cousins and friends. Make us proud." She set a hand on his cheek. "Thank you." *I love you.*

He looked at her for a moment, as if making sure she really was okay. How could she not be? Everything he'd just said made absolute sense and made her feel better.

"Okay, but if things don't go well, text me for a rescue." He kissed her on the mouth, and then he was gone.

She faced the door. *Here we go.* Opening it, she stepped inside to the familiar scents of pumpkin pie and roasting turkey. A roaring fire crackled, and she followed the voices coming from the kitchen.

She shed her jacket, tossing it over the back of a chair, and dropped her purse onto a side table. A mess of emotions, she headed toward her family. She wanted them to accept her, love her, draw her right back into the center of them where she'd once felt so safe and cherished.

She didn't want it to be awkward, to see resentment in their eyes.

Couldn't bear to have Lulu ignore her.

An adorable little girl came flying into the living room wearing gauzy silver wings and ballet slippers. Right behind her, Coco came out with a baby in her arms.

The little girl saw Stella and ran over to her. "Is that my auntie Stella?"

Coco smiled and came closer. "It sure is."

"Why is she just standing there?"

Coco's fingers sifted through the girl's hair. "Good question."

Stella burst out laughing. "I'm sorry. I'm just so excited to meet you." Forcing her body to move, her legs felt like they hadn't been attached correctly.

As she looked at Stella's boots, the little girl's eyes went wide. "Mommy. Those shoes sparkle." Her gaze swung up to her mom. "Can I wear boots like that?"

"When you're thirty." Coco pulled Stella into a hug. "You okay?" She smelled like baby shampoo and cocoa powder.

"I think if I sit at the kids' table, I'll be all right."

"Oh, so that's how it is? Posie sits by herself in a separate room, while the rest of us feast?"

"I'm not sitting by myself." The little girl sounded offended. "I sit with my daddy."

"Oh, I know, honey. Auntie Stella was…never mind. It was a joke. A bad one. Come on in."

Stella ran her hands down her dress, but she didn't follow Coco into the kitchen.

"If you're worried about Lulu, don't be. She's just as nervous about seeing you. You guys need to break through the wall. One conversation, and you'll back to being thick as thieves."

"That's optimistic."

"What do you want me to say?" Coco shifted the baby. "Don't turn your back on her, she's packing a shiv?"

"At least that's better than not knowing what to expect."

"Sometimes in life, you just have to take that first step. Like right now." She handed over her baby. "Welcome to being an aunt."

Stella took in the denim-blue eyes, sandy blonde hair, and bow-shaped pink lips of the most beautiful infant she'd ever seen. "She's precious. And heavy."

Coco laughed. "What were you expecting? A ball of fluff?"

Posie tugged on her mom's jeans. "I'm hungry, Mommy. When can we eat?"

"Ask Daddy to cut you an apple." When her daughter ran off, Coco turned back to her. "You look like you're about two seconds from dropping my baby and pulling a runner."

"No, it just feels weird, you know? The last time I saw you, you'd just graduated college. You were going to start a business with…Keith?"

"Yeah, that fucker ghosted me." Coco smiled. "Thank God."

"And now you have a husband, two daughters, and a really successful chocolate shop." She stroked the baby's downy hair. "I missed getting to know your children."

Coco wrapped an arm around her. "Yeah, you did. So, let's not waste one more minute, okay? Come on. Let's get this over with. It's kind of like a crème brûlée. Just give the crust a good, hard whack so you can get to the creamy custard underneath." She squeezed Stella's hand as if to say, *I got you.* And then she led her to the kitchen.

When she got to the threshold, Stella took in the scene. Her mom basted the turkey, Gigi ran a hand mixer in a silver bowl, and her dad leaned a hip against the counter as he handed a piece of sausage to Posie and set another on the charcuterie board he was putting together.

"Stella's here," Coco called. "Can we eat now?"

Everyone stopped talking. The room went silent, as all eyes turned to her.

At that exact moment, Lulu stepped out of the panty. "Okay, Dad, you've either got water crackers or—"

Their eyes met. Lulu's jaw went slack.

A volatile cocktail of fear, joy, and shock exploded in Stella's chest, sending hot pinpricks raining down on her skin. The air left the room, and a deep, unfathomable longing rumbled, burst, and crashed over her.

Please don't run.

Please, please, please don't run.

And then her sister tossed the crackers on the counter and disappeared back into the pantry.

Her mom set the baster on a plate and gave Stella a hug. "Hey, sweetheart. You want to start setting the table?"

Oh, my God. "Yeah, sure." Stung, embarrassed…she didn't really know what she was feeling. She almost couldn't believe it when conversation resumed as though her sister hadn't just annihilated her.

Cassian headed over. "Hey, Stella. Great to see you."

She took in his height, his muscles, and all that radiant star quality. "Well, you grew up." As hard as she tried to pretend she was all right, she knew the slight tremble in her voice gave her away.

Gigi joined them. "Right?"

"Look at you two. Together, finally." Her last memory of them had been Gigi curled up in a ball, crying her eyes out, inconsolable, the night Cassian kissed her sister's friend at a party right in front of her.

Doing her damnedest to ignore the pain of Lulu's rejection, she gave Cassian a playful smack on the shoulder. "I'm so glad you figured out your shit."

"Yeah, I was an asshole. But it all worked out in the end. I got the girl." He wrapped an arm around Gigi's shoulders and hugged her tightly.

A tall, muscular, extremely handsome man approached them.

Coco lit up. "And *this* is Beckett."

With the baby snuggled in one arm like a football, Coco's husband gave her a firm handshake. "Great to meet you. I've heard—"

"A lot about me? Yeah, I know. Despite that, maybe you'll give me a chance?"

His features broke into a devastatingly handsome grin. "I've heard way more good, and to be honest, the other stuff's more badass than bad."

Acutely aware of Lulu coming out of the pantry and lingering at her dad's side, Stella nodded. "I can live with that."

Her dad handed off the charcuterie board, and Lulu had to walk right past her to bring it out to the living room.

Stella abruptly—possibly rudely—excused herself from the others and reached for Lulu's arm. "You need help with that?"

Lulu faltered, her gaze catching Stella's.

When she didn't pick up any anger, hope sped through Stella's bloodstream, radiating heat through her body.

"I got it." Coco took the board, and all four of them headed into the living room.

That left Stella alone in the entryway of the kitchen with Lulu. She'd had years to go over what she'd say when she finally got the chance, but nothing came to her mind at that moment. Because there was only one thing she wanted to say. "I miss you."

The three simple words hang in the air, drenched with emotion and pulsing with tension. Lulu swallowed. She smoothed her hands on her blouse. And right then, their dad tried to get past them, arms loaded with bottles of wine.

"Everything okay?" he asked.

Before either could answer, their mom called, "Girls, hurry up and set the table."

And then…Lulu turned and walked away.

While everyone groaned and patted their bellies, Stella had hardly eaten a thing. Hard to do when Lulu sat across the long dining room table, actively ignoring her. After dinner, they'd gathered around the fireplace and told stories, and it felt like old times. They never ran out of conversation and laughter.

She'd made sure to give light, happy answers to all the expected questions, never delving too deep. Not in this setting. It was a holiday, after all.

But time had gotten away, and now Coco and Beckett needed to get the babies home. Panic fluttered in Stella's throat, knowing Lulu had to leave, too, to pick Xander up at the airport.

In the flurry of activity, as everyone got their coats and said their goodbyes and talked about future plans, Stella knew she had to take her shot. She glanced at her sister, who stood at the bottom of the stairs, talking quietly on the phone. Xander hadn't seen the point of Lulu missing Thanksgiving with her family for a game, so after winning, he'd literally run off the field, showered, and caught a jet to Calamity. His plane was just landing.

Coco crouched, snapping the baby into the car seat while Beckett held Posie in his arms.

"Hey, Stella, do you need a ride?" Coco asked.

"Oh, no, thanks. Dad's taking me."

"Okay, 'Night." Her sister gave her a hug.

Stella reached up to give Beckett a kiss on the cheek. "It was great to meet you."

"Come for dinner, okay?" he said.

"I will." Stella brushed the hair out of Posie's eyes. "I had fun with you tonight."

"Are you going to come over and make cookies with us?"

She'd heard all about the kitchen cabinet stuffed with sprinkles and glitter. "I would love that. Bye, Sweetie." After the family left, Stella closed the door, and when she turned around, she found Lulu heading for the kitchen. Which meant she was grabbing car keys and heading out the back door.

Stella hurried over. "Lulu?"

Everyone turned to her in surprise, and she guessed she had sounded a little aggressive. But her time was up, and she wasn't going to let another minute pass with her sister not knowing how sorry she was for hurting her. "Can I talk to you a second?"

"I have to go." Lulu sounded half helpless, half annoyed. "Xander's landing."

It's true. I had all night.

And I waited until the very last moment. "I know. It won't take long, and it's important."

Lulu gave a shrug of surrender, and then Stella led them into the kitchen, where the counters were littered with pots and pans, the turkey platter, and leftover pies. Standing there facing her sister, her mind went blank, and she tried to pull together any of the sentences she'd rehearsed over the years.

But none of those sentences mattered when she was face to face with the person she'd hurt so badly. "I'm sorry, Lulu. I'm sorry for not trusting you to figure things out on your own. I'm sorry for assuming I knew what was best for you."

Slowly, her sister's tension eased.

"I'm sorry for humiliating you in front of everyone we know. And I'm sorry I wasn't mature enough to understand that my job was to be there for you when you needed me."

"Well, that's…a very different kind of sorry than you gave me seven years ago."

"Back then, I still believed I'd done the right thing in the wrong way. I still thought I was saving you from a bad marriage."

"Well, I mean, you did. I would've married him, and he would've cheated. And I would've fought with him and cried a lot and spent months agonizing over what to do. I would've left him in a big dramatic scene. You did save me from all that."

"I didn't want you to go through any of that. You feel things so deeply, and I was…oh, forget what I was. I thought it was my job to protect you, to save you, and really my job was to be your best friend."

"You know, I've had a lot of time to think about it,

and the real problem was our dynamic. You were always this dazzling creature, and since socializing came so easily to you, I just stood in your shadow and let you lead the way. If you hadn't kissed Trace, I'm not sure we ever would have broken that dynamic. It wasn't until I moved away that I stopped trying to be more like you and started being *me*."

"Can you forgive me?"

"Oh, I did that a while ago. The issue was whether I wanted you in my life. I mean, not only was your apology mostly about defending your actions, but then you ran off and never came back. I think I've been angrier about that more than anything else." Her sister looked disappointed in her. "I thought you were the strongest woman I knew, but you weren't. By disappearing, you took away my option to rant at you or even forgive you. It was just another way for you to take away my choice. You know it takes me longer to process things than you, especially something as enormous as that night. And that's what I'm not sure I've forgiven you for."

"I honestly never thought about it like that. I'm sorry. I was devastated and scared and…immature. I'd lost my best friend and the love of my life, and it was all my fault, and I just couldn't live with myself."

"Well, you got him back." Lulu reached for her hand, lifting it to show the engagement ring. "Congratulations."

Oh, God. Here it is. The big lie.

Her hands went clammy, and her stomach twisted. "Thank you."

Her sister's gaze flicked to hers, alert, aware.

Stella cleared her throat. "Thank you." She said it more strongly this time. Because she had no choice.

But Lulu knew. And she dropped her hand, still warily watching her. "I have to go."

Stella didn't know what to say. *Can I call you? Can we talk again?*

Have we worked anything out at all?

Because she'd just lied to her sister.

And how could they move forward when Lulu still couldn't trust her?

Chapter Eighteen

Anxious, Griffin parked his truck in the garage.

He'd stayed longer than he'd wanted tonight because he kept waiting to hear from her. But she'd never even looked at the text message he'd sent asking if she needed a ride.

Climbing the steps to the house, he entered and tossed his keys on the counter. He headed straight for the back door, peering into the night. The carriage house was dark.

That's good. It meant the reunion had gone well.

He could relax. She wouldn't still be out if things had gone badly.

He'd grab a beer. Watch some TV.

But he was full, and he didn't really watch much TV.

That's fine. I'll read.

He checked his phone again. Nothing from Austin or Stella.

Griffin: How's it going?

Austin: Fine.

Griffin cracked a smile. Hard to get pissed when

Griffin gave the same kind of responses. He needed to be more specific.

Griffin: What room of the house are you in?

Austin sent a photo of his legs, feet tenting the cream and beige comforter.

Griffin: In bed already?

Austin: Don't be late picking me up.

Griffin: Am I ever late?

When Austin didn't respond, Griffin felt bad. The boy needed his assurance. Right then, he likely felt lonely, isolated, and judged.

Griffin: I missed you today. I won't be late.

Austin: k

He should go upstairs, get ready for bed. That way, he could be a creeper and look out the window to see if there was a light on somewhere in the carriage house.

She's not there. She's with her family.

He could picture her sitting on the couch, surrounded by her parents and sisters and brothers-in-law, having a great time, laughing. Stella did everything with her whole heart—including laugh. It came from her belly, and she didn't care what it sounded like. It was contagious. No matter your mood, if Stella was cracking up, you couldn't help but smile with her.

But what if she was sitting there, feeling like an outsider?

He couldn't stand that idea. He pulled his phone out. She still hadn't read his message.

Dammit, where are you, Stella?

Opening the back door, he stepped out into the frigid air and jogged across the short stretch of lawn. He knocked at the same time he turned the knob and let himself in. He didn't see her, and yet his body went on alert because he felt a presence.

Her presence.

Who was he kidding? He caught her scent in the air, felt her sorrow in his heart. Shutting the door, he rushed forward, heading for the bedroom.

Clothes rustled on the couch. "Griffin?" Sitting up. she sounded groggy.

"I woke you." He headed to her, wishing he could turn on a light to see her.

"No, I'm up."

He sat beside her—almost on top of her because he needed to be close, to make it all better—and wrapped an arm across her shoulders. She fell against him. For long moments, he stroked his fingers through her silky hair, keeping his mouth shut.

Because he had questions. Like who the hell hurt her?

But he waited. Because he knew it would come. Stella kept nothing inside. That was one of her best qualities. She got it out, which meant you always knew where you stood with her, what she was feeling, and what she needed.

"You smell like a frat party."

"Oh." He laughed. "After dinner, we went back for another game of flag football."

"Did you have a good day?"

"Yeah, it was great." *Except for the parts when I couldn't stop thinking about you, wondering how it was going and how Lulu treated you.*

"Was it awful, lying to them?" she asked.

"Yeah, but I changed the subject pretty quickly."

"And your mom let that happen? She didn't try to talk about wedding dates and venues and food?"

"I shut it down before it got there, told them it was

new, and we needed time." He couldn't take it anymore. He had to know. "How'd it go with Lulu?"

"Not so great." She played with the fringe on the throw pillow. "It was going well, until she congratulated me on my engagement. And it's that sister thing, you know? She could tell I was lying, and I think knowing I was playing her just killed everything. She shut down the conversation and left to pick up Xander."

"I can understand that." Because it had sucked to lie to his family. "We can call it off if you want, end the engagement."

"I don't think we should do that, not so close to the holidays. We agreed to wait until you get the letter of guardianship."

"Right, but not if it's causing problems with your family."

"No, it's okay."

"Then why do you sound so sad?"

"Because you'll get that letter soon, and then we won't be together. I know it sounds stupid. I know it's all fake. But…I'd rather be fake engaged than not have you in my life."

"I'm in your life, Stella." Sliding a hand under her ass, he shifted her onto his lap, pushed the hair off her shoulders, and kissed her. He poured his damn heart into that kiss.

Her fingers sifted through his hair, and nothing in the world felt better than this. His woman pressed to him, their mouths joined, tongues swirling in a sweet, slow dance that was as romantic as it was erotic.

When she squirmed, signaling she wanted more, he tipped her gently onto her back, deepening the kiss and letting his hand slip under her shirt to caress the warm, soft skin of her belly. He glided up until he reached her breast, full, bouncy, and bare.

Every nerve-ending in his body lit up, and he scooped her into his arms, carrying her into the bedroom. Tonight, he'd make her feel like the goddess she was.

Setting her gently down, he flicked on the lamp. When she blinked, quickly turning away from the light, he said, "I want to see you." He pulled down her leggings, bringing the panties with them, and she sat up long enough to yank the sweatshirt over her head, leaving her gloriously naked.

He'd never seen anything more beautiful, that lavishly feminine figure, the blonde hair tousled and fanned out on the pillow, and that overlarge mouth, so pink and lush.

"I love the way you look at me." She got on her knees and crawled over to him, all seduction and hunger. "You make me feel like I could have horns and a mustache, and you'd still adore me because you're not seeing my flesh and bone. You're seeing *me*."

He swallowed back the tide of emotion that threatened to crash over him, let her pull off his shirt, and unbutton his jeans. Sitting on the edge of the bed, he untied his boots and kicked them off. Then, he gathered her into his arms and kissed her, his hand taking a slow glide down her back, tracing each bump of her vertebrae and pausing on the curve of her ass.

Lifting her, he set her head on the pillow, and then he left a trail of kisses from the corner of her mouth, down to her jaw, and along the column of her neck. He'd show her how right she was about the way he saw her.

With her hands in his hair, her hips shifting restlessly on her unmade bed, he knew she understood.

He pressed a necklace of kisses along her collarbone,

his hand cupping her breast, loving the weight and suppleness, his thumb flicking the nipple. As he made his way down her beautiful body, he reached between her legs and found her hot, slick, and ready for him.

With a hand under each thigh, he lifted her, opened her, and kissed her feminine core with all the passion pounding in his blood, all the desperation making his heart beat so fast he thought he might die.

This. This connection, this perfect fucking intimacy—it was like plugging into a life force, an energy source. His world narrowed to the scent and heat of her, the cries, moans, and gasps…love, desire, want. It all swallowed him whole until his very essence melded with hers.

He needed to be inside her right the fuck now.

Fingers gripping the blanket, she arched off the mattress. His hands clamped her ass, holding her in place, as he brought her to a climax that had her crying out his name over and over.

And then he set her down, surged over her, gripped his cock, and drove home. Sensation tore across his skin, a flash fire that engulfed him, and he captured her mouth, kissing her, devouring her, as he thrust into her. He wanted it to last, couldn't bear losing this feeling of intimacy.

Jesus, he wanted to hold onto this blissful realm of tension right before a climax, when his body was strung tight, as it drove closer and closer to the euphoria it sought. But he couldn't hold off. He was going to come.

Not yet. He needed more.

He pulled out and sat back on his heels. Smacking her ass, he said, "Roll over."

She got up on her knees, her hair spilling forward, pooling on the pillow, and he yanked her hips back, easing himself back inside. *Yes, this. So fucking good.* When he plunged in deep, she rocked back on him, and the sound of their skin slapping drove him wild. He stroked a hand up her back and around to her breast, cupping, kneading, squeezing her. Her hips rammed back and ground against him.

"Fuck, fuck, *fuck*." It was too much. Noise roared in his head, and he couldn't think, couldn't stop this tsunami of emotion from crashing over him, pummeling him, leveling him.

Clutching her hips, he slammed into her, held her tightly, and came so hard his vision went white. He pumped in hard, short bursts, releasing again and again and again.

And when he settled, he felt wrung out. Shaky.

He felt like he'd burned his house down to the foundation.

And now, he could finally let go of the past and build something fresh, new.

Exhausted, he fell to his side. She curled up next to him, her hands on his face, stroking. She pressed kisses to his cheek, her body shaking.

He held her close. He had no words. Emotion still had control of him. No rational thought.

Except one.

Now that he had her, how could he ever go back to a life without her?

Friday morning, Griffin and Stella headed up the walkway to the Pilson's modest ranch house on a cul-de-sac near town.

"Is it weird that I can't wait to see him?" she asked

quietly in the early morning stillness. "He hasn't even been gone forty-eight hours."

"No." Griffin was eager, too. He'd texted Austin this morning, letting him know they were on their way but hadn't heard back. "I'm just glad we're getting him today and not Sunday." They climbed the porch steps.

"Same," she whispered. "How much damage can they do in a day and a half?"

It took a couple of knocks, but when the judge answered the door—dressed in slacks, loafers, and a cashmere sweater—he looked stern.

"Happy Thanksgiving." Stella beamed at him, the heat of her smile capable of melting a polar ice cap.

But not this man. He stepped out onto the porch, not inviting them in. "We don't appreciate you cutting short our time with him. He's our grandson, and we've made plans for the weekend that include him."

"I understand that," Griffin said. "He only recently decided to audition for the show. But, given that he's new to school and hasn't found it easy to make friends, we felt it was a step in the right direction for him to become involved. And then, when Gigi offered to perform with him, it became an opportunity we couldn't pass up."

"He can come back after he practices with her."

Austin pushed past his grandfather, bristling with anger. He skimmed around them and raced to the truck.

Griffin swung around. "Austin?"

The boy didn't answer. But there was no hair hanging out of the wool cap that covered his head.

Two things struck him at once. First, Austin didn't wear hats. He rarely bothered with a coat.

Secondly, if he were to wear a hat, his shoulder-length hair would surely be visible.

Stella tugged on his arm. "We should go."

But rage burned in his body, and smoke curled from hidden recesses. *What the fuck did they do to my boy?* He turned back to the judge, fire and accusation in his eyes.

But the older man met his gaze with a challenge. "Let us know when he'll be back." And then he stepped back into the house, ready to shut the door.

Griffin's boot kicked out, jamming it open. "What did you do?" When the older man looked at him with no remorse, he said, "What the fuck did you do?"

"If you wondered why he received a suspension for something he didn't do, if you couldn't figure out why nobody questioned him before issuing a punishment, it was because he looks like a delinquent."

"He looks exactly how he wants to look." Griffin leaned into the house. "You fucked up your own kid. I'm not letting you do it to Austin." And then he turned and walked away.

Stella's hand slid down to his, forcing him to thread their fingers together. "What did you just do?"

"They're not getting away with this shit."

"But you can't start a war with them. Not until you get that letter."

"Too late." He hurried to the truck and got in. Griffin sat there for a moment, his pulse racing. The tension in the car was thick. Looking in the rearview mirror, he found Austin staring out the window, the same mask he'd worn when he'd first shown up in Calamity.

Fuck. In three weeks, Stella had managed to get this boy to open up, and not even two days with the Pilsons had wiped out all her progress.

"What happened?" His tone was too harsh. *This isn't Austin's fault.* "What'd they do?"

When Austin didn't answer, Griffin twisted around.

"Can we just go?" Austin asked.

Griffin hesitated.

"Just go, okay?"

It was the plea in Austin's voice that got him moving. "Fine." Griffin started the truck and slowly backed out, checking carefully behind him. Once on 191, he said, "Now, tell me what happened."

"They cut my hair."

"*Who* did?" He needed clarification, or he'd go ballistic.

"Their friend."

"They invited a barber to Thanksgiving?" Griffin cut Stella a look. *They planned this.*

"No, one of the ladies cut my hair."

"How did it happen?" Stella asked softly.

"My grandmother was telling everyone about the show, and this lady said I should get a haircut if I'm going to stand in front of the whole school."

"And you agreed?" *Why?*

"No. I said I was fine. And then, after dinner, the lady asked if she could just trim it a little. She said I looked like a sheepdog with all the hair in my eyes." He gave Stella a look that asked, *Did I?*

She shook her head. "You have gorgeous hair. It's shiny and healthy and thick."

Austin looked utterly crestfallen.

"And it will grow back," she quickly added.

"So, what happened?" Griffin asked the boy. "You went along with it?"

"They were watching football, and she said I could watch the game while she trimmed."

"You don't watch sports."

"But that's what they were doing. I wasn't paying attention because she promised she wouldn't take much off."

"And then?"

"And I saw this piece of hair drop to the carpet." He sounded choked up. His features turned red.

"They had no right to do that," Griffin said.

"Did you tell them to stop?" Stella asked.

"No. There's nothing to say. It's done."

Griffin had reached his limit. Slowing the truck, he wheeled it around.

"Where are you going?" Austin sounded anxious.

"Back to see your grandparents. They don't get to cut your hair against your will." Taking away his guitar was bad enough. *Backing the car over it was sick.*

But cutting his hair? They'd stolen his identity.

"No, don't." Austin sounded scared.

"They stepped way the hell over the line, and we need to get some things straight."

Gripping the back of Griffin's seat, he sat forward. "Stop it. You're just going to make it worse. I want to go home."

"They can't keep getting away with this, Austin." he said. "We have to talk to them."

"If you talk to them, they'll twist everything around and make it sound like you're a bad person. Because they want me to live with them. And if you give them a reason, they'll take it."

Right. He knew that. He was just surprised that Austin understood it so clearly.

And he supposed the only thing he could do was help Austin deal with them. Agitated, he pulled to the side of the road. He let himself sit there for a minute, trying to calm down. "I'll take you home, but I need you to know that you're perfect just how you are."

Stella's attention jerked to him, but he kept connected with Austin through the rearview mirror. "Do you understand me? They took away your guitar because they didn't want you to turn out like your dad. But your dad's a good man. You might not like moving from one Army base to another, and you might hate his deployments, but you should know that every choice he makes comes from wanting to be the best father he can be."

He had Austin's attention, and it mattered. He needed the boy to understand.

"This time, they cut your hair because somehow they think the length determines what kind of man you become. They don't get to make those decisions. You do. Only you. If you don't want to spend time with them anymore, you don't have to. Okay?"

Austin nodded.

And maybe—it was hard to tell with this kid—he saw a little relief in his eyes.

Good. Because Griffin had meant every word of it.

Chapter Nineteen

Savannah, I wanna, I gotta,
I'm gonna be your man
Savannah, my only, my truly,
I'm your number one fan
Oh, oh, oh, life is fine when you're on my mind
Oh, oh, oh, wherever I look you're who I find

STELLA LOVED THIS LIFE. SITTING AT THE DINING room table, she typed up her notes from the video conference she'd had with a couple from North Dakota who wanted a destination wedding here. Throughout the call, she couldn't stop smiling as she listened to Gigi help Austin.

She wondered when the two of them would work on their song for the show, but she loved that Austin was getting a lesson in songwriting.

I could get used to this.

Something had changed between her and Griffin after Thanksgiving. That night, they'd made love, and it seemed to tear down the last of his walls. It was like he was free to be with her. She almost felt safe with him.

Almost.

She couldn't say why, but she had a sense of foreboding, that this was too good to be true. That something would come along to tear it all away from her again. And maybe it was because he'd dumped her before, something she'd never expected in a million years.

Maybe it was nothing more than the muscle-memory of rejection.

Gigi clapped her hands. "Woo hoo, you got it. That's a great bridge."

Austin murmured something, and then Gigi said, "Okay, now that we fixed your song, we need to come up with a song for the show."

Her sister went quiet again, listening. And then, "Are you sure? Because it's usually holiday songs and dances."

"I'm sure." Austin spoke louder now and with confidence.

"Um, okay, in that case, we have to work on the structure a little more. You've got the verse, that's the 'once upon a time section,' you know, where we set up the song. You knew that intuitively. And we've already tweaked the bridge. It's got great energy now. I love it. But we need to work on the outro, which is where you want to give the listener a sense of the ending."

"I don't know the ending yet."

"Well, let's break down the song and figure out the best way to give an emotional punch."

"No, I mean, *I* don't know the ending yet."

A shock of worry pierced her heart. Does he know Savannah?

Is he thinking he'll sing her a love song in front of the entire school?

"Songs aren't real life," Gigi said.

"Some are."

"No, I hear you. They can definitely start out like that, but when you're creating a piece of art, the purpose goes beyond expressing yourself. It becomes about making people feel something. With this song, since the narrator's into her, it would be really effective to end it with them not getting together."

"I don't want that."

"Well, it's a reversal, right? Like, the singer's clearly into this girl, and the melody is upbeat and rockin', so we're in a good mood, expecting her to give him the thumbs up...but then, you but drop the word 'fan.' And that makes us wonder what's going on here—he's her *fan*, not her friend, not her equal. So, now you've got the listener pulled in, waiting. And the bridge is happy and hopeful so we could end it with something like this." Gigi strummed her guitar and sang, "Here I am, once again, watching you walk by, here I am watching you, wondering if I'll catch your eye."

Stella swung around to see Austin's reaction.

He was smiling.

Yeah, for real. Austin was smiling.

"You like that?" Gigi grinned.

He nodded.

"Okay, let's do it." Her sister wrote something down.

Who's Savannah, though? Does she go to school with him? "This is such a great song." Stella got up. "When did you write this?"

"A few weeks ago."

"So, it's not about an old girlfriend? Someone you knew in San Diego?"

He grew uncomfortable.

"Does Savannah go to Calamity High?" *Please say no.*

"She's in my snowboarding class."

Oh, my God. "Is she your age?"

He nodded.

I have to fix this. "And her name's Savannah?"

"Yeah." He sounded almost defensive.

"Wait, have you been talking to her?" she asked. "Texting?" *Does she know you exist?*

He shook his head, clearly embarrassed.

"I'm sorry if I'm making you uncomfortable. I'm just trying to understand this, and I'm worried about you getting up on stage in front of the entire high school and singing a love song to Savannah when everyone else is doing holiday songs."

His chin tipped in defiance.

"Okay, what if we change the name? Call her Mariana? Angelina? Keep it similar."

"No." He was adamant. "It's Savannah's song."

Oh, wow. This boy…he was going to love deep and hard one day.

He might not be related by blood, but he was so much like Griffin it was scary.

But he couldn't expose himself like this at the Holiday Musicale. She looked to her sister. *Help me out here.* But Gigi just gave her a gentle smile. And Stella wanted to say, *Artistic integrity's great…unless you're a fourteen-year-old in a new school.*

But she needed to get through to him, so she sat on the arm of the couch. "Hear me out, okay? Let's say you're sitting in the auditorium, and some girl you've passed in the halls starts singing a song. And you hear your name. And it's a love song. What're you going to think?"

"I don't know, and I don't care what other people think of my song. It's for her. Not for anyone else."

"Right." *Hard to argue with that.* "But I just want you to imagine walking down the hallways the following Monday. Teenagers are a tough crowd. You're new at school. You don't want them making jokes at your expense, right?"

"I don't even know them. They don't mean anything to me. She does."

She wasn't getting through to him, and he was going to make a terrible mistake. One he wouldn't come back from. Teenagers had long memories, especially if he was the loner, the new kid who hadn't made any effort to make friends.

And what if Savannah was popular? What if she was mean to him?

Stella would die if anyone hurt this boy. She needed to talk to Griffin about this. He would help her figure out a way to get Austin to do *Frosty, the Snowman* or something instead of a song that had the potential to scar him for life.

"I'm starving." She headed into the kitchen. "You guys want me to make something?"

"I can't stay," Gigi called.

"Okay." She found her phone on the counter and pressed Griffin's number.

"Hey. Everything all right?" The whine of hydraulics and some hammering made it hard to hear him.

"Do you have a second?"

"Sure. Hang on." After a muffled sound, which she figured was Griffin walking to his office, he came back on the line. "What's up?"

She stood near the window and lowered her voice. "So, that song he wrote? *Savannah?* It's for a girl in his snowboarding class. That's what he's going to perform at the holiday show."

"What? He's dating someone?"

"No." *He gets it, thank God.* "He's never talked to her."

"And she goes to Calamity High?"

"Yes, but they're not friends. She might not even know he exists outside of being one of the kids in her class. I suggested he at least change the name from Savannah to Alannah or something similar, but he refuses."

"Did he say why?"

"Yes, because he wrote it for *her*. Because he likes her and doesn't care what the other kids say."

"He said that?" Griffin sounded impressed.

"I know, I know. It's really sweet, but he doesn't know what it feels like to be taunted. Remember Richard Bates?"

"Of course."

"Well, we can't let that happen to Austin."

"Richard Bates owns two car dealerships in Idaho Falls. He's doing great now."

"*Griffin.* You remember how badly he was teased and bullied. People were vicious."

"They were. But Austin isn't Richard Bates."

"No, he's not, but we can't sit back and do nothing. It's a holiday show. The other kids are going to be singing *Jingle Bells* and dancing to Run DMC's *Christmas in Hollis*. He'll be the only one putting his heart on his sleeve for a person he's never talked to. You know I'm right. It's a recipe for disaster. We need to stop him."

"I can talk to him when I get home, but other than giving him my opinion, I'm not sure what you want me to do. You want me to forbid him? Ground him the night of the show? Distract him with a trip to Vegas?"

"A trip to Vegas sounds a lot better. And if that'll save him from humiliation, then yes, offer him a trip."

"Offer who a trip?" Austin came into the kitchen with two empty glasses. Gigi followed him in.

"I have to go," Stella said to Griffin before disconnecting. *Well, damn.* He'd heard her. There was no covering for what she'd said. "That was Griffin. I told him I'm worried about you singing that song, and he joked about taking you to Vegas, so you don't perform at the holiday show. That's on me, though. Griffin says it's up to you."

"I'm performing." He opened the refrigerator and pulled out a yogurt. "It'll be fine." Peeling off the lid, he tossed it in the garbage and grabbed a spoon.

"What if Savannah doesn't like you back?"

He hunched a shoulder and turned to Gigi. "Thank you for teaching me today."

Her sister gave him a warm smile. "My pleasure. I'm leaving in the morning, but we can shoot for one more rehearsal over a video call, okay?"

"Okay." With a chin nod, he walked out of the room.

Stella waited until she heard his boots on the stairs. "I can't believe you and Griffin are being so chill about this."

"Because it's not our choice. He's obviously determined to do this."

"So? He's fourteen."

Gigi bit back a smile. "Do you remember your biker phase?"

She sure did. Griffin and his friends were into dirt biking at the same time the television show *Sons of Anarchy* was popular.

"I can remember coming home after a tour, and I

281

heard you and Lulu arguing in your room. She was trying to talk you out of wearing something, so I came in to see your outfit."

"You can stop right there." Stella laughed. "I don't need details."

"You were wearing a tight, cropped leather jacket with fringe and these tight, filthy, ripped black jeans."

"God, stop." How mortifying that her super-cool, older sister remembered this phase.

"And these brand new biker boots."

Stella covered her ears. "La la la la."

"You were going to wear a fake sleeve of tattoos on your arm." Gigi was cracking up.

"All right, enough. One more word out of you, and I'm going far, far away. Maybe New Zealand."

"Okay, fine, but my point is I tried to talk you out of it, and what did you do? You went to school in that ridiculous outfit. With your fake sleeves stuffed in your backpack."

"It was a very fashion-forward idea. That's my take on it, and I'm sticking to it. But no one made fun of me." In fact, some of the girls had actually copied her.

Thankfully, the fad hadn't lasted more than a few weeks. It was truly awful.

"Okay, but when you left for school that morning, you didn't know what the outcome would be. I warned you about it. Lulu warned you. Even Mom tried to talk you out of it, and you insisted on doing it anyway."

She could see her sister's point.

"And guess what? Austin might be quiet, but he's one of the most confident kids I've ever met. Very much like you."

"I hear you. And you're right, but can you just do me a favor? Can you practice a second song, just in case?"

"In case what?"

"In case I can talk him out of it. In case something happens between now and then, and the girl turns out to be a bitch. Then, we'll be ready to switch songs."

The humor left Gigi's eyes. "No, Stella. I'm not going to practice a second song with him, because that's not what Austin wants. Okay, I've got to go." She gave Stella a hug. "Love you. Talk soon."

"So fired up, man. Let's do this."

"Three, two, one…"

Heart racing, Griffin launched backward off the cliff, drawing his knees up and flipping. The moment he extended his legs, he pulled the chute. His canopy inflated, jerking his body. And then…

Freefall.

Elation.

And the eerie silence that always accompanied a jump.

In the dead of night, with his parachute fully extended, he couldn't see his friends, but he knew their expressions. The adrenaline rush from BASE jumping was fucking addictive.

They'd left a circle of lantern flashlights in the meadow for their landing zone, and it came hurtling up fast.

A gust of wind jerked his parachute. Terror struck, but he tugged the braces, leaned left, and righted his course.

Jesus.

It's all right. It's fine.

That scared the shit out of him.

Someone landed right in the circle.

I'm next.

Easy, easy, easy…

His boots hit the ground, the impact jarring his bones, and he jogged till he got his balance.

Fuckin' A. Perfect landing.

Yes.

They jumped on each other, high fiving, slapping backs.

"What a rush, man."

"That was awesome."

Jamie, Declan, Cole, Griffin…

Without a word, they all turned to look for Booker.

There he was, coming in. Fast.

A sudden burst of turbulence plastered his clothes to his body, and the canopy collapsed.

Booker pulled the braces.

He knows what to do. He's got this.

Except, he was coming in hard, too hard.

"Brake," Jamie shouted. "Fucking brake."

Griffin broke into a run. Fear pounded in his bloodstream. His pulse beat out of control.

"Booker!"

His friend hit the ground with a sickening thud.

Griffin jerked awake.

What the hell?

It took a moment to tear himself out of the dream, to remind himself Booker was fine. Everyone was fine.

Wait, were they? Sweating, he scrambled out of bed, reaching for his jeans.

Where's Austin?

He couldn't get his brain to fully wake up, and he had this terrible feeling something was wrong with his boy.

Still not used to this house, his shin clipped the edge of the dresser. Ignoring the sharp pain, he flung the door open and stalked down the hallway.

The dream still clung to him—his friend's unconscious body, the wrong angle of his leg, the panicked energy as they'd loaded him into the bed of the truck and raced to the hospital.

Only when he stood outside Austin's bedroom did he come back into the here and now. He remembered dinner with Stella. She'd made Austin laugh, telling stories about some of the guys on the football team she used to work for.

After, they'd played a video game together, all three of them. Not something Stella would choose to do on her own. She'd done it to give Austin a sense of home, security.

Everything's fine. Everyone's safe.

He stood outside Austin's door, but he didn't hear anything. Quietly turning the knob, he peered inside… and found the boy sleeping soundly. Griffin closed his eyes, let out a slow breath.

Then, he headed back to his room.

He'd never get over it, would he? Thinking Booker was dead, feeling for his pulse, the crushing silence in the truck. It had felt like sitting on a bed of needles the entire ride to the hospital. Then, the excruciating tension in the waiting room, not knowing if his friend would be paralyzed.

Closing himself in the bathroom, he splashed water on his face. As he dried his cheeks with a hand towel, he looked at himself in the mirror.

And found himself shaken to his core.

Booker had almost *died* because Griffin, Jamie, and

Cole were scared about the next phase of their lives. Because they'd wanted one more night together. Because…

They'd been reckless kids who flung themselves off cliffs, rode mountain bikes on uncharted terrain lined with boulders and unpredictable turns, and had no sense of their own mortality.

They'd never thought through the consequences.

Until that night.

Since then, I've been vigilant. He wouldn't let anything happen to the people he loved.

And it was killing him.

It's fucking exhausting.

Stella was right. Peyton could've asked any number of people to watch Austin while he was deployed.

He chose me because I won't let anything happen to his son.

Flicking off the light, he headed back to bed. Where Griffin controlled his external world to keep everyone safe, Stella threw herself into life.

I can't control her.

And so I cut her out of my life.

He lowered his head. *I might've lived my life without her if she hadn't come up with that stupid fake engagement idea.*

Right then, he almost didn't care that he'd lied to his family and friends. Well, he did. But it had been worth it. *Because I got Stella back.*

And he might be keeping Austin alive, but that boy wouldn't be coming into his own, experiencing life, if she hadn't barged into their lives.

Throwing on a hoodie, he hurried down the stairs. He

picked up his phone from the counter where it lay charging.

Griffin: You up?

He saw his text had been delivered. Three dots bounced on the screen.

Stella: I am now. Everything okay?
Griffin: Fine. Can I come over?
Stella: Of course.

Just in case Austin woke up, Griffin wrote him a note.

At Stella's. Be right back.

Shoving his bare feet into the boots he'd left by the back door, he let himself out. *Fuck, it's cold.* And it was just the wake-up he needed. Snow crunched under his soles as he jogged across the lawn and headed toward the yellow lights of the carriage house.

Stella opened the door. "Everything okay?" She reached for him, drawing him into the warmth of her home.

Closing the door behind him, he tipped her chin and gazed into those beautiful hazel eyes. "I'm an asshole."

She cracked a grin. "Okay?" But when she saw he was serious, the smile faltered. "What's going on? What've you done?"

He kicked off his boots and led her to the couch. "I love you."

Her eyes flared.

"I love everything about you, and it makes me sick to think you've doubted yourself all these years. That *I* made you feel there was something wrong with you. You love fiercely, and that's a gift. I need that kind of love. Austin needs it. If you hadn't crashed into our lives, Austin would still be eating Cheetos and playing video games. And my life would be nothing more than meeting obligations. I visit my family and pay my employees and deliver bikes on time. I eat to fuel myself and sleep so I can get up the next day and do it all over again. But with you, it's the opposite. With you, I eat pancakes because it's fun. I ice skate just to laugh, and it's fucking exhilarating. Everything with you—even a trip to the grocery store—is exhilarating. And that's how I want to live my life."

Her lips parted, went soft. "I love you, too. I love you more…" She caught her breath, overcome with emotion. "More than anything."

He kissed her. "I don't want you in the carriage house. I want you in our home, in our bed." He gestured around the room. "I hate that you're here. It's like you're banished. Marginalized. And that ends right now because you're the center of everything. You're the source."

"The source?"

"Of happiness." He cupped her chin. "You're my home, Stella. And I want—I need you with me. You make everything better."

Chapter Twenty

STANDING TO THE SIDE OF THE STAGE, STELLA panned Wild Billy's with her camera phone. "That's the bar. You can see we've transformed it into a formal dining room." She zoomed in on the linen-draped tables, votive candles, charming bouquets of stargazer lilies, and stunning crystal chandeliers. She was so proud of how it had turned out. It looked sophisticated and elegant. "And don't worry. The wait staff's been trained to serve royalty."

"Can they see the mechanical bull from that perspective?" Diane asked.

Stella turned the phone around. Her heart twisted for her boss, looking tired and pale. Her mother's stroke had taken a real toll. "Yes, but Rosie thinks they'll get a kick out of watching everyone dance and ride and have a good time." *As long as they don't have to participate.*

"I hope she's right. Fully half the guests are from St. Christophe. I can't imagine what they'll think when they see people riding a bull at a royal wedding."

Stella felt sick. "It's a risk, I know, but the bottom line is that this is the reception Rosie wants."

Diane looked skeptical.

Still, Stella's gut told her she'd done the right thing. "At least the other half will love it."

"They're not the half I'm worried about. But…I trust you."

Stella nearly dropped the phone. "You do?" She hadn't expected those words.

"Of course. If I didn't trust you, do you think I'd still be in New Jersey? Everything I've worked so hard to build with this business hinges on this event."

"Excuse me while I throw up real quick."

Diane smiled. "It'll be fine. You've shown me every detail along the way, and I'm confident you've created the wedding of Rosie's dreams. Her family's reaction is not within our realm of control. Rosie's the bride, and she's paying for it, so it's her show."

"Hey, so, how're things going with your mom?" *When will you be back?*

"We're not seeing the kind of progress we should after five weeks. We'll give it until the first of the year, and if she's still in this condition, we'll have to make arrangements."

"You'll put her in a home?"

"My mother devoted her entire life to her family. There's not a chance she'll spend her last days on earth in the care of strangers. No, she'll be moving in with me."

"Oh. So, she's coming to Calamity?"

"No, I can't do that." Exhaustion seemed to overcome the older woman. "All of her friends and everything she owns is in this town." She gave a resigned smile. "I'll have to move back here. But it's for the best. I want my mother to be comfortable and surrounded by everyone she loves."

"That's the most beautiful thing I've ever heard."

"All right." Diane flapped a hand. "Enough of this talk. You go on. Orchestrate the magic."

"I will. You take care and keep your phone nearby. I'll show you how it's going in real-time." She disconnected and climbed down the stairs to the dance floor.

The kitchen door punched open, and two of the wait staff helped Coco wheel out her Decadent Chocolate Cake. The queen had ordered a traditional white cake with flowers but, given that it was pretty much a duplicate of the one at the royal wedding in St. Christophe, Stella had decided to surprise the bride with a second cake, since Rosie lived for Coco's chocolates.

"Where do you want it?" her sister asked.

"Let's do it here, near the stage."

"Hey, girls." Her mom came in, looking sophisticated and gorgeous. "Here's your fix-it bag." She handed over the heavy tote Stella brought with her to weddings. It held everything a wedding planner could ever need, from safety pins and hair spray to pain relievers, mints, and clear nail polish.

"Thank you so much." She'd left it in the bridal room at the chapel.

"And here." Her mom handed her a plastic bag. "You've got your choice of cake cutters."

"You're the best." Gratitude rushed over her. "You guys, I'm so glad I'm home." To think she'd missed out on all this support and love for so many years... *God*. She had to blink back tears. She could *not* get emotional right now.

Her mom pulled her into a fierce hug. "You have no idea how happy I am to have our family whole again."

Another set of arms wrapped around them. "Can I get in on this?"

"Get over here," Stella said. "You smell like chocolate."

"Curse of my profession," Coco said.

"Thank you guys for being here for me and just… accepting me."

"We love you," her sister said.

Her mom rubbed her back. A phone vibrated, and they pulled back. Her mom read the screen. "The shuttles are arriving. It's go-time."

The doors opened, and in walked the guests. First came the Bowie brothers and their gorgeous wives, followed by Griffin and Austin.

Hands thrust into the pocket of his dress slacks, cuffs rolled to his elbows, Griffin stood out in the room full of rugged mountain men. His inked forearms were on full display, all-powerful muscles and bold designs. He must've felt her watching because he glanced over, and a thrill shot through her at the intensity of his look.

She flashed him a private smile, and his eyes flared.

"Look at you two." Her mom came up beside her. "Hard to believe it isn't real."

"I think it is real, Mom."

"What're you saying? Are you actually engaged?"

"No, but he had a dream the other night. About the accident."

"With Booker?"

She nodded. "I think he's got PTSD from it. Is that possible?"

"Absolutely. I don't know all the details, but from what I understand, the boys were right there when Booker crashed. They were the ones who rushed him to the hospital. I don't know who drove, but I know the others were in the back of the truck with Booker, scared out of their minds. It was a traumatic experience. They thought…well, you can imagine what they thought."

"Yeah, so, I think my impulsiveness, my…recklessness reminds him of how he used to be…and the consequences of it."

"I never thought of it like that. You've made some mistakes—who hasn't?—but I don't connect them with what happened to Booker."

"On an emotional level, though. But I think he gets it now, Mom. Which means…"

Her mom nodded. "We can only change what we're aware of." She rubbed Stella's arm. "It won't be overnight. You realize that, right? What he experienced left a deep imprint. It's going to take time."

"Oh, believe me, I know that for myself. You should've seen how hard I tried to come up with some stupid scheme to get Austin to sing a different song for the Musicale. I thought I was saving him from a world of hurt. But then I remembered that I didn't save Lulu from hurt. I just gave her a more brutal hit by betraying her."

Her mom broke into a sad smile, but before she could speak, someone said, "You did."

Both of them turned to find Lulu right behind them. Her mom patted her arm. "I'll let you two talk." She took off to help organize the wave of guests that had just come in from the second shuttle.

"That's all I've ever needed to hear you say," Lulu said.

"I don't think I could've said it until now."

"I've imagined seeing you a million times over the years, and I thought I was ready. I thought I was all mature and confident, but…I guess I'm still that little girl who thinks her sister is dazzling. I mean, look at you, Stella. You're gorgeous." She made a sweeping motion around the venue. "You did this wedding by yourself. And from what I understand, you've only been in Events for three months. You're just an amazing person, and I guess I don't know how to be the woman I've become when I'm around you."

Stella had no words. "That's…yes. You nailed it. That's exactly what it's been like for me since I got home. I don't know how to be the woman I've become when everyone in Calamity's seeing me as the girl I was when I left."

"Well, I guess there's only one thing for us to do, and that's get to know each other as the women we've become."

"But do you want to? Get to know me again?" Her heart beat so loudly in her ears it drowned out the buzz of conversation in the room.

"Of course, I do. You were my best friend. And no one has ever replaced you in my heart. No one ever could."

"I feel the same way."

They reached for each other at the same time, and all the affection and love she'd missed over these long years poured in, filling her, healing her. "I want you to know I've learned my lesson." They pulled apart. "I don't know if you know the story, but Austin's grandparents are super controlling. And I get so angry when they do what they think is best for him…until I realized I was doing the same thing. The Musicale I was talking about? It helped me see that I want to love him, not overpower him. I want to give him a voice, not take it away."

She could've sworn she saw appreciation in her sister's eyes, but her phone vibrated with a text message, and she had to look away.

Mom: Royal family just pulled up.

"Okay, it's show-time." She didn't want to leave her sister, not when they'd finally started talking. But she had to get to work, so she blurted out, "Will you cater Gigi's wedding?"

"Cater it?" Lulu asked. "Do you mean Harley and Lu's?"

"No, I mean you personally. I want to spend time with you, and if we can work together...both of us doing the things we love best? I mean, how fun would that be?"

"I'd love that." For the first time since seeing her sister, Lulu smiled, and it was warm, sweet, and full of affection. "We have so much to catch up on. Can we get started on your teenage *marriage?*"

As the band found their places on the stage and picked up their instruments, Stella laughed. "We'll need wine for that one. Lots of wine." And then, standing there facing the enormous room, her heart was so full she wanted to shout, *I just made peace with my sister! We're good, you guys! Everything's good!*

Her phone chimed again.

Mom: The limo just pulled up.

Stella turned to the band. "You guys ready?"

"You bet," the lead singer said.

The drummer held up his sticks, the keyboard player set his fingers on the keys, and the bass player fiddled with the amp.

And then Princess Rosalina, wearing a jean mini skirt and red cowboy boots, entered the bar holding hands with Brodie, who wore jeans and a black T-shirt. Both grinned widely as they raised their clasped hands over their heads.

Stella reached for the microphone. "Ladies and gentlemen, please welcome the bride and groom!"

The band launched into a song, and Stella's dad closed the door behind the newlyweds.

Before she got too busy, Stella called Diane on Face-Time and showed her the lively scene.

When she glanced at the screen, she found her boss looking pleased and relieved. "And the royal family?"

Stella panned the crowd to the dining area. The king and queen stood watching their daughter surrounded by her friends, laughing...positively glowing. They smiled, eyes glassy, and that's when Stella knew she'd done all right. She turned the phone back to face Diane. "I think they're happy."

"I'd say so. Congratulations, Stella. The job is yours if you want it."

Standing with his friends, Griffin had his eye on Stella as she handled yet another situation. He didn't know what this particular problem was, but the reception had given him a first-hand view of how stressful her job was. No surprise, but she handled everything like a pro. The coolest thing was that she spoke to everyone like they were all in this together—not like they worked for her.

At that moment, she tipped her head back and blew out a breath, and it was the first break in her calm demeanor. He excused himself and headed over. Pressing a hand to her lower back, he kissed her cheek. "Best reception ever. You killed it."

"Thank you." She stepped into his arms and slumped against him. "I think we pulled it off."

"Not surprising." Her stroked her hair. "Anything I can do to help?"

"I love that you ask. You have no idea what an important question that is to someone who's in the thick of things. But no, at the moment, I'm good."

They swayed together, even though the song was Sara Evans' *Suds in a Bucket*. "Diane happy?"

"She said the job's mine."

"Yeah?"

She peered up at him with a humble, almost surprised grin. "Yeah."

"Proud of you." He pulled her in for a hug—only meaning to congratulate her, but these crazy feelings rose up and crested over him. He wanted her so damn much, all the time. He breathed in the scent that drove him wild.

Her cell buzzed, and she pulled away as she read the screen. "Oh, my God."

"What's wrong?"

"Here's one I didn't anticipate." Laughing, she shook her head. "Come on. We've got to get to the mechanical bull. The king's about to ride."

"The *king*?" He hurried alongside her, making their way through the crowd. He noted the formal dining area, once crowded, now only had a handful of people. Everyone else was either on the dance floor two-stepping or waiting their turn to ride the bull.

"Can you excuse me, please?" Stella, always graceful and elegant, pushed through to climb the steps to the operator's box. She reached the woman behind the control panel. "Hi, I'm Stella Cavanaugh."

"Of course. Nice to put a face to a voice."

"That man who's getting on the ride? That's the king of a small principality in Europe."

The woman, in her pearl button shirt and pink bandana, stared at her, mouth hanging open. "Seriously?"

"For real. He's also sixty-one years old, so if you could go easy on him, I'd be forever grateful."

"You got it. And thanks for the tip, but for the record, I adjust according to age and athleticism."

"Oh, good. Okay, thank you." Instead of joining the others, they stood off to the side on the platform and watched the king remove his suitcoat and vest. His wife, the queen, took it from him, clearly unhappy with his life's choices. But Rosie's father didn't notice. He was giddy with anticipation.

"You think I should stop him?" Stella asked. "Maybe interrupt everything for toasts?"

"Now, why would you do that? Look at that smile."

She turned toward him. "This, coming from Mr. Cautious?"

Griffin smiled, pointing to the side of the pen. "His daughter's right there, and she's laughing, so I think it's all good."

And then the elegant, scholarly gentleman tried to hoist a leg onto the horse but failed. Chuckling, he tried again.

"Be right back." Gripping the banister, Griffin leaped over, landing on the padding in the enclosed area. He knelt beside the king and laced his fingers together.

With a regal nod of gratitude, the older man held onto the pommel, stepped into the cradle of Griffin's hands, and hefted himself onto the saddle.

"Let your center of gravity work for you," Griffin said. "You're going to want to lean forward but stay centered." Since he held onto the handle with his right hand, Griffin said, "Keep your left hand in the air, and your knees bowed inward—you're using your thighs to stay on. Most of all, have fun."

"Thank you," the king said. "That was very kind of you."

Stepping out of the ring, Griffin motioned to the ride operator. Slowly, the machine started rocking, and the king burst out laughing.

"Go, Papa," Rosie shouted.

"Woo hoo," Vivi, the princess's sister—who looked nothing like the refined, elegant Rosalina, called.

Stella came up beside him and reached for his hand. "That was nice of you."

He leaned down. "Soon as we get home, I'm not going to be nice at all."

She shivered and gave him that wicked smile that set his blood on fire. "I can't wait."

They didn't get home till after two in the morning. Stella had gone straight for the shower, while he'd gotten Austin to bed.

The house quiet, Griffin boiled water for her tea—her nightly ritual—and made a plate with some crackers and cheese. Maybe he'd slice an apple, too. He knew she hadn't stopped to eat tonight, so yeah, he'd add that.

He couldn't believe how well the reception had gone. His heart filled with affection for Stella. She'd risked her career to give Rosie the reception she wanted. Diane hadn't done that—she'd gone along with the queen's wishes. Because it was the right choice for the business.

But Stella always went with her gut. She was strong, fierce, and loving.

And if he didn't fuck her right now, he was going to lose his shit.

Carrying the mug and plate up the stairs, he realized

he'd stopped listening to his instincts the night of the accident. But for eighteen years, they *had* worked for him. He'd never gotten hurt or injured, and he'd done some damn risky things.

When he compared the first half of his life—the wild, crazy adventures he'd had as a kid, the whole-hearted way he'd loved Stella, to today, when he lived in an apartment over the shop and kept his business running and little else…well, it became pretty clear he had a problem.

And there was no one better to fix it than Stella. His uninhibited, free-spirited, gorgeous woman.

And all he wanted to do was show her how much he appreciated her.

He pushed open the bedroom door, the air humid from the shower. The lights were on, the bathroom door open…and Stella was passed out, face-down on the pillow.

He set the food on the tall dresser and went to her side. Brushing the hair away, he kissed her cheek. "Let's make it real." The words tumbled out, and his heart pounded. Even though she was asleep, panic teased the edges of his mind, stirring shit up.

But he meant it. He did.

"Let's get married."

No, he couldn't control his world with her in it.

But then the world isn't made for us to control it.

He'd failed her once before.

He wouldn't do it again.

Chapter Twenty-One

Damn, it was cold out here, but Stella wanted a Christmas tree, and by God, he'd get her the biggest, best Douglas Fir on the farm.

For whatever reason, she'd figured the better choices would be farthest from the parking lot, so they'd hiked deeper into the woods. Griffin lagged behind, listening to her happy chatter and Austin's quiet replies. It made him happy, this little temporary family they'd created.

Not a real one, he knew that. Peyton would come home and take Austin back to San Diego…

Peyton would come home, right? That now-familiar sense of fear buzzed his nerves. It was going on five weeks without a word from his friend. They watched the news every night but hadn't heard anything about skirmishes or fighting. He just needed one text from his friend, one sign that everything was all right.

"This one," Stella declared. "Griffin, we found it. Come here."

He supposed after what he'd lived through, he couldn't

really help catastrophizing. Since that night, the world just seemed scary.

But there was no point in imagining the worst, so he put his fears in his back pocket and stepped up his pace. When he reached them, he found Austin crouching, pushing aside branches to get to the base of the trunk.

"Where do I cut?" the boy asked.

"As close to the ground as possible," Stella said. "We'll need enough trunk to fit into the stand." She smiled up at Griffin. "And that kind of knowledge comes from being the baby of the family. When my older sisters lost interest in holiday stuff, my dad hunted Easter eggs and cut down Christmas trees with me."

He listened to her, but his focus was on the box saw in Austin's hand.

"He's fourteen, and we're right here," Stella whispered.

"I know that. It's fine."

"Uh-huh." She tried to pry his fist open. "You're totally picturing the movie *Saw*."

He laughed, wrapping an arm around her.

As she leaned against him, she tipped her head back. "This is a big one. We might need a wagon."

He wasn't going anywhere. Not while Austin held a saw. "Between the three of us, we got this."

"Yeah, but the branches are going to drag on the ground. And we're pretty far. Let me get a wagon. Be right back." She took off.

Griffin watched Austin's body shake with the effort of sawing. "How's it going?"

"Not good."

He crouched beside him. "You need a hand?"

"No."

Of course not.

But then, Austin's head came out from under the tree, and he sat back on his heels. He didn't say anything, just wiped the perspiration off his forehead.

"It's a thick trunk. We could take turns."

Austin nodded, but he didn't hand over the saw. He seemed distracted. And then he looked down at the snow and said, "Uncle Griffin?"

Usually, he only referred to him as uncle when he talked about him to other people, as though explaining the validity of the relationship. It seemed like an answer for why he wasn't staying with his grandparents.

So, to hear it now? In that…thin voice?

"Yeah?" he said it quietly, gently, appreciating this rare moment of vulnerability.

Austin drew the side of his hand under his nose and wiped, his breath coming out in a white fog. Looking at the saw, he asked, "What happens if my dad doesn't come back?"

The words made a clean slice right through his heart. Okay, he hadn't expected that.

But if it's on my mind, it's got to be consuming Austin's thoughts.

I should've addressed it sooner, dammit.

He wanted to reassure him, but empty words and promises wouldn't help him sleep at night. And if he thought about it, Austin hadn't asked if his dad was okay.

What will happen to me.

That's what's on his mind. That's the question that needs to be addressed.

And it's a good one. "What do you want to happen?"

"I want to live with you." He cut a glance to Griffin, hesitant, wary…unsure.

But again, he couldn't give empty promises. "I can't

tell you for certain what will happen because your dad's got a will, and I don't think he listed me as your guardian."

A flare of anxiety lit his eyes.

"But you're fourteen now, and the court will listen to you." He touched Austin's shoulder to emphasize his next point. "You're going to have to tell the judge what you want, and you'll have to need to be very honest and very real."

"Will they listen to me?"

Great question. "It depends on the judge who hears your case, but again you're fourteen."

"But my grandpa was a judge, and everyone listens to him."

"True, but you'll be fifteen in a few days. That gives you a say."

"If you and Stella got married, would that help?"

His body warmed at the thought. "It could. But I'm not sure imagining what-if scenarios in this situation is helpful. First of all, the probability of your dad not coming back is low. Secondly, yeah, you'd probably go live with your grandparents, but I'm not going anywhere. I was there when you learned how to ride a bike, and I'll be right by your side when you graduate high school. I'll probably be wheeling you down the hallway in your old folks' home." In the perfect quiet of the woods in early December, Griffin could almost feel the boy's fears. "Austin."

The boy looked up with cautiously hopeful eyes.

"I will always be here for you. And if you want me to fight the Pilsons for custody, I'll do that. My family's powerful, too."

"So's Stella's."

"That's right. Your grandparents aren't bad people. They just have a very fixed idea about how to live. Their daughter went off the rails, and they're convinced they know how to keep you from doing the same thing."

"By cutting my hair?"

"I know. It's stupid, but they do love you."

"I don't like their love."

Whoa. This kid... "Then, I'll fight to keep you with me. Because I love you, and I want you to feel safe and happy." He tipped the boy's chin with a gloved hand. "You believe me?"

His eyes turned glossy, and he swallowed hard. "Yes."

Griffin brought him in for a hug. "I will always fight for you."

A fire crackled in the hearth—yeah, he had a fuckin' hearth—Christmas carols played on the built-in speakers, and the living room was aglow in strings of tiny white lights.

The house smelled of woodsmoke, pine, and sugar cookies.

His dad and Lulu were in the kitchen cooking up a storm, and Mrs. Cavanaugh was leading the charge on decorating the tree. Mr. Cavanaugh sat in a chair by the fireplace, Rocco curled up on his lap, reading a book aloud.

And Austin...

Austin was chasing Posie around the room, flapping his arms like he was a fairy, too, both of them laughing.

Stella came up just then, sliding an arm through his. "It's perfect."

Now it is. "Yeah."

And right then, Griffin knew he could have this life. It was his to take. He lifted her hand. "You like that ring?"

Hope flared in her eyes. "I don't like what was in your heart when you bought it."

"Good point." He kissed her knuckles. Tomorrow, he'd go back into town. There was only one fine jewelry store in Calamity. Nothing he'd seen a month ago had been quite right, so he'd have them make something.

Something as dazzling as the woman who would wear it.

Oven mitts on her hands, Lulu came out of the kitchen and set a big serving dish on the dining room table. "Dinner's ready."

Only his brothers dropped what they were doing and headed over to grab plates. It was a buffet, so people could do whatever they wanted. Eat, decorate, cook, or fly around the room.

And it was honestly the first time in a very long time that he felt part of his family.

Like instead of being a bodyguard to the people he loved, he could actually hang out with them.

He gazed down at his love. "This is going to be a great Christmas. And I wouldn't have any of this if it weren't for you."

Stella hadn't been inside the auditorium at Calamity High in seven years. She'd been in Theater Arts, so she'd spent a lot of time backstage waiting for her audition. She could remember her stomach heaving at the thought of performing, the anxiety of wanting a lead role, and fearing she'd wind up wife number three in the *King and I.*

Tonight, she experienced a whole different kind of worry. She reached for Griffin's hand. "Are you freaking out?"

"No."

And yet, his jaw was tight. If Griffin was worried about the performance…that made her anxiety skyrocket.

Please don't let Savannah be in the audience.

Or, if she is, please let her like Austin.

Or, if she doesn't, can the kids at least be nice and think he's an awesome musician?

After the Run DMC *Christmas in Hollis* song came to an end, and the group of dancers left the stage, the MC stepped up to the microphone. "That was fun. Let's hear it for the Dancers in 4G. Aren't these kids talented?"

After scattered applause, he continued. "All right, for our next act, we've got a big surprise for you. Austin Greene moved here from San Diego, and he's with us this year while his dad serves in Afghanistan."

The response was thunderous, boots stomping on the ground and shoutouts.

The MC nodded, letting the acknowledgement run its course. And then he made a *settle-down* motion with one hand. "That's right. Austin, we thank your dad for his service. Now, let's welcome him to the stage. Austin will be performing a song he wrote and composed."

The popular kids got catcalls and whistles, the others got a few cheers, but Austin…got pretty much nothing.

And that pissed Stella off. At the very least, the teachers and parents knew better. So, she started clapping. Between her and Griffin's family, they'd taken up two entire rows, and the entire block of them got rowdy, raising the roof.

True to himself, Austin ignored them completely. He just came out on stage, adjusted the microphone, and said, "Okay, settle down."

Stella and Griffin cracked up.

"Yeah, so, I can't take all the credit for the song I'm playing tonight because I had a lot of help. And I'd like to invite my collaborator out here to perform with me. Gigi?"

Her sister came out to pure, shocked silence. And then someone said, "Wait, is that Gigi Cavanaugh?"

"Oh, my God, that's Gigi Cavanaugh."

But before the audience got carried away, her sister grabbed the mic. "Hey, guys. How fun is it to be back at my alma mater? Let's not talk about how long it's been since I've walked these halls." She gestured to Austin. "Okay, so just to clarify, the song we're performing tonight is one hundred percent Austin's. All I did was tweak it a little. Now, sit back and let him show you how awesome he is."

"I'm so scared," Stella whispered.

Griffins squeezed her hand. "It's a great song,"

She knew that. She just didn't know how the kids would react. "You think he's as calm as he seems?"

"Doubt it."

"Thank God my sister's up there with him."

Griffin kissed her palm. "And we're here. He's got a whole army of supporters."

With his guitar out of the case, Austin scraped a hand through his hair and then scanned the audience. Without thinking, Stella's hand shot up, and she waved. He just shook his head and chuckled. He had so much more confidence than she'd ever realized.

Over the low roar of conversation and excitement in the auditorium, Austin began strumming and singing. She wanted to stand up and tell everyone to shut up, forget about Gigi, and just listen to this beautiful song.

But that happened on its own. Because it wasn't a sappy love song. It wasn't even a pop tune. It was lively, it was edgy, and it was Austin's own unique brand of rock 'n' roll. "He's so good."

But Griffin was captivated. Pride lit him up so brightly he practically glowed.

Stella scanned the audience, thrilled to see everyone so into it, moving their heads and rocking out.

And then someone called, "Who's Savannah?"

Oh, God, it's starting. "Shh." Stella couldn't help herself.

"Savannah Owen," someone else shouted.

"Savannah." The taunting began.

"I'm going to kill them." Stella shifted in her seat so she could look around, scouting the audience for a mortified teenage girl.

"Stop." Griffin squeezed her hand. "Watch him."

He's right. She sat back and turned her attention to the stage and found Austin completely focused on his song, his voice never wavering. He was knocking it out of the park. Stella let out a breath. "You're right. He's in his element."

When the song ended, there was complete silence in the auditorium. Fear ricocheted throughout her body. What if—

But then it came, that crack of applause. Austin

looked up as people slowly but surely got to their feet and gave him and Gigi a standing ovation.

Stella grinned so wide her cheeks hurt.

Even if there was fall-out from the Savannah issue, he would always have this memory. He'd won them over with his talent.

"You were phenomenal." Stella pushed through the crowd and pulled Austin in for a bear hug. And—*glory be*—he hugged her back.

She wanted to look in his eyes, make sure he was okay about the heckling—though, it really hadn't been that bad —but more arms pulled him in and took him away from her.

Her mom, dad, Coco, Beckett, and Gigi, Griffin's entire family…the boy was enveloped in love and affection.

And she saw it clearly for the first time right then. Even if the kids did make fun of him, even if Savannah rejected him, Austin would be okay because he had so much support.

As Lulu would have been.

"Who wants to go to Bliss?" her mom asked.

Everyone was excited about that. "Let's do it."

Griffin wrapped an arm around Austin. "Sound good?"

"Sure. Just give me a sec" Austin scanned the crowd milling around the auditorium.

"Half the audience will be heading there right now, so you guys go ahead and get us a table," Stella said. "We'll be right behind you."

As they left, Stella moved to the other side of Austin,

she and Griffin like a brace of bodyguards, both instinctively wanting to protect him. And when Austin stiffened, they both followed his gaze.

"That's her?" Griffin said it low.

Austin gave a curt nod. Strong, courageous boy that he was, he made his way to the tall, pretty girl with long, wavy, red hair.

"She's not smiling," Griffin said.

"But at least she's not with a boyfriend."

"She's fourteen."

"I loved you at fourteen."

He cut her a look, his features softening. "Don't remind me how I felt about you at that age. Even though we weren't dating."

"If Lulu hadn't been crushing on you, believe me, we'd have been dating."

He chuckled. "And I'd have gone to jail."

She let out an exaggerated huff. "Do you honestly not have a single romantic bone in your body?"

"You don't seem to mind the bone I do have."

A laugh burst out of her. "It's one of my favorite things about you." She shut her mouth when Austin reached the girl. "If she so much as gives him a funny look, I'm going to—"

"To what, exactly? I really want to hear this. You going to punch her? Rough her up? What're you going to do to the fourteen-year-old girl who doesn't want to date our boy?"

"It's crowded in here. I could trip her."

"Very mature." When her elbow jabbed into his gut, he grunted.

They watched as the two teenagers talked easily. The girl even laughed at something Austin said.

"Well, would you look at that?" Griffin said. "He has an actual personality. Looks like he's talking in whole sentences."

"What the hell is he giving her?" Stella caught a glimpse of a glossy black box with a gold bow. "That's from Coco's. Please don't tell me he carried a box of chocolates under his shirt? Or in his pocket? He must know better than that."

"It was in his guitar case."

"You saw? And you didn't tell me?"

Savannah looked surprised—and impressed—as she accepted the gift.

"She seems cool with everything," Griffin said.

"She really does. I thought she'd be embarrassed by his song, but she doesn't look it." The couple laughed, and then Austin turned around. "He's coming back. Pretend we're having a conversation."

"We are having a conversation."

She tugged on his shoulder to make him face her. "What, um, flavor ice cream are you getting?"

"You're not nearly as smooth as you used to be."

Laughing, she whacked his arm. "This is a big deal."

"We might not have to worry about flavors."

"What does that mean?"

"If she shot him down, he's not going to want ice cream with our entire families staring at him, asking how it went with Savannah."

"Good point. If that happens, we'll text our moms and go home." *Home.* Happiness infused her. She and Griffin James were making a home together.

Last night, at the tree trimming, he'd asked if she liked the engagement ring.

He's going to propose.

He's going to ask me to marry him, and I'm going to cry like a baby and throw myself into his arms. And then I'm going to text my family and shout it from the rooftops. I'M MARRYING GRIFFIN JAMES.

Waiting for it would absolutely kill her.

As Austin approached, she gave him a big smile…but he breezed right past them.

They quickly fell into step on either side of him.

"Well?" Stella asked. "How'd it go?"

"All right." He depressed the bar that led them out into a bitterly cold night. Headlights flicked on in the parking lot, and engines rumbled.

"She looked happy with the chocolates." In her high-heeled boots, she had to work harder to keep pace their long legs.

Griffin clicked the keypad, and the lights flashed on his truck. They got in, and Stella rubbed her hands on her pants. "Turn on the heat. It's freezing."

"If I turn it on now, it'll just blow cold air on you." He fired up the engine.

Stella glanced at Austin—and the boy smiled back at the inside joke.

Oh, my God. He smiled.

That means he's happy.

Yes.

Night made.

She tried to keep her voice casual, but she was dying for the details. "Looks like it went well with Savannah."

He murmured a quiet, *Mm-hm.*

"So, what happens now?"

"Nothing. I didn't do it to get something out of her. I just like her."

"Oh, my God, Austin. What did she say?" Stella twisted around to see his face in the dark interior.

Austin glanced out the window. "She said it was a good song." And then his gaze swung back to her. "She liked the chocolates."

The way he looked at her felt like he was thanking her, and it made her heart swell. "I'm glad it worked out so well." When he didn't say more, she asked, "So, where did you guys leave things?"

"She said she'll see me in class."

"Do you want to have her over?"

"To the house? No."

Stella flicked a glance to Griffin to see if he understood why a boy would write a girl a song and buy her chocolates and not want to spend time alone with her.

But Austin caught it. "I like her. I think she's cool, but I don't know her. I'll talk to her at lunch and at the training center." He held up his phone. "I got her number."

"You know that small party we're having for your birthday? Just family?"

He nodded, wary.

"What if we change it? What if we invite some of the kids in the snowboarding class instead?"

He caught Griffin's gaze in the rearview mirror, and they had some kind of silent communication she assumed had to do with the Pilsons.

Idling in the middle of a long line of cars waiting to leave the school parking lot, the red taillights cast a glow on Griffin's strong, handsome features. "If you want to invite a few friends, that's fine."

Austin's tension broke. "Yeah, okay."

"Perfect. We'll have a family dinner Friday night, and

then on your birthday, we'll do something with your friends." Stella settled back in her seat. She didn't want him to see how excited she was. This kid had been through so much, and he was good and smart and mature...she just wanted to make him feel special and loved.

By the time they reached town, the streets were lined with cars.

"You were right," Griffin said. "Everyone had the same idea."

"I'm glad I sent them early." Through the window, she could see their families had dragged two tables together, and they already held ice cream cones. The line was out the door. "Let's park at Coco's. She and Beckett are in for the night."

"You guys get out," Griffin said. "I'll catch up with you."

She kissed his cheek before stepping into the street. The moment she hit the sidewalk, she looped her arm through Austin's, and they entered the crowded parlor.

Hit with the warmth inside, she loosened the scarf around her neck.

Her mom got up to greet them. "Here's the star of the night." She gave Austin a big hug.

The others joined in—Griffin's brothers, his parents, her Dad, Gigi—everyone surrounding him, praising his performance, and Austin just stood in the center of it and drank it all in. Quiet as usual, only tonight he looked as far from broody as she'd ever seen him.

"I'm proud of you, sweetheart." Her dad slung an arm around her shoulders.

"Me?"

"Yes, you. You did a great thing for that boy. He's come a long way since he moved here, and that's because he's been touched by the Stella magic." He wrapped her in his arms. "I'm so damn glad you're home. We've missed you, your special energy."

"Got you your fave." Gigi held out a cone.

She stepped back from her dad and accepted the caramel dark chocolate ice cream. "Thank you." She took a lick. "Yum. So good." She touched her sister's arm. "Thank you so much for working with him."

"Oh, honestly, it was no big deal. It was my pleasure."

"It was a big deal, though. Just you getting up there with him means he won't be the loner new kid anymore. But it's so much more than that. He's only ever played his guitar secretly in his room. If we tried to come in, he'd hide it. So, for him to perform in front of the school? I think you opened up the world of music for him."

"Aw, that's really sweet to hear. But, really, fuck them for trying to suppress his talent."

"Yep. Fuck them."

"Girls." Her mom joined them. "'Screw' them would convey the same meaning."

Gigi and Stella looked at each other, pretending to contemplate the word choice. At the same time, they shook their heads and said, "Nope." And burst out laughing.

"So, what happened with Savannah?" her mom whispered.

"I think it went well. I suggested he invite her and some of the other kids from the snowboarding class to a birthday party next week, and he said yes. So, let's have the family dinner on Friday, and then I'll do something for his friends on Saturday."

"What about having an indoor pool party at the Owl Hoot resort?" her mom asked.

"That's a great idea."

Stella had never been happier in her life. She had her family back, she had her dream career…

And she had Griffin.

Riding high, she gave her mom and Gigi hugs.

Five weeks ago, she hadn't thought any of this was possible.

And now she had it all.

She wouldn't do anything to jeopardize this new life.

Chapter Twenty-Two

THE MOMENT AUSTIN LEFT FOR SCHOOL, GRIFFIN got busy. He had a flight to catch.

First, he called Bryce. As he waited for his shop manager to answer, he watched Stella type up her notes from her early morning meeting. She brushed a lock of hair off her shoulder, exposing the feminine curve of her neck.

Unable to resist, he headed over and dropped a kiss on that soft, scented skin.

Her hand curled around his head, holding him there, and she turned to press a kiss on his cheek. But he tilted so he could catch her lips instead. Everything went hot so fast, just from the touch of her tongue, the softness of her mouth.

Jesus, how could a simple kiss make his heart beat out of control?

"Yeah?" Bryce answered, sounding groggy.

He headed to the sink and poured Stella a glass of water. "Hate to do this to you, but I need you to get up, grab a shower, and get over to the shop."

"What the fuck? Where's the fire?" He sounded more alert.

Griffin brought the glass to Stella, and she mouthed, *Thank you.* "Donny wrecked his bike." Since the winter months were only about repairs, a lot of the temp guys went south, where they could ride their motorcycles. A nomad, Donny spent four months of the year on the road. He'd wiped out in Arizona.

"Is he okay?" A rustling sound in the background made Griffin picture his manager throwing back the covers and getting out of bed.

"Don't know. He texted from the ER. That was the last I heard."

"Where is he?"

He'd already packed a bag, so now he just needed to fuel up and head to the airport. "Small town outside Scottsdale."

"Anyone with him? Who was he riding with?"

"I don't know the details, but as far as I understand he's alone."

"He likes to be off the grid." Bryce sounded exerted like maybe he was hiking up his jeans.

"Which is great until he gets clipped by a semi on a major highway."

Bryce exhaled into the receiver. "Let me guess. He's got no insurance?"

"Right. So, I'm heading to the airport, and I need you to handle the shop while I'm gone."

"'Course. How long?"

"I'll be back on Saturday."

"For Austin's party." Bryce chuckled. "You know, you don't have to be there for it, right? No one's going to drown just because you're not there."

Griffin jolted. Funny how he thought he hid his anxiety. He'd never realized how obvious he'd been. "My kid, my responsibility." The conversation caught Stella's attention, and she turned away from her laptop to watch him. "Look, I have to go. Just tell me you've got the shop."

"I've got the shop."

"Thanks, man." There weren't many people he could trust in this world outside of his family, but he could count on Bryce.

As soon as Griffin disconnected, Stella got up and came over to him. "What did he say that upset you?"

"Nothing." *Oh, what the hell. Just say it.* "He made a joke about me getting back in time for the party because I'm worried someone will drown."

"Ooh, so seen." Her teasing grin made the clouds in his mind scatter.

He wrapped his arms around her. "You probably don't know this, but your smile makes everything better."

"And for a man of few words, you sure have a way with them." She ran her hands up his chest. "Know what *I* have a way with?" Her arms wrapped around his neck, and she licked the shell of his ear. "My tongue."

"True." He watched her unbutton his jeans.

"You think you can spare a few minutes so I can show you?"

Heat flooded him, and his spine tingled. "I think if I missed the flight and had to walk to Arizona, it'd be worth it."

She sank to her knees, yanking his jeans and black boxer briefs down. His cock sprang free, and she watched his expression as she grasped him and swiped the head.

The shock of desire made him sizzle. "You weren't overselling."

"Oh, I haven't even begun."

His hands went to the top of her head, and his hips rocked. Fuck, he needed in that hot mouth.

"Don't rush me."

"Wouldn't dream of it." Though, he was dying for the suction.

She licked the length of him, then ran her open mouth up and down, all wet and warm and luscious.

A flash fire raced down his spine. *So good. Jesus.* His legs shook, and his fingers curled into her hair.

Back and forth, her mouth slid, tongue flicking, working him into a frenzy of need.

And then, with no warning, she sucked him in deep, all the way to the back of her throat. And swallowed.

His back bowed, and he shouted, "Fuck." And then he was thrusting, hands cradling her head. His balls tightened. There was no chance he could last. Because this was Stella. Blowing him. And she was fun and sexy, smart and warm, kind…she was everything, and he was so damn lucky she'd chosen him. "You make me crazy." The words came out a growl. But sensation burst in his chest, a spray of sparks lighting him up from the inside. "Yes, fuck. *Yes.*"

She knew he was about to come because she clamped her hands on his ass, held him close, and let him release right down her throat.

Holy shit. Each shot electrified him. When he had nothing left to give, she kissed the tip of his cock and stood up. "Hope you don't miss your flight. Shame to have to walk all that way."

He laughed, pulling her in for a hug. "I wish I didn't have to leave you."

"Same."

Aftershocks still pulsed through his body, and his legs

were weak, but he grabbed his keys. "I'll see you in two days."

She walked him to the door, fingers tangling with his. "Call me when you land."

"Stella?" He dropped his duffle bag and cupped her cheeks.

"Yes?" she sounded all breathy.

"I'm going to miss the fuck out of you." And then he left.

Because the sooner he took care of things, the sooner he'd be home.

With Austin's gorgeous birthday cake on the backseat, Stella pulled away from the curb. Her sister stood in front of Coco's Chocolates, waving. A rush of affection had her nearly bumping into the car in front of her, but she grabbed the steering wheel and corrected just in time.

She was just so damn happy because getting to know her sisters as adults was a whole different experience. As the youngest, she'd always felt left behind. They'd stopped believing in Santa Claus long before she did. They'd had boyfriends and interests that kept them away from home. She'd just never really been part of their worlds.

And now she was.

As she turned down Sundance Street, she passed the Music Box. She had *so* many memories of that place. Founded by students, the coffeehouse was funded by the town's Youth Commission. A drug-free, alcohol-free space, it held live concerts and gave teenagers a cool place to hang out.

She doubted Austin knew about it since it closed

during the mountain town's harsh winter months. She'd have to tell him. Oh, maybe he could even perform there when they opened in the spring.

Wait a minute.

Oh. My. God.

Pulling over, Stella grabbed her phone out of the cupholder and called her mom.

"Stella?" Her mom answered after the third ring, sounding winded.

"Hey, Mom. Did I catch you at a bad time?"

"No, it's fine. Where are you?"

"I just picked up the cake, and I was driving past the Music Box—"

Her mom laughed. "I'm two blocks away at the yoga studio."

"I interrupted your class? I'm so sorry."

"No, no, we just finished. It's fine. Want to meet for coffee?"

"We might not have time." She could barely suppress her excitement.

"I'm intrigued."

"What if instead of having Austin's party at the hotel tonight, we switched it to the Music Box?"

"That's a great idea, but it's closed in the winter."

"But you must know people on the Youth Commission."

"I do, but it's a pretty large venue for only twelve kids."

"True, but can you imagine Austin and Gigi playing a few songs?"

"I like the idea…I think we'd need a little more for them to do, though. They won't want to just stand around listening to Austin sing."

"You're right." Part of her deflated…but the other part resisted. She could make this work. "Unless we could come up with something else for them to do. Do we know any other local bands who could play?"

"Well, wait a minute. I'm standing outside the Exhibition of Broken Hearts. Callie had the AV department at the high school put up big screens. What if we did the same thing? We could get some video games and controllers."

"Yes. Oh, my God, yes. This is a thousand times cooler than a pool party."

"Let me run in and talk to Callie, see if she can tell me who set her—oh, what am I thinking? I'll just call Aaron. He does all the tech stuff for the foundation."

"Before you do that, let's make sure we can get the space."

"Your dad's on the commission. We can get the space. Okay, let me go. I've got to call him. Oh, and I have to call Harley and Lu, get them to deliver to the Music Box instead. Are we doing decorations?"

"No, this is enough." In fact, it was perfect.

Now, she just needed to convince Griffin. But he wouldn't mind. It was a great idea and totally safe. And her family would be there to make sure everything went smoothly.

Nothing could possibly go wrong.

After Stella hit send, she pocketed her phone. For Griffin's peace of mind, she'd been sending him footage of the party. Sixteen kids had shown up—and that was okay because some were siblings, and one was a friend in town visiting—and she had her parents, Coco, Beckett, and Gigi.

It was just…he hadn't read her original text yet, telling him about the change of venue.

Not that it was a big deal. In fact, it was safer at the Music Box than it was at a pool party.

So, it would probably be all right.

She just didn't know why he hadn't looked at his phone all day.

Sure, he was traveling. He'd had to handle Donny's arrangements—and there were a lot. Without insurance, the hospital had wanted to transfer him to another facility. But Griffin had insisted he have the best care.

Since then, he'd had to check out of the hotel, return his rental car, catch his flight…and then he had a two-and-a-half-hour drive home from the Idaho Falls airport.

When he did read her text, he'd worry. She knew he would. He might flip out at first. But she'd keep sending him brief recordings to show how chill the party was.

Stella: It's going great. Kids are happy. Everyone's well-behaved.

She'd left Austin mostly alone, but as she passed by him, she said, "Hey, guys. Need anything?"

Her mom had ordered more food than four football teams could eat in a week, but she understood. Everyone wanted things to go well for this boy who'd won their hearts. He didn't need friends in school as long as he had the kids in his snowboarding class.

"No, this is great," Savannah said. "Thank you so much."

"It's my pleasure." Austin didn't seem mortified at her intrusion, so she continued. "So, you have your first competition on Friday. You guys ready?"

"Oh, it's not a big deal," one of the girls said. "It's not a real competition."

"It's just us and some other beginner classes," Savannah said.

"It doesn't have to be the X Games for it to be real," Stella said. "But I think with that attitude, you'll do great. You won't be nervous."

Austin said nothing, of course, but he seemed happy.

"What do you think, should we open gifts?"

But just as Stella asked the question, Gigi got up on stage and turned on the microphone. "All right, you guys, you ready to rock?"

The kids shouted and clapped. *Awesome.* They were really into it.

"Get up here, Austin," Gigi called.

"Oh, my God, go." His friends pushed him toward the stairs. "Do it."

He grinned and headed over. Bypassing the stairs, he placed his hands on the stage and leaped up. Gigi had already set his guitar by the mic stand. "We're taking requests so, what have you got?"

The kids moved closer, shouting out familiar song titles.

This is so great. Wanting to share the awesomeness, she looked for her parents and found them guarding the door. She texted her mom.

Stella: Everything all right?

Just then, Gigi and Austin started strumming, and she whipped around to watch.

After a moment, her mom came up to her. "He's so good."

"I know." Stella glanced behind her to find her dad still at the door. "Everything all right?"

Her mom shrugged. "Eh. You know how it goes with teenagers."

"What does that mean?"

"A group of kids tried to get in. We explained it was a private party, and they went away."

A *group*? "So, we're good?"

"We're good."

They turned back to the stage, and all her worries went right down the drain when she saw Austin in his element, and the kids rocking out to the performance. She pulled out her phone and recorded for a minute, then hit send.

Stella: He's a star. It's going so well.

Stella: Can't wait to see you.

Before she could drop her phone into her purse, it vibrated. *Griffin.* She answered while already on the move toward a quieter space. In the hallway that led to the bathrooms, she said, "Hey. Where are you?"

"What the hell's going on?"

Her heart started pounding. *But it's all right. I expected this.* "No, it's okay. I promise. It's going great."

"Stella, we agreed on a pool party. Not a rock concert."

"Have you landed? Are you on your way here?"

"Just got in my truck and plugged in my phone. I ran out of power last night because I wound up not checking into the hotel. I've been dealing with Donny and insurance issues. Look, I need you to shut this down."

"What? Why?"

"Come on, Stella. You know how it works. Someone posts pictures on social media, the word spreads, and pretty soon we've lost control of the situation."

"We're not…Griffin, it's not going to be like that. My parents are here. Gigi, Beckett, Coco…we've got this."

"Gigi Cavanaugh's playing. Of course, kids are going

to try to crash the party. Think back. You would've done the same thing."

I would. "But we won't let them. I'm telling you, we've got this."

A cluster of girls came out of the bathroom, and she stepped out of their way. "Besides, I can't shut it down. That would mortify him, and he's having a really good time. He's with Savannah. Griff, he's really happy."

"Fine. Let him play a song or two, play a few games, but then I need you to kick everyone out. I'd rather embarrass him than have him go live with the Pilsons." The line went dead.

Oh, fuck.

He's really pissed.

Anxiety had her racing back to the main room. She just needed confirmation that everything was under control.

Only, by the time she got back, her guest list of sixteen had doubled.

A chill skittered down her spine.

It's okay. Everyone's behaving well. She hurried over to her mom. "How did they get in?"

"Your dad checked. Looks like the bathroom window."

Shit. "Griffin wants me to shut down the party."

"What? Why?" She tipped her chin toward Austin. "He's having the time of his life."

Laughing, he was surrounded by three guys and Savannah. He was making friends.

"Mom, if I send everyone home, that's what they're going to remember. Not how cool the party was, not how great Austin is, but how we kicked everyone out an hour into the party."

"It's your call, but if you want to keep it going, we've got six adults covering the entry points."

"Except the bathroom."

"No, we sent Beckett that way. No one's getting past him."

"I'm not sure what to do."

"We'll do whatever you want."

The only reason to shut it down was for Griffin's peace of mind. But he was a little irrational about these things, thanks to what happened with Booker. With so many adults here, she just didn't think it could get out of hand.

If she weighed one against the other, the worse outcome would be embarrassing Austin right when he was making friends and having fun with Savannah.

Okay, she knew what to do. "We leave it going, but the minute it starts to get out of hand, we send everyone home."

"That makes sense."

But there was something she could do. Stella climbed the stairs onto the stage. She leaned into the mic. "Hey, guys, remember I told you this is a private party? Well, it looks like some of you invited friends, and that's not cool. We worked hard to make this a special night, but we'll absolutely shut it down if anyone else comes in, okay?" She smiled at the group. "Now, let's have some fun."

There's no way they'd invite more people—not when they'd miss out on Gigi's performance and the video game that hadn't even been released yet.

Thank you, Cassian, for your awesome endorsements.
It'll be fine.

Chapter Twenty-Three

THIS CAN'T BE HAPPENING.

Pacing the length of the police station, Stella watched the officers release the last two kids to their parents. Now, it was just her and Austin. And they wouldn't let her take him home.

Because she wasn't his guardian.

The Pilsons were. And they were on their way.

This is so bad.

Never in a million years could she have anticipated kids breaking in through a basement window. She hadn't even known the Music Box *had* a basement. But the teens had come flooding in. And when the fire marshal had shut down the party, the police found alcohol, so the parents had to come pick up their kids.

The kids who couldn't get ahold of their parents were brought to the station.

When a cop emerged from a room, she rushed towards him. "Hey, I'm Griffin James's fiancée and Austin's staying with us, so I really wish you'd let me take him home."

"I'm afraid we can't release him to anyone but a legal guardian."

"I'm the guardian's fiancée." She flashed her ring.

"Yeah, I know. But to be honest, even if Griffin were here, I'd still have to release him to his grandparents." Given his expression, the officer knew what it meant for Austin to go home with them.

"Please, that can't happen. He lives with us."

"Ma'am, I'm sorry. This is all over social media. That's how they found out. Judge Pilson called us."

"We didn't do anything wrong. It was a good, nice party. None of the kids we invited drink. Austin doesn't drink. We did everything—"

"I'm here." A gust of cold air swirled around her ankles, rising like a wind tunnel until she was fully enveloped in it. Griffin stalked over to them. "Where is he?"

They looked behind him where Austin sat on a bench playing on his phone. Shoulders hunched, body slouched, he'd turned into himself. Griffin strode over there. "Hey, man. Happy birthday." When the boy ignored him, Griffin turned back to the officer. "He's staying with me while his dad's deployed. I'm taking him home."

"I'm afraid it's not that simple. I have to release him to his grandparents."

"No, he's staying with me. He's been with me since his dad left in October."

"I'm sorry, Griffin. They're his family, so you can resolve this with them when they get here. If they let you take him home, it's fine with me."

"He's not drunk. He didn't take drugs. And now I'm here, so why can't I take him home? He didn't do anything wrong. He *lives* with me."

"They're on their way," the officer said. "Hang tight." He went behind the desk to do some paperwork.

Griffin brushed past her to sit beside Austin. "This isn't your fault. You know that, right?"

Austin lowered his phone. "I don't want to go with them."

"I know that. I'm going to take care of it."

"You can't. If my grandfather comes in and says he's taking me home, he's taking me home. And he's going to be pissed at me."

"They won't hurt you, right?" Stella sat on the other side of him. "They've never physically hurt you?"

"No, it's worse. My grandfather will ignore me and take my phone away. He'll ground me, and I won't be able to train anymore."

"But you didn't do anything wrong," Stella said. "There's no reason to do any of that."

"I'll talk to them when they get here," Griffin said.

"If I go with them, I can't have guitar lessons with Gigi."

"You'll still have your lessons when you come visit us," Stella said.

"If he lives with the Pilsons, he'll follow their rules." Griffin didn't look at her when he spoke. "We're not going to have him sneak around and lie to them. It'll just make things worse."

"I'm not going home with them." Austin sat up. "I don't want to."

"And you'll tell them that," Griffin said. "You'll look them in the eyes and tell them you're fifteen years old and you want to stay with me."

Austin let out a huff of breath. "You don't know what you're talking about."

"I can tell them that Peyton wants you with me. I can tell them that *I* want you with me, but I can't tell them you're better off with me. That has to come from you."

"They don't listen to me." He lurched forward, elbows on his knees, pulling on the short strands of his hair.

Stella had never felt worse in her life. The one thing Griffin had tried to avoid—the reason he'd lied to his own family—was now on the verge of happening.

He's going to lose Austin.

Because of me.

Because a simple pool party hadn't been enough.

She'd gone over the top. And now Austin was in jeopardy. "Can I talk to you a second?"

Reluctantly, Griffin got up.

At the counter, she got an officer's attention. "Do you have a room where we can have a little privacy?"

"Yeah, sure." The officer pointed. "That one right there."

They entered a plain room that overlooked the parking lot. It had an empty desk and a few chairs. She shut the door behind them. "I'm so sorry it turned out like this. Everything was going so well, we had all the access points covered, but they—"

"I don't want to hear it. I told you this would happen. I told you to shut it down."

"I know that, but he was so happy. You should've seen him. He was having fun, making friends."

"Yeah, I get it. You wanted to do something great for Austin but look how it turned out. *Exactly* how I said it would. If I'd gotten your first message, I would've told you it's not happening. Because if you'd thought about it for one second, you'd have realized that every kid there was going to upload pictures of Gigi Cavanaugh performing at a birthday party. And those videos would go viral just like that." He snapped his fingers. "So, *this* was going to happen no matter what."

How could she argue? He was right.

He pointed to the door. "And now the boy that I'm responsible for has to go live with the grandparents who demoralize him. Because you just can't stop yourself, I've failed the job that matters the most to me: keeping that kid safe until his dad gets back." He waved her off. "I'm done talking. I have to get out there."

"Wait, I have an idea."

He turned furious. "I don't want any more of your ideas, Stella. It's your stupid fucking ideas that got me into this ugly mess, that has me lying to my own family. Everything was going fine, and the minute you come back into my life, you turn it into chaos. The first time I see you in seven years, you lie about us being engaged? Jesus fucking Christ, the reason we broke up was your crazy plan to kiss your sister's fiancé at her rehearsal dinner. It never stops."

"Lower your voice. I can fix this."

"With more lies? Because I'm done with them. That boy has had enough upheaval in his life to last a lifetime. The only thing I want for him is stability. And now, because you couldn't do a simple damn pool party with a couple bags of chips, he might have to go live with the people who strip away everything that makes him happy. Everything that makes him Austin."

"I'm sorry. I didn't mean for—"

"You never mean for the bad consequences because you never consider them. You had us engaged and buying a house without knowing anything about the situation. I can't even keep track of all the lies. I'm sorry, Stella, but I don't want to live on this razor's edge with you anymore.

This is over. We're done." He threw open the door and came to a hard stop.

A dozen people stood stock-still staring at them.

The police officers, her parents, Gigi, Coco and Beckett, Mr. and Mrs. James…and the Pilsons.

Her stomach heaved, and she went boiling hot. In the next instant, her blood went ice cold.

They'd heard everything.

For one brutal moment, she witnessed Griffin's pain as he looked at his parents.

"We thought it would help if we came," his dad said.

But then Griffin scrubbed his face clean of emotion and faced the Pilsons. "I'm sorry about tonight. About the lies. I hope you understand we were only trying to keep Austin safe."

"That's been our point all along," Mrs. Pilson said. "He's *not* safe with you."

"You haven't changed at all," the judge said with disgust. "We'll be filing a court order in the morning. You've done enough damage to our grandson." And with that, the Hanging Judge of Calamity gripped Austin's arm and led him out of the station.

When Griffin made a move to go, the officer blocked him. "He's been through enough tonight. Let him go. Talk to them tomorrow when everyone's cooled down."

Griffin gave a curt nod and approached his parents.

Stella wanted to follow him, to apologize, explain… she really couldn't take it if he were done with her again. Instead, she reluctantly headed toward her family. Her parents looked at her with nothing but pity, but Gigi and Coco were bristling with anger.

"Are you serious?" Coco asked. "You've been lying to us this whole time?"

"You have to hear the whole story. The first day I got here, I was bringing Austin home, and I overheard—"

"Are. You. Engaged. To. Griffin?" Coco asked.

"No."

"You are unbelievable." And with that, her sister grabbed Beckett's hand and walked out of the station.

"Why?" Gigi looked caught between anger and a willingness to understand.

"Because I love them, and I was trying to make things better."

"Yeah, well, the road to hell is paved with good intentions. God, Stella, when will you finally get that?"

Griffin paced the length of the pit room.

Cue in hand, Declan perched on the edge of the pool table. "I don't know why you're freaking out."

"Because he's with them." Fuck, the way the Pilsons had looked at him...

He's not *safe with you.*

You haven't changed at all.

"Okay, but you said they don't physically hurt him."

What have I done? "You know how bad they are."

"I know it sucks he's there, but it's not going to ruin him. At best, he'll be there a night or two. At worst, he'll stay until you hear from Peyton. But however long, he's a good kid. He's got balls. He'll be fine."

Declan was right. It wasn't the end of the world. *I'm overreacting.* "I'm just so pissed at her. Even knowing what's at stake, she still goes ahead and throws a blow-out fucking party."

"No, that's not what she did. She threw a party for

sixteen kids. And she had her parents, her sisters, and brother-in-law there. She did a good job of covering all the angles. This could have happened to anyone."

If everything Declan said made sense, why was Griffin so damn agitated? "Whose side are you on?"

"I'm on yours. Always yours. But you've got to look at this from a different perspective. You're pissed at a woman who loves that kid enough to get him guitar lessons, put him in a snowboarding class, and throw him a fuckin' awesome party." He huffed out a breath. "You're an asshole to let her go."

"I have an obligation to Peyton, and as long as I'm with Stella, I can't meet it."

"Right because she's out of control, that girl. She brought in strippers, had bowls of condoms in the bathrooms. She's a real menace." Declan tapped him with the pool cue. "She's the best thing that ever happened to that kid. Even better than you."

"Yeah, I'd almost bought into that for a minute there, but you're wrong. The reason I'm not the 'fun' parent is for this exact reason. I'm trying to keep him safe until his dad gets home."

"And she's trying to help him grow into a good, strong man." Leaning over, Declan lined up his shot, slid the cue between his fingers, and...*crack*. They both watched the ball drop into the pouch.

"The only thing on my mind is getting Austin back home with me."

"You get him back by picking him up from his grand-parents' house." Declan gave a chin nod. "So, do it."

"I'm going to. I've got a message in for Peyton. As soon as he makes me legal guardian, I'll be able to get him."

"What the fuck's the matter with you?" Declan tossed the cue onto the table. "We're not those same kids standing in his courtroom. Look, I get it. What he said to us still haunts me—*kidnapped*? *Prison…wrath of fucking justice*?"

Griffin would never forget that terrifying day when he'd stood before the Hanging Judge of Calamity.

"By the facts of the law, you kidnapped a young man who ended up severely injured, cheating him of the life he'd worked so hard for. By the needs of justice, the four of you should go to prison for a long time. However, after taking into account the wishes of the Langstons and the community, the court hereby releases you." The judge narrowed his eyes on them. *"But know that if any of you show up in my court again, I will deliver the wrath of justice upon you."*

"But he said those words in the heat of the moment," Declan said. "When it was fresh, when we didn't know if Booker would get better. Everyone was scared and pissed at us. But Booker did get better, and we're not those assholes anymore, so why're you letting the judge swing his big dick around and intimidate you? He can't *do* anything to you, Griff."

"But he can do something to Austin."

"So, get your ass over there, and give no apologies because you did nothing wrong, and get your boy back." His friend shook his head like he couldn't believe Griffin was so dense. "And then…you get your woman back." He gave Griffin an incredulous look. "You dumped *Stella*. Again."

He knew that. And that was the problem. He loved her. He didn't want to live without her but look what she'd done. "She knew what was at stake, and she still couldn't help herself. That woman's nothing but chaos."

"Nothing?" Declan asked. "She's not the most positive person you've ever known?"

"You don't have to sell me on her. I'm the one who's so fucking in love with her I let her back into my life." He was having a hard time breathing, and his friend just stared at him. "But I can't live with her—not when I've got Austin."

"Jesus Christ, how do I get through to you? You think if we could go back to that night and shut off our phones, ignore Jamie's text, that we wouldn't do it? You think, if any of us had a shot at a do-over, that we wouldn't take it? *This* is your do-over. It's right here, man. She's here." Declan exhaled. "I get it. You're shook. We're all still shook. But I don't want to watch you give up your second chance at happiness because you can't move on from something we did when we were *eighteen*."

Griffin had to admit the truth. "I don't know how to do that."

"You want to let go of the past? Then start living in the present. And if you can't tell the difference between the two, check and see if Stella's in bed next to you. If she's not, you'll have your answer. You're stuck in the past."

Griffin was going to fix everything.

Last night, he'd barely slept. How could he when the house was so damn silent?

No stairs creaking or guitar strumming, no voices murmuring as Stella and Austin talked downstairs. The energy was gone, making him acutely aware of what he'd done.

He'd handled everything wrong.

Austin was with the Pilsons, and his heart was home with her parents.

Declan's right. I'm stuck in the past.

That night ten years ago had smashed his sense of safety and immortality. It had shattered his idea of himself and his place in the world, and now it lived in him like a shard of glass pushing its way to the surface. If he rubbed his finger over the spot, he could feel the sharp edge. It was a constant reminder.

It was just…how did he get the image out of his head? Watching Booker's body hit the ground…

He smacked the steering wheel. Seeing his friend's crumpled body…Jesus, Griffin had never known terror like that. The heart-pounding, deal-making-with-God fear that Booker had died. The foreverness of it all. The stupidity of their reckless choices.

Heading north on 191, he neared the intersection where he'd turn right to get to the Pilsons.

His gut churned at the thought of confronting the judge. The shame, the remorse…the fucking guilt—

Wait a minute.

Guilt for what? I didn't do anything wrong.

So, we threw a birthday party for Austin. So what—

And then it hit him.

Emotionally, he was stuck in that courtroom facing a judge who'd ripped his character to shreds.

But I'm not that kid.

I'm a grown man with a business.

I'm a good enough man that Peyton trusted me with his son.

I'm not bad.

I'm not reckless.

I'm not an irresponsible asshole.

Jesus, the revelation was fucking empowering.

It was as if he'd had Judge Pilson's hands on his shoulders all this time, holding him down, and now he'd finally shrugged them off.

At the stop sign, he turned right because he had to get Austin back. That was the priority.

After, he'd get Stella.

Because he loved her. With everything in him, he loved that woman.

And he'd gone and hurt her again.

She hadn't done anything wrong. And he didn't think he could stand to let her think for another second that she had.

His stomach squeezed into a fist because…

This blow could be lethal. She might not forgive him for shutting her out a second time.

Griffin stomped on the brake. Jerking the gearshift, he backed up the truck in someone's driveway and turned around.

Sorry, Austin. You're going to have to get through breakfast with those fuckers.

It was time to *live* his life. Be a whole man.

And for the first time, he felt like one. A man.

And this man is going to get his woman.

Maybe he'd live with the trauma of that night for the rest of his life, but he didn't have to let it control him anymore.

When he reached the Cavanaugh's gate, he rolled down his window. Before he could press the intercom button, he heard her mom's voice. "She's not here."

His stomach lurched. "Okay, where is she?"

"At your house." He'd never heard that tone from Joss before. Cold, detached.

The edge of finality chilled him to the bone.

His heart nearly flipped over. "Okay, thanks, I'll—"

"Packing up."

"She's moving out," Tyler said.

"Is she moving in with you?"

"No, she's not." Joss's tone held an edge of, *Thanks a lot, asshole.*

"I'll take care of this. Thank you." He had to get home before she left. Backing out, he turned onto the highway, hit the accelerator, and gunned it home.

It's okay. I've got this. He finally understood what had been holding him back. He was finally free and clear.

She loved him. She'd hear him out. She'd understand.

There was very little traffic this Saturday morning, so he parked at the curb, cut the engine, and strode across the lawn. Throwing open the door, he shouted, "Stella?" Her scent filled the house.

She's here.

At the bottom of the stairs, he gripped the banister and propelled himself up. "*Stella.*"

He burst into the bedroom to find an open suitcase on the bed. *No.* Adrenaline crashed his system.

It's okay. I got here in time.

She came out of the closet with an armful of lingerie, saw him, and jerked to a stop. "Hey." She skimmed around him. "I'll be out of your hair in twenty minutes."

"Nope." He pulled the lingerie out of her arms and tossed it on the bed. "I don't want you out of anything. I want you in my heart, in my bed, and in my life. I fucked up, and I'm sorry. You have no idea how sorry I am."

"Well, that's nice." She went back into the closet and yanked dresses off hangers. "I'd appreciate it if you'd leave. Like I said, I only need about twenty minutes."

"Stella, I made a mistake. You know where that fear comes from."

"Sure do."

"But I see it now, and I don't want to be like this anymore."

"I don't blame you. Shitty way to live. Must be pretty lonely in that little box."

"I'm done with that. Last night was a knee-jerk reaction."

She dumped the pile of dresses into the suitcase.

"Stella, listen to me. I only just figured out the impact that night had on me, how the *judge* affected me. But I see it now. I'm working on it. Now, I can check it when it rears up."

"That's great." She moved around him to scoop up shoes from the floor of the closet. "I'm happy for you."

All those crazy high heels, some glittery, some shiny, all expensive and totally Stella.

He grabbed her shoulders and forced her to look at him. "Stella, I love you." His voice cracked, along with his heart. "I love you so much, and I hate myself for pushing you away last night. I panicked, thinking I'd lost Austin. That I'd failed Peyton."

Finally, she stopped moving. "Griffin, stop. Your words don't mean anything to me. I care about your *actions*. And when we should've been a team, figuring out how to fix the problem together, you turned on me. You questioned my integrity and insulted who I am as a person. And I'm done with that. Do you hear me? I'm done feeling bad about myself because I don't fit into your safe little box. I am always going to be a woman with a big personality and big ideas, and I'm not going to change, not even for you. So, you go back to your cold cereal life, and I'm going to keep on being lemon ricotta pancakes today and cinnamon roll French toast tomorrow."

"No, that's not what I want. That's not what you want. Don't give up on us."

"Now, see, I'm not the one who did that. You did. *Twice*."

"Where are you going?"

"New York. I'm getting my job back."

"What? No. You don't want to work for that woman. You want to run the show here. Diane gave you the job."

"My sisters aren't speaking to me, your family thinks I'm awful, and I'm sorry, but I just don't want to live in a town that thinks of me as the sum of every bad decision I've ever made. This is who I am, and I'm obviously not going to change."

"I don't want you to change. I'm the one who has to change. And I will. I *am*."

"Well, you go on and do it. I wish you the best—for your and Austin's sake. But I can't live my life waiting for the next shoe to drop, worrying that I'm going to make another mistake you can't forgive. Waiting for those two words that break my heart every time. I'm always going to be too much chaos in your small, ordered world. So, this time, it's my turn to say them." She straightened her shoulders and tipped her chin.

Looking him right in the eyes, she said, "We're done."

Chapter Twenty-Four

TWENTY MINUTES LATER, GRIFFIN STOOD ON THE Pilson's front porch in a daze. Before he knocked, he had to get his head on right, transition from the loss of Stella, and focus on bringing his boy home.

Drawing in a breath, he rapped on the door.

"Griffin, now isn't the best time." Mrs. Pilson peered out at him. "I wish you'd called. Let me get Leonard—"

Hard leather soles clacked on hardwood, and then the door swung open. Mr. Pilson, dressed formally in slacks and a cardigan sweater over a button-down shirt, gave him a stern look.

"Looks like you're on your way out." Griffin had no diplomacy left in him.

Seven years ago, Stella had fought for him with everything she had.

This morning…she'd let him go.

She wasn't hurt. She was teary. She wasn't angry.

She was flat.

She didn't care.

I did that to her.

"We're having friends over for brunch, so we don't have time for a visit." Mr. Pilson didn't invite him in.

"I won't be long. I'm just here to pick up Austin."

The stern man narrowed those reptile eyes on him. He opened his mouth to speak, but Griffin was done walking on eggshells with these people.

"This isn't a request. We're not having a conversation about it. I'm responsible for Peyton's son while he's deployed, so I'm taking him home with me."

"Does Peyton know what you did ten years ago?" Mr. Pilson asked.

He was done with intimidation, too. "Ten years ago, five best friends who thought they were invincible acted like dumbass eighteen-year-olds. Since that night, we've lived with the guilt of our bad choices. But I'm not that kid anymore, and I'm not going to be judged by a decision I made ten years ago."

"You never paid the price of your actions, and therefore you never changed," the man said. "That boy's family should have pressed charges, and you should have gone to prison."

"You know what's really cool?" He grinned because he'd never felt lighter, freer, than in that moment. "Those words don't make me shit my pants anymore. And it's because now I know you were wrong about me. You were wrong then, and you're wrong now. That night, we were all scared about the next phase of my life—Calamity was all we'd ever known, and we were heading off in different directions in a big, scary world—so we did something stupid. But you know what else I was? I was a good brother. I was a good student—good enough to get into USC. I was a good son. And a good friend. Now, step aside and let me get my boy. Because the fact is you're not a judge anymore, and you've got no power in the courts or over me."

"Do not underestimate my reach, young man."

"Mr. Pilson, you don't have any legal authority to keep him. You're related by blood to a mother who has no legal custody and has never been in his life. If you don't release him to me right now, I'll go to the police department and have you charged with kidnapping, and I can assure you, Peyton will back me up because he was very clear that he wanted Austin with me and not you."

The man took a step forward, features livid. "Don't you dare threaten me—"

"Stop it." Austin came out of the dark hallway in his bare feet, a long-sleeve T-shirt, and sweatpants. "Stop fighting." His chest rose and fell with labored breaths. "I like living with Griffin. And I like Stella."

"Well, liking them isn't what's important here," the man said. "You need good role models. You need structure."

"You need family," Mrs. Pilson said.

"That's the thing," Austin said. "You don't know what I need because you don't know me. You don't ask questions, and you don't do anything with me. And you're mad at them for lying, but *you* lie to me all the time. You try to trick me into doing things your way." He tugged his hair at the roots. "I hate this haircut. You told me I was getting a trim, and you pretended to watch a football game." He shot a look at his grandfather. "You don't even watch sports, but you pretended you were into it so I wouldn't notice that lady cutting my hair. So, you do it, too. You just tell yourself you're doing it for my own good. But you're not. You're doing it because you want me to be like you. But I don't want to play soccer or join the choir. I want to play my guitar." His accusing glare toggled between his grandparents.

For a moment, neither responded. Both seemed a little uneasy. And then Mr. Pilson said, "You were playing the guitar deliberately to defy me." But he'd lost some of his power.

"I was playing it because I like it. It makes me feel right in my head. I *need* to play it." Austin took a breath, lowering his hands. "You say you want to give me structure but you really just want me to fit in some box. Griffin does all the things you want him to do like make sure I do my homework and eat vegetables and get enough sleep, but he also lets me be me." He took a few breaths. "I'm going home with Griffin because that's where I want to be, and that's where my dad wants me to be. And if you have a problem with it, you can talk to my dad." He turned and went into his bedroom.

Silence hung in the room. Pride filled him, and Griffin wanted to hug that boy. "I've been waiting for that."

"To get your way?" Mrs. Pilson asked in a bitter tone.

"No, for him to find his voice." But at the same time, it crushed him, because the only reason Austin had gotten there was because of Stella.

And they'd lost her.

The steak they'd grilled last night lingered in the air, along with the pine from the Christmas tree.

Which meant the house didn't smell like her anymore.

To make things cheerful, he'd kept the lights on the tree, but it wasn't working. It wasn't about decorations or presents or a crackling fire or hot chocolate. It was about people. Relationships. Love.

It was about Stella. She was a star, and he was forever caught in her orbit.

He and Austin sat at the kitchen table, the only sound the clinking of spoons against bowls as they ate their cereal. He needed to talk to the boy like Stella did. "What did your dad say about the chocolate?"

"He said now they have to stay over there longer since there's no way they can eat everything Coco sent them."

They'd awakened this morning to an email from Peyton. He couldn't talk on the phone, but he was okay, and he promised to write the Pilsons and tell them to back off. "Good to know he's okay."

"Mm-hm." Austin spooned more cereal into his mouth.

Why did Stella find conversation with a teenager so easy? *Try.* "There's no training this week because of the holiday break."

"I know."

"So, I thought we could go snowboarding ourselves every day after school."

Austin stopped eating, his mouth just above the rim of the bowl. "Can I see if some of my friends want to come?"

"No, it'll just be us. I don't want to be responsible for your friends." The words landed on the table like a dead fish.

I can't believe I said that.

"You're not *responsible* for them. We're just boarding with them on the same slope."

"I know. Sorry. Of course, you can invite them."

"'K."

Again, silence descended on them. Maybe he should keep those Christmas songs going all day long. That might cheer things up. "Juice?"

"Orange juice tastes gross after milk."

Griffin grew exasperated. He'd relied on Stella to fill the silence—

No, that's wrong. She had things to say because she was an interesting person who tried things, who put herself out there. She lived life. And she got Austin living his.

Stella told stories. She shared her thoughts.

What stories did Griffin have? "You want to come with me to the shop one day? I'll show you this sick Ducati 900 I just finished."

"Cool." Austin shook out the last of the cereal into his bowl.

Griffin scraped his chair back. "You want me to make your lunch?"

"Nobody brings lunch. It's lame."

What? "You always bring lunch."

"That's because Stella made it."

"Are you saying you didn't want to hurt her feelings?"

"No, she made cool lunches. Everyone came over to see what I got."

"So, I'll make what she makes."

"You can't. You're not like that."

"Like what?"

"Fun."

"I'm not fun? I'm taking you snowboarding after school."

"Yeah, but that's different. Stella's always coming up with fun ideas. I never know what I'm going to get when I open my lunch." He caught Griffin's eye, obviously picking up on his confusion. "You're a good person. You make my life good. But Stella makes it fun." He slurped the rest of the milk out of the bowl. Finished, he dropped the spoon in and pushed his chair back. "It's boring without her."

"It really is." When he was nineteen, he'd had stolen moments with her. It had been thrilling, exciting, and wild.

This time, he'd gotten to play house with her. He'd gotten to live with her, and no question about it, she brought joy and laughter and depth to his life.

He missed her. Only this time it was so much worse.

This was a soul-deep ache.

Griffin exhaled. "I blew it."

"Obviously. So, why you're just sitting around here? Get her back."

"She moved to New York. She took a job."

"No, she didn't." Disgusted, he put his bowl in the sink. "She told Diane she'd stay through the holidays because of all the weddings." He started out of the kitchen but stopped, holding onto the frame of the door. "Ever since I was little, I put myself to sleep at night making up songs in my head. I only got to play them because of Stella. She'd just met me, but she got me better than anybody. You're a dumbass if you let her go."

When Griffin entered Calamity Joe's, he found the three Cavanaugh sisters seated at a round table. He cut across the room and pulled out the fourth chair. "Hey, thanks for meeting me."

Each had an espresso drink, and there was a basket of baked goods between them.

"I only have a few minutes," Coco said. "It's a huge week for us. Everyone buys last-minute chocolates for hostess gifts."

He nodded. This wouldn't take long. "I love your sister."

They all stopped chewing.

"And I've lost her again. Last time, she fought for me, but I was too stupid to get out of my own head and be with her. This time, she's not fighting. She's done."

"Well, that's what she does," Gigi said. "She runs. At least this time, she's self-sufficient instead of taking off with my parents' emergency credit card."

"She's taking off because we all kicked her to the curb."

"Well, she lied to us," Lulu said. "I can't even wrap my head around the fact that I trusted her. I let her back into my life, and she…she was just lying to me the whole time."

"And I'm here to tell you why."

"It doesn't matter," Lulu said. "There are only so many times you can let someone back in."

"God, I hope not, or else I've lost her for good. Let me ask you something." He spoke to Coco. "Imagine you come home from work, you've got Posie with you, and you overhear someone telling Beckett that they just don't understand why a grown man wanted to spend so much time with a baby girl."

Coco bristled. "I'd tell them to fuck right off."

"Okay, but what if the person was trying to take the baby away from Beckett? Because the Pilsons have been escalating their battle from the minute Peyton dropped Austin off with me. They found out before I did that he'd gotten suspended and showed up at my house. Would you tell them to fuck off if you knew they had the legal rights to take your baby away?"

"No." Coco eased back in her seat.

That took the righteousness out of all three women.

"Right. Well, you know how hard Stella loves. She heard what the Pilsons said, and she was standing right next to Austin. So, she said we were engaged. And I could've told them we're not. Right then and there, I could've debunked the whole thing. But…Christ, do you know what it's like living with that threat every minute of the day? Peyton gave me a big responsibility, and then I've got these powerful people working behind the scenes to prove I'm unfit. I was relieved that the lie got them off my back. Trust me. She hated lying to you guys as much as I hated lying to my family. But for Austin?"

"It was worth it," Lulu said.

"Damn right. And I'm going to bet you feel the same way I do, that having Stella in my corner makes me feel pretty damn invincible. If the ship's going down, she's not letting go of my hand and drifting off alone on her raft. She's not only going to tread freezing water with me, but she's going to send up flares and get the damn Coast Guard to come rescue us in the next five minutes." He gave them a look that said, *Am I right?*

All three sisters cracked a smile, and Gigi nodded. "She'd absolutely do that."

"You're right," Lulu said.

"So, what are you going to do?" Gigi asked "What do you want us to do?"

"I'm glad you asked. I have a plan, and I need all of you to help me pull it off."

───────

Stella threw open the door to find her entire family in the living room, waiting for her. "Sorry, I'm late. One of my brides had a total meltdown. After a year of planning, she's decided she hates the cold, hates the mountains, and wants to get married on a beach." She rolled her eyes.

Lulu sat stiffly, Gigi smiled, and Coco was changing a diaper, so it was only her mom who responded. "So, how did you talk her down off the ledge?"

"I told her she could totally do that, she'd just have a smaller guest list since a lot of people can't afford the airfare, hotel, and the babysitting costs of a tropical wedding. Of course, she didn't like that, so I suggested a beach *honeymoon* instead. And then she was back to the original plan and discussing hors d'oeuvres." She dropped her purse on a side table. "Okay. Thank you guys for coming. I have something to say, and I'd rather talk to everyone at the same time."

Finished snapping the onesie, Coco lifted her baby and set her on her lap.

"Number one, I'm staying in Calamity. I like my job —no, I love my job, and I'm damn good at it, so there's no way I'm going back to running errands for Taji Nash."

"I'm so happy to hear that." Her mom started to get up, but Stella raised a hand. *Hold on, please.*

"Number two, it sucks being the baby of a family like this. I'm not like you guys. I don't have an amazing singing voice or a passion for…well, anything."

"You have a passion for life." Lulu said it quietly but surely.

Startled, Stella took a moment to decide whether Lulu was slamming her or complimenting her. "Thank you. I think you're right about that. And I think that's what makes me a good party planner because when I'm pitching a certain menu or stock card, it comes from a place of truth. I really am that excited about finding just the right font. Anyhow, I decided that if I pick up and move every time I screw up, I'll wind up being a nomad."

"You didn't screw up," Lulu said.

Shocker number two had Stella's jaw snapping shut. Was her sister seriously defending her right now?

"If I heard anyone insinuating Xander was a pedophile…who's to say I wouldn't have done the same thing?" Lulu said. "With Austin standing right next to you, you had a split second to turn the tide. And you said what you said."

"I just wish you'd trusted us enough to tell us the truth," Coco said. "There's a cone of trust with sisters."

"She would have eventually," Gigi said.

"Okay, this is not what I was expecting when I walked in here." *But it was damn nice.* "What I wanted to say is there's never a good reason to lie or manipulate to get things done. Instead of telling the Pilsons we were engaged, I could've said I've known him for years and can verify he's an amazing man and that my entire family and most of the town would back that up. And then I could've stood beside him as he continued to deal with whatever they'd thrown Griffin's way."

"Yes, you could've done that," her dad said. "But then you wouldn't be you. And, Stella, sweetheart, you've got big, bright ideas. You shine."

"Thank you, Dad." They were making this conversation awfully easy on her. "But the thing is, growing up the daughter of a Hall of Fame quarterback and a supermodel, the sister of a rock star and a world-class chef…you guys were larger than life. You're all talented and driven and ambitious and…amazing. And I just wasn't. And I think I learned to rely on my personality. I mean, seriously, you don't know what dinner conversation was like for me. You guys had such big news to share, and what could I talk about? I got hit in the head by a volleyball. I didn't get the lead role in the play."

"Well, I didn't have big news, either," Coco said. "I don't have any particular talent."

"But you were driven, and you were involved in so many things. In any event, the only thing that worked for me was my ideas. I could just see it in people's eyes when I'd suggest something, and when you get reinforcement like that…you run with it."

"You're so much more than your ideas, sweetheart," her mom said.

"Well, thank you." Leaning into her finale, she turned to Lulu. "So, I'm sorry I kissed Trace. Worst idea ever. And I'm sorry I lied to Austin's grandparents. Second worst idea ever. But I'm not sorry for who I am. So, I'm staying. I'm keeping my job. And you guys can either accept me"—*love me*—"for who I am, or you can go back to hating me."

Her mom stood up. "We love you."

"No one hates you, drama queen." Coco passed the baby over to her dad, got up, and hugged her. "You're my sister, and I love you, and you don't need to run away whenever you do something stupid."

Tears spilling down her cheeks, Stella choked on a laugh.

"I think you're pretty badass, and there's no one I'd rather have in my corner." Lulu joined the hug.

Stella found herself in the middle of a circle of love and affection, and she let it sink in.

I'm finally home.

Now, she had to figure out what to do about Griffin.

Chapter Twenty-Five

Stella thumbed through two weeks of Griffin's texts.

Griffin: I wish you'd talk to me. I miss you so fucking much.

Griffin: Wish you were here. I miss the way your perfume lingers in the house.

Griffin: We keep the Christmas lights on, but we both agree your smile shines brighter.

Griffin: Are you okay? I miss talking to you.

Griffin: I hate how I treated you in the police station. Been thinking about it a lot, the way I shut you out.

Griffin: The other day, I realized I've been stuck in that courtroom when the judge made me feel like the lowest form of humanity for what we did that night. Wanted to tell you that in person. Think we could meet up?

Griffin: I love you.

Griffin: I fucking love you.

Griffin: Wish you'd talk to me.

Griffin: Can we talk? I just miss you so much. I can't stand it.

Griffin: I don't know if you're aware of this, but when you're thinking, you get this little divot right between your eyes. It's cute. I want to kiss it.

Griffin: You know what I miss? Just talking to you. You make me laugh. You make me feel good. Do I do that for you?

Griffin: Can't sleep. For a long time, I wanted to go back in time to that night with the guys and make a different choice. Now, I want to go back to that night in the police station. I want to walk in the door and go right up to you, pull you into my arms, and say, You all right? I want to hold your hand as we face the Pilsons, the officers, and our families. I want us to be a team.

Griffin: I promise to never turn on you like that again.

With each text, she felt herself weakening.

Oh, another text came in. Right then.

Griffin: I love you.

She ached for him. She was coming dangerously close to forgiving him.

But he'd always been great with words.

It was his actions she couldn't trust.

Her cell phone vibrated on her desk. *Austin.*

Well, that cheered her up. "Hey. How's it going over there?" Even though she and Griffin were kaput, Austin continued to get off the bus at the hotel and spend some afternoons with her. She loved that boy.

Actually…confronting the judge and taking Austin home…that was definitely action.

Maybe he really is changing…

"It's all wrong," Austin said.

Fear sped through her so fast, her fingertips burned. "What?" She got up. "What's wrong?" They were setting up for a New Year's Eve wedding. It had to be perfect.

"You said it shouldn't look like Christmas."

"That's right." She pulled her parka off the hanger in the closet. "What's he doing? Is he putting up garlands? Don't they have my schematics?"

"They've got strings of lights. Red and green. Big bulbs. It's ugly."

"*Christmas lights*? What in the world? Put Carl on the phone."

"I can't."

"What do you mean you can't?" She grabbed her purse off the hook and reached into the inside pocket for her keys. "Where is he?"

"He went to the storage room to get more lights."

"*More* lights? Are you serious?" She raced across the office. It was Christmas Eve, so of course, Quinn hadn't come in. No one had. "Don't go anywhere. I'm on my way."

She was already late for Christmas Eve at her parent's house. She should just text Carl and tell him to go home. They could meet next week and fix things then.

But wait, what's Austin doing at the chapel?

Oh, dammit.

She'd just run over there and check on things.

She'd only be a few minutes late for dinner.

Stella fumed the entire ride. Carl should've waited until next week to work on this wedding. He certainly shouldn't have enlisted the help of a fifteen-year-old boy. She was going to have a conversation with that man.

Strangely, when she got to the parking lot, she found it full.

Maybe there was a service going on?

Cutting the engine, she flipped down the visor to check her lipstick. She'd been so busy all day she'd barely looked up. When had she last eaten?

Griffin wasn't around to fill her minifridge anymore.

And didn't that depress the hell out of her.

Forget it. Let's see what's going on, and then I get to my parent's house and eat with my family.

Her heels clicked on the asphalt. As soon as she reached the walkway, she noticed spots of pink. She reached down and picked one up. Rose petals. She breathed in the lovely, fresh scent.

Wait, what are those? Laminated photographs were strewn along the entire path to the chapel.

She picked up the first one. It was old, a blurry shot of her family at the lake. *That's me.* She must've been two or three. In a striped bikini, she stood at the shoreline watching her sisters play in the water. Other kids were there, but there was one in particular who caught her eye. A dark-haired boy wearing board shorts. He was reaching for her.

Oh. My. God.

That's Griffin. A memory flickered, as subtle as a breeze lifting the edge of a curtain. He'd been reaching for her hand, walking her into the water. Because she'd been scared?

No, because she'd been left behind. Her sisters had gone in, not even thinking about her.

And she'd wanted to play with them more than anything in the world.

In the next photograph, she was seven. She knew because she was blowing out seven candles on her cake in the main dining room of the Homesteader Inn. Her mom had taken her for high tea, just the two of them.

She was sitting up on her knees, leaning forward to blow out the candles, and there were fingers curled around the back of her chair. *Griffin*. She laughed out loud, glancing up the walkway. "Where are you, Griffin James?"

But no one answered.

She picked up the next one. It was the Fourth of July, and the whole town had gathered for fireworks at the lake. Her ten-year-old self gazed up at the sky, utterly in awe of the display. Beside her, Griffin was looking at *her*.

He was *scowling* at her.

She smiled so wide it hurt. "You even wanted to kiss me back then, didn't you?"

Where is he?

Another image showed a bunch of kids snowboarding. She did a hasty scan, looking for them. There, in the back row. *That's Griffin*. In the front of the group was a girl in a white and navy designer snowsuit, her arms thrown open wide.

Show-off.

The next one was Stella's Sweet Sixteen. There were balloons, streamers, and a stack of presents. A handsome, muscular teenager stood to the side of the cake table, arms crossed, watching Stella blow out candles on her birthday cake. Stella had her lips pursed, ready to blow, but the camera had captured the moment she'd glanced at Griffin.

She looked so happy, so full of joy.

She'd loved him her whole life.

Now, the next one, she recognized. *This one's mine.* She'd brought it to Dallas and New York and kept it in a drawer in the carriage house. *How did he get it?* Her mom had to be in cahoots with him.

Wait, Austin had called her.

There's no problem with the staging at the chapel.

What in the world is going on?

She loved this picture. It was a selfie she'd taken of her and Griffin in bed when she was seventeen, the first night they could freely be together. They looked giddy and so in love.

Walking forward, she picked up the next one. Her heart twisted. It was taken at Lulu's rehearsal dinner, well before she'd gotten drunk and messy. She'd never seen this one before. They were gazing at each other with pure adoration.

She loved that man with all her heart. Every fiber in her body ached for him.

And then, at the end of the path, she picked up the most recent one. *This is from the tree trimming.* Arms around each other, she was gazing up at him, while he smiled down at her, their faces bathed in the soft glow of fairy lights.

The promise in their eyes said, *Let's do this forever, okay?*

Her heart thundered. *I can't believe he did this.*

It's so romantic. She neatly tucked the photos into her purse. Whatever he had planned, she wanted to remember this moment forever.

And when she looked up, Griffin was there, kneeling in front of the closed chapel doors.

Stella broke into a run. "*Griffin.*"

He got up just in time to catch her, lifting her and

swinging her around. "I missed you." Setting her down, he kissed her like he'd nearly lost her. Like he never, ever wanted to let her go. But then, arms trembling, he pulled away, resting his forehead against hers. "I'm going to need to stop kissing you for about twenty minutes, okay?"

"No. Don't stop kissing me. Not yet." What was she saying? *Yet? No.* "Not ever."

"You're the love of my life, and I'll never stop kissing you." Cupping her face, his thumbs caressed her cheeks. "But right now, I'm trying to go big, so bear with me." Holding one of her hands, he got back down on a knee and gazed up at her. "Stella Cavanaugh, I have loved you my entire life. I love *everything* about you. Your big personality, your bright, glowing energy, your kindness, and your great big heart. You make me whole, you make me happy, and I never, ever want to be without you again." He pulled a ring out of his pocket, gazing up at her with love and adoration. "Will you stand by my side through whatever life throws our way and love me for the rest of our lives?"

"Well, I'm not keen on an end date because I can't imagine an existence where I'm not madly in love with you, but I'll take what I can get. Yes, Griffin, I'll marry you."

Grinning, he slid the ring onto her finger. It took a moment to get the right alignment since both their hands were shaking. Her heart was just so full.

She held her hand out in front of her to take it in. "This is stunning."

"I know diamonds are traditional, but they're not you. You're passion and joy and zest, and this ring…is you."

"But *five* rubies?" Joy spilled hot and wet onto her cheeks. "It's so extravagant."

"Exactly. You're extravagant with your love. You've filled me up with it, and I want to do the same for you."

"You do, you sweet man, you do."

He stood up. "I'm glad you said yes." Pulling open the door, he said, "It would've been really embarrassing if you hadn't."

Someone whispered loudly, "They're here. Sit down."

The chapel was bursting with people. She was so stunned she just stood there and took it all in. Her parents, sisters, and brothers-in-law took up the first pew on the left, and Griffin's family had the right side. Panning the faces, she recognized her friends, teachers, coaches... pretty much everyone she'd ever known had shown up for...

She leaned closer to Griffin. "This isn't an engagement party, is it?"

But before she could answer, a profusion of sparkling blush-pink tulle hustled toward her. When it arrived, Knox peeked around it. "You ready to get dressed?"

"Me?" She shot a look to her fiancé. For real this time. "We're getting married?"

"Yes, ma'am."

"Right now?"

"That's what I'd like. You in?"

"You bet I am." She threw her arms around his neck and kissed him. "You take my breath away." She rubbed the lipstick off his mouth with a thumb. "See you in a minute."

As she followed Knox, she noticed her sisters and mom breaking away and racing up the aisle. They all convened in the bridal dressing room, and when Knox hung the dress on a hook, Stella recognized it immediately.

"That's the one in your shop?"

Her mom said, "It sure is."

"You should see the cake," Coco said. "You're going to die. It's this luscious tower of strawberries and cream."

"And for the reception, I made all your favorites," Lulu said.

For the first time in her life, Stella was rendered speechless. Her family saw it, and they crowded around her, wrapping her up in their love and support.

"Are you disappointed that you don't get to plan your own wedding?" Lulu asked.

"You've given me literally every single thing I've ever wanted." And, no, she planned weddings for a living. She definitely didn't want to plan her own on top of that.

"Well, let's get you dressed." Her mom ushered her into the changing room.

"Hair up or down?" Gigi stood at the dressing table with an array of hair and beauty products.

"Down, please."

"You got it."

Lulu smiled. "Let's get you married."

Flowers scented the air, candles flickered, and moonlight spilled in through the stained glass windows. Then, in the most spectacular gown she'd ever seen, Stella headed down the aisle on the arms of her mom and dad.

She couldn't stop smiling.

She'd waited for this moment for so long.

All through the years of thinking she'd lost him for good, she'd had this deep-down gut feeling of resistance. Hope had never died because they were meant to be.

And now...

She lost her step. "Oh, my God. I'm marrying Griffin James."

Her dad laughed. "Only if you want to."

"I want to more than anything."

"Then, let's not keep him waiting."

The standing guests smiled warmly as they headed down the aisle. They knew. Everyone knew how long she'd loved this man.

At the altar, her mom took her bouquet and handed it off to Lulu. After a hug and a kiss, her parents took their seats.

With a deep breath, she turned to her groom. "I get to marry you."

Laughter rippled across the room.

She'd meant to whisper it. Well, actually, she'd meant to say that in her head. *Oh, well.* It was true, and she just wasn't the type of person to suppress her joy.

Griffin brought her hand to his mouth and kissed it. Beside him, Austin stood looking grown up in a suit and tie. She mouthed, *Handsome* to him, and his cheeks flamed.

And then the officiant spoke, snatching her attention away from her guys.

"Please be seated." Declan flashed her a grin. "Don't worry. I got a certificate in the mail. I know what I'm doing." He flicked a glance to Griffin. "Pretty much."

Griffin gave him an impatient roll of his hand. *Go on.*

"Right." Declan cleared his throat. "Griffin wants me to thank everyone for joining us at this impromptu affair. He knows it's Christmas Eve, and the fact that you've made their wedding a priority is the very reason he asked you to witness and celebrate the lifelong commitment they're about to make. Because you're their people."

Stella shot a glance over her shoulder and smiled at the crowd, so grateful for their love and support.

"He also asked that I keep it quick, so here we go." Declan unfolded the piece of paper in his hand and read from it. "The road Griffin and Stella took to this moment hasn't been easy, and it's been filled with challenges they weren't prepared for. But they've taken each one and used it to not only grow stronger themselves but to deepen their bond and commitment." He gestured toward Stella. "Since you didn't have time to prepare your vows, how about we let Griffin go first?"

"Oh, I don't need time. I've been rehearsing my vows since I was twelve years old and doodling his name all over my notebook."

Once again, laughter rippled across the chapel.

Declan nodded to her. *Go for it.*

She was so in awe of her groom she could hardly think. *Look at him. This gorgeous man with his thick, dark hair, the sleeves of his button-down rolled neatly to his elbows, exposing the colorful ink on his forearms, is mine.* For good this time.

His eyes glistened, and he swallowed past what she knew was a lump in his throat.

This man was her whole heart and the other half of her soul. "Griffin James, I love you. I love the way you care about your family and your employees and your entire community, and I'm just so lucky to be the one you chose to fall in love with." She clutched his hand. "I vow to love you big and bold. I will love you through chaos and quiet nights, through diapers and rolling walkers, and everything in between. I vow to love you, fight with you, support you, laugh with you, and never, ever leave your side. And I vow to give one hundred percent of myself to you, to us, and to our family."

"Think you can beat that?" Declan asked Griffin.

Their friends and family chuckled, but her groom didn't. He'd grown intense, urgent. "Stella, you're my best friend and the love of my life. I was told to write my vows, but that's not what they are. They're privileges. It's my privilege to wake up to your beautiful face every morning. It's a joy to get to laugh with you, play with you, sleep with you, scheme with you, and watch you change the world with your brilliant ideas. I vow to never give up on us, to love you through good and bad, and to never walk away from us again." He drew in a slow, unsteady breath. "I still can't believe I get to marry you, but tonight, I give you my heart, my commitment, my attention, and my whole self. Wherever life takes us, wherever we wind up, I know that as long as you're with me, that's where I'm meant to be."

Declan looked impressed. "That's good, man. Okay, it's time to exchange the rings."

She gazed helplessly into Griffin's eyes. "I don't have one."

"We got this." Austin dug two gold bands out of his pocket. He handed her one and dropped the other in Griffin's palm.

"I give you this ring as a symbol of my eternal love and commitment." Griffin slid the lovely ruby-studded band onto her finger.

Never taking her eyes off him, she said, "I give you this ring as a symbol of my eternal love and commitment."

"I now pronounce you husband and wife." He looked beyond them. "You might want to cover the kids' eyes for this next bit. Now, you can seal this pact you made tonight with a kiss."

They reached for each other at the same time, their mouths joining, their hearts beating in sync, and their lives forever joined.

Epilogue

GRIFFIN JUMPED OUT OF THE HELICOPTER FIRST. Then, he grabbed his wife's waist and lifted her out. Once Austin cleared the rotors, he waved the pilot off.

"Can I see now?" Touching the blindfold, Stella had to shout over the whumpa whumpa whumpa of the departing chopper.

"Go for it."

"And why is it so cold? It's *June*." Lifting the scarf, she blinked against the bright sunlight. "Oh, my God." She took in the view from the top of the glacier. To the southeast, they could see Idaho. On the other side, the valley of Jackson Hole lay spread out before them, a tableau of neatly delineated ranchland, wildflower-covered meadows, and patches of blue from lakes, ponds, and the Snake River. She burst out laughing. "You guys, what is going on? We have a party to get to."

"Exactly, and we're on our way." Griffin pointed down the mountain. "It's right there."

They'd told Austin they were throwing their first-annual summer solstice party for both of their large families in a small park surrounding a cirque lake. They'd hired a caterer to set up tents, games, and a bounty of food and drinks.

But really, they had an amazing surprise for him.

"You're crazy," she said. "We couldn't just take the shuttle like everyone else?"

"Where's the fun in that?" Griffin asked.

"Are you kidding?" Austin took in the summit. "We're snowboarding down a glacier. In a million years, I never thought he'd let me do this. I haven't even been taking lessons for a year."

What he didn't know—and Griffin wouldn't mention it—was that he'd checked it out first to make sure this particular line was safe. With no crevasses or ice, Fin Bowie had given his approval. Besides, it wasn't a long descent.

"So, this was Griffin's idea, huh?" she asked in a teasing tone.

"It was." Austin nudged him with an elbow. "You're a good influence on him."

"Okay, but I'm the *host*." The sparkle in Stella's eyes belied her objection. "How long will it take to get there?"

"Not long. Let's grab a snack for our growing boy and then head down." Griffin gestured to the tent he'd arranged.

Her hands clapped over her mouth. "What have you done?" They stepped inside to find their snowboards, three backpacks filled with hoodies, helmets, and gloves, and a small café table covered with a white tablecloth. On it sat a bucket filled with ice, champagne, and a bottle of orange juice, and a pewter tray of chocolate-covered strawberries. "This is amazing." She spun around to him. "I can't believe you did this."

"*We* did this. The boarding was my idea, but the snacks…that's all him." Griffin popped the cork and filled two of the flutes. The raspberries at the bottom floated to the top. "What can I say? We know you like to arrive in style. And…" He kissed her cheek. "We love you."

"I love you guys, too." She hugged them each in turn. "So much." And then she pressed a hand over Griffin's heart. "And I love being married to you. These have been the best seven months of my life."

People called married life "settling down." But his life with Stella was full of adventures and surprises. Thanks to her, the bindings had snapped, liberating him…and he was just so damn grateful. "Stella, you're the most amazing person I know, and there isn't a day that goes by that I don't thank the forces that be for letting me share this journey with you." He gripped Austin's shoulder. "You're fearless, and you're smart, and watching the way you live your life, well, it's gotten me here, to this moment when I can trust us all to board down a glacier together." Handing him his orange juice and Stella a glass, Griffin raised his champagne in a toast. "To us."

The three of them clinked and then sipped. Well, Austin guzzled, but that just made Griffin smile.

She reached for a strawberry. "I can't believe you did this. It's amazing and fun and just…perfect." She bit into it. "Mm, this is so good."

"Should be. Coco made them." Since there'd be so much food at the party, he'd only brought two for each of them. So, when they finished, Griffin wiped his hands on a linen napkin and said, "Who's ready to carve this glacier?"

"Wait." Austin set his strawberry stem down. "I know my dad's coming home in a few weeks, and I'll be moving back to San Diego, but I want you to know I'm glad I got to stay with you." He swallowed, running his hands down his jeans. "You make me happy." He fidgeted with the edge of the tablecloth. "I love you guys."

Stella rushed forward and pulled him to her. At first, Austin's arms stayed at his side, but then he wrapped one around her back and used the other to reach for Griffin.

Standing on top of a glacier on a cloudless summer day, the three of them hugged long and hard.

Griffin would miss this kid.

More than he'd ever expected.

But he had the love of his life right here in his arms, in his heart, in his bed, and nothing had ever felt more perfect.

Life is good.

Stella nudged him. Yeah, it was time. They shared a secret smile.

"Let's get going." Griffin picked up a backpack and handed it to Austin.

The boy shook his head. "You guys aren't nearly as clever as you think you are. I already know about the big surprise."

"What?" How the hell had he found out?

"I know you pulled Savannah out of camp and flew her here for the party. We don't keep secrets from each other."

And with that, he went to grab his snowboard, not even trying to hide his smile.

It was a clear shot down the summit, and the untouched powder made the ride unreal.

Stella led the way, Austin followed, and Griffin took

up the rear so he could keep an eye on them. For the past seven months, the three of them had spent a lot of time boarding together. As Griffin got a handle on his anxiety, they'd gradually increased the risk level.

And now? He felt free. The wind whistled in his ears, the sun glittered on the snow, and his heart fucking soared. He'd lost a lot of years to fear, but he was back. And with Stella by his side, he'd live the rest of his life to its fullest.

Breathless, they reached the bottom of the slope. All three of them eager for the surprise, they popped their bindings and headed into the white tent to change into their party clothes. Griffin was so damn excited that he was already on his way out when Austin called, "You think you might want to take off your helmet?"

Griffin's hands went to his head, and he burst out laughing.

As they headed out, sunshine glinted off the two shuttle buses. Their friends and family had already gathered around the picnic tables. He reached for Stella's hand and gave it a squeeze.

As soon as he saw his friends, Austin took off.

When they reached their guests, Stella got up on a picnic table and said, "Hey, guys, listen up real quick. We want to thank you for coming to our first annual summer solstice celebration. Maybe next year you can be as cool as us and board a glacier instead of taking a wimpy ole bus."

Everyone laughed, and one of his brothers called, "I didn't know it was an option."

"Honestly, I didn't either." She grinned at Griffin, and his heart expanded.

It was perfect, this moment. His family, Austin…and

his wife. *Look at her.* That dazzling smile, that sexy body, her happy, fierce spirit.

The only thing that could make this day better would be having his friends here. If they could heal the rift, find a way to forgive each other…but they'd gone off in different directions, and he just couldn't think of a single thing that could ever pull them back together.

"Anyhow, the food's just about ready, and we've got a huge bin of toys for you to play with." She gestured toward the volleyball and badminton sets. "We want you all to have a great time. In the meantime, while the caterer's setting up for lunch, some appetizers will be coming around. Enjoy."

She hurried over to Griffin's side, and they watched the server come out of the tent holding a tray. He moved quickly, ignoring everyone who reached out to grab one of his bruschetta, focused wholly on Austin.

But the boy was talking to Savannah, both of them so deep into conversation they didn't notice the tray.

The man inched forward—he even nudged the boy to get his attention, but it wasn't until Savannah noticed him, that Austin grabbed a bruschetta, said thank you, and kept talking.

"He didn't even look," Stella said. "Are you kidding me?"

Savannah said something that made Austin laugh.

"When she's around, no one else exists." Griffin could relate.

"Okay, that's it. I'm going over there."

He reached for her hand. "Nope, you'll spoil the fun. Just keep watching."

The server cut in between Austin and Savannah to offer the tray to some of the other kids.

And Austin *still* didn't notice him.

Anticipation wound through him, and he chuckled. "Come on, kid."

"Oh, my God, this is killing me." Stella marched over there. "Hey, Austin, can you grab me one before they're all gone?"

"Sure?" Looking confused, like…*can't you get one yourself?*…the boy tapped the server on the shoulder.

The man turned around.

Austin's jaw fell open. "Dad?" His cheeks went red, his eyes glassy, and he flung himself into his father's arms. "Dad." His voice broke.

For the first time in nine months, Peyton and his son were together. They clung to each other so hard they were rocking back and forth.

When Austin tucked his face into his dad's shoulder, Griffin gave into the tears. Stella clung to him, hiding her face in his sleeve.

Her mom joined them. "Is that *Peyton*?"

Griffin could only nod.

"He's back early?" her mom asked.

"Yep."

Joss's lower lip trembled. "You arranged this?"

Stella tugged on his arm. "It was his idea."

And then everyone stopped talking to watch Austin smiling, cheeks glistening, as he said, "You're home."

"I'm home, son."

Thank you for reading YOU'RE STILL THE ONE! If you love a grumpy, tattooed hockey player and want to see him fall head over heels in love with the spoiled princess he's forced to live with for a month, you're going to love THE DEEPER I FALL!

Do you subscribe to my newsletter? Get on that right now because I've got an EXCLUSIVE novella for my readers in 2022! You'll get 2 chapters a month of this super sexy, fun romance! #rockstarromance #whenyourcelebritycrushbecomesyourboyfriend #teenidol

Need more Calamity Falls, where the people are wild at heart?

KEEP ON LOVING YOU
WE BELONG TOGETHER
THE VERY THOUGHT OF YOU
JUST THE WAY YOU ARE
IT WAS ALWAYS YOU
CAN'T HELP FALLING IN LOVE
COME AWAY WITH ME
WHOLE LOTTA LOVE
YOU'RE STILL THE ONE
THE DEEPER I FALL
LOVE ME LIKE YOU DO

Have you read the Rock Star Romance series? Come meet the sexy rockers of Blue Fire:

YOU REALLY GOT ME
I WANT YOU TO WANT ME
TAKE ME HOME TONIGHT

MORE THAN A FEELING

Look for LOVE ME LIKE YOU DO in September 2022! Grab a FREE copy of PLANES, TRAINS, AND HEAD OVER HEELS. And come hang out with me on Facebook, Twitter, Instagram, Goodreads, and Pinterest or in my private reader group.

Excerpt from The Deeper I Fall

TWO YEARS AGO

Tonight, Seraphina Maud Crutchley was a superstar.

She didn't feel like one very often. Rarely, in fact. But in this moment, with the spotlight trained on her as she stood in the middle of the ballroom surrounded by every single luminary in London's elite, she felt a wild mix of emotion: pride, certainly, but also the teensiest sense of imposter syndrome.

Honestly, she didn't know what to do with all the attention, so she smiled and kept her focus on the stage.

"The Lumley Foundation has hosted this ball for over a century." The CEO, in his black tailcoat and white bow tie, addressed the crowd of glittering donors. "Thanks to the addition of Phinny to our team, we've seen our donations quadruple. With her sparkling personality and boundless compassion, she is most certainly a bright star among us. Thank you, Phinny, for putting together such a spectacular array of auction items." He gave her a nod, and the audience broke into applause.

Her stepfather squeezed her shoulder, and her mum whispered in her ear, "I'm so proud of you, darling."

It was the most glorious moment of her life. Thanks to the blinding light in her eyes, she couldn't see the audience, so she just waved her appreciation. When the applause didn't die down, she began to wonder what was going on. The acknowledgement was lovely, but surely, she hadn't done anything *that* exceptional.

She supposed getting the use of a reclusive billionaire's superyacht for a week was quite a coup, but still…

This response is a bit much.

It was only when the spotlight turned away from her that she discovered the reason for the crowd's enthusiasm. Cameron Lumley had taken the stage. Shaking the CEOs hand, he grabbed the microphone. Then, her elegant, handsome boyfriend graced the room with his movie star smile. "Good evening."

Even though his family ran the foundation, he had no reason to be on stage right then. He didn't run events. But he sure was an impressive sight. His custom-made suit hugged his broad shoulders and muscular thighs while his commanding presence captured the attention of everyone in the room. "On behalf of my family, I'd like to thank you all for your support this evening. As you know, the charity is my life's work, so it's only fitting that the woman who owns my heart now plays such a central role in it."

Surprise jolted her.

I own his heart?

They might've been together a while, but they hardly had some grand love affair. Not even close.

What's he going on about?

Her parents moved to stand on either side of her, enormous smiles stretching across their faces.

Cameron extended a hand. "Darling, please come up here."

She almost shouted *Why?* She didn't need to get up on stage. The band should start playing, and the patrons should go back to dancing and chatting. That was the order of events.

Her mum took the champagne glass out of her hand. "Don't just stand there. Go."

With all eyes on her, what choice did Phinny have? But while her brain sent the signal to her legs, they refused to cooperate. A wave of nausea hit, and she went hot all over.

Her stepfather set his hand on the small of her back and gave her a nudge. "Don't embarrass us."

That got her moving. As the crowd parted, she made her way to the steps. On some level, she knew what was happening, but her mind was racing, and she couldn't think clearly.

Please don't do this.

We're nowhere near ready for this. They'd grown up together but had only begun dating during their last year at university.

Casually dating.

Cameron stood center stage, while the CEO reached for her hand and helped her up the stairs. It was hard enough to move in her ball gown and shapewear undergarments, but with her legs shaking, she moved like a newborn foal.

Which was fitting since her heart was positively *galloping*.

"Darling…" Cameron reached for her hand, kissing her palm.

And then, he dropped to a knee.

In the middle of the grandest charity event of the year, her boyfriend—emphasis on friend—was about to propose. "I have loved you my entire life, but it was only when I saw you coming out of Trinity Hall that I knew it was time to start our future together. Every day has gotten better, and I can't wait to spend my life with you. Seraphina, will you do me the honor of becoming my wife?"

With the audience's collective gasp, the air was sucked out of the room.

She couldn't breathe. Blood roared in her ears, and her vision blurred around the edges.

In the silence, she had the strangest sensation of floating. She could picture herself grabbing a handful of strings attached to helium balloons and drifting off the stage, out the window, and sailing over the rooftops of London.

Cameron's smile faltered, and it jerked her back to the moment. She couldn't embarrass him. "Yes. Of course, yes."

Relief washed over his handsome features, and he stood to his full height. He wrapped an arm around her and faced the ballroom, raising their clasped hands as though she were a trophy.

Among the sea of smiles, Phinny found her parents. She'd never seen them so happy.

But why? The moment felt surreal. She'd never gushed about him to her parents. Never once talked about marriage or babies or any kind of future with him. Two people from similar backgrounds who had fun together, they were just dating.

Marriage?

Standing on that stage, she felt like a paper doll cut-out.

With a tug, she was led back down the stairs. Immediately, well-wishers swarmed them. His family, their friends…everyone was gleeful.

And it was all a lie.

Because she couldn't marry him.

Flee. It wasn't a thought so much as an alarm that rang through her body. She wrenched her hand out of his grip and made her way out of the ballroom. When she saw a sign for a powder room, she ducked inside and locked the door.

Oh, God. What is happening?

As she ran cold water over her hands, she looked up into her wild-eyed reflection. Her pulse pounded violently. Why had he proposed publicly? Now, calling it off would create a scandal.

It didn't have to be like this.

A hard rap jerked her attention from the mirror.

"Phinny?" *Cameron.* "Open up."

Angry that he'd put her in a terrible position, she opened the door, grabbed his wrist, and pulled him inside the lavender-scented bathroom. "What was that?" They'd have to manage the situation in a way that would cause the least embarrassment to their families, which meant waiting several months, and then quietly calling it off.

His eyes flickered with hurt. "What do you mean, what was that? It was a marriage proposal."

"But why? Cameron, we're not ready for that."

"We've been dating three years. When did you think we should be ready?"

"I don't know." *Never.* "We haven't talked about it."

"What on earth do you think we've been doing all this time?"

"We've been *dating.*"

"Yes, on a course toward marriage. Why else would I be exclusive with someone if not with the intention of marrying her? Why are you acting like this came out of nowhere? You can't pretend you didn't know it was the path we've been on."

She couldn't argue his point, and it flustered her. Because, really, it uncovered a truth that would only hurt his feelings. *I don't love you.* "I can't possibly get married now. I haven't done anything with my life."

His jaw snapped shut, like he was trying to contain his anger. "Whatever you want to do with your life, what better way to do it than as Cameron Lumley's wife?"

Obviously, that made perfect sense. Marrying into one of the wealthiest families in the United Kingdom would afford her any opportunity her heart desired. And it wasn't like Cameron cared what she did. That wouldn't change once they got married. He'd still go off with his mates on trips, and she'd go clubbing with hers. Sometimes, they'd do the holidays together, while other times, they'd be with their own families.

She knew exactly what her life with him would look like because that was the kind of marriage his parents had. And she didn't want to wind up like his mum, spending more time with her wine than her husband.

She pulled off the engagement ring. "I'm sorry, but I'm not ready to get married."

He just stared at her as though waiting for her to laugh and say *Gotcha. Of course, I'll marry you, silly!* "Are you serious?"

"Quite." His presumption that she'd just fall in line with some plan he'd never voiced irked her. "Cameron, come on. Do you even love me?"

"Of course, I do." He seemed calmer, as if they could

now settle things. "I like you better than anyone else we know."

Well, there's a ringing endorsement for marriage. "And I like you. But I need more time."

"How much time?"

"I don't know."

"Are we talking a few weeks?"

Weeks? "I'm twenty-four. What's the rush?"

His expression shuttered. "Waiting these three years has cost me nearly two million pounds."

She flinched as if he'd flicked cold water at her face. As soon as he married, he tapped into his trust fund. With each child he added to his family, the monthly allowance rose.

Quite the incentive to keep the Lumley line going.

She'd known that. So, why did it sound so ugly to hear him say it out loud?

He must not have liked her crestfallen expression because he reached for her elbows and bent his knees to look her in the eyes. "Darling, there's no one I'd rather spend my life with than you. You make me laugh…you make me happy."

"Well, yes, because I don't require anything of you."

He chuckled. "Most definitely, that's one for the plus column. But it works both ways. We give each other room to live our lives. Trust me, that's a good thing. We'll never grow restless or resentful."

I want more.

And what a bombshell revelation that was. She'd just been going along, having fun, not questioning anything, and she'd given no thought to where she was heading. Now that he'd forced her to think about it, she had to accept she hadn't done a damn thing with her life.

She couldn't say what she wanted to do exactly, but for the first time, she felt something missing. Something between the phases of parties, clubs, and shopping and getting married and popping out babies. "I need more time."

The smile vanished. He straightened. "No."

Fear sliced through her. She might not be ready to marry him, but she'd never contemplated a life without him. Like her parents, he was a major cog in the machine of her world, and she didn't know how to operate without all of them. "No, you won't wait?"

"I have waited. Three years is more than enough." He softened. "Look, you'd make a smashing stylist. Or you and your mum could open a boutique. Once we're married, you can use a portion of the extra fifty thousand pounds a month to do whatever you want. It doesn't matter to me, but we either get married now or it's done."

"It's done? Or we're done?"

"We're done. If you're not ready to marry me after three years, then I've got no reason to believe you'll be ready by four years or even five."

"I can't imagine my life without you, but I can't marry you because you've run out of patience with me. I'm sorry, Cameron." She took in the proud jut of his chin and the look in his eyes that screamed *Are you seriously going to walk away from me?* She liked him very much. They'd had a lot of fun together. But she didn't love him.

And so, she walked out the door.

Cut from her mooring, she felt adrift…uneasy. She hustled toward the exit as though the manor were on fire. The tight silk liner of her dress and the five-inch stilettos hampered her progress, though, as people rushed toward her, eager to share the happy occasion.

She couldn't talk to anyone right then, so she hurried on. Pulling out her phone, she texted her parents' driver, but her trembling fingers kept tapping the wrong pads, making her delete and start over.

"Seraphina?" Her mum glided along the hallway.

"Where are you going?" her stepfather asked. "We've just opened the bubbly to toast your wonderful news. Let's find Cameron. Come along."

The moment her mum reached her, the smile faded. "What's going on?"

Phinny handed over her phone. "Can you please ask Fergus to come round?"

Her stepfather snatched it. "We'll do no such thing. All of our friends are here to celebrate with you."

"There's nothing to celebrate." Phinny let out a tight breath. "We're not getting married."

"Of course, you are." Andrew's eyebrows shot up. "Don't be ridiculous."

When she'd met him as a little girl, she'd called him by his first name, but since she couldn't pronounce Andrew, she'd wound up saying Dewzy. For the first time since he'd come into her life, that term of endearment didn't fit. In this moment, when he cared more about his reputation than her feelings, he was purely her stepfather. "I gave the ring back. I'm not marrying him."

"Seraphina." Her mother sounded appalled.

"I told him I needed more time, and he said he wouldn't give me any."

With a grip on her upper arm, Andrew led them to an alcove. "You've known each other your entire lives. How much more time could you possibly need?"

"There are things I still want to do."

"Like what?" her mum whispered harshly. "You want

to shop more? Travel more? Have more spa days? What exactly are you so eager to do?"

Like a can on the road flattened by a tire, Phinny's spirit compressed under the weight of her mum's words. She'd never considered herself frivolous. She'd been living the only life she'd ever known. "I don't know. But I would rather find out than get married to a man I don't love."

Her stepfather had always indulged her, and in return she'd tried very hard to please him. So, to see the tick in his jaw, the color flood his cheeks, truly upset her. "What on earth do you think we've been doing, Seraphina?"

"What do you mean?" A sickening feeling rolled through her.

"You don't have a proper job, you live in an apartment we own, you use a credit card we've given you…why do you think we've been supporting you all this time?"

The great beast of fear loomed over her like a dark, menacing shadow. "I——" Her mind went blank.

"We've supported you because you were going to marry Cameron," her mum said. "And Lumleys do philanthropy, just as I've done. Just as you've been doing. *That* has been our expectation. If we thought for a moment you had no intention of marrying him, you'd have been polishing your CV and applying for jobs your last year at university. You'd have been paying your own bills upon graduation."

"Now, go and find your fiancé," her stepfather said. "And get things back on track. Or the locks to your Knightsbridge apartment will be changed by morning."

"What?" She could barely process his words. He couldn't possibly mean to throw her out onto the streets?

"Darling, please." Her mum patted his arm.

Oh, thank God. Her mum would always take care of

her. They were a team. Her parents were upset. She understood that. But they'd never make her marry a man she didn't love.

But then her mum's features hardened. "Give her a few days to see which of her friends will allow her to sleep on their couch until she gets a job."

About the Author

Award-winning author Erika Kelly writes sexy and emotional small town romance. Married to the love of her life and raising four children, she lives in the southwest, drinks a lot of tea, and is always waiting for her cats to get off her keyboard.

https://www.erikakellybooks.com/

facebook.com/erikakellybooks

twitter.com/ErikaKellyBooks

instagram.com/erikakellyauthor

goodreads.com/Erika_Kelly

pinterest.com/erikakellybooks

amazon.com/Erika-Kelly/e/B00L0MLWUY

bookbub.com/authors/erika-kelly

Printed in Great Britain
by Amazon

17075158R00233